9/7/8
27/7/8
30/6/16

E
e
f
v
f
h
f
f
v

Cleopatra, is digging in again!'
Philadelphia Enquirer

'Shines with charm and wit…and the winsome personality of Amelia Peabody.'
Chicago S

**Titles in this series currently
available from Constable & Robinson Ltd**

Crocodile on the Sandbank
First Amelia Peabody mystery

The Curse of the Pharaohs
Second Amelia Peabody mystery

The Mummy Case
Third Amelia Peabody mystery

Lion in the Valley
Fourth Amelia Peabody mystery

The Deeds of the Disturber
Fifth Amelia Peabody mystery

The Snake, the Crocodile and the Dog
Seventh Amelia Peabody mystery

The Hippopotamus Pool
Eighth Amelia Peabody mystery

Seeing a Large Cat
Ninth Amelia Peabody mystery

The Ape Who Guards the Balance
Tenth Amelia Peabody mystery

The Falcon at the Portal
Eleventh Amelia Peabody mystery

Thunder in the Sky
Twelfth Amelia Peabody mystery

Lord of the Silent
Thirteenth Amelia Peabody mystery

The Golden One
Fourteenth Amelia Peabody mystery

Children of the Storm
Fifteenth Amelia Peabody mystery

Guardian of the Horizon
Sixteenth Amelia Peabody mystery

The Serpent on the Crown
Seventeenth Amelia Peabody mystery

Tomb of the Golden Bird
Eighteenth Amelia Peabody mystery

THE LAST CAMEL DIED AT NOON

Elizabeth Peters

ROBINSON
London

Constable & Robinson Ltd
3 The Lanchesters
162 Fulham Palace Road
London W6 9ER
www.constablerobinson.com

First published in the UK in hardback by
Judy Piatkus (Publishers) Ltd 1991

First published in the UK in paperback by Robinson,
an imprint of Constable & Robinson Ltd 2002

This paperback edition published by Robinson,
an imprint of Constable & Robinson Ltd 2006

A copy of the British Library Cataloguing in
Publication Data is available from the British Library

ISBN-13: 978-1-84529-389-5
ISBN-10: 1-84529-389-4

Printed and bound in the EU

1 3 5 7 9 10 8 6 4 2

For Ellen Nehr
with the compliments of the author
and Ahmet, the camel

Acknowledgments

I owe the translation of Ramses's Latin note to the kindness of Ms Tootie Godlove-Ridenour; if there are errors, they are due to my careless transcribing or (more probably) to the haste of Ramses himself.

A tip of the chapeau as well to Charlotte MacLeod for coming up with a particularly loathsome method of rendering an enemy hors de combat, and a tip of the pith helmet to Dr Lyn Green, who supplied me with copies of hard-to-find Egyptological research materials.

My greatest debt will of course be obvious to the intelligent Reader. Like Amelia (and, although he refuses to admit it, Emerson) I am an admirer of the romances of Sir Henry Rider Haggard. He was a master of a form of fiction that is, alas, seldom produced in these degenerate days; having run out of books to read, I decided to write one myself. It is meant as an affectionate, admiring, and nostalgic tribute.

AMELIA PEABODY, born in 1852, found her life's work and life partner in 1884, when on a trip to Egypt she married Egyptologist, Radcliffe Emerson. Their son Walter 'Ramses' Emerson was born three years later, and their adopted daughter, Nefret, joined the family in 1898. Other important members of the family include several generations of Egyptian cats.

Although the Emersons own a handsome Queen Anne mansion in Kent, they spend half of each year digging in Egypt and fighting off criminals of all varieties. Amelia is planning to draw her last breath holding a trowel in one hand and her deadly parasol in the other.

Contents

BOOK ONE

1 'I Told You This Was a Harebrained Scheme!'   3
2 'My Son Lives!'   22
3 'He Promised All the Ladies Many Sons'   45
4 Stone Houses of the Kings   66
5 'He Is the Man!'   95
6 The Ghost of a Bowman of Cush   118
7 Lost in the Sea of Sand   141

BOOK TWO

8 The City of the Holy Mountain   161
9 'Touch This Mother at Your Peril!'   190
10 Assaulted at Midnight!   214
11 'Another Pair of Confounded Young Lovers!'   236
12 'When I Speak the Dead Hear and Obey!'   259
13 'I Would as Soon Leave Ramses'   284
14 Into the Bowels of the Earth   307
15 'The God Has Spoken'   335
16 'Sleep, Servant of God'   361

EGYPT AND THE SUDAN ▴ 1897

Mediterranean Sea

Suez Canal

ALEXANDRIA

SUEZ

GIZA ● ▴ ● SUEZ
CAIRO

WESTERN DESERT

EASTERN DESERT

Gulf of Suez

EGYPT

● LUXOR

Red Sea

● ASWAN

ABU SIMBEL ●

NUBIAN DESERT

● WADI HALFA

KERMA ●

● ABU HAMED

DONGOLA ●

NAPATA

● MEROWE

SUDAN (NUBIA)

● MEROË

N

OMDURMAN ●

W — E

▴ KHARTOUM

S

BOOK ONE

'I Told You This Was a
Harebrained Scheme!'

Hands on hips, brows lowering, Emerson stood gazing fixedly at the recumbent ruminant. A sympathetic friend (if camels have such, which is doubtful) might have taken comfort in the fact that scarcely a ripple of agitated sand surrounded the place of its demise. Like the others in the caravan, of which it was the last, it had simply stopped, sunk to its knees, and passed on, peacefully and quietly. (Conditions, I might add, that are uncharacteristic of camels alive or moribund.)

Those conditions are also uncharacteristic of Emerson. To the readers who have encountered my distinguished husband, in the flesh or in the pages of my earlier works, it will come as no surprise to learn that he reacted to the camel's death as if the animal had committed suicide for the sole purpose of inconveniencing him. Eyes blazing like sapphires in his tanned and chiselled face, he plucked the hat from his head, flung it upon the sand, and kicked it a considerable distance before turning his furious glare towards me.

'Curse it, Amelia! I told you this was a harebrained scheme!'

'Yes, Emerson, you did,' I replied. 'In those precise words, if I am not mistaken. If you will cast your mind back to our first discussion of this enterprise, you may remember that I was in full agreement with you.'

'Then what – ' Emerson turned in a circle. Boundless and bare, as the poet puts it, the lone and level sands stretched far away. 'Then what the devil are we doing here?' Emerson bellowed.

It was a reasonable question, and one that may also have occurred to the reader of this narrative. Professor Radcliffe Emerson, F.R.S. F.B.A., LL.D. (Edinburgh), D.C.L. (Oxford), Member of the American Philosophical Society, et cetera, pre-eminent Egyptologist of this or any other era, was frequently to be encountered in unusual, not to say peculiar, surroundings. Will I ever forget that magical moment when I entered a tomb in the desolate cliffs bordering the Nile and found him delirious with fever, in desperate need of attentions he was helpless to resist? The bond forged between us by my expert nursing was strengthened by the dangers we subsequently shared; and in due course, Reader, I married him. Since that momentous day we had excavated in every major site in Egypt and written extensively on our discoveries. Modesty prevents me from claiming too large a share of the scholarly reputation we had earned, but Emerson would have been the first to proclaim that we were a partnership, in archaeology as in marriage.

From the sandy wastes of the cemeteries of Memphis to the rocky cliffs of the Theban necropolis, we had wandered hand in hand (figuratively speaking), in terrain almost as inhospitable as the desert that presently surrounded us. Never before, however, had we been more than a few miles from the Nile and its life-giving water. It lay far behind us now, and there was not a pyramid or a broken wall to be seen, much less a tree or a sign of habitation. What indeed were we doing there? Without camels we were marooned on a sea of sand, and our situation was infinitely more desperate than that of shipwrecked sailors.

I seated myself upon the ground with my back against the camel. The sun was at the zenith; the only shade was cast by the body of the poor beast. Emerson paced back and forth, kicking up clouds of sand and swearing. His expertise in this latter exercise had earned him the admiring title of 'Father of Curses' from our Egyptian workmen, and on this occasion he surpassed himself. I sympathised with his feelings, but duty compelled me to remonstrate.

'You forget yourself, Emerson,' I remarked, indicating our companions.

They stood side by side, watching me with grave concern, and I must say they made a ludicrous pair. Many of the native Nilotic peoples are unusually tall, and Kemit, the only servant remaining to us, was over six feet in height. He wore a turban and a loose robe of woven blue-and-white cotton. His face, with its clean-cut features and deeply bronzed skin, bore a striking resemblance to that of his companion, but the second individual was less than four feet tall. He was also my son, Walter Peabody Emerson, known as 'Ramses,' who should not have been there.

Emerson cut off his expletive in mid-syllable, though the effort almost choked him. Still in need of a 'went' for his boiling emotions, he focused them on me.

'Who selected these da— these cursed camels?'

'You know perfectly well who selected them,' I replied. 'I always select the animals for our expeditions, and doctor them too. The local people treat camels and donkeys so badly – '

'Don't give me one of your lectures on veterinary medicine and kindness to animals,' Emerson bellowed. 'I knew – I knew! – your delusions about your medical knowledge would lead us into disaster one day. You have been dosing these da— these confounded animals; what did you give them?'

'Emerson! Are you accusing me of poisoning the camels?' I struggled to overcome the indignation his outrageous accusation had provoked. 'I believe you have taken leave of your senses.'

'Well, and if I have, there is some excuse for me,' Emerson said in a more moderate tone. He edged closer to me. 'Our situation is desperate enough to disturb any man, even one as even-tempered as I. Er – I beg your pardon, my dear Peabody. Don't cry.'

Emerson calls me Amelia only when he is annoyed with me. Peabody is my maiden name, and it was thus that Emerson, in one of his feeble attempts at sarcasm, addressed me during the early days of our acquaintance. Hallowed by fond memories, it has now become a private pet name, so to speak, indicative of affection and respect.

I lowered the handkerchief I had raised to my eyes and smiled at him. 'A few grains of sand in my eye, Emerson, that is all. You will never find me succumbing to helpless tears when firmness is required. As you are well aware.'

'Hmph,' said Emerson.

'All the same, Mama,' said Ramses, 'Papa has raised a point worthy of consideration. It is surely stretching coincidence to the point of impossibility to assume that all the camels should die, suddenly and with no symptoms of disease, within forty-eight hours of one another.'

'I assure you, Ramses, that consideration had already occurred to me. Run and fetch Papa's hat, if you please. No, Emerson, I know your dislike of hats, but I insist that you put it on. We are in bad enough case without having you laid low by sunstroke.'

Emerson made no reply. His eyes were fixed on the small figure of his son, trotting obediently after the sun helmet, and his expression was so poignant that my eyes dimmed. It was not fear for himself that weakened my husband, nor even concern for me. We had faced death together not once but many times; he knew he could count on me to meet that grim adversary with a smile and a stiff upper lip. No; it was the probable fate of Ramses that brought the moisture to his keen blue eyes. So moved was I that I vowed not to remind Emerson that it was his fault that his son and heir had been condemned to a slow, lingering, painful death from dehydration.

'Well, we have been in worse situations,' I said. 'At least we three have; and I presume, Kemit, that you are no stranger to peril. Have you any suggestions, my friend?'

Responding to my gesture, Kemit approached and squatted down next to me. Ramses immediately squatted as well. He had conceived a great admiration for this taciturn, handsome man; and the sight of them, like a stork and its chick, brought a smile to my lips.

Emerson was not amused. Fanning himself with his hat, he remarked sarcastically, 'If Kemit has a suggestion that can get us out of this dilemma, I will take off my hat to him. We – '

'You cannot take off your hat until you put it on, Emerson,' I interrupted.

Emerson slapped the offending article onto his unruly black head with such force that his eyelashes fluttered wildly. 'As I was saying, we are more than six days from the Nile, as the camel trots; considerably longer on foot. If the so-called map we have followed is to be trusted, there is a water hole or oasis ahead. It is a journey of approximately two days by camel, of which we have none. We have water for perhaps two days, with strict rationing.'

It was an accurate and depressing summary. What Emerson did not say, because the rest of us knew it, was that our desperate condition was due to the defection of our servants. They had departed, in a body, the night before, taking with them all the waterskins except the partially filled containers we had had with us in our tent and the canteen I always carry attached to my belt. They might have done worse; they might have murdered us. I cannot, however, attribute their forbearance to kindness of heart. Emerson's strength and ferocity are legendary; many of the simple natives believe he is armed with supernatural powers. (And I myself have a certain reputation as the Sitt Hakim, dispenser of mysterious medicines.) Rather than challenge us, they had stolen away in the dead of night. Kemit claimed he had been struck unconscious when he attempted to prevent them, and indeed he had a sizable lump on his head to prove it. Why he had not joined the mutineers I could not explain; it might have been loyalty – though he owed us no more than did the others, who had worked for us as long – or it might have been that he had not been invited to join them.

There was a great deal about Kemit that wanted explaining. Expressionless as the nesting bird he somewhat resembled at that moment, his knees being on approximately the level of his ears, he was not at all a comic figure. Indeed, his chiselled features had a dignity that reminded me of certain Fourth Dynasty sculptures, most particularly the magnificent portrait of King Chephren, builder of the Second Pyramid. I had once remarked to Emerson on the resemblance; he had replied that it was not surprising, since the ancient Egyptians were of mixed racial stock and some of the Nubian tribes were probably their remote descendants. (I should add that this theory of Emerson's – which he regarded not as theory but as fact – was not accepted by the great majority of his colleagues.)

But I perceive that I am wandering from the plot of my narrative, as I am inclined to do when questions of scholarly interest arise. Let me turn back the pages of my journal and explain in proper sequence of time how we came to find ourselves in such an extraordinary predicament. I do not do this in the meretricious hope of prolonging your anxiety as to our survival, dear Reader, for if you have the intelligence I expect my Readers to possess, you will know I could not be writing this account if I were in the same state as the camels.

I must turn back not a few but many pages, and take you to a quiet country house in Kent, when the turning of the leaves from green to golden bronze betokened the approach of autumn. After a busy summer spent teaching, lecturing, and readying the publication of our previous season's excavations, we were about to begin preparations for our annual winter's work in Egypt. Emerson was seated behind his desk; I walked briskly to and fro, hands behind my back. The bust of Socrates, oddly speckled with black – for it was at this bust that Emerson was wont to hurl his pen when inspiration flagged or something happened to irritate him – watched us benevolently.

The subject of discussion, or so I fondly believed, was the future intellectual development of our son.

'I fully sympathise with your reservations concerning the public-school system, Emerson,' I assured him. 'But the boy must have some formal training, somewhere, sometime. He is growing up quite a little savage.'

'You do yourself an injustice, my dear,' Emerson murmured, glancing at the newspaper he was holding.

'He has improved,' I admitted. 'He doesn't talk quite as much as he used to, and he has not been in danger of life or limb for several weeks. But he has no notion how to get on with children his own age.'

Emerson looked up, his brow furrowed. 'Now, Peabody, that is not the case. Last winter, with Ahmed's children – '

'I speak of English children, Emerson. Naturally.'

'There is nothing natural about English children. Good Gad, Amelia, our public schools have a caste system more pernicious than that of India, and those at the bottom of the ladder are abused more viciously than any Untouchable. As for "getting on" with members of the opposite sex – you do not mean, I hope, to exclude female children from Ramses's social connections? Well, I assure you that that is precisely what your precious public schools aim to achieve.' Warming to his theme, Emerson leapt up, scattering papers in all directions, and began to pace back and forth on a path at right angles to mine. 'Curse it, I sometimes wonder how the upper classes in this country ever manage to reproduce! By the time a lad leaves university he is so intimidated by girls of his own class it is almost impossible for him to speak to them in intelligible sentences! If he did, he would not receive an intelligible answer, for the education of women, if it can be dignified by that term – Oof. I beg your pardon, my dear. Are you hurt?'

'Not at all.' I accepted the hand he offered to assist me to rise. 'But if you insist on pacing while you lecture, at least walk with me instead of at right angles to my path. A collision was inevitable.'

A sunny smile replaced his scowl and he pulled me into a fond embrace. 'Only that sort of collision, I hope. Come now, Peabody, you know we agree on the inadequacies of the educational system. You don't want to break the lad's spirit?'

9

'I only want to bend it a little,' I murmured. But it is hard to resist Emerson when he smiles and . . . Never mind what he was doing; but when I say Emerson's eyes are sapphire-blue, his hair is black and thick, and his frame is as trim and muscular as that of a Greek athlete – not even referring to the cleft or dimple in his chin or the enthusiasm he brings to the exercise of his conjugal rights . . . Well, I need not be more specific, but I am sure any right-thinking female will understand why the subject of Ramses's education ceased to interest me.

After Emerson had resumed his seat and picked up the newspaper, I returned to the subject, but in a considerably softened mood. 'My dear Emerson, your powers of persuasion – that is to say, your arguments – are most convincing. Ramses could go to school in Cairo. There is a new Academy for Young Gentlemen of which I have had good reports; and since we will be excavating at Sakkara . . .'

The newspaper behind which Emerson had retired rattled loudly. I stopped speaking, seized by a hideous premonition – though, as events were to prove, not nearly hideous enough. 'Emerson,' I said gently, 'you have applied for the firman, haven't you? You surely would not repeat the error you made a few years ago when you neglected to apply in time, and instead of receiving permission to work at Dahshoor we ended up at the most boring, unproductive site in all of Lower Egypt?* Emerson! Put down that newspaper and answer me! Have you obtained permission from the Department of Antiquities to excavate at Sakkara this season?'

Emerson lowered the newspaper, and flinched at finding my face only inches from his. 'Kitchener,' he said, 'has taken Berber.'

It is inconceivable to me that future generations will fail to realise the vital importance of the study of history, or that Britons will be ignorant of one of the most remarkable chapters in the development of their empire. Yet stranger things have happened; and in the event of such a catastrophe (for I would

The Mummy Case

10

call it nothing less), I beg leave of my Readers to remind them of facts that should be as familiar to them as they are to me.

In 1884, when I made my first visit to Egypt, most English persons persisted in regarding the Mahdi as only another ragged religious fanatic, despite the fact that his followers had already overrun half the Sudan. This country, encompassing the region from the rocky cataracts of Assouan to the jungles south of the junction of the Blue and White Niles, had been conquered by Egypt in 1821. The Pashas, who were not Egyptians at all but descendants of an Albanian adventurer, had proceeded to rule the region even more corruptly and inefficiently than they did Egypt itself. The benevolent intervention of the great powers (especially Britain) rescued Egypt from disaster, but matters continued to worsen in the Sudan until Mohammed Ahmed Ibn el-Sayyid Abdullah proclaimed himself the Mahdi, the reincarnation of the Prophet, and rallied the forces of rebellion against Egyptian tyranny and misrule. His followers believed he was the descendant of a line of sheikhs; his enemies sneered at him as a poor ignorant boat-builder. Whatever his origins, he possessed an extraordinarily magnetic personality and a remarkable gift of oratory. Armed only with sticks and spears, his ragtag troops had swept all before them and were threatening the Sudanese capital of Khartoum.

Against the figure of the Mahdi stands that of the heroic General Gordon. Early in 1884 he had been sent to Khartoum to arrange for the withdrawal of the troops garrisoned there and in the nearby fort of Omdurman. There was a good deal of public feeling against this decision, for abandoning Khartoum meant giving up the entire Sudan. Gordon was accused, then and later, of never meaning to comply with his orders; whatever his reasons for delaying the withdrawal, he did just that. By the autumn of 1884, when I arrived in Egypt, Khartoum was besieged by the wild hordes of the Mahdi, and all the surrounding country, to the very borders of Egypt, was in rebel hands.

The gallant Gordon held Khartoum, and British public opinion, led by the Queen herself, demanded his rescue. An expedition was finally sent but it did not reach the beleaguered city until February of the following year – three days after Khartoum fell and the gallant Gordon was cut down in the courtyard of his house. 'Too late!' was the agonised cry of Britannia! Ironically, the Mahdi survived his great foe by less than six months, but his place was taken by one of his lieutenants, the Khalifa Abdullah el-Taashi, who ruled even more tyrannically than his master. For over a decade the land had groaned under his cruelties, while the British lion licked its wounds and refused to avenge the fallen hero.

The reasons, political, economic and military, that led to a decision to reconquer the Sudan are too complex to discuss here. Suffice it to say that the campaign had begun in 1896 and that by the autumn of the following year our forces were advancing on the Fourth Cataract under the gallant Kitchener, who had been named Sirdar of the Egyptian Army.

But what, one might ask, do these world-shaking affairs have to do with the winter plans of a pair of innocent Egyptologists? Alas, I knew the answer only too well, and I sank into a chair beside the desk. 'Emerson,' I said. 'Emerson. I beg of you. Don't tell me you want to dig in the Sudan this winter.'

'My dear Peabody!' Emerson flung the newspaper aside and fixed the full power of his brilliant gaze upon me. 'You know, none better, that I have wanted to excavate at Napata or Meroë for years. I'd have tackled it last year if you hadn't raised such a fuss – or if you had consented to remain in Egypt with Ramses while I did so.'

'And waited to learn that they had put your head on a pike, as they did Gordon's,' I murmured.

'Nonsense. I'd have been in no danger. Some of my best friends were Mahdists. But never mind,' he continued quickly, to forestall the protest I was about to make – not of the truth of his statement, for Emerson had friends in very strange places – but of the common sense of his plan. 'The situation is entirely different now, Peabody. The region around Napata is already in Egyptian hands. At the rate Kitchener is going, he will take

Khartoum by the time we reach Egypt, and Meroë – the site I favour – is north of Khartoum. It will be quite safe.'

'But Emerson – '

'Pyramids, Peabody.' Emerson's deep voice dropped to a seductive baritone growl. 'Royal pyramids, untouched by any archaeologist. The pharaohs of the Twenty-Fifth Dynasty were Nubians – proud, virile soldiers who marched out of the south to conquer the degenerate rulers of a decadent Egypt. These heroes were buried in their homeland of Cush – formerly Nubia, now the Sudan – '

'I know that, Emerson, but – '

'After Egypt lost its independence to the Persians, the Greeks, the Romans, the Moslems, a mighty kingdom flourished in Cush,' Emerson continued poetically – and a trifle inaccurately. 'Egyptian culture survived in that far-off land – the same region, as I believe, from which it had originally sprung. Think of it, Peabody! To investigate, not only the continuation of that mighty civilization, but perhaps its roots as well. . .'

Emotion overcame him. His voice failed, his eyes glazed.

There were only two things that could reduce Emerson to such a state. One was the idea of going where no scholar had gone before him, of being the discoverer of new worlds, new civilisations. Need I say that I shared that noble ambition? No. My pulse quickened, I felt reason sink under the passion of his words. One last faint ray of common sense made me murmur, 'But – '

'But me no buts, Peabody.' He grasped my hands in his – those strong bronzed hands, which could wield pick and shovel more vigorously than any of his workmen but which were capable of the most sensitive, the most exquisite touch. His eyes held mine; I fancied the brilliant rays of sapphirine-blue struck from his orbs straight into my dazzled brain. 'You are with me, you know you are. And you will be with me, my darling Peabody – this winter, in Meroë!'

Rising, he drew me once more into his masterful embrace. I said no more; indeed I was unable to say more, since his lips were pressed to mine. But I thought to myself, Very well, Emerson. I will be with you – but Ramses will be at the Academy for Young Gentlemen in Cairo.

I am seldom wrong. On those rare occasions when I am wrong, it is usually because I have underestimated the stubbornness of Emerson or the devious wiles of Ramses, or a combination of the two. In defence of my powers of precognition, however, I must say that the bizarre twist our expedition was to take resulted not so much from our little familial differences of opinion as from a startling development that no one, not even I, could possibly have anticipated.

It took place on a wet autumn evening not long after the conversation I have just described. I had a number of reservations about Emerson's projected plans for the winter, and once the euphoria of his persuasive powers had subsided, I was not shy of expressing them. Though the northern Sudan was officially 'pacified' and under Egyptian occupation as far south as Dongola, only an idiot would have assumed that travel in the region was completely safe. The unfortunate inhabitants of the area had suffered from war, oppression, and starvation; many were homeless, most were hungry, and anyone who ventured among them without an armed escort was practically asking to be murdered. Emerson brushed this aside. We would not venture among them. We would be working in a region under military occupation, with troops close by. Furthermore, some of his best friends . . .

Having resigned myself to accept his plans (and I will admit that the thought of pyramids, my consuming passion, had some effect), I hastened to complete our arrangements for departure. After so many years I had the process down to a routine, but additional precautions and many extra supplies would be necessary if we were to venture into such a remote region. Of course I had no help whatever from Emerson, who spent all his time poring over obscure volumes on what little was known of the ancient inhabitants of the Sudan, and in long conversations with his brother Walter. Walter was a brilliant linguist who specialised in the ancient languages of Egypt. The prospect of obtaining texts in the obscure and as yet undeciphered Meroitic tongue raised his enthusiasm to fever pitch. Instead of trying to dissuade Emerson from his hazardous project he actually encouraged him.

Walter had married my dear friend Evelyn, the granddaughter and heiress of the Duke of Chalfont. Theirs had been an exceedingly happy union, and it had been blessed with four – no, at the time of which I speak I believe the number was five – children. (One tended to lose track with Evelyn, as my husband once coarsely remarked, overlooking, as men are inclined to do, that his brother was at least equally responsible.) The young Emersons were staying with us on the evening of which I am about to speak. Greatly as I enjoyed the opportunity to spend time with my dearest friend, and a brother-in-law whom I truly esteem, and their five (unless it was six?) delightful offspring, I had an additional reason, this particular year, for encouraging the visit. I had not entirely abandoned hope of persuading Emerson that Ramses should be left in England when we set out on our hazardous journey. I knew I could count on Evelyn to add her gentle persuasion to mine. For reasons which eluded me, she doted on Ramses.

It is impossible to give a proper impression of Ramses by describing his characteristics. One must observe him in action to understand how even the most admirable traits can be perverted or carried to such an extreme that they cease to be virtues and become the reverse.

At that time Ramses was ten years of age. He could speak Arabic like a native, read three different scripts of ancient Egyptian as easily as he could read Latin, Hebrew, and Greek – which is to say, as easily as English – sing a wide variety of vulgar songs in Arabic, and ride almost anything with four legs. He had no other useful skills.

He was fond of his pretty, gentle aunt, and I hoped she could help persuade him to stay with her that winter. The presence of his cousins would be an inducement; Ramses was fond of them too, although I am not certain the feeling was reciprocated.

I had gone off to London that day with less trepidation than I usually felt when leaving Ramses because it was raining heavily and I assumed Evelyn would insist that the children remain indoors. I had strictly forbidden Ramses to conduct any chemical experiments whatever, or continue his excavations in the wine cellar, or practice knife-throwing in the house, or show little Amelia his mummified mice, or teach his cousins any Arabic songs. There were a number of other things; I forget them now, but I felt reasonably sure I had covered everything. I was therefore able to pursue my errands with a mind at ease, though the same could not be said about my body; the coal smoke that hangs over London had combined with the rain to form a blackish smut that clung to clothing and skin, and the streets were ankle-deep in mud. When I got off the train late that afternoon I was glad to see the carriage waiting. I had arranged to have most of my purchases shipped, but I was loaded with parcels and my skirts were wet to the knee.

The lights of Amarna House shone warm and welcoming through the gathering dusk. How joyfully I looked forward to my reunion with all those I loved best, and to lesser but nonetheless pleasant comforts – a hot bath, a change of clothing, and a cup of the beverage that cheers but does not inebriate. Feeling the chill of wet feet and clinging skirts, I reflected that I might instead indulge in the beverage that does inebriate – but only when taken in excessive quantities, which I never do. There is, after all, nothing so effective in warding off a cold than a stiff whiskey and soda.

Gargery, our excellent butler, had been watching for the carriage; as he assisted me to remove my wet outer garments he said solicitously, 'May I venture to suggest, madam, that you take something to ward off a cold? I will send one of the footmen upstairs with it at once, if you like.'

'What a splendid idea, Gargery,' I replied. 'I am grateful to you for suggesting it.'

I had almost reached my room before I realised that the house was uncommonly quiet. No voices raised in genial debate from my husband's study, no childish laughter, no . . .

'Rose,' I cried, flinging open my door. 'Rose, where . . . Oh, there you are.'

'Your bath is ready, madam,' said Rose, from the open door of the bathroom, where she stood wreathed in steam like a kindly genie. She seemed a trifle flushed. It might have been the warmth of the bathwater that had brought the pretty colour to her cheeks, but I suspected another reason.

'Thank you, Rose. But I was about to ask – '

'Will you wear the crimson tea gown, madam?' She hastened to me and began wrenching at the buttons on my dress.

'Yes. But where . . . My dear Rose, you are shaking me like a terrier with a rat. A little less enthusiasm, if you please.'

'Yes, madam. But the bath water will be cold.' Having divested me of my gown, she began attacking my petticoats.

'Very well, Rose. What has Ramses done now?'

It took me a while to get the truth out of her. Rose is childless; no doubt that fact explains her peculiar attachment to Ramses, whom she has known since he was an infant. It is true that he showers her with gifts – bouquets of my prize roses, bunches of prickly wildflowers, small furry animals, hideous gloves, scarves, and handbags, selected by himself and paid for out of his pocket money. But even if the gifts were appropriate, which most are not, they hardly compensate for the hours Rose has spent cleaning up after him. I long ago gave up trying to comprehend this streak of irrationality in an otherwise sensible woman.

After Rose had stripped me of my garments and popped me into the tub, she deemed that the soothing effect of hot water would soften me enough to hear the truth. In fact, it was not as bad as I had feared. It seems I had neglected to forbid Ramses to take a bath.

Rose assured me that the ceiling of Professor Emerson's study was not much damaged, and she thought the carpet would be all the better for a good washing. Ramses had fully intended to turn off the water and no doubt he would have remembered to do so, only the cat Bastet had caught a mouse, and if he had delayed in rushing to the rodent's rescue, Bastet would have dispatched it. As a result of his prompt action the mouse was now resting quietly, its wounds dressed, in Ramses's closet.

Rose hates mice. 'Never mind,' I said wearily. 'I don't want to hear any more. I don't want to know what forced Ramses to the dire expedient of bathing. I don't want to know what Professor Emerson said when his ceiling began spouting water. Just hand me that glass, Rose, and then go quietly away.'

The whiskey and soda had been delivered. An application of that beverage internally and of hot water externally eventually restored me to my usual spirits, and when I went to the drawing room, trailing my crimson flounces and looking, I fancy, as well as I have ever looked, the smiling faces of my beloved family assured me that all was well.

Evelyn wore a gown of the soft azure that intensified the blue of her eyes and set off her golden hair. The gown was already sadly crushed, for children are drawn to my dear friend as bees are drawn to a flower. She had the baby on her lap and little Amelia beside her, in the maternal clasp of her arm. The twins sat at her feet, mashing her skirts. Raddie, my eldest nephew, leaned over the arm of the sofa where his mother sat, and Ramses leaned against Raddie, getting as close to his aunt's ear as was possible. He was, as usual, talking.

He broke off when I entered, and I studied him thoughtfully. He was extremely clean. Had I not known the reason I would have commended him, for the condition is not natural to him. I had determined not to mar the congeniality of the gathering by any reference to earlier unpleasantness, but something in my expression must have made Emerson aware of what I was thinking. He came quickly to me, gave me a hearty kiss, and shoved a glass into my hand.

'How lovely you look, my dearest Peabody. A new gown, eh? It becomes you.'

I allowed him to lead me to a chair: 'Thank you, my dear Emerson. I have had this dress for a year and you have seen it at least a dozen times, but the compliment is appreciated nonetheless.' Emerson too was extremely clean. His dark hair lay in soft waves, as it did when it had just been washed. I deduced that a quantity of water, and perhaps plaster, had fallen on his head. If he was prepared to overlook the incident, I could do no less, so I turned to my brother-in-law, who stood leaning against the mantel watching us with an affectionate smile.

'I saw your friend and rival Frank Griffiths today, Walter. He sends his regards and asked me to tell you he is making excellent progress with the Oxyrynchos papyrus.'

Walter looks like the scholar he is. The lines in his thin cheeks deepened and he adjusted his eyeglasses. 'Now, Amelia dear, don't try to stir up a competition between me and Frank. He is a splendid linguist and a good friend. I don't envy him his papyrus; Radcliffe has promised me Meroitic inscriptions by the cartload. I can hardly wait.'

Walter is one of the few people who is allowed to refer to Emerson by his given name, which he detests. He flinched visibly, but said only, 'So you stopped by the British Museum, Peabody?'

'Yes.' I took a sip of my whiskey. 'No doubt it will come as a great surprise to you, Emerson, to learn that Budge also proposes to travel to the Sudan this autumn. In fact, he has already left.'

'Er, hmmm,' said Emerson. 'No! Indeed!'

Emerson considers most Egyptologists incompetent bunglers – which they are, by his austere standards – but Wallis Budge, the Keeper of Egyptian and Assyrian Antiquities at the British Museum, was his particular bête noire.

'Indeed!' Walter repeated. His eyes twinkled. 'Well, that should make your winter's activities even more interesting, Amelia. Keeping those two from one another's throats – '

'Bah,' said Emerson. 'Walter, I resent the implication. How you could suppose me so forgetful of the dignity of my

19

profession and my own self-esteem... I don't intend to come within throat-grasping reach of the rascal. And he had better stay away from me, or I will throttle him.'

Always the peacemaker, Evelyn attempted to change the subject. 'Did you hear anything more about Professor Petrie's engagement, Amelia? Is it true that he is soon to be married?'

'I believe so, Evelyn. Everyone is talking about it.'

'Gossiping, you mean,' said Emerson, with a snort. 'To see Petrie, who was always wedded to his profession and had no time for the softer emotions, fall head over heels for a chit of a girl... They say she is a good twenty years younger than he.'

'Now who is engaging in ill-natured gossip?' I demanded. 'By all accounts she is an excellent young woman and he is utterly besotted with her. We must think of a suitable wedding present, Emerson. A handsome silver epergne, perhaps.'

'What the devil would Petrie do with an epergne?' Emerson asked. 'The man lives like a savage. He would probably soak potsherds in it.'

We were discussing the matter when the door opened. I glanced up, expecting to see that Rose had come to take the children away, for it was approaching the dinner hour. But it was Gargery, not Rose, and the butler's face wore the frown that betokened an unwelcome announcement.

'There is a gentleman to see you, Professor. I informed him that you did not see callers at this time of day but he – '

'He must have urgent reasons for disturbing us,' I interrupted, seeing my husband's brows draw together. 'A gentleman, you said, Gargery?'

The butler inclined his head. Advancing upon Emerson, he offered the salver on which rested a chaste white calling card.

'Hmph,' said Emerson, taking the card. 'The Honourable Reginald Forthright. Never heard of him. Tell him to go away, Gargery.'

'No, wait,' I said. 'I think you ought to see him, Emerson.'

'Amelia, your insatiable curiosity will be the death of me,' Emerson cried. 'I don't want to see the fellow. I want my whiskey and soda, I want to enjoy the company of my family, I want my dinner. I refuse – '

The door, which Gargery had closed behind him, burst open. The butler staggered back before the impetuous rush of the new-comer. Hatless, dripping, white-faced, he crossed the room in a series of bounds and stopped, swaying, before Walter, who stared at him in astonishment.

'Professor,' he cried. 'I know I intrude – I beg you to forgive me – and to hear me – '

And then, before Walter could recover from his surprise or any of us could move, the stranger toppled forward and fell prostrate on the hearthrug.

'My Son Lives!'

E merson was the first to break the silence.
'Get up at once, you clumsy young ruffian,' he said irritably.
'Of all the confounded impudence – '

'For pity's sake, Emerson,' I exclaimed, hastening to the side
of the fallen man. 'Can't you see he has fainted? I shudder to
think what unimaginable horror can have reduced him to such
straits.'

'No, you don't,' said Emerson. 'You revel in unimaginable
horrors. Pray control your rampageous imagination. Fainted,
indeed! He is probably drunk.'

'Fetch some brandy at once,' I ordered. With some difficulty
– for the unconscious man was heavier than his slight build had
led me to expect – I turned him on his back and lifted his head
onto my lap.

Emerson folded his arms and stood looking on, a sneer wreathing
his well-cut lips. It was Ramses who approached with the glass of
brandy I had requested; I took it from him, finding, as I had expected, that the outside of the glass was as wet as the inside.

'I am afraid some was spilled,' Ramses explained. 'Mama, if I
may make a suggestion – '

'No, you may not,' I replied.

'But I have read that it is inadvisable to administer brandy or
any other liquid to an unconscious man. There is some danger
of – '

'Yes, yes, Ramses, I am well aware of that. Do be still.'

Mr Forthright did not appear to be in serious condition. His colour was good, and there was no sign of an injury. I estimated his age to be in the early thirties. His features were agreeable rather than handsome, the eyes wide-set under arching brows, the lips full and gently curved. His most unusual physical characteristic was the colour of the hair that adorned his upper lip and his head. A bright, unfashionable but nonetheless striking copper, with glints of gold, it curled becomingly upon his temples.

I proceeded with my administrations; it was not long before the young man's eyes opened and he gazed with wonder into my face. His first words were 'Where am I?'

'On my hearthrug,' said Emerson, looming over him. 'What a da—er–confounded silly question. Explain yourself at once, you presumptuous puppy, before I have you thrown out.'

A deep blush stained Forthright's cheeks. 'You – you are Professor Emerson?'

'One of them.' Emerson indicated Walter, who adjusted his spectacles and coughed deprecatingly. Admittedly he more nearly resembled the popular picture of a scholar than my husband, whose keen blue eyes and healthy complexion, not to mention his impressive musculature, suggest a man of action rather than thought.

'Oh – I see. I beg your pardon – for the confusion, and for my unpardonable intrusion. But I hope when you hear my story you will forgive and assist me. The Professor Emerson I seek is the Egyptologist whose courage and physical prowess are as famous as are his intellectual powers.'

'Er, hmmm,' said Emerson. 'Yes. You have found him. And now, if you will remove yourself from the arms of my wife, at whom you are staring with an intensity that compounds your initial offence . . . '

The young man sat up as if he had been propelled by a spring, stammering apologies. Emerson assisted him to a chair – that is to say, he shoved him into one – and, with a scarcely less heavy

23

hand, helped me to rise. Turning, I saw that Evelyn had gathered the children and was shepherding them from the room. I nodded gratefully at her and was rewarded by one of her sweet smiles.

Our unexpected visitor began with a question. 'Is it true, Professor that you are planning to travel in the Sudan this year?'

'Where did you hear that?' Emerson demanded.

Mr Forthright smiled. 'Your activities, Professor, will always be a subject of interest, not only to the archaeological community but to the public at large. As it happens, I am in an indirect manner connected with the former group. You will not have heard my name, but I am sure you are familiar with that of my grandfather, for he is a well-known patron of archaeological subjects – Viscount Blacktower.'

'Good Gad!' Emerson bellowed.

Mr Forthright started. 'I – I beg your pardon, Professor?'

Emerson's countenance, ruddy with fury, might have intimidated any man, but his terrible frown was not directed at Mr Forthright. It was directed at me. 'I knew it,' Emerson said bitterly. 'Am I never to be free of them? You attract them, Amelia. I don't know how you do it, but it is becoming a pernicious habit. Another cursed aristocrat!'

Walter was unable to repress a chuckle, and I confess to some amusement on my own part; Emerson sounded for all the world like an infuriated sans-culotte, demanding the guillotine for the hated aristos.

Mr Forthright cast an uneasy glance at Emerson.

'I will be as brief as possible,' he began.

'Good,' said Emerson.

'Er – but I fear I must give you some background if you are to understand my difficulty.'

'Curse it,' said Emerson.

'My . . . my grandfather had two sons.'

'Curse *him*,' said Emerson.

'Uh . . . my father was the younger. His elder brother, who was of course the heir, was Willoughby Forth.'

'Willie Forth the explorer?' Emerson repeated, in quite a

different tone of voice. 'You are his nephew? But your name
– '

'My father married Miss Wright, the only child of a wealthy merchant. At his father-in-law's request, he added the surname of Wright to his own. Since most people, hearing the combined name, assumed it to be a single word, I found it simpler to adopt that version.'

'How accommodating of you,' said Emerson. 'You don't resemble your uncle, Mr Forthright. He would have made two of you.'

'His name is familiar,' I said. 'Was it he who proved once and for all that Lake Victoria is the source of the White Nile?'

'No; he clung doggedly to the belief that the Lualaba River was part of the Nile until Stanley proved him wrong by actually sailing down the Lualaba to the Congo, and thence to the Atlantic.' Willoughby Forth's nephew smiled sardonically. 'That, I fear, was the sad pattern of his life. He was always a few months late or a few hundred miles off. It was his great ambition to go down in history as the discoverer of . . . something. Anything! An ambition that was never realised.'

'An ambition that cost him his life,' Emerson said reflectively.

'And that of his wife. They disappeared in the Sudan ten years ago.'

'Fourteen years ago, to be precise.' Forthright stiffened. 'Did I hear someone at the door?'

'I heard nothing.' Emerson studied him keenly. 'Am I to expect another uninvited visitor this evening?'

'I fear so. But pray let me continue. You must hear my story before – '

'I beg, Mr Forthright, that you allow me to be the judge of what must or must not be done in my house,' said Emerson. 'I am not a man who enjoys surprises. I like to be prepared for visitors, especially when they are members of the aristocracy. Is it your grandfather whom you expect?'

'Yes. Please, Professor, allow me to explain. Uncle Willoughby was always the favoured son. Not only did he share my grandfather's archaeological and geographical interests, but he had the physical strength and daring his younger brother lacked. My poor dear father was never strong – '

I could tell by Emerson's expression that he was about to say something rude, so I took it upon myself to intervene. 'Get to the point, Mr Forthright.'

'What? Oh – yes, I beg your pardon. Grandfather has never accepted the fact that his beloved son is dead. He must be, Professor! Some word would have come back, long before this – '

'But no word of his death has come either,' Emerson said.

Forthright made an impatient gesture. 'How could it? There are no telegraphs in the jungle or the desert wastes. Legally my uncle and his unfortunate wife could have been declared dead years ago. My grandfather refused to take that step. My father died last year – '

'Aha,' said Emerson. 'Now we come to the crux of it, I fancy. Until your uncle is declared to be dead, you are not legally your grandfather's heir.'

The young man met his cynical gaze squarely. 'I would be a hypocrite if I denied that that is one of my concerns, Professor. But believe it or not, it is not my chief concern. Sooner or later, in the inevitable course of time, I will succeed to the title and the estate; there is, unhappily, no other heir. But my grandfather – '

He broke off, with a sharp turn of his head. This time there was no mistake; the altercation in the hall was loud enough to be heard even through the closed door. Gargery's voice, raised in expostulation, was drowned out by a sound as loud and shrill as the trumpeting of a bull elephant. The door exploded inward, with a shuddering crash; and on the threshold stood one of the most formidable figures I have ever seen.

The mental image I had formed, of the pathetic, grief-stricken old father, shattered like glass in the face of reality. Lord Blacktower – for it could be no other than he – was a massive brute of a man, with shoulders like a pugilist's and a mane of coarse reddish hair. It was faded and liberally streaked with grey, but once it must have blazed like the setting sun. He seemed far too young and vigorous to be the grandfather of a man in his thirties, until one looked closely at his face. Like a stretch of sun-baked earth, it was seamed with deep-cut lines – a map of violent passions and unhealthy habits.

The suddenness of his appearance and the sheer brute dominance of his presence kept all of us silent for several moments. His eyes moved around the room, passing over the men with cool indifference, until they came to rest on me. Sweeping his hat from his head, he bowed, with a grace unexpected in so very large a man. 'Madam! I beg you will accept my apologies for this intrusion. Allow me to introduce myself. Franklin, Viscount Blacktower. Do I have the honour of addressing Mrs Radcliffe Emerson?'

'Er – yes,' I replied.

'Mrs Emerson!' His smile did not improve his looks, for his eyes remained as cold and opaque as Persian turquoise. 'I have long looked forward to the pleasure of meeting you.'

Advancing with a ponderous rolling stride, he extended his hand. I gave him mine, bracing myself for a bone-crushing grip. Instead he raised my fingers to his lips and planted a loud, lingering, damp kiss upon them. 'Mmmm, yes,' he mumbled. 'Your photographs quite fail to do you justice, Mrs Emerson.'

I fully expected Emerson would object to these proceedings, for the mumbling and kissing went on for a protracted period of time. There was, however, no comment from that source, so I withdrew my hand and invited Lord Blacktower to take a chair. Ignoring the one I had indicated, he sat down on the couch beside me, with a thud that made me and the whole structure vibrate. There was still no reaction from Emerson, or from Mr Forthright, who had sunk back into the chair from which he had started when his grandfather burst in.

'May I offer you a cup of tea, or a glass of brandy, Lord Blacktower?' I asked.

'You are graciousness itself, dear madam, but I have already taken too great advantage of your good nature. Allow me only to explain why I venture to burst in upon you so unceremoniously, and then I will remove myself – and my grandson, whose presence is the cause, if not the excuse, for my rudeness.' He did not look at Mr Forthright, but went on with scarcely a pause. 'I intended to approach you, and your distinguished husband, through the proper channels. Learning by chance, this afternoon, that my grandson had taken it upon himself to anticipate me, I was forced to act quickly. Mrs Emerson ...' He leaned towards me and placed his hand on my knee. 'Mrs Emerson! My son lives! Find him. Bring him back to me.'

His hand was heavy as stone and cold as ice. I stared at the veins squirming across the skin like fat blue worms, at the tufts of greyish-red hair on his fingers. And still no objection from Emerson! It was unaccountable!

Only maternal sympathy for a parent driven into madness by the loss of a beloved child kept me from flinging his hand away. 'Lord Blacktower,' I began.

'I know what you are about to say.' His fingers tightened. 'You don't believe me. Reginald there has probably told you that I am a senile old man, clinging to an impossible hope. But I have proof, Mrs Emerson – a message from my son, containing information only he could know. I received it a few days ago. Find him, and anything you ask of me will be yours. I won't insult you by offering you money – '

'That would be a waste of your time,' I said coldly.

He went on as though I had not spoken. ' – though I would consider it an honour to finance your future expeditions, on any scale you might desire. Or a chair in archaeology for that husband of yours. Or a knighthood. Lady Emerson, eh?'

His accent had coarsened, and his speech, not to mention his hand, had grown increasingly familiar. However, it was not the insult to his wife but the implied insult to himself that finally moved Emerson to speak.

'You are still wasting your time, Lord Blacktower. I don't buy honours or allow anyone else to purchase them for me.'

The old man let out a rumbling roar of laughter. 'I wondered what it would take to rouse you, Professor. Every man has his price, you know. But yours – aye, I'll do you justice; none of the things I've offered would touch you. I've got something I fancy will. Here – have a look at this.'

Reaching into his pocket he drew out an envelope. I re-arranged my skirts; I fancied I could still feel the imprint of his hand, burning cold against my skin.

Emerson took the envelope. It was not sealed. With the same delicacy of touch he used on fragile antiquities, he drew from the envelope a long, narrow, flat object. It was cream-coloured and too thick to be ordinary paper, but there was writing on it. I was unable to make out the words.

Emerson studied it in silence for a few moments. Then his lip curled. 'A most impudent and unconvincing forgery.'

'Forgery! That is papyrus, is it not?'

'It is papyrus,' Emerson admitted. 'And it is yellowed and brittle enough to be ancient Egyptian in origin. But the writing is neither ancient nor Egyptian. What sort of nonsense is this?'

The old man bared his teeth, which resembled the papyrus in colour. 'Read it, Professor. Read the message aloud.'

Emerson shrugged. 'Very well. "To the old lion from the young lion, greetings. Your son and daughter live; but not long, unless help comes soon. Blood calls to blood, old lion, but if that call is not strong enough, seek the treasure of the past in this place where I await you." Of all the childish – '

'Childish, yes. It began when he was a boy, reading romances and tales of adventure. It became a kind of private code. He wrote to no one else in that way – and no living man or woman knew of it. Nor knew that his name for me was the old lion.'

He resembled one at that moment – a tired old lion with sagging jowls and eyes sunk in wrinkled sockets.

'It is still a forgery,' Emerson said stubbornly. 'More ingenious than I had believed, but a forgery nonetheless.'

'Forgive me, Emerson, but you are missing the point,' I said. Emerson turned an indignant look upon me, but I went on. 'Let us assume that the message is indeed from Mr Willoughby

Forth, and that he has been held prisoner, or otherwise detained, all these years. Let us also assume that some daring couple – er – that is to say, some daring adventurer – were willing to go to his aid. Where would that adventurer go? A man asking for help ought at least give directions.'

'I,' said my husband, 'was about to make that very point, Amelia.'

The old man grinned. 'There is something else in the envelope, Professor. Take it out, if you please.'

The second enclosure was more prosaic than the first – a single sheet of ordinary writing paper, folded several times – but its effect on Emerson was remarkable. He stood staring at it with as much consternation as if it had been a death threat (a form of correspondence, I might add, with which he was not unfamiliar). I jumped up and took the paper from his hand. It was grey with age and dust, tattered with much handling, and covered with writing in the English language. The handwriting was as familiar to me as my own.

'It looks like a page from one of your notebooks, Emerson,' I exclaimed. 'How on earth did this come into your hands, Lord Blacktower?'

'The envelope and its contents were left on the doorstep of my house in Berkeley Square. My butler admitted he had half a mind to pitch it into the trash. Fortunately he did not.'

'It didn't come through the post,' Emerson muttered, inspecting the envelope. 'So it must have been delivered by hand. By whom? Why didn't the messenger identify himself and claim a reward?'

'I don't know and I don't care,' the old man said irritably. 'The handwriting on the envelope is my son's. So is the writing on the papyrus. What more proof do you want?'

'Anyone who knew your son, and had received a letter from him, could imitate his handwriting,' I said gently but firmly. 'To my mind, the page from my husband's notebook is a far more intriguing clue. But I don't understand what bearing it has on Mr Forth's disappearance.'

30

'Turn it over,' said Lord Blacktower.
I did as he directed. At first glance the faded lines appeared to be random scribbles, like those made by a small child. From Lord Blacktower's throat came a horrible grating sound. I presumed it was a laugh.

'Are you beginning to remember, Professor Emerson? Was it you or my son who sketched the map?'

'Map?' I repeated, studying the scrawl more closely.

'I remember the occasion,' Emerson said slowly. 'And under the present circumstances – taking into consideration the suffering of a bereaved father – I will make an exception to my general policy of refusing to answer impertinent questions from strangers.' I made a little sound of protest, for Emerson's tone of voice – especially when he mentioned the suffering of a bereaved father – made the speech even ruder than the words themselves convey. Blacktower only grinned.

'This is not a map,' Emerson said. 'It is a fantasy – a fiction. It can have no possible bearing on your son's fate. Someone is playing a cruel trick on you, Lord Blacktower, or is planning to perpetrate a fraud.'

'That is precisely what I told my grandfather, Professor,' Mr Forthright exclaimed.

'Don't be a fool,' Blacktower snarled. 'I couldn't be deceived by an impostor – '

'Don't be so sure,' Emerson interrupted. 'I saw Slatin Pasha in '95, after he had escaped from eleven years' starvation and torture by the Khalifa. I didn't recognise him. His own mother wouldn't have known him. However, that wasn't the kind of fraud I had in mind. How much were you prepared to offer me to equip and undertake a rescue expedition?'

'But you refused to be bribed, Professor.'

'I refused, period,' Emerson said. 'Oh, the devil with this! There is no point in my offering you my advice, because you wouldn't take it. As my family will tell you, Lord Blacktower, I am the most patient of men; but my patience is wearing thin. I bid you good evening.'

The old man heaved himself to his feet. 'I too am a patient man, Professor. I have waited for my son for fourteen years. He lives; I know it, and one day you will admit that I was right and you, sir, were wrong. Good evening, gentlemen. Good evening, Mrs Emerson. Don't trouble yourself to ring for the servant. I will let myself out. Come, Reginald.'

He went to the door and closed it quietly behind him.

'Good-bye, Mr Forthright,' said Emerson.

'Let me add one last word, Professor – '

'Be quick about it,' Emerson said, his eyes flashing.

'This may be precisely the sort of filthy game you described. But there is another possibility. My grandfather has enemies – '

'No! You astonish me!' Emerson exclaimed.

'If there is no further communication – if he can't find a qualified man to lead such an expedition – he will go himself. You look sceptical, but I assure you I know him well. He is convinced of the authenticity of this message. Believing that – '

'You said one word, and I have let you utter sixty or seventy.'

'Before I let my grandfather risk his life on such a scheme, I will go,' Forthright said quickly. 'Indeed, if I could believe there was the slightest chance – '

'Confound it,' Emerson shouted. 'Must I evict you bodily?'

'No.' The young man backed towards the door, with Emerson following. 'But if you should change your mind, Professor, I insist upon accompanying you.'

'A very pretty speech, upon my word,' Emerson declared, splashing whiskey into his glass with such force that it fountained up onto the table. 'How dare he suggest I might change my mind? I never change my mind.'

'I suspect he is a more acute judge of character than you give him credit for,' Walter said. 'I too detected something in your manner ... You haven't been completely candid with us, Radcliffe.'

Emerson winced – whether at the unpopular appellation or the implied accusation, I cannot tell. He said nothing.

I went to the window and drew the curtain aside. The rain had stopped. Mist veiled the lawn, and carriage lamps glowed through the dark. They were obscured as a shapeless bulk heaved itself between them and my vision. It was Lord Blacktower, mounting into his coach. In his caped coat, wrapped round with wisps of fog, his shape was scarcely human. I had the unpleasant impression that I saw not a man or even a beast, but some elemental force of darkness.

Hearing the door open, I turned to see Evelyn. 'Cook is threatening to leave your service if dinner is not served instantly,' she said with a smile. 'And Rose is looking for Ramses. He did not come up with the others; is he . . . Ah, there you are, my boy.'

And there he was indeed, rising up from behind the sofa like a genie from a bottle – or a flagrant eavesdropper from his place of concealment. Irritation replaced my eerie forebodings, and as my son obediently hastened towards his aunt, I said sharply, 'Ramses, what have you got there?'

Ramses stopped. He looked like the reverse image of a small saint, for the mop of curls crowning his head was jet-black and the face thus framed, though handsome enough in its way, was as swarthy as any Egyptian's. 'Got, Mama? Oh . . .' With an air of surprised innocence he glanced at the paper in his hand. 'It appears to be the leaf from Papa's notebook. I picked it up from the floor.'

I did not doubt that in the least. Ramses preferred to tell the truth whenever possible. I had placed the paper on the table, so he must have pushed it off onto the floor before he picked it up.

After he had handed over the paper and gone through the lengthy process of saying good night, we made our way to the dining room.

I had long since given up trying to prevent Emerson from discussing private family matters in front of the servants. In fact, I had come round to his point of view – that it was a cursed silly, meaningless custom – for the servants always knew everything that was going on anyhow, and their advice was often helpful since on the whole they had better sense than their purported superiors. I fully expected that he would discuss the extraordinary events that had just taken place. Gargery, our butler, obviously shared this anticipation; though he directed the serving of the meal with his usual efficiency, his face was beaming and his eyes alight. He always enjoyed participating in our little adventures, and the peculiar behaviour of our visitors certainly justified the suspicion that another was about to occur.

Conceive of my surprise, therefore, when, after having satisfied the first pangs of hunger by polishing off his soup, Emerson patted his lips with his napkin and remarked, 'Inclement weather for this time of year.'

'Hardly unusual, though,' said Walter innocently.

'I hope the rain will let up. You will have a wet journey home otherwise.'

'Quite,' said Walter.

I cleared my throat. Emerson said hastily, 'And what are you giving us tonight, Peabody? Ah – roast saddle of lamb. And mint jelly! I am particularly fond of mint jelly. A splendid choice.'

'Mrs Bates is giving us the lamb,' I said, as Gargery, visibly pouting, began serving the plates. 'You know I leave the menu to her, Emerson. I have no time for such things. Especially now, with so many extra supplies to order – '

'Quite, quite,' said Emerson.

'Mint jelly, sir?' said Gargery, in a voice that ought to have frozen that wobbly substance into a solid chunk. Without waiting for an answer, he proceeded to give Emerson approximately half a teaspoonful.

Like his brother, Walter was inclined to ignore conventions, not because he necessarily shared Emerson's radical social theories but because he forgot all else when professional enthusiasm overcame him. 'I say, Radcliffe,' he exclaimed. 'That bit of papyrus was quite fascinating. If an ancient Egyptian scribe had known how to write English, the result would have looked precisely like that message. I wish I had had a chance to examine it more closely.'

'You may do so after dinner,' I said. 'By a strange coincidence, and in the haste of his departure, Lord Blacktower forgot to take it with him. Or was it a coincidence, Emerson?'

'You know as well as I do that it was deliberate,' Emerson snarled. '*Pas devant les domestiques*, Peabody, as you are always telling me.'

'Bah,' I replied pleasantly. 'Ramses has probably told Rose all about it by now. I know you well, my dear Emerson; your countenance is an open book to me. That supposedly meaningless scrawl on the back of the notebook page had meaning for you. I know it. His lordship knew it. Will you take us into your confidence, or force us to employ underhanded means to discover the truth?'

Emerson glowered – at me, at Walter, at Evelyn, and at Gargery, who was standing guard over the mint jelly, his nose in the air and wounded dignity in every lineament of his face. Then Emerson's own face cleared and he burst into a hearty laugh. 'You are incorrigible, my dear Peabody. I won't inquire what particular underhanded methods you had in mind. . . In fact, there is no reason why I shouldn't tell you what little I know of the matter. And now, Gargery, may I have more mint jelly?'

This delicacy having been supplied, Emerson went on. 'I spoke the truth when I told Blacktower that piece of paper could have no bearing on Forth's fate. Yet it gave me an eerie feeling to see it again after all these years. Rather like the hollow voice of a dead man echoing from his tomb. . .'

'Now who is allowing a rampageous imagination to run away with him?' I inquired playfully. 'Get on with it, Emerson, if you please.

'First,' said Emerson, 'we must tell Evelyn what happened after she left with the children.'

He proceeded to do so, at quite unnecessary length. Gargery found it most interesting, however. 'A map, was it, sir?' he asked, giving Emerson more mint jelly.

'Take that cursed stuff away,' Emerson said, studying the green puddle with loathing. 'Yes, it was a map. Of sorts.'

'Of the road to King Solomon's diamond mines, I suppose,' said Walter, smiling. 'Or the emerald mines of Cleopatra. Or the gold mines of Cush.'

'It was a fantasy almost as improbable, Walter. It is coming back to me now – that strange encounter, the last meeting I ever had with Willie Forth.' He paused to give Gargery time to remove the plates and serve the next course before resuming.

'It was the autumn of 1883 – the year before I met you, my dearest Peabody, and a year when Walter was not with me. Having no such engaging distractions, I found myself at loose ends one evening in Cairo, and decided to visit a café. Forth was there; when he saw me, he jumped to his feet and called my name. He was a great bull of a fellow with a head of wiry black hair that always looked as if it had not seen scissors or brush for weeks. Well, we had a friendly glass or two; he demanded I drink a toast to his bride, for he had just been married. I ragged him a bit about this unexpected news; he was a confirmed old bachelor of forty-odd and had always insisted no woman would ever tie him down. He only grinned sheepishly and raved about her beauty, innocence, and charm like any infatuated schoolboy.

'Then we got to talking about his plans for the winter. He was cagey at first, but I could see that something besides marital bliss had fired him up, and after another friendly glass or two he admitted that his ultimate destination was not Assouan, as he had initially told me, but somewhere farther south.

'"I understand you have excavated at Napata," he said casually.

'I was unable to conceal my surprise and disapproval. The news from the Sudan was extremely disquieting, and Forth had told me he planned to take his wife with him. He brushed my objections aside. "The worst of the trouble is in Kordofan, hundreds of miles from where I mean to go. And General Hicks is on the way there; he'll settle those fellows before we reach Wadi Halfa."' Turning to the butler, he explained, 'Wadi Halfa is at the Second Cataract, Gargery, several hundred miles south of Assouan.'

'Yes, sir, thank you, sir. And that other place – Nabada?'

'Hmm, well,' said Emerson. 'There has been some debate about that. The Cushites, or Nubians, had two capitals. Meroë, the second and later of the two, was near the Sixth Cataract, just north of Khartoum. Its ruins have been visited and identified. We have a fairly good idea of where Napata, the earlier capital, was situated, because of the pyramid cemeteries in the area, but its exact location is uncertain.

'Well, we all know what happened to Hicks. (His army was annihilated by the Mahdi, Gargery, contrary to all expectations except mine.) Word of that disaster did not reach Cairo until after Forth had left. All I could tell him that night was that I had visited a site I believed to be Napata and that – to put it mildly – it was not the spot I would have chosen for a honeymoon. "You surely don't mean to take your bride to a primitive, fever-ridden, dangerous place like that?" I demanded.

'Forth was feeling the effects of four or five friendly glasses. He gave me a drunken grin. "Farther than that, Emerson. Much farther."

'"Meroë? It's even more remote and dangerous than Gebel Barkal. You're mad, Forth."

'"And you're still off the mark, Emerson." Forth leaned forward, planting both elbows on the filthy table, and fixed me with burning eyes. I felt like the Wedding Guest, and indeed, as he went on, I would not have been surprised to see the albatross hung about his neck. "What happened to the royalty and nobility of Meroë after the city fell? Where did they go? You've heard the Arab legends about the sons of Cush who marched towards the setting sun – westward through the desert to a secret city. . ."

'"Stories, legends, fictions," I exclaimed. "They are no more factual than the tales of Arthur being carried off to the Isle of Avalon by the three queens, or Charlemagne sleeping under the mountain with his knights – "

'"Or the Homeric legends of Troy," said Forth.

'I swore at him – and at Heinreich Schliemann, whose discoveries had encouraged lunatics like my friend. Forth listened, grinning like an ape and fumbling in the pockets of his coat – for his pipe, as I thought. Instead he took out a small box and handed it to me, inviting me, with a sweeping gesture, to lift the lid. When I did so . . . Peabody, do you remember the Ferlini Collection in the Berlin Museum?'

Caught unawares by the question, I started to shake my head and then exclaimed, 'The jewellery brought back from Meroë by Ferlini half a century ago?'

'Quite.' Emerson whipped a pencil from his pocket and began to draw on the tablecloth. Gargery, who was familiar with this habit of Emerson's and with my reaction to it, deftly inserted a piece of paper under the pencil. Emerson finished his sketch and handed the paper to Gargery, who, after inspecting it closely, handed it round the table like a platter of vegetables. 'What I saw in the box was a gold armlet,' Emerson continued. 'The designs, consisting of uraei, diamond shapes, and lotus buds, were inlaid with red and blue enamel.'

Walter frowned at the paper. 'I have seen a lithograph of a piece of jewellery resembling this, Radcliffe.'

'In Lepsius's *Denkmäler,*' Emerson replied. 'Or perhaps the official guide to the Berlin Museum, 1894 edition. An armlet of the same type, with similar decoration, was found by Ferlini at Meroë. I saw the resemblance at once, and my first reaction was that Forth's armlet must also have come from Meroë. The natives have been plundering the pyramids ever since Ferlini's time, hoping to find another treasure trove. Yet the cursed thing was in virtually pristine condition – a few scratches here and there, a few dents – and the enamel was so fresh it might have been newly made. It had to be a modern forgery – but what forger would use gold of such purity it could be bent with one's fingers?

'I asked Forth where he had got it, and he proceeded to tell me a preposterous story about being offered the piece by a ragged native who offered to lead him to the source of such treasures. A source far in the western deserts, in a secret oasis, where there were huge buildings like the temples of Luxor and a strange race of magicians who wore golden ornaments and performed blood sacrifices to demonic gods. . .' Emerson shook his head. 'You can imagine how I jeered at this absurd story, all the more so when he told me that the unfortunate native had suffered from a fever to which he succumbed a few days later.

'My arguments had no effect on Forth; he was drinking quite heavily, and when I finally gave up my attempt to dissuade him from his lunatic plan I could see he was in no condition to be left alone. Late at night, in that district, he would have been robbed and beaten. So I offered to escort him to his hotel. He agreed, saying he was anxious to introduce me to his wife.

'She had waited up for him, but she had not anticipated he would bring a stranger with him; she was wrapped in some sort of fluffy white stuff, all trembling with lace and ruffles; part of her bridal getup, I suppose. An exquisite creature, looking no more than eighteen; great misty blue eyes, hair like a fall of spun gold, skin white as ivory. And cold. An ice maiden, with no more human warmth than a statue. They made a bizarre contrast, Forth with his ruddy beaming face and mane of black hair, his wife all white and silvery pale – Beauty and the Beast personified. I thought of that flowery-white skin of hers baked and scourged by blowing sand, of her gleaming hair dried by the sun – and by heaven, Peabody, I felt only the regret one might feel at seeing a work of art disfigured – no human pity at all. She would have received none; she would have felt none. No, the pity I felt was for Willie Forth. The idea of taking a frozen statue like that into one's arms, into one's . . . Er, hmmm. You understand me, Peabody.'

I felt myself blushing. 'Yes, Emerson, I do. Yet one can't help but feel for her. She can have had no idea of what she was about to experience.'

'I tried to tell her. Forth had collapsed onto the bed and lay snoring, with both hands clenched over the box that contained the armlet. I spoke to her like a brother, Peabody; I told her she was mad to go, that he was madder to let her. I might have been speaking to a chryselephantine statue. At last she intimated that my presence displeased her, so I left, and I am sorry to say I slammed the door behind me. That was the last I saw of either of them.'

'But the map, Emerson,' I said. 'When did you – '

'Oh.' Emerson coughed. 'That. Well, curse it, Peabody, I'd had a few friendly drinks myself, and I'd been reading some of the medieval Arabic writers . . .'

'*The Book of Hidden Pearls?*'

Emerson grinned sheepishly. 'Confound you, Peabody, you're always a step or two ahead of me. It's that rampageous imagination of yours. But there is often a germ of truth in the most fantastic of legends. I am quite willing to believe that there are unknown oases in the western desert, far to the south of the known oases of Egypt. Wilkinson names three, in his book published in 1835; he had heard about them from the Arabs. The people of Dakhla – one of the known oases in southern Egypt – tell tales of strangers, tall black men, who came out of the south. And El Bekri, who wrote in the eleventh century, described a giantess who was captured at Dakhla; she spoke no known language, and when she was released, so that

40

her captors could not track her to her home, she outran them and escaped.'

'Fascinating,' Evelyn breathed. 'But the *Book of Hidden Pearls?*'

'Ah, there we enter into pure legend,' Emerson said, smiling affectionately at her. 'It is a magical work, written in the fifteenth century, containing stories of buried treasure. One such location is in the white city of Zerzura, where the king and queen lie asleep on their thrones. The key to the city is in the beak of a bird carved on the great gate; but you must take care not to wake the king and queen if you want the treasure.'

'That is simply a fairy tale,' Walter said critically.

'Of course it is. But Zerzura is mentioned in other sources; the name probably derives from the Arabic zarzar, meaning sparrow, so Zerzura is "the place of the little birds." And there are other stories, other clues. . .' Emerson's face took on the pensive, dreamy look few of his acquaintances are privileged to see. He likes to be thought of as a strictly rational man, who sneers at idle fancies, but in reality the dear fellow is as sensitive and sentimental as women are purported to be (though in my experience women are far more practical than men).

'Are you thinking of Harkhuf?' Walter asked. 'It is true that that mystery has never been solved, at least not to my satisfaction. Where did he go on those expeditions of his, to procure the treasures he brought back to Egypt? Gold and ivory, and the dancing dwarf that so delighted the child-king he served. . . Then there are Queen Hatshepsut's voyages to Punt – '

'Punt doesn't enter into it,' Emerson said. 'It must be somewhere on the Red Sea coast, east of the Nile. As for Harkhuf, that was over four thousand years ago. He may have followed the Darb el Arba'in. . . There, you see the fascination of such idle speculation? We speculated, and had those friendly drinks, and drew meaningless lines on a piece of paper. If Forth was fool enough to follow that so-called map, he deserved the unpleasant death that undoubtedly came to him. Enough of this.

41

Peabody, why are you sitting there? Why haven't you risen from your chair to indicate that the ladies wish to retire?'

This question was mean to provoke me; Emerson knew quite well that the custom to which he referred was never followed in our house. 'We will all retire,' I said.

Walter hastened to open the door for me. 'It is an odd coincidence, though,' he said innocently. 'The Dervish uprising had just begun when Mr Forth disappeared. Now it appears to be almost over, and the message arrives – '

'Walter, don't be so naive. If fraud is contemplated, the timing is no coincidence. The news of Slatin Pasha's escape, after all those years in captivity, may well have inspired some criminal mind – '

He broke off with a choking sound. The blood rushed into his cheeks.

I knew what he was thinking. I always know what Emerson is thinking, for the spiritual bond that unites us is strong. The dark shadow of the Master Criminal, our old nemesis, would always haunt us – me, especially, since I had (much to my astonishment, for I am a modest woman) inspired an intense passion in that warped but brilliant brain.

'No, Emerson,' I exclaimed. 'It cannot be. Remember his promise, that never again would he – '

'The promise of a snake like that is worth nothing, Peabody. This is just the sort of scheme – '

'Remember your promise, then, Emerson. That never again would you – '

'Oh, curse it,' Emerson muttered.

Though she did not (at least I hoped she did not) know whereof we spoke, Evelyn tactfully introduced another subject. 'Explain to me, dear brother, what it is you hope to accomplish at Meroë, and why you can't work in Egypt as you have always done? It terrifies me to think of you and Amelia running such risks.'

Emerson responded, though he kept tugging at his collar as if it were choking him. 'To all intents and purposes, ancient

Cush is an unknown civilisation, Evelyn. The only qualified scholar who visited the site was Lepsius, and he could do little more than record what was there in 1844. That is the most important task awaiting us – to make accurate records of the monuments and inscriptions, before time and treasure hunters destroy them completely.'

'Especially the inscriptions,' Walter said eagerly. 'The script is derived from Egyptian hieroglyphs, but the language has not been translated. When I think of the rate at which the records are vanishing, never to be recovered, I am tempted to come with you. You and Amelia cannot possibly – '

At this Evelyn let out a cry of alarm and clutched at Walter's arm as if he were about to depart instantly for Africa. Emerson reassured her in his usual tactful fashion. 'Walter has grown soft and flabby, Evelyn. He wouldn't last a day in Nubia. A strict course of physical training, that is what you need, Walter. If you work hard at it this winter, I may allow you to accompany us next season.'

In such animated and pleasant domestic intercourse the next hour passed. Both men had asked permission to smoke their pipes, permission which was, of course, granted; Evelyn was too kind to refuse anyone she loved and I would never dream of attempting to prevent Emerson from doing anything he liked in his own drawing room. (Though I have been forced, upon occasion, to request that he postpone a particular activity until a more appropriate degree of privacy could be attained.)

At last I went to the window to admit a breath of fresh air. The clouds had cleared away and moonlight spread its silvery softness across the lawn. As I stood admiring the beauty of the night (for I am particularly fond of nature), a sharp cracking sound broke the dreaming peace. It was followed in rapid succession by a second and a third.

I turned. My eyes met those of Emerson.

'Poachers,' said Walter lazily. 'It's a good thing young Ramses is asleep. He'd be out that door – '

Emerson, moving with pantherlike quickness, was already

out that door. I followed, delaying only long enough for a quick explanation. 'Not poachers, Walter. Those shots came from a pistol. Stay here with Evelyn.'

Hitching up my crimson flounces I sped in pursuit of my husband. He had not gone far; I found him on the front lawn, gazing out into the darkness. 'I see nothing amiss,' he remarked. 'From what direction did the sounds come?'

We were unable to agree on that question. After a rather brisk discussion – in the course of which Emerson firmly negated my suggestion that we separate in order to search a wider area more quickly – we set out in the direction I had suggested, towards the rose garden and the little wilderness behind it. Though we investigated the area carefully, we found nothing out of the way, and I was about to accede to Emerson's demand that we wait until morning before pursuing the search when the sound of a wheeled vehicle came to our ears.

'That way,' I cried, pointing.

'It is only a farmer's wagon going to market,' Emerson said.

'At this hour?' I started across the lawn towards the belt of trees that bounds our property on the north. The grass was so wet it was impossible for me to attain my usual running speed in fragile evening shoes, and Emerson soon forged ahead, ignoring my demands that he wait for me. When I caught him up, he had passed through the gate in the brick wall – which constitutes a side entrance to the estate – and was standing still, staring down at something on the ground.

Turning, he put out his arm and held me back. 'Stop, Peabody. That's one of my favourite frocks; I would hate to see it ruined.'

'What – ' I began. But there was no need to finish the question. We were on the edge of the belt of trees. A narrow track used by carts and farm vehicles ran along the side of the wall. On the beaten earth the pool of liquid was black as ink in the moonlight, which stroked its surface with tremulous silver fingers. But the liquid was not ink. By daylight it would be another colour entirely – the same shade as my bright crimson skirts.

'He Promised
All the Ladies
Many Sons'

With the conspicuous absence of intelligence that marks the profession, our local constabulary refused to believe that murder had been committed. They agreed with me that no living creature could have survived the loss of such a quantity of the vital fluid; all the more reason, they declared, to assume that the crime had been perpetrated against one of the lower animals and was therefore not a crime, or at least not the crime of murder. When I pointed out that poachers seldom employ hand weapons, they only smiled politely and shook their heads – not at this self-evident fact, but at the idea that a mere female could have distinguished between the different sounds – and inquired, even more politely, why my hypothetical murderer should have removed the body of his victim.

They had me there. For no body had been found, nor even a trail of bloodstains. Clearly the perpetrator had carried it away by means of a cart or wagon, the sound of whose wheels Emerson and I had heard, but I was forced to admit that without a corpus delicti my case was considerably weakened.

Emerson did not support me with the ardour I had every right to expect. He was particularly annoyed by my suggestion that the fatality was in some way connected with the Forth family. I am sure the Reader will agree with this conclusion, as any sensible person would; two mysterious events on the same evening cannot be unrelated. Yet it appeared that they were. Inquiries, which I insisted upon making, resulted in the discovery that both Lord Blacktower and his grandson were in perfect health and at a loss to understand my concern.

The viscount also took pleasure in telling me that no one had approached him demanding money for information or for equipping a rescue expedition. He seemed to think this was proof Emerson's analysis of the message had been mistaken, but to me it made the situation even more baffling. Certainly, if fraud had been intended, further communications were to be expected, but the same was true if the appeal was genuine. How had the message got from – wherever it was? – to London, and why did not the messenger make himself known to the recipient? And what bearing – if any – had the ghastly puddle in the lane upon the matter?

As for the documentary evidence – the scrap of papyrus and the page from Emerson's notebook – closer examination confused the situation even more. The papyrus was ancient; traces of an earlier text could be seen under the modern writing. This phenomenon was of frequent occurrence in ancient Egypt, for papyrus was expensive and was often erased so that it could be reused. Pieces of ancient papyrus were (I regret to say) easily obtained by any traveller to Egypt. Similarly, the page from Emerson's notebook might have come into the possession of a person or persons unknown. Emerson admitted that he could not remember what had happened to it; Forth might have put it in his pocket, or he might have left it on the café table.

The case, such as it was, appeared to have reached a dead end. Even I could think of nothing more to do. I decided reluctantly to abandon it, especially since other problems were trying Emerson's temper to the utmost.

Emerson likes to think that he is the master of his fate and the lord of all he surveys. It is a delusion common to the male sex and accounts for the sputtering fury with which they respond to the slightest interference with their plans, no matter how impractical those plans may be. Being ruled by men, most women are accustomed to irrational behaviour on the part of those who control their destinies. I was therefore not at all surprised when Emerson's plans received their first check. Instead of advancing towards Khartoum, the Egyptian Expeditionary Force settled into winter quarters at Merawi, not to be confused with Meroë, which is several hundred miles farther south.

Rather than resign himself to the inevitable, as a woman would do, Emerson wasted a great deal of time trying to think of ways to get around it. He also refused to accept the obvious arguments against working in a region where food was scarce and trained workmen were in exceedingly short supply.

'If we could find something to feed them, we would have workers enough,' he growled, puffing furiously on his pipe. 'These stories about the congenital laziness of the Sudanese are only European prejudice. I don't see how we can manage it, though. All transport south of Wadi Halfa is controlled by the military; we can hardly commandeer a railway carriage, load it with supplies . . .' He fell silent, his eyes brightening as he considered this idea.

'Not without being somewhat conspicuous,' I replied dryly. 'You would also have to commandeer an engine to pull the carriage, and wood to stoke the boiler, and an engineer, among other necessities. No, I fear the idea is impractical. We must give it up, Emerson, for this year at least. By next autumn our brave lads will have taken Khartoum and wiped out the stain of dishonour that has soiled the British flag since we failed to succour the gallant Gordon.'

'Gallant nincompoop,' said Emerson. 'He was sent to evacuate Khartoum, not squat like a toad in a puddle daring the Mahdi to come and murder him. Well, well, perhaps it is all for the best. Even if the country were pacified, it has suffered greatly. Not a fit place for our boy, hardy though he is.'

'Ramses does not enter into it,' I replied. 'He will be at school in Cairo. Where shall we excavate then, Emerson?'

'There is only one place, Peabody. Napata.'

'Napata?'

'Gebel Barkal, near Merawi. I am convinced it is the site of the first capital of Cush, which flourished for six hundred years before the Cushites moved upriver to Meroë. Budge is already there, curse him,' Emerson added, clenching his teeth so violently on the stem of his pipe that a cracking sound was heard. 'What he is doing to the pyramids I dare not think.'

Poor Mr Budge was at fault because he had had the audacity to be already in the Sudan. It was no use for me to point out that he had only done what Emerson himself would have done, given the opportunity – i.e., accept an invitation from the British authorities. 'Invitation, my –' Emerson would roar, employing language that made me clap my hands over my ears. 'He invited himself! He bullied, pushed, and toadied his way into going. Good Gad, Peabody, by the time that blackguard finishes, there won't be one stone left on another in Nubia, and he will have stolen every portable antiquity in the country for his cursed museum. . .'

And so on, at considerable length.

Though as a rule I attempted to defend Mr Budge against Emerson's more unreasonable complaints, I was a trifle out of sorts with him myself. A dispatch sent through military channels boasted of his making the arduous journey from Cairo to Kerma in only ten and one half days. I knew too well what the effect of this claim would be on my irascible spouse. Emerson would insist on bettering Budge's record.

The first stage, from Cairo to Assouan, was one we had made many times, and I anticipated no particular difficulty there. So it proved; but Assouan, which had been a sleepy little village, was now transformed into a vast depot for military supplies. Though we received every courtesy from Captain Pedley, he was tactless enough to tell Emerson he ought not allow his wife to travel into such a desolate and dangerous region. 'Allow!' Emerson repeated. '"Allow," did you say?'

Though scarcely less annoyed, I thought it best to change the subject. One must recognise the limitations of the military mind, as I later pointed out to Emerson. After a certain age – somewhere in the early twenties, I believe – it is virtually imposs-ible to insert any new idea whatever into it.

Since travel by boat through the tumultuous, rocky rapids of the First Cataract is hazardous, we had to leave the steamer at Assouan and take the railroad to Shellal, at the south end of the cataract. There we were fortunate enough to find passage on a paddle wheeler. The captain turned out to be an old acquaintance of Emerson's. A good many of the inhabitants of Nubia turned out to be old acquaintances of Emerson's. At every wretched little village where the steamer took on wood for the boiler, voices would hail him 'Essalâmu 'aleikum, Emerson Effendi! Marhaba, Oh Father of Curses!"' It was flattering, but somewhat embarrassing, especially when the greetings came (as they did upon one occasion) from the painted lips of a female individual inadequately draped in a costume that left little doubt as to her choice of profession.

Our quarters on the steamer, though far from the standards of cleanliness upon which I normally insist, were commodious enough. Despite the inconveniences (and the awkwardness I have referred to earlier), I greatly enjoyed the trip. The territory south of Assouan was new to me. The rugged grandeur of the scenery and the ruins lining the banks proved a constant source of entertainment. I took copious notes, of course, but since I plan to publish an account elsewhere, I will spare the Reader details. One sight must be mentioned, however; no one could pass by the majestic temple of Abu Simbel without a word of homage and appreciation.

Thanks to my careful planning and the amiable cooperation of Emerson's friend the captain, we came abreast of this astonish-ing structure at dawn, on one of the two days each year when the rays of the sun lifting over the eastern mountains strike straight through the entrance into the farthest recesses of the sanctuary and rest like a heavenly flame upon the altar. The effect was awe-inspiring, and even after the sun had soared higher and the arrow-shaft of golden light had faded, the view held us motionless at the rail of the boat. Four giant statues of Ramses II guard the entrance, greeting with inhuman dignity the daily advent of the god to whom the temple was dedicated, as they have done morning after morning for almost three thousand years.

Ramses stood beside us at the rail, and his normally impassive countenance showed signs of suppressed emotion as he gazed upon the mightiest work of the monarch whose namesake he was. (In fact, he had been named for his uncle Walter; his father had proposed the nickname for him when he was an infant, claiming that the child's imperious manner and single-minded selfishness suggested that most egotistical of pharaohs. The name had stuck, for reasons which should be apparent to all Readers of my chronicles.)

But what, you may ask, was Ramses doing at the rail of the steamer? He should have been in school.

He was not in school because the Academy for Young Gentlemen in Cairo had been unable to admit him. That is the word the headmaster used – 'unable.' He claimed they had no room for another boarder. This may have been so. I had no means of proving it was not. I cannot conceive of any other reason why my son should not have been admitted to a school for young gentlemen.

I do not speak ironically, though anyone who has read certain of my comments concerning my son may suspect I do. The fact is, Ramses had improved considerably in the past few years. (Either that, or I was becoming accustomed to him. It is said that one can become accustomed to anything.)

He was at this time ten years old, having celebrated his birthday late that summer. Over the past few months he had shot up quite suddenly, as boys do, and I had begun to think he might one day have his father's height, though probably not the latter's splendid physique. His features were still too large for his thin face, but just lately I had discovered a dent or dimple

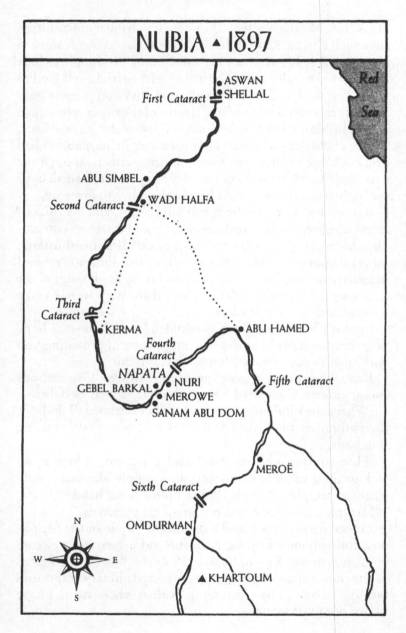

NUBIA ▲ 1897

Red Sea

ASWAN
First Cataract SHELLAL

ABU SIMBEL

Second Cataract WADI HALFA

Third Cataract KERMA

ABU HAMED

Fourth Cataract

NAPATA
GEBEL BARKAL NURI
MEROWE
SANAM ABU DOM

Fifth Cataract

MEROË

Sixth Cataract

OMDURMAN

N
W E
S

▲ KHARTOUM

in his chin, like the one that lent Emerson's handsome countenance such charm. Ramses disliked references to this feature as much as his father resented my mentioning his dimple (which he preferred to call a cleft, if he had to refer to it). I am bound to admit that the boy's jet-black curls and olive complexion bore a closer resemblance to a young Arab – of the finest type – than an Anglo-Saxon; but that he was a gentleman, by birth at least, no one could deny. A distinct improvement in his manners had occurred, due in large part to my untiring efforts, though the natural effects of maturation also played a part. Most small boys are barbarians. It is a wonder any of them live to grow up.

Ramses had lived, to the age of ten at least, and his suicidal tendencies seemed to have decreased. I could therefore contemplate his accompanying us with resignation if not enthusiasm, especially since I had little choice in the matter. Emerson refused to join me in bringing pressure to bear on the headmaster of the Academy for Young Gentlemen; he had always wanted to take Ramses with us to the Sudan.

I put my hand on the boy's shoulder. 'Well, Ramses, I hope you appreciate the kindness of your parents in providing you with such an opportunity. Impressive, is it not?'

Ramses's prominent nose quivered critically. 'Ostentatious and grandiose. Compared with the temple of Deir el-Bahri – '

'What a dreadful little snob you are,' I exclaimed. 'I do hope the antiquities of Napata will measure up to your exacting standards.'

'He is quite right, though,' said Emerson. 'There is no architectural subtlety or mystery in a temple like that – only size. The temples of Gebel Barkal, on the other hand – '

'Temples, Emerson? You promised me pyramids.'

Emerson's eyes remained fixed on the facade of the temple, now fully illumined by the risen sun and presenting a picture of great majesty. 'Er – to be sure, Peabody. But we are limited in our choice of sites, not only by the cursed military authorities but by . . . by . . . by a certain individual whose name I have sworn not to pronounce.

It was I who had requested he abstain from referring to Mr Budge if he could not do so without swearing. (He could not.) Unfortunately I could not prevent others from referring to Budge. He had preceded us, and everyone we met mentioned him, hoping, I suppose, to please us by claiming an acquaintance in common.

Ramses distracted Emerson by climbing up on the rail, thus prompting a stern lecture on the dangers of falling overboard. I rewarded my son with an approving smile; there had never been any danger of his falling, he could climb like a monkey. With such distractions and a few animated arguments about archaeological matters, the time passed pleasantly enough until we disembarked at Wadi Halfa.

Halfa, as it is now commonly termed, was once a small cluster of mud huts; but in 1885, after the withdrawal of our forces from Khartoum, it was established as the southern frontier of Egypt. It had now become a bustling depot of supplies and arms for the forces farther south. Following the advice of the young military officer whom I consulted, I purchased quantities of tinned food, tents, netting, and other equipment. Emerson and Ramses had wandered off on some expedition of their own. On this occasion I did not complain of their dereliction, for Emerson does not get on well with military persons, and Captain Buckman was a type of young Englishman who particularly annoyed him – prominent teeth, no chin to speak of, and a habit of tossing his head when he laughed in a high-pitched whinny. He was a great help to me, though, and full of admiration for Mr Budge, whom he had met in September. 'Quite a regular chap, not like your usual archaeologist, if you take my meaning, ma'am.'

I took his meaning. I also took my leave, with appropriate thanks, and went in search of my errant family. As I had come to expect, Emerson had a number of 'old acquaintances' in Halfa; it was at the home of one of them, Sheikh Mahmud al-Araba, that we were to meet. The house was palatial by Nubian standards, built of mud brick around a high-walled central courtyard. I had braced myself for an argument with the doorkeeper, for these persons often tried to take me to the harîm instead of into the presence of the master of the house, but on this occasion the old man had evidently been warned; he greeted me with salaams and repeated cries of *marhaba* (welcome) before escorting me into the salon. Here I found the sheikh, a white-bearded but hearty man, and my husband seated side by side on the mastaba-bench along one wall. They were smoking narghiles (water pipes) and watching the performance of a young female who squirmed around the room to the undulating beat of an orchestra consisting of two drummers and a piper. Her face was veiled; the same could not be said of the rest of her.

Emerson sprang to his feet. 'Peabody! I had not expected you so soon.'

'So I see,' I replied, returning the dignified greetings of the sheikh and taking the seat he indicated. The orchestra continued to wail, the girl continued to squirm, and Emerson's high cheekbones took on the colour of a ripe plum. Even the best of men exhibit certain inconsistencies in their attitude towards women. Emerson treated me as an equal (I would have accepted nothing less) in matters of the intellect, but it was impossible for him to conquer completely his absurd ideas about the delicate sensibilities of the female sex. The Arabs, for all their deplorable treatment of their own women, showed far more common sense in their treatment of ME. Having decided that I ranked as a peculiar variety of female-man, they entertained me as they would any masculine friend.

When the performance ended I applauded politely, somewhat to the surprise of the young woman. After expressing my appreciation to the sheikh, I inquired, 'Where is Ramses? We must be on our way, Emerson; I left instructions for the supplies to be delivered to the quay, but without your personal supervision – '

'Yes, quite,' said Emerson. 'You had better fetch Ramses, then, he is being entertained by the ladies. Or vice versa.'

'Oh, dear,' I said, hastily rising. 'Yes. I had better fetch him –

and,' I added in Arabic, 'I would like to pay my compliments to the ladies of your house.'

And, I added to myself, I would also have a word with the young woman who had – I suppose she would have called it 'danced' – for us. I would have felt myself a traitor to my sex if I had missed any opportunity to lecture the poor oppressed creatures of the harîm on their rights and privileges – though heaven knows, we Englishwomen were far from having attained the rights due us.

An attendant led me through the courtyard, where a fountain trickled feebly under the shade of a few sickly palm trees, and into the part of the house reserved for the women. It was dark and hot as a steam bath, for even the windows opening onto the courtyard were covered with pierced shutters, lest some bold masculine eye behold the forbidden beauties within. The sheikh had three of the four wives permitted him by Moslem law, and a number of female servants – concubines, to put it bluntly. All of them were assembled in a single room, and I heard them, giggling and exclaiming in high-pitched voices, long before I saw them. I expected the worst – Ramses's Arabic is extremely fluent and colloquial – but then I realised that his was not among the voices I heard. At least he was not entertaining them by telling vulgar jokes or singing rude songs.

When I entered the room, the ladies fell silent, and a little flutter of alarm ran through the group. When they saw who it was they relaxed, and one – the chief wife, by her attire and her air of command – came forward to greet me. I was used to being swarmed over by the women of the harîms; poor things, they had little enough to amuse them, and a Western woman was a novelty indeed. On this occasion, however, after glancing at me they turned their attention back to something – or, as I suspected, someone – hidden from me by their bodies.

The heat, the gloom, the stench of the strong perfumes used by the women (and the aroma of unwashed bodies those perfumes strove to overcome) were familiar to me; but I seemed to smell some other, underlying odour – something sickly sweet

Elizabeth Peters

and subtly pervasive. It may have been that strange scent that made me forget courtesy; it may have been the uncertainty as to what was happening to my son. I pushed the women aside so I could see.

A rug or matting, woven in patterns of blue and red-orange, green and umber, had been spread across the floor. On it sat my son, cross-legged, with his cupped hands held out in a peculiarly rigid position. He did not turn his head. Facing him was the strangest figure I had ever seen – and I have seen a great many strange individuals. At first glance it appeared to be a folded or crumpled mass of dark fabric, with some underlying structure of bone or wood jutting out at odd angles. My reasoning brain identified it as a squatting human figure; my mother's heart felt a thrill of fear bordering on horror when my eyes failed to find a human countenance atop the angular mass. Then the upper portion of the object moved; a face appeared, covered with a heavy veil; and a deep murmurous voice intoned, 'Silence. Silence. The spell is cast. Do not wake the sleeper.'

The elder wife came to my side. She put a timid hand on my arm and murmured, 'He is a magician of great power, Sitt Hakim – like yourself. An old man, a holy man – he does the boy honour. You will not tell my lord? There is no harm in it, but – '

The old sheikh must be an indulgent master or the women would not have dared introduce a man, however old or holy, into their quarters, but he would be forced to take notice of such a flagrant violation of decency if someone like myself brought it to his attention. I whispered a reassuring, *'Taiyib mâtakhâfsh* (It is good; do not fear)' – though, as far as I was concerned, it was not at all good.

I had seen such performances in the sûks of Cairo. Crystal-gazing, or scrying, is one of the commonest forms of divination. It is all nonsense, of course; what the viewer sees in the crystal ball or pool of water or (as in this case) liquid held in the palm of the hand is nothing more than a visual hallucination, but the deluded audience is firmly convinced that the diviner is able to foretell the future and discover hidden treasure. Often a child is employed by the fortune-teller in the (naive) belief that the innocence of youth is more receptive to spiritual influences.

I knew that to interrupt the ceremony would be not only rude but dangerous. Ramses was deep in some sort of unholy trance, from which he could be roused only by the voice of the magician, who now leaned forwards over the boy's cupped hands, mumbling in a voice so low I could not make out the words.

I did not blame the poor bored women for allowing the ceremony, or even the seer, who undoubtedly believed sincerely in his own hocus-pocus. However, I was not about to stand idly by and wait upon the latter's convenience. Very softly I remarked, 'As is well known, I, the Sitt Hakim, am also a magician of great power. I call upon this holy man to bring back the soul of the boy to his body, lest the efreets [demons] I have set to protect my son mistake the holy man's purpose and eat up his heart.'

The women gasped in delighted horror. There was no immediate reaction from the 'holy man,' but after a moment he straightened and moved his hands in a sweeping gesture. The words he addressed to Ramses were unfamiliar to me; either he spoke some unknown dialect, or they were meaningless magical gibberish. The result was dramatic. A shudder ran through the stiff frame of Ramses. His hands relaxed, and a dribble of dark liquid poured into the cup the magician held below them. The cup vanished into some hidden pocket in the crumpled robe, and Ramses turned his head.

'Good afternoon, Mama. I hope I have not kept you waiting?'

I managed to repress my comments through the long and tedious process of leave-taking, first of the ladies and then of the sheikh who insisted upon escorting us to the very door of the house – the highest honour he could pay us. Not until we were standing in the dusty street and the door had closed behind us did I let the words burst forth. I was considerably agitated, and Emerson had to ask me to stop and elaborate on the story several times before the full meaning of it dawned on him.

'Of all the confounded nonsense,' he exclaimed. 'What were you thinking of, Ramses, to allow such a thing?'

'It would have been rude to refuse,' said Ramses. 'The ladies had set their hearts on it.'

Emerson burst out laughing. 'You are becoming quite a gallant, my boy. But you must learn that it is not always wise, or safe, to indulge the ladies.'

'Upon my word, you take this very lightly, Emerson,' I exclaimed.

'I imagine it was curiosity, rather than gallantry, that induced Ramses to try this experiment,' Emerson replied, still chuckling. 'It is his most conspicuous character trait, and you will never change it; just be thankful that this adventure, unlike so many earlier ones, turned out to be harmless.'

'I hope you are right,' I muttered.

'Nothing worse than dirty hands,' Emerson went on, inspecting the palms Ramses held out. They were darkly stained and still damp. I snatched out a handkerchief and began wiping them; the stuff came off more readily than I had expected, but I caught a whiff of that same odd scent I had smelled before. I threw the handkerchief away. (A toothless street beggar pounced on it.)

As we walked on, Emerson, who suffers from a certain degree of curiosity himself, questioned Ramses about his experience. Ramses said it had been most interesting. He claimed to have been fully conscious throughout, and to have heard everything that was said. However, his responses to the questions of the seer were made without his own volition, like hearing another person speak 'It was mostly about having babies,' he explained seriously. 'Male babies. He promised all the ladies many sons. They seemed pleased.'

'Ha,' I said.

The next stage of our journey was made by rail, along the line laid with such remarkable rapidity from Halfa to Kerma, thus avoiding the rocks of the Second and Third Cataracts. This part of the trip tried even my strength. We had been given the best accommodations available – a battered, ramshackle railroad coach affectionately known as 'Yellow Maria,' which had been built for Ismail Pasha. It had come down in the world since then; most of the window glass was missing, and on the sharp curves and steep gradients of the roadbed it swayed and rattled so violently that one expected it to bounce off the track. The engines were old and in poor repair. Blowing sand and over-heating necessitated frequent stops for repairs. By the time we reached our destination Ramses was a pale shade of pea-green and my muscles were so stiff I could hardly move.

Emerson, however, was in fine fettle. Men have it so much easier than women; they can strip down to a point that is impossible for a modest female, even one so unconventional as I. I have always been an advocate of rational dress for women; I was one of the first to imitate the scandalous example of Mrs Bloomer, and the full, knee-length trousers I was accustomed to wear on the dig anticipated by several years the bicycling costumes daring English ladies eventually adopted. Fashions in sport and in costume had changed, but I retained my trousers, which I had had made in a variety of cheerful colours that would not show the effects of sand and dust as did navy blue and black. With the addition of a neat cotton shirtwaist (long-sleeved and collared, of course), a pair of stout boots, a matching jacket, and a wide-brimmed boater, this made up a costume as becoming and modest as it was practical.

During the dreadful train ride I had ventured to unfasten the top two buttons of my shirt and turn up my cuffs. Emerson had of course abandoned his coat and cravat as soon as we left Cairo. Now his shirt gaped open to the waist, and his sleeves had been rolled above his elbows. He wore no hat. After assisting me to alight from the carriage he took a deep breath of the steaming, stifling, sand-laden air and exclaimed, 'The last stage! We will soon be there, my darling Peabody. Isn't this splendid?'

I had not the strength to do more than glare at him.

However, I am nothing if not resilient, and a few hours later I was able to share his enthusiasm. A troop of Sudani soldiers – which included several of Emerson's acquaintances – had removed our luggage and helped us set up our tents. We had declined with thanks the offer of the harassed captain in charge of the encampment to share his cramped quarters; after assuring us that there would be places for us on the steamer leaving next day, he bade us farewell and bon voyage with obvious relief. As the sun sank rapidly in the west, Emerson and I strolled hand in hand along the riverbank, enjoying the evening breeze and the brilliance of the sunset. The silhouettes of the palm trees stood black and shapely against the glory of gold and crimson.

We were not alone. A troop of curious villagers trailed us. Whenever we stopped they stopped, squatted on the ground and stared with all their might. Emerson always attracts admirers and I had become more or less used to it, though I did not like it.

'I hope Ramses is all right,' I said, turning to look at the rapidly dimming outline of the tent where he slept. 'He was most unlike his normal self. Hardly a word out of him.'

'You said he was not feverish,' Emerson reminded me. 'Stop fussing, Amelia; the train ride was tiring, and even a gritty little chap like Ramses must feel its effects.'

The sun dropped below the horizon and night came on with startling suddenness, as it does in those climes. Stars sprang out in the cobalt vault of the heavens, and Emerson's arm stole around my waist.

It had been a long time since we had enjoyed an opportunity for connubial exchanges of even a modest nature, but I felt bound to protest. 'They are watching us, Emerson. I feel like some poor animal in a cage; I decline to perform for an audience.'

'Bah,' Emerson replied, leading me to a large boulder. 'Sit down, my dear Peabody, and forget our audience. It is too dark for them to observe our actions, and if they should, they could hardly fail to find them edifying – inspiring, even. For instance, this . . .'

It certainly inspired me. I forgot the staring spectators until a strengthening glow of silvery light illumined the beloved features so close to mine. The moon had risen. 'Oh, curse it,' I said, removing Emerson's hand from a particularly sensitive area of my person.

'It was a refreshing interlude, though,' Emerson said with a chuckle. Reaching into his pocket, he took out his pipe. 'Do you mind if I smoke, Peabody?'

I really did not approve of it, but the soft moonlight and the stench of tobacco smoke recalled tender memories of the days of our courtship, when we faced the sinister Mummy in the abandoned tombs of Amarna.* 'No, I don't mind. Do you remember Amarna, and the – '

'The time I set my – er – myself on fire by neglecting to knock the ashes out of my pipe before I put it in my pocket? And you let me do it even though you knew perfectly well . . .' Emerson burst out laughing. 'Do you remember the first time I ever kissed you – lying flat on the floor of that cursed tomb, with a maniac shooting at us? It was only the expectation of imminent death that gave me the courage to do it. I thought you detested me.'

'I remember that moment and many others,' I replied with considerable emotion. 'Believe me, my darling Emerson, that I am fully cognizant of the fact that I am the most fortunate of women. From first to last, it has been outstanding.'

'And the best is yet to come, my dearest Peabody.'

His strong brown hand closed over mine. We sat in silence watching the moonlight spread silvery ripples across the dark surface of the river. So clear and bright was the illumination that one could see for a considerable distance. 'The rock formations are extremely regular,' I remarked. 'So much so that one might wonder whether they are not in fact the ruins of ancient structures.'

'They may well be, Peabody. So little has been done in the way of excavation here, so much needs to be done. . . My

Crocodile on the Sandbank

colleagues – curse them – are more interested in mummies and treasure and impressive monuments than in the slow, tedious acquisition of knowledge. Yet this region is of vital importance, not only for its own sake, but for the understanding of Egyptian culture. Not far from this very spot are the remains of what must have been a fort or a trading post or both; within its massive walls were stored the exotic treasures brought as tribute to the pharaohs of the Egyptian Empire – gold and ostrich feathers, rock crystal and ivory and leopard skins.' He pointed with the stem of his pipe towards the moonlight lying like a white path along the river and across the sand. 'The caravans went there, Peabody, into the western desert, through the oases, toward the land called Yam in the ancient records. One such caravan route may have gone west from Elephantine – Assouan, as it is today. A series of wadis run westward from this very region; they are dried-up canyons today, but they were cut by water. Three thousand years ago . . .'

He fell silent; gazing at his stern, strong profile, I felt a sympathetic thrill, for he seemed to be looking not across distance but across time itself. No wonder he felt a kinship with the bold men who had braved the wilderness so many centuries before. He too possessed the unique combination of courage and imagination that leads the noblest sons (and daughters) of humanity to risk all for the sake of knowledge!

With all due modesty I believe I may claim that I possess those qualities myself. The bond of affection that unites me and my dear Emerson left me no doubt of the direction in which his thoughts were tending. Into those distances, so deceptively cool and silver-white in the moonlight, had gone Willoughby Forth and his beautiful young bride, never to return.

However, in addition to courage, imagination, et cetera, I also possess a great deal of common sense. For a time I had – I admit it! – entertained a romantic notion of going in search of the missing explorer. But now I had seen with my own eyes the dreadful desolation of the western desert; I had felt the burning heat of the day and the deadly chill of darkness. It was impossible that anyone could have survived in that arid waste for fourteen long years. Willoughby Forth and his wife were dead, and I had no intention of following them, or allowing Emerson to do so.

A shiver passed through my frame. The night air was cold. Our audience had vanished, as silently as shadows. 'It is late,' I said softly. 'Shall we . . .'

'By all means.' Emerson jumped to his feet.

At that moment the quiet air was rent by a weird, undulating cry. I started. Emerson laughed and took my hand. 'It is only a jackal, Peabody. Hurry. I feel a sudden, urgent need for something only you can supply.'

'Oh, Emerson,' I began – and said no more, because he was pulling me along at such a pace I lost my breath.

Our tents had been placed in a small grove of tamarisk trees. Our boxes and bags were piled around them; theft is almost unknown among these so-called primitive people, and Emerson's reputation was enough to deter the most hardened of burglars. I was startled, therefore, to see something moving – a slight white shape slipping through the trees with an unpleasantly furtive motion.

Emerson's night vision is not as keen as mine, and perhaps he was preoccupied with the subject he had mentioned. Not until I shouted, 'Halt! Who goes there?' or something to that effect, did he behold the apparition – for so it appeared, pale and silently gliding. As one man (figuratively speaking) we leapt upon it and bore it to the ground.

An all-too-familiar voice exclaimed in plaintive protest. With a loud oath Emerson struggled to his feet and raised the fallen form to its feet. It was Ramses, looking quite ghostly in the white native robe he wore as a nightshirt.

'Are you injured, my boy?' Emerson asked in faltering accents. 'Have I hurt you?'

Ramses blinked at him. 'Not intentionally, Papa, I am sure. Fortunately the ground is soft. May I venture to ask why you and Mama knocked me down?'

'A reasonable question,' Emerson admitted. 'Why did we, Peabody?'

Having had the breath knocked out of me by the fall, I was unable to reply at once. Observing my state, Emerson considerately assisted me to rise; but he took advantage of my enforced silence to continue, 'I hope you understand, Peabody, that the question was not meant to imply criticism, but only inquiry. I reacted instinctively, as I hope I will always do, my dear, when you have need of my assistance. Did you see or hear something I failed to observe that prompted such impetuous activity?'

Normally I would have resented this cowardly attempt to put the blame on me – so typical of the male sex, from Adam on down. But to be honest, I was as bewildered as he. 'No, Emerson, I confess I did not. I too reacted instinctively, and I am at a loss to explain why. I had the strangest feeling – a premonition of danger, of – '

'Never mind,' Emerson said hastily. 'I know those premonitions of yours, Peabody, and with all respect, I prefer not to discuss them.'

'Well, but it was only natural that seeing someone prowling around our stores, I should assume the worst. Ramses ought to have been asleep. Ramses, what were you . . . Oh.'

The answer seemed self-evident, but it was not the one Ramses gave. 'You called me, Mama. You called me to come, and of course I obeyed.'

'I did not call you, Ramses.'

'But I heard your voice – '

'You were dreaming,' Emerson said. 'What a touching thing, eh, Peabody? Dreaming of his mama and, even in sleep, obedient to her slightest command. Come along, my boy, I will tuck you in.'

With a meaningful glance at me, he pushed Ramses into the tent and followed after. I knew he would sit by the boy until he had fallen asleep; Emerson is somewhat self-conscious about being overheard, especially by Ramses, when he and I are actively demonstrating the deep affection we feel for one another. Instead of retiring to prepare for this activity, I lingered in the shadows of the trees, gazing all around. Moonlight sifted through the leaves and formed strange silvery hieroglyphs upon the ground. The night was not silent, sounds of activity came from the direction of the military base, where the barges were being loaded for the morning's departure. And from across the river, lonely as the cry of a lost and wandering spirit, came the mournful call of a jackal.

Four days later, after an uncomfortable but uneventful voyage, we saw a ruddy mountain loom over the tops of the palm trees. It was Gebel Barkal, the Holy Mountain of the Nubian kingdom. We had reached our destination.

Stone Houses of
the Kings

I f I have not done so already, I should make it clear that Napata is not a city but an entire region. In modern times several towns and villages occupy the site. Merawi, or Merowe, was the best known; it is a confusing name, resembling so closely that of Meroë, the second of the ancient capital cities of Cush, which is much farther south. Across from Merawi, on the opposite bank of the Nile, was the headquarters of the Frontier Field Force of the Egyptian Army, near the small village of Sanam Abu Dom. The encampment stretched along the river for over a mile, tents neatly aligned in a manner that clearly betrayed the presence of British organisation.

Emerson was unimpressed by this demonstration of efficiency. 'Curse them,' he growled, surveying the scene with a scowl. 'They have put their cursed camp smack on top of a ruined temple. There were column bases and carved blocks here in '82.'

'You weren't planning to excavate here,' I reminded him. 'The pyramids, Emerson; where are the pyramids?'

The steamer edged in towards the quay. 'All over the place,' Emerson replied somewhat vaguely. 'The main cemeteries are at Nuri, several miles upstream from here, and Kurru, on the opposite bank. There are three groups of pyramids near Gebel

Barkal itself, as well as the remains of the great temple of Amon.'

The sandstone mass of Mount Barkal was an impressive sight. It is (as we later determined) only a little over three hundred feet high, but because it rises so abruptly from the flat plain it looks higher. Late-afternoon sunlight turned the rock a soft crimson and cast fantastic shadows, like the weathered remains of monumental statues, across the face.

With some difficulty I persuaded Emerson that it would be courteous, not to say expedient, to announce ourselves to the military authorities. 'What do we need them for?' he demanded. 'Mustapha has everything arranged.'

Mustapha flashed me a broad grin. He had been the first to greet us when we disembarked, and his followers had promptly set to work unloading our baggage. Emerson had introduced him as 'Sheikh Mustapha abd Rabu,' but he certainly lacked the dignity one associates with that title. He was no taller than I and thin as a skeleton; his dirty, ragged robe flapped wildly about his body as he performed a series of respectful bows to Emerson, to me, to Ramses, and again to Emerson. His wrinkled face showed the mixture of races that distinguishes this region. The Nubians themselves are of the Brown race, with wavy black hair and sharply cut features, but from time immemorial they have intermarried with Arabs and with the Black peoples of central Africa. I could not see Mustapha's hair, for it was covered by an extravagant turban, once white in colour but white no longer.

I returned Mustapha's smile; it was impossible to be aloof, he seemed so very respectful and so very glad to see us. However, I felt bound to express some reservations. 'Where are they taking our luggage?' I asked, indicating the men who were already trotting away, heavily laden, and with an energy one does not expect to find in warmer climes.

'Mustapha has found a house for us,' Emerson replied. Mustapha beamed and nodded. He was so very agreeable, I hated to cast cold water on the scheme, but I had the direst suspicions of what Mustapha would consider a suitable house. No man, of any race or nationality, has the least notion of cleanliness.

Humming in the tuneless baritone expressive of high good humour, Emerson led me along the path towards the village. From a distance it looked quite charming, surrounded by palm trees and boasting a number of houses built of mud brick. Other huts, commonly known as tukhuls, were built of palm branches and leaves interwoven on a wooden framework. Mustapha, trotting along beside us, kept up a running commentary, amusingly like that of a tourist guide: that large, impressive house was occupied by General Rundle; the pair of tukhuls near it was the headquarters of the Intelligence Service; that hut had belonged to the Italian military attaché, and then to the British Museum gentleman. . .

'Grrr,' said Emerson, setting a faster pace.

'Is Mr Budge still there?' I asked.

'That is what we must determine,' Emerson growled. 'I am determined to stay as far away from Budge as I possibly can; I will not settle on a site until I find out where he is working. You know me, Peabody, I go to great lengths in order to avoid controversy and confrontations.'

'Hmmm,' I said.

One unexpected and welcome feature of the village was a small market operated by Greek merchants. The mercantile instincts of these fellows never cease to amaze me; they are as bold as they are businesslike, moving into an area right on the heels of the fighting men. I was delighted to find that I would be able to procure tinned food and soda water, fresh-baked bread, soap, and all kinds of pots and cutlery.

Emerson found several old acquaintances there, and while he was engaged in friendly banter with one of them I had leisure to look around me. I hope I am no ignorant tourist; I had become accustomed to the wide diversity of racial and national types that are to be found in Cairo. But I had never seen such variety as in this remote corner of the world. The complexions ranged from the 'white' of the English soldier (more sickly yellow than white, and often bright red with heat) through all the shades of brown, tan, and olive to a shining blue-black. Handsome, hawk-faced Beduin rubbed elbows with Sudani women draped in bright-coloured cottons. Bisharin tribesmen, whose hair was oiled and braided into small, tight plaits, mingled with ladies of the stricter Moslem sects hidden by dusty black draperies that left only their eyes exposed. Particularly interesting to me were a pair of tall handsome men jingling with ornaments and topped with hair the size, colour, and consistency of black mops. They were Baggara from the distant province of Kordofan – the earliest and most fanatic of the Mahdi's followers. This extravagant and characteristic hairstyle had won them the affectionate nickname of Fuzzy-Wuzzies from the British troops whom they had fought with such desperate and often successful ferocity. (I have never been able to understand how men can feel affection for individuals who are intent on massacring them in a variety of unpleasant ways, but it is an undeniable fact that they can and do. Witness the immortal verses of Mr Kipling 'So 'ere's to you, Fuzzy-Wuzzy, at your 'ome in the Soudan; You're a pore benighted 'eathen but a first-class fightin' man!' One can only accept this as another example of the peculiar emotional aberrations of the male sex.)

And the variety of languages! I understood Greek and Arabic, and had learned a little Nubian, but most of the babble was in dialects I could not identify, much less understand.

Emerson finally finished exchanging tall stories with his friend and turned to me. 'Yussuf says he can find some workers for us. We had better go on and . . . Ramses! Where the devil has he got to? Peabody, you were supposed to keep an eye on him.'

I could have pointed out that it was impossible to keep track of Ramses by keeping one eye on him; the task required one's total attention and a firm hand on the collar. Before I could do so, Yussuf said in Arabic, 'The young effendi went that way.'

Muttering, Emerson plunged off in the direction Yussuf had indicated, and I followed. We soon found the miscreant; he was squatting in front of one of the booths, engaged in animated conversation with a man wrapped in a voluminous robe or mantle, a fold of which had been drawn over his head to protect it from the sun.

Emerson bellowed, 'Ramses!' whereupon Ramses jumped up and turned to face us. In his hand he held a short wooden skewer upon which were impaled chunks of meat whose origin I could not (and did not care to) determine. He waved it at me, swallowed the mouthful he had been chewing, and began, 'Mama and Papa, I have just found a most interesting – '

'So I see,' said Emerson. '*Essalâmu 'aleikum,* friend.'

The man had also risen, with a slow dignity that verged on arrogance. Instead of touching brow, breast, and lips in the traditional Arabic greeting, he inclined his head slightly and lifted his hands in a curious gesture. 'Greetings, Emerson Effendi. And to the lady of your house, good health and life.'

'You speak English,' I exclaimed.

'A few words, lady.' He shrugged out of the mantle, which was nothing more than a long strip of cloth, and laid the folds across his shoulders like a shawl. Under it he wore only a pair of loose, knee-length trousers, which displayed to excellent advantage his lean, athletic form and sinewy limbs. On his feet were red leather sandals with long, upward-curving toes. Such sandals were a mark of distinction among the Nubians, most of whom went barefoot. But this man was no ordinary Nubian, though his skin was a dark reddish-brown. His chiselled, regular features bore a certain resemblance to those of the Baggara, but his black hair was cut close to his head.

'He speaks a most interesting dialect, which is unfamiliar to me,' Ramses said. 'I could not resist asking him where – '

'We will discuss your inability to resist interesting dialects later, Ramses,' I said. 'And throw away that – '

It was too late. The skewer was bare.

The tall man repeated his gesture. 'I go now. Farewell.'

Inclining his head, he addressed a brief speech to Ramses in a language that was unfamiliar to me. Ramses, however, had the audacity to nod, as if he had understood it.

'What did he say?' I demanded, taking hold of Ramses. 'Don't tell me you learned enough of the language in five minutes to – '

'You are about to contradict yourself, Amelia,' said Emerson, watching with furrowed brow the dignified yet brisk retreat of Ramses's new acquaintance. 'If he has not learned enough of the language to understand what was said, he can't tell you. Er – what did he say, Ramses?'

Ramses shrugged, looking as enigmatic as any Arab master of that annoying gesture. 'I am sorry, Papa, I am sorry, Mama, that I wandered off. I will not do it again.'

'Come along, come along,' said Emerson, before I could express the incredulity this promise naturally provoked. 'We have delayed too long, and lost our guide. However, we need only continue along the path. On the other side of the market, Yussuf said . . . I say, Peabody, one can hardly blame Ramses for being intrigued. I have never heard that dialect, and yet a word or two in the last speech was oddly familiar.'

'He is not a Baggara, then?'

'Definitely not. I know something of that speech. Some of the people of the upper White Nile are tall and well-built; the Dinka and Shilluk, for example. He may be from that region. Ah, well, we had better get on. Ramses, stay close to your mama.'

The accommodations Yussuf had found were about what I had expected, i.e., uninhabitable by humans. There were certainly rats in the palm-leaf roof, and the insect life was varied and aggressive. I requested the men to pitch our tents, tactfully explaining that we would reserve the hut for storage, and then, finally, I got Emerson to agree to call on the authorities. We took Ramses with us, though he did not want to come, claiming he preferred to stay with the men and improve his knowledge of Nubian dialects.

However, Ramses perked up when Emerson announced his intention of calling on Slatin Pasha, who was assisting the

Intelligence Department. I myself looked forward to meeting this astonishing man whose adventures had become the stuff of legend.

Rudolf Carl von Slatin was Austrian by birth, but like a number of European and English military men, he had spent most of his life in the East. When the Mahdi overran the Sudan, Slatin was serving as governor of Darfur, the province to the west of Khartoum. Though he fought gallantly against overwhelming odds, he was finally forced to surrender; and for eleven years he was held prisoner under conditions so appalling that only courage and will could have kept him alive. His most terrible experience occurred after the capture of Khartoum, when, as he sat in chains upon the ground, a party of Mahdist soldiers approached him, carrying some object wrapped in a cloth. Gloating, the leader unwrapped the cloth to display the head of Slatin's friend and leader, General Gordon. He finally made good his escape, and those who saw him shortly afterwards said he looked like a withered old man of eighty.

Imagine, then, my surprise when we were shown into the presence of a stout, hearty, red-cheeked gentleman, who rose politely from his chair to bow over my hand. He and Emerson greeted one another with the familiarity of old acquaintances, and Slatin asked how he could help us. 'We were warned of your coming, but frankly I could hardly believe – '

'Why not?' Emerson demanded. 'You ought to know that when I say I will do something, I do it. As for Mrs Emerson, she is even more bull – er . . . determined than I.'

'I have heard a great deal about Mrs Emerson,' Slatin said, smiling. 'And about this young man. *Essalâmu 'aleikum*, Master Ramses.'

Ramses promptly replied, '*U'aleikum es-salâm warahmet Allah warabakâtu. Keif bâlak?* (And with you be peace and God's mercy and blessing. How is your health?)' and went on in equally fluent Arabic, 'But my own eyes inform me, sir, that it is excellent. I am surprised to see how very stout you are, after the privations you endured at the hands of the followers of the Mahdi.'

'Ramses,' I exclaimed.

Slatin bellowed with laughter. 'Don't scold him, Mrs Emerson; I am proud of my girth, for every pound represents a triumph of survival.'

'I would like very much to hear of your adventures,' Ramses said.

'One day, perhaps. At the moment I am fully occupied gathering reports from men who have returned from enemy territory. Intelligence,' he added, addressing Ramses, whose fixed stare he probably took for boyish admiration, 'is the nerve network of any army. Before we begin the next stage of the campaign, we must find out all we can about the strength and disposition of the Khalifa's forces.'

'If that's your excuse for going into winter quarters instead of continuing to Khartoum . . .' began Emerson.

'Our excuse is that we wish to save lives, Professor. I don't want to lose a single brave man through stupidity or lack of preparation.'

'Hmph,' said Emerson, who could hardly deny the sense of this. 'Well, then, to business. You are a busy man and so am I.'

Upon inquiry, Slatin told us that Mr Budge had already investigated the pyramid fields of Nuri, Kurru, Tankasi, and Zuma, and was now working at Gebel Barkal. 'There is, or was, a temple of considerable size there,' Slatin said. 'Mr Budge believes it was built by the pharaoh Piankhi – '

'Mr Budge doesn't know what he is talking about,' Emerson interrupted. He turned to me. 'Good Gad, Peabody, can you believe it? Four separate cemeteries in a few months! And now he is ransacking the temple, scooping up objects for his bloo – his precious museum. Curse it, we must go there at once! I'll run him off before he can do any more damage, or my name – '

'Now, Emerson, remember your promise,' I said in some alarm. 'You said you intended to stay away from Mr Budge.'

'But curse it, Peabody – '

'Pyramids, Emerson. You promised me pyramids.'

'So I did,' Emerson grumbled. 'Very well, Peabody. Where shall it be?'

Slatin had followed the exchange with openmouthed interest, 'You make the decisions, Mrs Emerson?'

Emerson's brow darkened. He is a trifle sensitive about being considered henpecked. Before he could comment, I said smoothly, 'My husband and I have discussed the subject at length. He is making a courteous gesture, that is all. We had agreed on Nuri, Emerson, had we not?'

In fact, the decision was not a difficult one; the only thing that could have kept me from Nuri was learning that Budge was there. Nuri had a number of advantages. In the first place, it was ten miles away from the military base. That made it inconvenient from the point of view of fetching supplies, but the distance reduced the chances of unpleasant encounters with Mr Budge and with the army. In the second place, the reports I had read, by Lepsius and others, made me suspect that the Nuri tombs were the oldest and hence the most interesting, dating, as they might, from the period of the Nubian conquest of Egypt in 730 B.C. They were also more solidly built, being of cut stone throughout instead of a mere outer layer of stone over a core of loose rubble.

'It makes no difference to me,' Emerson said moodily.

It was therefore decided that we would leave the following morning, which gave me the rest of the afternoon to shop and make arrangements for transport. Slatin informed us that the trip across the desert by camel required approximately two hours, but he recommended that we go by water instead, even though it would take longer. Camels were very hard to find, owing to the devastation wrought by the rebels and the fact that the army had first call on them.

After I had appealed to him as a gentleman and a scholar, he promised to do all he could to help us. Men are very susceptible to flattery, especially when it is accompanied by simpers and fluttering lashes. Fortunately Emerson was still brooding on the sins of Mr Budge and did not interfere.

In fact, it was after noon the next day before we got under way. Washing the camels took longer than I had anticipated. Where Yussuf had found them I did not ask, but they were a sorry-looking group of animals, which had obviously never been under the care of the officer in charge of the military camels. I had had a most interesting chat with this gentleman; he operated a kind of hospital for ailing camels outside the camp, and I was

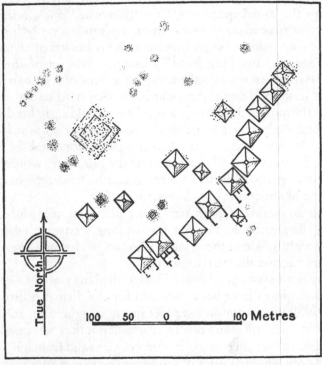

"We'll pitch our tent between the two southernmost pyramids."

pleased to find that his views on the care of animals agreed with mine. I had had the same problem with donkeys while in Egypt. The poor beasts were shamefully overloaded and neglected, so I had made it a policy to wash the donkeys and their filthy saddlecloths as soon as they came under my care. Captain Griffith was good enough to give me some of the lotions and medicines he used, and most efficacious they proved. However, camels – like other animals, including human beings – are not always aware of what is good for them, and the ones Yussuf supplied did not take kindly to being washed. I had become fairly expert at dealing with donkeys, but washing a camel is a much more complicated procedure, owing in part to the greater size of the latter animal and in part to its extremely irascible disposition. After some futile experiments, which left everyone except the camel quite wet, I finally worked out a relatively effective procedure. I stood upon a temporary platform of heaped-up sand and stone blocks, with my bucket of water and lye soap and my long-handled brush, while six of the men endeavoured to restrain the camel by means of ropes attached to its limbs and neck. It would have been hard to say which made the most racket, the camel or the men holding it, for despite my best endeavours some of the soapy water splashed onto them. However, this was all to the good, for some of them needed washing too. (I must add that the procedure would have gone more smoothly had Emerson condescended to help me instead of collapsing in helpless mirth.)

The pyramids of Nuri stand on a plateau a mile and a half from the riverbank. The sun was sinking westward when we came within sight of them, and their shadows formed grotesque outlines across the barren ground.

My heart sank with the sun. I had studied the work of Lepsius, and I ought to have been prepared for the dismal reality, but hope will ever triumph over fact in my imagination. Some of the pyramids still stood relatively intact, but they were pathetic substitutes for the great stone tombs of Giza and Dahshûr. Most were only tumbled piles of stone, with no sign of a pyramid shape. The whole area was strewn with fallen blocks and heaps of debris. It would take weeks, perhaps months, of arduous labour to make sense of the plan, even if we had had the necessary number of workers.

I had hoped to find a tomb chapel or other structure that could be converted into a residence, but my sand-and sun-strained eyes searched in vain for any such convenience. The temperature was approximately one hundred degrees Fahrenheit, the camel's jolting gait had reduced my muscles to jelly, and blowing sand had scoured the skin from my face and seeped into every crevice of my clothing. I turned a look of bitter reproach (for my throat was too parched for speech) on my husband, who had ignored the sensible advice of the military authorities and insisted on travelling by camel instead of waiting until we could hire a boat.

Impervious to my distress, Emerson urged his camel to kneel. Dismounting with the agility of a boy half his age, his face beaming, he hastened to me and addressed the animal upon which I perched '*Adar ya-yan!* Come along now, you heard me – *adar ya-yan*, I say.' The cursed camel, which had grumbled and protested every order I had given it, promptly obeyed Emerson. Those among my Readers who are acquainted with the habits of camels know that they lower the front end first. Since they have extraordinarily long limbs, this procedure tilts their bodies to a considerable degree. Stiff and exhausted, caught unawares by the quickness of Emerson and the camel, I slid down the slope and fell to the ground.

Emerson picked me up and dusted me off. 'Quite all right, are you, Peabody?' he asked cheerfully. 'We'll pitch our tents there, between those two southernmost pyramids, don't you think? Quite. Come along, Peabody, don't dawdle, it will be dark soon. Mohammed – Ahmet – Ramses – '

Spurred by his enthusiasm and his friendly curses – and no doubt by the desire for food, rest, and water – the men began to unload the camels. I leaned against mine, which had lowered its back section and lay upon the sand. It turned its head to look at me. I cleared my throat. 'Don't even think of it,' I said hoarsely. The camel coughed, in the irritating way they have, and looked away.

Some water from the small canteen attached to my belt restored me to my usual self, and I hastened to assist Emerson. After I had pointed out that he had picked the wrong place for the camp, and found a better one, matters went smoothly. By the time the sun had sunk below the western hills I was able to retire to the privacy of a tent and remove my sandy, perspiration-soaked garments. The relief was indescribable. When I emerged I found Emerson and Ramses sitting cross-legged on a bit of carpet. A small fire crackled merrily; some distance away was the fiery glow of a larger fire, and I could hear the cheerful voices of the men and smell dinner cooking. Emerson quickly jumped up and led me to a chair, placing a glass in my hand.

The cool night breeze stirred the damp tendrils of my hair. The vault of heaven blazed with stars that cast a mystical glow along the sides of the pyramid. Feeling like a queen enthroned, surrounded by kneeling courtiers, I sipped my whiskey and opened my senses to the allure of the desert wastes. And when Emerson sighed deeply and remarked, 'Ah, my dear Peabody; life cannot hold any greater charm than this,' I was forced to agree that he was right.

We began next morning to make key plans of the pyramids. A certain amount of excavation was necessary to establish, as far as was possible, the original dimensions, but our main focus, as Emerson insisted, was that of recording. Since my dear Emerson's real passion is digging things up, this was a sign of his genuine concern for scholarship over treasure-hunting. After comparing the plans of Lepsius, drawn in 1845, with what remained, I was shocked to find how much the monuments had deteriorated in half a century. Finding traces of recent and hasty excavation at the base of the best preserved of the pyramids, Emerson blamed all of the depredation on Budge, but as I pointed out, even Budge could not have done so much damage in a few hours. Time, and the treasure-hunting instincts of the local villagers, must be partially responsible.

From these villages, scattered along the riverbank, we procured our workers, and being old hands at organising excavations, we soon had a routine worked out. The men were divided into three groups, under the command of Emerson, myself, and Ramses. I must admit that Ramses was a great help, though I soon got tired of hearing Emerson congratulate himself on insisting the boy come with us. Ramses, of course, was in his element, and it was rather amusing to hear his shrill voice shouting out orders in his extremely colloquial Arabic and increasingly fluent Nubian. His linguistic abilities impressed the men, who had been inclined at first to treat him with the same amused tolerance they showed their own progeny.

By the end of the work week we had a pretty fair idea of the general plan of the site. A pyramid of considerable size must once have dominated the area; it had completely collapsed, and additional work would be necessary to determine its original dimensions. In front of it, in a rough semicircle, were four smaller pyramids, with another row of ten pyramids to the southeast. Lepsius's original plan showed a number of smaller, shapeless masses of stone clustered west and north of the great(!) pyramid and scattered at random among the others. We found ten such mounds not shown on his map. At that point we were forced to break off work for the inevitable day of rest. Our men were Moslems, most of the Hanafi sect; their holy day was, of course, Friday. Emerson was all for continuing the work without them, pointing out, with perfect truth, that the surveying itself required no more than three people. However, I persuaded him that we also deserved, if not a day of rest, at least a brief period spent at the camp and the nearby market. We needed supplies, more camels, and, if possible, more workers.

We had offered to let our men leave on the Thursday evening, but they refused with thanks and with a great shuffling of feet and sidelong glances. They were afraid of jinn and ghosts, which as all men knew came out in the dusk. So the following morning they all scattered to their villages and we set out for the camp. In the relative cool of the morning the ride was pleasant enough, and as we drew near Sanam Abu Dom, the view of the great mountain across the river became increasingly impressive. I was particularly struck by several oddly shaped rock formations that resembled the great statues of Ramses II at Abu Simbel. Emerson, who had been staring at the mountain with greed writ clearly across his handsome countenance, muttered, 'That is the greatest temple of Nubia, Peabody. Excavation there would undoubtedly produce invaluable historical material. Since we are at loose ends today – '

'We are not at loose ends; I have a great deal to do,' I said firmly. 'Furthermore, Mr Budge is working at Gebel Barkal, and you swore to me you would stay away from him.'

'Bah,' said Emerson, as I had expected he would.

Pleased to have had my stratagem of keeping Emerson and Mr Budge apart succeed, I was extremely annoyed to find that I had overlooked one fact. Mr Budge's workmen, too, were enjoying their day of rest, and Mr Budge had decided to pay a visit to his friends at the camp.

Fortunately Emerson was not with me when I made this discovery. He and Ramses had gone off to the village, ostensibly for the purpose of trying to hire more men, though, knowing their habits, I had the direst suspicions of what they would actually do. It had been left to me to strengthen our ties with the military establishment. I therefore rode directly to the camel hospital (my humorous term for it), since the beast I bestrode had an eye infection concerning which I was anxious to consult Captain Griffith. After a delightful and useful conversation, he informed me that General Rundle, having heard of my arrival, had invited me to join him and some of the other officers at luncheon. 'And the professor too, of course,' he added.

'Oh, I have not the slightest idea where Emerson may be at this time,' I replied. 'No doubt he is lunching with a Dervish or a Greek shopkeeper or a Beduin sheikh. So I will be happy to accept the general's invitation.'

I tucked the tube of ointment he had given me into one of the pouches at my belt. Captain Griffith studied this accessory curiously. 'Pardon me, Mrs Emerson, but you seem to be somewhat – er – encumbered. Would you care to leave your – er – accoutrements here? They will be quite safe, I assure you.'

'My dear Captain, I would as soon think of going about without my – er – my hat as without my belt,' I replied, taking the arm he offered. 'It is a trifle noisy, I confess; Emerson is always complaining about how I jangle and clank when I walk; but every object has proved not only useful but, upon occasion, essential to survival. A compass, a small canteen, a notebook and pencil, a knife, a waterproof box containing matches and candles – '

'Yes, I see,' the young man said, his eyes shining with interest. 'Why waterproof, may I ask?'

I proceeded to tell him about the time Emerson and I had been flung into the flooded burial chamber of a pyramid,* and then, as he seemed to be genuinely fascinated, went on to explain my theories of appropriate attire for excavation. 'One of these days,' I declared, 'women will boldly usurp your trousers, Captain. That is to say – not yours in particular – '

We enjoyed a hearty laugh over this, and the captain assured me that my meaning had been quite clear. 'I have no designs on them myself,' I went on. 'These full, divided skirts are more flattering to a female figure, and yet they allow perfect freedom of movement. Furthermore, I suspect that the flow of air through their folds renders them more comfortable in a hot climate than those close-fitting nether garments of yours.'

He quite agreed with me; and in such interesting conversation the brief walk seemed even briefer. The general occupied a 'mansion' – two rooms and a walled courtyard, plus a separate shed which served as a kitchen – built of mud brick instead of

---

The Mummy Case

the usual interwoven branches. Emerson is always going on about the decadence of military officers, who have to have their personal servants wherever they go, but after the random efforts of our camp cook whose regular occupation was that of camel driver, I was looking forward to a decent meal prepared by a trained servant. My pleasure received only a slight check when I saw Mr Budge among the men who rose to greet me.

'I believe you know Mr Budge,' General Rundle said, after he had introduced the others.

'Yes, yes, we are old friends,' said Mr Budge, beaming all over his round, red face and transferring his glass to his left hand in order to give me a damp handshake. 'And where have you left the professor, Mrs Emerson? You are making great discoveries at Nuri, I understand.'

The grin that accompanied the last sentence explained his good humour; having appropriated the best site for himself and having made certain that there was nothing of obvious value at ours, he could afford to gloat. I replied with perfect courtesy, of course.

We took our places at the table. I was, naturally, seated next to General Rundle. He was an amiable man but his conversational efforts did not tax me unduly; I was able to observe that Budge kept shooting glances at me, and something in his look aroused the direst of suspicions. It was as if he knew something I did not know – and if it amused Budge, it was certain not to amuse me. Sure enough as the last course was being cleared away and a lull fell upon the conversation, Budge addressed me directly.

'I do hope, Mrs Emerson, that you and young Ramses aren't planning to go with the professor when he sets off in search of the Lost Oasis.'

'I beg your pardon?' I gasped.

'Do try to dissuade him from such a fruitless and dangerous quest,' Budge said, pursing his lips in the most hypocritical look of concern I have ever seen on a human countenance. 'A fine fellow, the professor – in his way – but given to these little fancies – eh?'

'Quite right, ma'am,' the general rumbled. 'No such place, you know. Native tales and idle rumours – never thought the professor would be so gullible.'

'I assure you, General,' I assured him, 'that "gullible" is not the word for Professor Emerson. May I ask, Mr Budge, where you heard this piece of idle and inaccurate gossip?'

'I assure you, ma'am, it is not idle gossip. My informant was a certain Major Sir Richard Bassington, who arrived yesterday on the paddle wheeler from Kerma, and he got it direct from the source – Mr Reginald Forthright, grandson of Lord Blacktower. Major Bassington met him at Wadi Halfa, some days ago. He was looking for transport south – without success – '

'I should hope not,' General Rundle exclaimed. 'Don't want a lot of civilians hanging about. Er – present company excepted, of course. Who is this fellow and what put this particular bee in his bonnet?'

Budge proceeded to explain, at quite unnecessary length. The name of Willoughby Forth made an impression; several of the older officers had heard of him, and General Rundle appeared to know something of his history. 'Sad case, very,' he mumbled, shaking his head. 'Hopeless, though. Quite hopeless. The damned – excuse me, ma'am – the confounded Dervishes must have got him. Can't imagine why that old reprobate Blacktower would allow his grandson to go haring off on such a ridiculous jaunt.'

'Forthright seemed very determined,' Budge said smoothly. 'He had a message from Professor Emerson, inviting him to join in the expedition. Dear me, Mrs Emerson, you look quite thunderstruck. I hope I have not been indiscreet.'

Rallying, I said firmly, 'I am only surprised at the folly of people who invent such stories, and the greater folly of those who credit them. General, I have greatly enjoyed your hospitality; I won't detain you and your officers any longer from the labours that await you.'

With a last mocking salutation, Budge strutted off in the company of some of the younger officers, and I took my leave.

The Reader can well imagine the bitterness of spirit that filled me as I hastened on towards the sûk, where Emerson and I had agreed to meet. My husband – my other half – the man who had sworn his eternal devotion, and to whom I had given mine – Emerson had deceived me! If he had really asked young Mr Forthright to join him, he must be planning to pursue the quest he had so often derided as folly. And if he had not consulted me, he must be planning to go without me. It was treachery of the vilest and most contemptible kind; never would I have believed Emerson could be capable of such betrayal.

The rich, malodorously mingled scents of the market assaulted my nostrils. It is said that the olfactory sense is the quickest to adapt; certainly I had found that within a day or so after arriving in Egypt, I no longer noticed the distinctive odours of the country, which many Europeans find distasteful. I cannot claim that I breathed them in with the same pleasure I would have found in the aroma of a rose or a lilac, but they brought back delightful memories and were thereby rendered tolerable. Today, however, the stench made me feel a trifle ill, compounded as it was of rotting vegetation, dried camel dung, and sweating unwashed human bodies. I rather regretted having eaten quite so much.

I traversed the sûk from end to end without seeing any sign of my husband and son. Retracing my steps, I settled myself on a bench in front of one of the more prosperous establishments and prepared to purchase foodstuffs. The Greek shopkeepers do not engage in the long exchange of courtesies that precedes any purchase in the sûks of Cairo, but I expected I would have to do some bargaining, and so it proved. Rice, dates, tinned vegetables, and some water jars – of the coarse, porous type that permits cooling by evaporation – had been acquired when the shopkeeper broke off his discussion and began a series of extravagant bows. Turning, I saw the familiar form of my husband approaching.

He was bareheaded, as usual, and his waving dark locks shone with bronze highlights. His smiling face, the strong brown throat bared by the open collar of his shirt, the muscular forearms, also bared, had their usual softening effect; after all, I thought, perhaps he had not deceived me. The story I had heard had been third-hand; it might have been distorted, especially by Budge, who was always eager to think the worst of Emerson.

I did not see Ramses, but I assumed he was there, his slighter form hidden by the crowd, for Emerson would not have looked so pleased if he had managed to lose the boy. However, it would have been hard to overlook the individual who followed my husband at a respectful distance. The folds of his mantle shadowed his features, but his height and lithe movements made his identity unmistakable.

'My dear Peabody!' said Emerson.

'Good afternoon, Emerson,' I replied. 'And where is ... Oh, there you are, Ramses. Don't try to hide behind your father; you are even dirtier than I expected you would be, but I can't do anything about that now. What is that brown stain all down your shirtfront?'

Ramses chose to ignore the direct question in favour of the accusation. 'I was not hiding, Mama. I was talking with Mr Kemit here. He has taught me a number of useful phrases in his language, including – '

'You may tell me later, Ramses.' The brown stain appeared to be the residue of some kind of food or drink – something sticky, to judge by the number of flies that clung to it. I transferred my attention to Ramses's tutor, who replied with one of his curious gestures of greeting. 'So your name is Kemit, is it?'

'He has agreed to work for us,' Emerson said happily. 'And bring two others of his tribe. Isn't that splendid?'

'Very. And where do your people live, Mr – er, Kemit?'

'It is a tragic story,' said Ramses, squatting with a supple ease no English lad should have demonstrated. 'His village was one of many destroyed by the Dervishes. They cut down the date palms, killed the men and boys and dishonoured – '

'Ramses!'

'I see that as always you have made good use of your time, Peabody,' Emerson said quickly. 'Are we ready to go back to Nuri?'

'No. I want to buy some trinkets – beads, mirrors, and the like – as gifts for the men to take their wives. You know I always try to become friendly with the women, in the hope of instructing them in the rights and privileges to which their sex is morally entitled.'

'Yes, Peabody, I do know,' Emerson said. 'And while I am in full sympathy with the justice of that cause, I do feel – as I have had occasion to mention before, my dear – that your chances of bringing about any lasting change . . . Well, but that is by the by; shall we finish making our purchases and be on our way?'

Followed by porters carrying our goods, we made our way to another booth. Ramses chose to honour me with his company. 'You would like Kemit's people, Mama,' he remarked. 'Their women are highly respected – except by the Dervishes, who, as I told you, dishonoured – '

'Kindly refrain from referring to the subject again, Ramses. You don't know what you are talking about.'

However, I had an uneasy feeling that he did know.

Like all men, Emerson grows very impatient over the necessary deliberations of shopping. If it were left to him, he would simply point to the first object of its kind he saw and order a dozen. His grumbling and fidgeting were checked, however, when I had the pleasure of telling him that I had got the loan of five more camels from Captain Griffith.

'How the devil did you do that?' he asked admiringly. 'These cursed military men – '

'Are British officers and gentlemen, my dear. I persuaded them that since the animals in question are not yet fit for the arduous trips the Camel Corps makes, they can just as well recuperate at our camp as here. Captain Griffith was kind enough to express full confidence in my veterinary skills.'

'Hmph,' said Emerson. But he said it very softly.

We picked up the camels and a supply of medication for them, and loaded our purchases. The weight of them was negligible compared to the loads camels are accustomed to carry, and I was careful to see that it was done properly, placing pads over the healing sores on the beasts' backs and sides and adjusting the saddles to protect them. I was surprised to see how quick Kemit was to understand the reasoning behind these procedures, and how adept at carrying them out.

'He seems quite an intelligent individual,' I said to Emerson, as we rode side by side out of the village. 'Perhaps he can be taught some of the excavation techniques, as you did with the men of Aziyeh. How I miss our friends, dear old Abdullah and his son and grandsons and nephews!'

'I was thinking the same thing, Peabody. Kemit is clearly a mentally superior individual. If his fellow tribesmen are as capable . . . Ha! Speak of the devil!'

Two men had appeared from among the palm trees, so suddenly and silently that they might have materialised out of thin air. They were attired in the same short trousers and long mantles. Kemit advanced to meet them; after a brief conversation he came back to Emerson. 'They will come. They speak no English. But they will work. They are faithful.'

We mounted Kemit's friends on two of the camels – which they bestrode with a facility that indicated considerable familiarity with that means of transport – and resumed our journey. The gait of the camel does not permit comfortable conversation; I resolved to wait until Emerson and I were alone before raising the subject of Reginald Forthright and my husband's unacceptable behaviour.

However, when the desired condition of privacy was at last attained, other considerations soon intervened, and when they had been concluded (to the satisfaction of both parties), I am bound to confess that Reginald Forthright was the last subject on my mind.

Kemit and his two attendants proved to be all that he had claimed and more. They not only worked tirelessly and carefully at any task assigned them, following directions to the letter, but they all – Kemit especially – proved astonishingly quick at learning the methods of excavation we used. Naturally we rewarded them by giving them increased responsibility and respect (though I hope I need not tell the Reader that we treated all our men with the same courtesy we would have accorded English servants). They were not popular with the villagers, whose insular parochialism made them view even members of nearby tribes as strangers, but the trouble I half expected did not occur. Kemit's crew kept aloof from the others; they built themselves a little tukhul some distance away from the men's camp and retired there as soon as the working day was over.

We usually began work at an early hour, after only a cup of tea, and then paused for breakfast in mid-morning. It was while we were at this meal on the day after our return from the camp that I found an opportunity of speaking with Emerson about Mr Forthright. He had mentioned Mr Budge, remarking, in his bluff manner, 'I caught a glimpse of a familiar fat form strutting around camp yesterday, in the company of some of the officers. Did you happen to run into him, Peabody?'

'Indeed I did,' said I. 'He and I had the honour of lunching with General Rundle. You were invited, Emerson.'

'They couldn't invite me because they couldn't find me,' Emerson said smugly. 'I had a notion some such thing would happen; that is why I kept out of the way. And you see, Peabody, how well it turned out. It's difficult enough to be civil to a group of military blockheads; Budge would have been too much for me. Bragging and boasting as usual, I suppose?'

'To some extent. But it was not his bragging that would have been too much for you.'

'What, then?' Emerson's countenance darkened. 'Did he have the effrontery to admire you, Peabody? By heaven, if he so much as touched your sleeve – '

'Oh, come, Emerson. You must get over this notion (flattering though it may be) that every man I meet falls madly in love with me. Mr Budge has never shown the slightest indication of doing so.'

'He has not the delicacy of taste to appreciate you,' Emerson agreed. 'So what did he do, Peabody?'

'He was kind enough to inform me – and the officers – that Mr Reginald Forthright is on his way here, having been invited by you to join an expedition in search of the Lost Oasis.'

Fortunately Emerson had finished his tea. Otherwise I am convinced he would have choked. I will spare the Reader a description of the broken, incoherent outcries that escaped his lips. With his accustomed quickness he had immediately grasped that the result of Budge's statement must be to make him an object of ridicule, and this seemed to be the major theme of his complaints. Interspersed with the curses which have made Emerson famous along the length of the Nile Valley, his comments rose to a pitch that was audible at some distance. The men turned to stare, and Kemit, who was waiting for instructions, opened his eyes very wide – the first sign of emotion I had seen on his composed countenance.

I suggested that Emerson moderate his voice. He fell silent, and I went on, 'When last heard of, Mr Forthright had got as far as Wadi Halfa. I had not expected the young man would have such determination. He must have had strong encouragement to proceed, don't you think?'

'I do not engage in idle speculation concerning the motives of individuals with whom I am barely acquainted,' Emerson replied.

'Then you did not invite – '

'Curse it, Amelia. . .' Emerson caught himself. It creates a bad impression for leaders of an expedition to quarrel openly before the men – or for the parents of a child like Ramses to disagree. He went on in a more moderate voice. 'I certainly did not encourage Mr Forthright to come to Nubia. Quite the reverse.'

'Ah. So you did communicate with him before we left England.'

Emerson's cheeks turned a handsome mahogany shade and the dimple in his chin quivered ominously. 'And you, Peabody – weren't you moved to send a sympathetic message to the bereaved old father?'

It was a shrewd hit. I believe my countenance remained relatively unmoved, but Emerson knows me too well to be deceived. His tight lips relaxed and a humorous gleam brightened the brilliant blue of his eyes. 'Cards on the table, Peabody. If this young idiot is about to descend upon us, we must know precisely where we stand. I did write to Forthright. I assured him that we would make inquiries, and that if – I underlined the word twice, Peabody – if we discovered anything that substantiated the possibility of Forth's survival, we would communicate with him and his grandfather at once. I fail to see what was wrong with that, or how he could possibly have construed it as a promise or an invitation.'

'I said essentially the same thing,' I admitted. 'To Lord Blacktower.'

Ramses had been uncharacteristically silent up to this point, his wide dark eyes moving from my face to that of his father as we spoke. Now he cleared his throat. 'Perhaps Mr Forthright has received additional information. It would be difficult for him to pass it on to us through the usual channels; the telegraph is reserved for the military, and our whereabouts have been uncertain.'

'Hmph,' said Emerson thoughtfully.

'Well, we can only wait and see,' I remarked. 'There is no way of heading Mr Forthright off, so we had better get as much work as possible accomplished before he arrives.'

Emerson scowled at me. 'His arrival will not affect my activities in the slightest, Peabody. How many times must I repeat that I have no intention of going off on a wild-goose chase?'

'But if it were not a wild-goose chase, Papa?' Ramses asked. 'One could not abandon a friend if there was any hope of rescue.'

Emerson had risen. Fingering the cleft in his chin, he looked down at his son. 'I am glad to find, Ramses, that your principles are those of an English . . . that is, of a gentleman. I would move heaven and earth to save Forth, or his wife, if I truly believed either of them still lived. I don't believe it, and it would take overpowering evidence to convince me I am wrong. So much for that. Now, Kemit. I want to do some digging around the second of the pyramids in line – this one.' Unrolling his plan, he indicated the structure in question. 'Lepsius shows a chapel on the southeast side. There are no signs of it now, but the cursed scavengers can't have carried away every cursed stone; there must be some traces left. Confound it, we need to find some inscriptional material, if only to identify the builders of these structures.'

'Why do you lecture the poor fellow, Emerson?' I inquired softly. 'He doesn't understand a word you are saying.'

Emerson's lips curved in an enigmatic smile. 'No? Did you understand, Kemit?'

'You want to know who made the stone houses. They were the great kings and queens. But they are gone. They are not here.'

Arms folded across his broad breast, he intoned the words like a priest reciting a mortuary formula.

'Where have they gone, Kemit?' Emerson asked.

'They are with the god.' Kemit's hand moved in a curiously fluid gesture from the horizon to the vault of the sky, now pale with heat.

'I pray that is so,' said Emerson courteously. 'Well, my friend, let us get on with it; our work will make their names live again, and in that, as you know, was their hope of immortality.'

They went off together, and I thought, not for the first time, what an impressive pair they made – and Emerson not the lesser of the two.

'Ramses,' I said absently – for part of my attention was concentrated on the graceful and athletic movements of my spouse's admirable form – 'as soon as you have finished at number six, I want you to move your crew to the largest pyramid, and join me.'

'But Papa said – '

'Never mind what Papa said. He has succumbed to his lust – er – he has postponed his surveying in favour of excavation; he cannot complain if I do the same. The largest pyramid surely belongs to one of the great kings, Piankhi or Taharka or Shabaka. The superstructure has completely collapsed, but there must be a burial chamber underneath.'

Ramses stroked his chin. For a moment he looked uncannily like his father, though the resemblance was one of gesture and expression rather than physical likeness. 'Yes, Mama.'

A few days later my crew had moved several tons of stone without finding any trace of the entrance to the burial chamber, and Emerson had shifted his crew from the pyramids of the southeast row to a smaller, half-fallen structure behind them. Shortly after sunrise on the Wednesday I was electrified by a cry that echoed weirdly across the sandy waste. I at once hastened to the scene, and found Emerson hip-deep in his excavation trench. 'Eureka!' he cried in greeting. 'At last! I think we've hit on the chapel, Peabody!'

'Congratulations, my dear,' I replied.

'Get the rest of the men over here at once, Peabody. I want to deepen and widen the trench.'

'But, Emerson, I have not yet – '

Emerson wiped the sand from his perspiring face with his sleeve and gave me a comradely grin. 'My dear, I know you are aching to find some beastly collapsing tunnel into which you can crawl, at the risk of life and limb; but it is imperative that we clear this area as soon as possible. As soon as the locals get wind of our discovery, gossip and exaggeration will transform the find into a treasure of gold and gems, and every human rodent in the neighbourhood will start burrowing.'

'You are right, Emerson,' I said, sighing. 'I will of course do as you ask.'

It took several hours to enlarge the trench so as to expose fully the stones he had found, and to take careful notes of their precise location. As we measured and sketched, while the sun beat down and the sand filled our mouths and nostrils, I would have given a good deal to have a camera. I had proposed bringing one, but Emerson had vetoed the idea, pointing out that the cursed things were cumbersome and unreliable – except in the hands of a trained photographer, which we did not have – and that the efficient use of them required other equipment which was not easy to procure – clean water, chemicals, and the like.

Unfortunately one of the men turned up a few scraps of gold foil. I say unfortunately, for there is nothing that arouses the treasure-hunting instincts and the (alas!) concomitant willingness to commit violence for its possession more quickly than the aureus metal. Shining like the sun, soft enough to be easily worked, incorruptible, since time immemorial it has aroused in men a lust passing the love of women, not to mention their fellow men. The very name of Nubia is derived from the ancient Egyptian word for gold. It was for gold beyond all other treasures, that the pharaohs sent traders and armies into the land of Cush. I would not be at all surprised to find that it was for gold that Cain committed the first murder. (It happened a very long time ago, and Holy Writ, though no doubt divinely inspired, is a trifle careless about details. God is not a historian.)

There was undoubtedly a great deal of gold in Nubia at one time, but as Emerson remarked, studying the pitiful scrap in his big brown hand, there didn't seem to be a lot left. However, I felt it incumbent upon me to take over the task of sifting the soil removed from the trench – and a tedious, hot task it was.

The sun was far down the west and the shadows were lengthening, and I was looking forward to a sponge bath and a change of clothing (and perhaps a small whiskey and soda) when one of our less industrious workers, who spent more time leaning on his shovel than he did using it, cried out in surprise.

'Have you stabbed your foot again with your shovel, careless one?' I inquired sarcastically.

'No, Sitt Hakim – no. There is a camel coming, and a man upon the camel, and the camel is running, and the man is about to fall off the camel, I believe; for look, Sitt Hakim, he sits the camel as no man who wishes to remain upright sits upon – '

But I heard no more, for I had seen what he had seen and had realised that for once his appraisal of the situation was fairly accurate. The rider was not sitting on the camel, he was listing dangerously from side to side. Hastening to meet him, I addressed the camel with an emphatic '*Adar ya-yan*, confound you!'

The camel stopped. I whacked it with my parasol, but before it could kneel (supposing that it had intended to do so), the rider slid from the saddle and fell unconscious at my feet.

The rider was, of course, Mr Reginald Forthright. I had anticipated this, as I am sure the Reader must have done.

'He Is the Man!'

'Good Gad!' said Emerson. 'I wonder if the fellow makes a habit of introducing himself in this fashion, or if we have a particularly unfortunate effect on his nerves. Peabody, I absolutely forbid you to touch him. It may well be that your unnecessarily demonstrative attentions last time inspired this – '

'Don't be absurd, my dear.' With a strange sensation of déjà vu I knelt beside the young man. He was lying on his back this time, in a particularly graceful attitude; but what a change from the well-dressed, neatly groomed individual who had fallen upon our hearth-rug a few weeks earlier! His suit had been cut by an excellent tailor, but it was crumpled and stained. Sunburn had scorched his cheeks and peeled the skin from his nose. His hat (a fashionable but inappropriate tweed cap) had fallen from his head; from under the sweat-darkened curls on his brow a thin trickle of blood traced a path across one cheek.

Emerson had been the first on the scene, but the others soon followed, and curious spectators ringed us round as I dampened my handkerchief from the canteen at my belt and wiped the young man's flushed face. The response was prompt. As soon as consciousness returned, a flush of embarrassment further reddened Mr Forthright's cheeks, and he began stammering apologies.

Emerson cut them short. 'If you are stupid enough to wear wool clothing in this climate and go racing around in the hot sun, you must expect to be overcome by the heat.'

'It was not the heat that caused my collapse,' Forthright exclaimed. 'I was struck on the head by a stone, or some other missile. Another struck my camel, which bolted, and . . . Good heavens!' He sat up, catching at my shoulder for support, and levered an accusing finger. 'There is my assailant – that man there!'

He was pointing at Kemit.

'Nonsense,' Emerson said. 'Kemit has been working at my side all afternoon. Do you often suffer from hallucinations, Mr Forthright?'

'Then it was a man very like him,' Forthright said stubbornly. 'Tall, dark-skinned – '

'As are most of the male inhabitants of this region.' Emerson leaned over him and with ruthless efficiency parted the curls on his brow. Forthright flinched and bit his lip. 'Hmph,' said Emerson. 'There is no swelling, only a small nick in the scalp. No stone caused this injury, Mr Forthright; it was a sharp-edged object like a knife.'

'What difference does that make, Emerson?' I demanded. 'Mr Forthright was obviously attacked – though not by Kemit, who, as you have said, was with us at the time. I suggest we retire to the shade and partake of some liquid refreshment while we discuss the situation. Mr Forthright has a good deal of explaining to do.'

'That is certainly true,' said Emerson, his brows lowering. 'But I have no intention of stopping work early on his account. Take him away, Peabody, and see if you can get any sense out of him.' Beckoning the men to follow, he stalked off, still complaining. 'What the devil are we going to do with him? He can't go back to the camp alone, he'd get himself lost and fall off the cursed camel again and knock himself unconscious and die of exposure or thirst or both and it would be on my . . .'

The words died into an unintelligible but still audible grumble. 'He is right, you know,' I remarked, assisting Forthright to rise. 'It was extremely foolish of you to start out in search of us alone.'

'I was not alone,' Forthright replied gently. 'My servants were with me. It is not their fault that I so far outstripped them. They were attempting to follow when I last saw them, and I expect they will be here before long.'

'That must be them now,' said Ramses.

'"They," not "them,"' I corrected. 'Ramses, what the dev – why are you still here? Papa told you to get back to work.'

'I beg your pardon, Mama, but I did not hear Papa address a direct order to me. Admittedly the general tenor of his comments suggested that he wished the work to resume, but in view of his failure to make a specific – '

'Never mind,' I said.

'Yes, Mama. I had thought I might start a fire to boil water for tea.'

'What a thoughtful lad,' said Forthright, smiling at the boy. 'It is easy to see that he is devoted to his dear mama.'

'Hmmm, yes,' I said, studying my son with mixed emotions. Like his father he seized every excuse to remove his clothing, and since by hook or crook (design or accident, rather) he managed to ruin his nice little Norfolk suits, no matter how many of them I brought along, I was forced to allow him to rely to some extent on locally available attire. At this time he was wearing the trousers of one of his suits and a pair of boots, but from the waist up he might have passed for an Egyptian youth. Upon his black curls he had clapped a cap woven in bright red, yellow, and green patterns, and his coarse cotton shirt was one I had fashioned from a native robe by cutting off several feet of the length.

'Well,' I said, 'so long as you are here, Ramses, you may as well make yourself useful. Go and meet Mr Forthright's servants and take them ... somewhere. Anywhere that is suitable for a temporary camping site – er – so long as it is some distance from – '

'From the tent of Papa and yourself,' said Ramses.

'Quite. I am afraid you will have to rough it tonight, Mr Forthright. We have no extra tents or cots. We were not expecting guests.'

'But of course I brought my own equipment and supplies, Mrs Emerson,' said the young man, adding with a little laugh, 'You had no way of knowing when I might arrive, so I could hardly expect you to provide for me.'

His eyes were as candid as those of Ramses. (More so, in fact.) 'When you might arrive,' I repeated. 'Quite so. We have a good deal to talk about, Mr Forthright. Follow me, if you please.'

The shades of night had fallen before Emerson called a halt to the excavation and dismissed the men. The last half hour of work had been punctuated with curses and exclamations of pain as individuals fell into or over various obstacles, for it was really too dark by then to see what one was doing. Emerson had gone on beyond the usual time, in order to prove . . . Well, one wonders precisely what. But that is the way of the masculine sex, and a woman can only accept these minor aberrations in what is in many ways a thoroughly satisfactory part of the human race.

Mr Forthright and I were sitting in front of the tent, enjoying the crackle and colour of our little fire when Emerson brushed past us with a mumble of greeting and vanished into the tent. I had thoughtfully lit a lantern for his convenience; he promptly kicked it over and proceeded with whatever he was doing in utter darkness and relative silence. Only the splash of water and an occasional swear word betokened his presence. However, when he emerged at last, with his black hair curling on his brow and a clean shirt clinging to the muscular breadth of his shoulders, he was obviously in a better mood, for he gave me a surreptitious caress in passing and actually nodded at Mr Forthright. Our evening ablutions were a great deal of trouble because every drop of water had to be fetched from the Nile, over a mile away, and filtered before it could be used, but I felt they were a necessity rather than a luxury, raising the spirits even as they cleansed the body. I am sure I need not say that they were my idea. Left to himself, Emerson would not have changed his shirt from the beginning of the week to its end. If, that is, he wore a shirt at all.

'We have been waiting for you, my dear,' I said pleasantly. 'Late as it is, I believe there is time for a sip of our usual beverage. We should drink a toast to Mr Forthright, and the perils he has survived.'

Emerson filled the glasses and passed them around, ignoring the hand Ramses had extended. Ramses never gave up hope that Emerson would absent-mindedly include him in the evening ritual – not so much, I think, because he liked the taste of whiskey as because it represented maturity and equal status with his parents.

'And what perils has Mr Forthright survived?' Emerson asked sarcastically.

'Only the ordinary dangers of travel in this region,' the young man replied modestly. 'Mrs Emerson has convinced me that the attack this afternoon was one of them. A disaffected follower of the late and unlamented Mahdi, perhaps.'

'There are a good many disaffected persons in the area,' said Emerson. 'Myself among them. No doubt you have explained your presence to the satisfaction of Mrs Emerson; she is a kind-hearted individual with a peculiar weakness for romantic young idiots. You will find me harder to win over, Mr Forthright.'

'I don't blame you for being annoyed, Professor,' Forthright said. 'As soon as I arrived at Sanam Abu Dom, I found that Mr Budge's version of my mission had spread throughout the camp. It really is too bad! I had not imagined a man of his reputation would be so ill-natured. But perhaps he was only misinformed.'

'He was not misinformed,' Emerson growled.

'Well, you may be sure I immediately set the matter straight. On my honour, Professor, he or his informant completely misinterpreted my remarks and my motives. I have no intention of persuading you to risk your life for a hopeless cause. I simply wanted to be on the spot in case . . . You had said, you know, that if any further information came to light...' The explanation which had begun so glibly faltered into silence. Then Mr Forthright said simply, 'If there is a risk to be taken, I am the one to take it. You have heard nothing – learned nothing?'

'No,' said Emerson.

'I see.' The young man sighed. 'My grandfather has become very frail. It is hope alone that keeps him alive, I believe.'

I began, 'Mr Forthright – '

'I beg, Mrs Emerson, that you will do me the honour to call me Reginald – or Reggie, if you prefer. That is what my friends call me, and I hope I may number you among them.'

'You may indeed,' I said warmly. 'Emerson, Reggie has undergone considerable discomfort, not to say peril, in order to pursue this quest, or convince himself that it is hopeless. And all for the sake of his poor old grandfather. Proof of his son's death would be exceedingly painful to Lord Blacktower, but it would be less painful than the agonising uncertainty that has tormented him. Hope deferred can fester and grow – '

'Yes, yes,' Emerson said. 'So how do you intend to pursue this quest, Mr Forthright?'

Darkness was complete. A shining net of stars spanned the deep vault of heaven, and in the west a silvery glow outlined the ragged crest of the hills. It flooded the landscape in pallid light as the half-grown moon lifted slowly into view. From the cookfire a voice rose in poignant melody.

'How beautiful this is,' Reggie said softly. 'To have experienced such a moment makes the journey worthwhile. Travel broadens the mind, it is said; it has certainly broadened mine. I understand now what drew my uncle to these wild, yet magical regions.'

'Hmph,' said Emerson. 'It is one thing to sit comfortably in the cool of the evening with a glass of whiskey in one's hand and a servant preparing dinner. You wouldn't find it quite so magical if you were lost in the desert with an empty canteen and the sun broiling you like a chicken on a spit and your tongue as dry as a scrap of leather. You haven't answered my question, Mr Forthright.'

'Oh.' The young man started. 'I beg your pardon, Professor. There are refugees arriving daily, I am told, from the areas which have been held by the Dervishes. The officers of the Intelligence Department who question them have promised me they will ask about captives held in remote places.'

'That seems harmless enough,' Emerson muttered.

'And while I wait for news, I will take up the study and practice of archaeology,' Reggie went on gaily. 'Can you use another pair of hands, Professor? I have some knowledge of surveying, but I will wield a spade like the humblest native if that is what you want.'

This handsome offer was welcomed by Emerson with less enthusiasm than it merited, but after voicing the expected (by me) reservations concerning lack of experience and absence of a long-term commitment, he unbent so far as to produce his plan of the site. The ensuing explanation soon took on the length of a lecture, which was interrupted only by the appearance of the cook summoning us to the evening meal. As soon as it was consumed, Reggie expressed his intention of retiring, pleading fatigue, and we soon followed suit; for our working day began at sunrise.

As we prepared for bed I awaited with considerable interest Emerson's comments. He said nothing, however; so after he had put out the light and reclined at my side, I ventured to introduce the subject myself.

'Reggie's assistance will be helpful, don't you think?'

'No,' said Emerson.

'We should have realised that Mr Budge would put the worst possible interpretation on his presence in Nubia. I thought his reasons for coming were both sensible and admirable.'

'Hmph,' said Emerson.

'Who do you suppose it was who threw the rock at him?'

'It could not have been a rock that struck him.'

'I agree. You were quite right, my dear. A knife, a spear, an arrow – '

'Oh, an arrow, by all means,' said Emerson, goaded at last into sarcasm. 'The Bowmen of Cush formed one of the crack

units of the Egyptian Army; no doubt the ghost of one of them mistook Forthright for an ancient Nubian. The bow has not been employed in this region for over a thousand years.'
'A knife or a spear, then.'
'Piffle, Peabody. He probably fainted – it seems to be a habit of his – fell off the camel, and landed on his head. Naturally he would be embarrassed to admit it.'
'But then there would have been a bruise, Emerson.'
Emerson requested that we end the discussion, and reinforced the request by a series of gestures that rendered further conversation on my part inappropriate, if not impossible.

Despite a somewhat disturbed night Emerson was up betimes the following morning. I was awakened by his precipitate departure from our tent, and by his stentorian voice summoning the men to work. Knowing full well that his primary aim was to rouse Reggie and test that unfortunate young man's powers of endurance to the limit, I lingered over my cup of tea, enjoying the exquisite blush of the eastern sky as the stars faded, yielding their lesser light to the glorious lord of day.

The morning air was cool enough to make a wool shirt welcome, but by early afternoon, when Emerson called a temporary halt, we had all shed as many garments as modesty permitted. Reggie had held up better than I expected. To be sure, he had very little to show for his morning's work.
'It will take a while to familiarise yourself with the terrain and with our methods,' I said.
Reggie laughed. 'You are too kind, Mrs Emerson. The truth is, I was too fascinated by what you and the professor are doing to concentrate on my own tasks. Tell me . . .' And he went on to pepper me with questions. What did we hope to find? Why were we digging so slowly and laboriously by hand instead of battering our way into the pyramids?
If he really wanted information, he got more than he bargained for. Emerson simply rolled his eyes and shrugged, in

indication that he found Reggie's state of ignorance too abysmal to be capable of improvement, but Ramses was always ready to lecture.

'The goal of proper excavation, Mr Forthright, is not treasure but knowledge. Any scrap of material, no matter how insignificant, may supply an essential clue to our understanding of the past. Our primary purpose here is to establish the original plan and, if possible, the relative chronology...'

Und so weiter, as the Germans say. After a while Reggie threw up his hands, laughing heartily. 'That's enough for one day, Master Ramses. I don't think I am cut out for archaeology after all. But I am ready to resume work whenever you say, Professor.'

'We don't work during the hottest part of the day,' I informed him. 'You had better rest while you can. If you are ready to retire to your tent, I will accompany you; I may be able to make a few suggestions that will render your situation more comfortable.'

My real aim was to meet his servants and ascertain how they were getting on with the other men, and to inspect his camels. I took it for granted that they would be in need of attention. The campsite was some distance from ours, to the north of the ruins of the largest pyramid. Compared to our own modest quarters, Reggie's were positively palatial. The tent was large enough to accommodate several people, and every possible comfort had been supplied, from rugs upon the sandy floor to a folding bathtub.

'Good heavens,' I exclaimed. 'What, no champagne glasses?'

'Not even champagne,' said Reggie with a laugh. 'However, brandy travels well, I believe; I hope you and the professor will join me in a glass after dinner tonight.'

The camels were in need of my attention – which was not surprising, considering the loads they had carried. Reggie's servants looked on with ill-concealed derision as I applied ointment to the festering sores on the poor beasts' sides, but their grins disappeared when I addressed them in forcible and idiomatic Arabic. There were four of them, three Nubians and an Egyptian, a native of the Thebaid, who answered (like about half his countrymen) to the name of Ahmed. When I asked him what he was doing so far from home, he said, 'The Effendi offered much money, Sitt. What is a poor man to do?'

Reggie decided he did not need a rest, and followed me back to my tent. He was as cheerful and eager to please as a large, clumsy dog, so I allowed him to help me with the accounts. The men were to be paid that evening. We kept separate pay sheets for each individual, since the amount they earned depended upon the number of hours worked plus extra for each important discovery. 'By paying the fair market value for artifacts, we remove the incentive to theft,' I explained, adding wryly, 'Unfortunately, thus far we have had to pay very little extra.'

'The site does appear to have been thoroughly ransacked,' Reggie agreed, with a disparaging glance at the tumbled piles of stone that had once been pyramids. 'How much longer will you stay here if nothing of value turns up?'

'You still don't understand, Reggie. It is knowledge, not treasure, we seek. At the rate we are going, it will take the entire season to finish here.'

'I see. Well, this appears to be the last memorandum, Mrs Emerson. The men will be off to their villages this evening, I presume; do you and the professor stay here, or are you going to the encampment?'

After considerable discussion and a good deal of profane and fruitless argument, Emerson had finally agreed to let the men leave early so they could reach their homes before dark, providing they returned the following evening. I explained this to Reggie, adding that I had planned to visit the market in Sanam Abu Dom next day to purchase fresh vegetables and bread. 'But if you are going, Reggie, you could shop for me and save me the trip.'

A shadow crossed the young man's smiling face. 'I must go, Mrs Emerson. Having beheld the vast and threatening face of the desert, I begin to realise how fruitless my quest must prove, but . . .'

'Yes, of course. I will give you a list this evening, then. I suggest you wait until morning; travel after dark is fraught with perils.'

'You need not argue that,' Reggie replied. His hand went to the neat bandage I had applied to the cut on his brow, and he glanced over his shoulder at Kemit, who was resting in the shade nearby. 'I suppose it could not have been that fellow who attacked me, but I swear to you, Mrs Emerson, it was a man so like him it might have been his twin. What do you know of him?'

'His village, which was destroyed by the Dervishes, is south of here. He was not more precise; as you know, Western notions of distance and geography are unknown to these people.'

'You trust him, then?' Reggie's voice had dropped to a whisper.

'You need not lower your voice, he only understands a few words of English. As for trusting him, why should I not? He and his friends have worked faithfully and diligently.'

'Why is he staring at us?' Reggie demanded.

'He is looking, not staring. Come now, Reggie, admit that your suspicions of Kemit are unjust and unfounded. You couldn't have got a good look at your assailant, since by your own account you didn't realise anything was wrong until the missile struck you.'

After a few more hours of work, Emerson called a halt and summoned the men to the table where I sat ready to hand out their wages. 'Curse it,' he remarked, taking a seat at my side, 'we must think of another arrangement, Peabody. They are so anxious to get away, they haven't done a bloo – blooming thing all afternoon.'

'The only alternative is to return to our original plan of letting them leave early Friday morning,' I replied.

'Then they will have to return Friday night,' Emerson declared. 'Otherwise they won't be here until mid-morning on Saturday and will complain that they are too tired after their long walk to put in a good day's work.'

At least the men did not linger to argue about the amount of their pay; they were anxious to be safe at home before the dread demons of darkness came out of hiding. As they dispersed I closed the account book and remarked, 'Supper tonight will be out of tins, gentlemen; cooking is not an activity at which I excel or in which I care to do so.'

'My servant Ahmed is an excellent cook,' Reggie said. 'It was one of the skills for which I selected him. Perhaps you will all do me the honour of being my guests at dinner this evening.'

I accepted with proper expressions of appreciation. After Reggie had gone off to his tent, Emerson remarked sourly, 'It wouldn't surprise me to see him turn out in full evening kit. I warn you, Amelia, if he does I will go and dine with Kemit.'

'Mr Forthright brought a considerable quantity of luggage,' said Ramses, sitting cross-legged at my feet. 'In addition to a revolver, he has two rifles and quantities of ammunition as well as – '

'He probably plans to do some hunting,' I replied, thinking it best not to ask Ramses how he knew of these facts.

'Should that be the case, I will feel myself obliged to remonstrate,' said Ramses in his stateliest manner.

'Just so you don't run into the line of fire, as you have been known to do,' I said sternly. 'You spend far too much time interfering in other people's business, Ramses. Come and give me a hand; there are several hours of daylight left and I want to have a closer look at those small piles of debris south of number four. I suspect they may have been queens' tombs – for even in Cush, where women enjoyed considerable power, the ladies were shortchanged in the matter of pyramids.'

Emerson decided to join us, and we spent a most enjoyable hour poking around the rubble and arguing about where the burial chambers might be. Ramses, of course, had to disagree with me and his father. 'We cannot assume,' he claimed, 'that because the burial chambers in Egyptian pyramids were, for the most part, under the superstructure, that such was the case here. Remember Ferlini's description of the chamber in which he found the jewellery that is now in the Berlin Museum – '

'Impossible,' I exclaimed. 'Lepsius agrees with me that Ferlini must have made a mistake. He was no archaeologist – '

'But he was there,' said Ramses. 'Herr Lepsius was not. And with all due respect, Mama – '

'Hmmm, yes,' Emerson said quickly. 'But, my boy, even if Ferlini did find a burial chamber in the upper portions of one pyramid, that could have been an exception to the general rule.'

His attempt at compromise failed, as such efforts generally do. 'Nonsense!' I exclaimed.

'That is not the point, Papa, if you will excuse me,' said Ramses.

The debate continued to rage as we walked back to our tents. Few families, I venture to assert, share so many agreeable interests as ours, and the freedom and candour with which we communicate our opinions to one another only adds to our mutual pleasure.

I had brought along one good frock just in case – for one never knows when one may encounter persons of a superior social status. It was a simple evening dress of eau-de-Nil spotted net, the bodice cut low and square, the skirt flounced, with pink silk roses trimming the flounces and the short puffed sleeves. By allowing Emerson the privilege, which he much enjoys, of buttoning me into the frock, I managed to persuade him to wear a jacket and change his boots for proper shoes, but he refused to wear a cravat, claiming that he had taken up archaeology as a career primarily because a cravat was not part of the official costume for that profession. However, as I had to admit when he pressed me, Emerson's personal appearance is so striking that the absence of a particular article of clothing does not diminish the effect in the least.

I then went in search of Ramses, for it was safe to assume he would wash only the parts of him that showed. As I trailed my eau-de-Nil flounces across the sandy ground, wincing as pebbles pressed through the thin soles of my evening slippers, I could almost have wished that Emerson had not placed the boy's little tent so far from our own. His reasons for doing so were excellent, however, and on the whole the advantages far outweighed the disadvantages. (Even in the light of what happened soon afterwards I maintain that opinion.)

Ramses had not washed even the parts that showed. He was perched on a campstool in front of the packing case that served as desk and table combined. It was littered with scraps of paper and he was busily scribbling in the battered clothbound notebook that accompanied him everywhere.

He greeted me with his usual punctilious courtesy, more becoming a grave old gentleman than a little boy, and begged for another minute of delay so that he could finish his notes.

'Oh, very well,' I said. 'But you must hurry. It is rude to be late when one is invited to dine. What notes are those, that are so important?'

'A dictionary of the dialect spoken by Kemit and his friends. The spelling is, of necessity, phonetic; I am using the system derived from – '

'Never mind, Ramses. Just make haste.' Looking over his shoulder I saw that he had arranged the vocabulary by parts of speech, leaving several pages for each. None of the words was familiar to me, but then my knowledge of the Nubian dialects was extremely limited. I was happy to observe that Kemit's instruction had not included any words to which I could take exception, with the possible exception of a few nouns applying to certain portions of human anatomy.

When Ramses had finished he offered me his campstool, which I took outside, lowering the tent flap as I left. Several years earlier Ramses had requested the privilege of privacy when he performed his ablutions or changed his clothing. I was perfectly happy to accede to this request, for washing small dirty squirming boys had never been a favourite amusement of mine. (The nurserymaid in charge of Ramses at the time had made no objection either.)

I had asked Emerson to join us when he was ready, so I was content to wait; the sunset was particularly brilliant that evening, a blaze of gold and crimson that contrasted exquisitely with the

deepening azure of the zenith. Against this tapestry of living light
the jagged contours of the pyramids stood out in dark outline,
and as any thoughtful individual might do, I mused upon the
vanity of human aspiration and the brevity of human passions.
Once this tumbled wilderness had been a holy place, adorned
with every beautiful and good thing (as the ancients expressed
it). Chapels built of carved and painted stone served each stately
monument; white-robed priests hastened about their duties,
bearing offerings of food and treasure to be placed upon the altars
of the royal dead. As the shadows deepened and the night crept
across the sky, I heard the soft rush of beating wings. Was it the
human-headed soul bird, the *ba* of some long-vanished pharaoh,
returning to partake of food and drink from his chapel? No. It
was only a bat. The poor *ba* would have starved long ages ago if
it had depended on the offerings of its priests.

These poetic thoughts were rudely swept away by Emerson
blundering towards me. He can move as quickly and quietly as
a cat when he chooses; on this occasion he did not choose,
because he was not in the humour for a social engagement. I
must say that he seldom is.

'Is that you, Peabody?' he called. 'It is so dark I can scarcely
see where I am going.'

'Why didn't you bring a lantern?' I inquired.

'We won't need it; the moon will be up soon,' said Emerson,
with one of those bursts of striking illogic of which men
constantly accuse women. 'Where is Ramses? If we must do
this, let's get it over with.'

'I am ready, Papa,' said Ramses, lifting the flap of the tent. 'I
took pains to make myself as tidy as possible, given the circumstances, which are not conducive to the easy attainment of that
condition. I trust, Mama, that my appearance is satisfactory.'

Since he was only visible as a dark shape against the darker
interior of the tent, I was hardly in a position to make a valid
judgment. I suggested that he light a lantern, not so much
because I wanted to inspect him – further delay would have
driven Emerson wild – but because night had fallen and the

roughness of the ground made walking difficult, particularly for a lady wearing thin-soled shoes. So equipped, we set out. At my request, Emerson gave me his arm. He likes me to lean on his arm, and since Ramses preceded us with the light, he was able to make a few gestures of an affectionate nature, which further soothed his temper, so much so that he made only one rude remark when he saw the elegant arrangements Reggie had made for our reception.

Candles graced the table, which was covered with a cloth of gay printed cotton. This must have been purchased at the sûk, for I had seen others like it there. The pottery dishes had come from the same source, but I felt sure the wine had not; even the enterprising Greek merchants had not imported expensive German hock. The carpet on which the table had been placed was a beautiful antique Oriental, its deep wine-red background strewn with woven flowers and birds. I could only admire the taste that had chosen the best of the local crafts, and the kindly care that had taken so much trouble for guests. People make fun of the British for maintaining formal standards in the wild, but I am of the school that believes such efforts have a beneficial effect not only upon the participants but upon the observers.

Ahmed's cooking lived up to his master's claims and the wine was excellent. Emerson unbent so far as to take a glass, but he refused the brandy Reggie offered at the conclusion of the meal, despite the latter's urging. Out of politeness I joined the young man, and was pleased to observe that he was as abstemious as I, restricting himself to a single glass of brandy. 'It will keep,' he said with a smile, as Ahmed carried the bottle away. 'But perhaps I should share it with my men – a special treat, on the eve of their holiday – '

Emerson shook his head, and I said emphatically, 'On no account, Reggie. Liquor is one of the curses the white man has introduced into this country. The military authorities, quite rightly, keep a strict control over the amount of alcohol that is brought in. It would be doing these poor people a disservice to introduce them to drunkenness.'

'That is no doubt correct, Mama,' said Ramses, before Reggie could reply. 'But does not that view smack somewhat of condescension? Alcoholic beverages were not unknown before Europeans came here; the ancient Egyptians were particularly fond of both beer and wine. Even young children – '

'Beer and wine are not as harmful as spirits,' I said, frowning at my son. 'And all of them are harmful to young children.'

Emerson was beginning to fidget, so I thanked Reggie for his hospitality and we started back towards our tents. The moon had risen. It was only halfway to the full, but its light was bright enough to make the lantern unnecessary. The soft silvery rays of the goddess of the night cast their spell of magic and romance. (The wine may have had a certain effect as well.) Emerson's pace quickened, and I was not reluctant to be hurried along. We left Ramses at his tent with affectionate, though somewhat abbreviated, good-nights, and made haste to reach our own.

There is nothing like strenuous physical exercise to induce healthful slumber. I slept soundly that night. It was no ordinary, audible noise that roused me, but something I took to be a voice, penetrating my dreams with the shrill insistence of a cry for help. It summoned me with that imperative instinct which nestles deep within a mother's breast, oft-tried though it may have been. I tried to answer; my voice died in my throat. I attempted to rise; my limbs were weighted down.

The weight shifted, and Emerson, cursing sleepily, rose to hands and knees. He was gone before I could stop him, but I took comfort in the fact that he was wrapped in one of the loose native robes, the sudden drop in temperature during the night having apparently prompted this departure from custom. My own nightgown was voluminous enough to be modest, if not exactly suitable for walking abroad; I paused only long enough to slip my feet into my boots and snatch up my parasol before rushing in pursuit of my husband.

111

The source of the disturbance was, as I might have expected, near the tent of Ramses, where I saw a singular tableau. One body lay prone upon the ground. Another stood over it, fists on its hips. A third, smaller form sat, pallid and immobile as a limestone statue, several feet away.

'Peabody!' Emerson bellowed.

I put my hands over my ears. 'I am just behind you, Emerson, you needn't shout. What has happened?'

'The most extraordinary thing, Peabody. Look here. He's done it again! This is ridiculous. It's one thing to collapse at the slightest provocation, or none at all, I was becoming accustomed to that; but to wake people up in the middle of the night – '

'It is not a faint this time, Emerson. He is wounded – bleeding.'

It was not until my fingers actually touched the sticky wetness that I realised the truth. Like Emerson, Reggie wore a native robe, but his was dark blue in colour 'Light, Emerson,' I exclaimed. 'I must have light. Ramses, fetch the lantern. Ramses? Did you hear me?'

'I will light the lantern,' Emerson said. 'The poor lad is a trifle dazed still, after having been wakened so abruptly.'

I went to Ramses. Even when I bent over him he seemed to be unaware of my presence. I took him by the shoulders and shook him, insisting that he speak to me. (And I must say it made rather a change for me to ask Ramses to talk instead of trying to get him to stop.)

He blinked at me then, and said slowly, 'I think I was dreaming, Mama. But I came when you called.'

The chill that seized my limbs was not the product of the cold night air. 'I did not call you, Ramses. Not until just now. You called me.'

'How very odd.' Ramses stroked his chin thoughtfully. 'Hmmm. We must discuss this situation, Mama, and compare our impressions of what occurred. Is that Mr Forthright lying there on the ground?'

'Yes, and he is more in need of my attentions than you seem

to be,' I replied, considerably relieved to find that Ramses was himself again. 'Bring the lantern here, Emerson.'

Emerson let out a startled exclamation when the lamplight illumined the fallen man. 'I beg your pardon, Peabody, I thought you were up to your usual . . . Ahem. He does seem to have bled rather profusely. Is he dead?'

'No, nor likely to die, unless the wound becomes infected.' I turned Reggie onto his back and opened the robe to expose an arm and shoulder more admirably muscled than one might have expected. 'It is not so bad as I feared. The bleeding seems to have stopped. And – good heavens! Here is the weapon that wounded him. It was under his body.'

I picked it up by the haft and handed it to Emerson. 'Curiouser and curiouser,' he muttered. 'This is no native knife, Peabody, it is good Sheffield steel and bears the mark of an English maker. Could he have fallen on it?'

'Never mind that now, Emerson. He ought to be carried to his tent, where I can attend to him properly. Where the dev – the deuce are his servants? How could they sleep through such a racket?'

'Drunk, perhaps,' Emerson began. Then a voice from the darkness said quietly, 'I am here, Lady. I carry him.'

So it happened that the first sight to meet Reggie's eyes was the tall form of Kemit, advancing into the circle of lamplight. A sharp cry burst from the lips of the wounded man. 'Murderer! Assassin! Have you returned to finish me off?'

'Mr Forthright, you are becoming a bore,' Emerson said impatiently. 'My thanks, Kemit; I can manage him.' He lifted the young man into his mighty arms.

Reggie's head fell back against Emerson's shoulder. He had lost consciousness again. I had to agree with my husband; Reggie was becoming a bit of a bore, especially on the subject of Kemit. What had he been doing so far from his own camp in the middle of the night?

On hands and knees, his nose so close to the ground that he resembled a hunting dog on the trail of a rabbit, Ramses was examining the spot, hideously stained with blood, where Reggie had lain.

'Get up from there, Ramses,' I said in disgust. 'Your morbid curiosity is repugnant. Either return to your cot or come with me.'

As I had expected, Ramses chose to come with me. When we reached Reggie's tent, Ahmed was there, rubbing his eyes in an ostentatious and unconvincing fashion. 'Did you call, Effendi?' he asked.

'I certainly did,' said Emerson, who certainly had, his shouts having made the welkin ring. 'Confound you, Ahmed, are you blind as well as deaf? Can't you see your master is injured?'

Ahmed gave a theatrical start. '*Wallahi-el-azem*! It is the young effendi. What has happened, Oh Father of Curses?'

Emerson proceeded to prove his claim to that title, to such effect that Ahmed soon had the lamps lit and his master's couch prepared. Reggie had brought a well-equipped medical kit. It did not take long for me to clean the wound and bandage it. It was hardly more than a shallow cut and did not even require stitching.

A little brandy soon restored Reggie to his senses, and his first words were an apology for having caused me such trouble.

'What the devil were you doing outside my son's tent in the middle of the night?' Emerson demanded.

'Taking a walk,' Reggie replied faintly. 'I could not sleep, I know not why; I thought some exercise might do me good. As I drew near the boy's tent, I saw . . . I saw . . .'

'Don't talk anymore,' I said. 'You need to rest.'

'No, I must tell you.' His hand groped for mine. 'You must believe me. I saw the tent flap open and a pale, ghostly form appear. It gave me quite a start until I realised it must be Master Ramses. Naturally I assumed he was – he felt the need . . .'

'Yes, go on,' I said.

'I was about to withdraw when I saw another form, dark as a shadow, tall as a young tree, glide towards the boy. Ramses went slowly towards it. They met – and the dark shape stretched out its arms to grasp the boy. The gesture broke through my paralysis of surprise, realising that danger threatened Ramses, I rushed to his aid. Needless to say, I had no weapon. I grappled with the man – for a man it was, with muscles like bands of rope, who fought with the ferocity of a wild beast.' The effort of speech had exhausted him, his voice faltered, and he said feebly, 'I remember nothing more. Guard the boy. He . . .'

I put my finger on his lips. 'No more, Reggie. You are exhausted by shock and loss of blood. Have no fear, we will watch over Ramses. May the grateful thanks of his devoted parents console you for your injuries, and may you sleep in peace, knowing that you – '

'Harrumph,' said Emerson forcibly. 'If you want him to rest, Amelia, why don't you stop talking?'

It seemed a reasonable suggestion. I instructed Ahmed to watch over his master and call me at once if any change in his condition occurred. As we retraced our steps I suggested to Emerson that Ramses had better spend the rest of the night with us.

'He may as well,' said Emerson. 'There is not enough of the night left for . . . Ramses, what have you got to say for yourself?'

'Quite a good deal, Papa,' said Ramses.

'I thought as much. Well?'

Ramses took a deep breath. 'To begin with, I have no recollection whatever of leaving my tent. I saw no mysterious dark form, I saw no struggle.'

'Ha,' Emerson exclaimed. 'Then Forthright lied.'

'Not necessarily, Papa. He may have exaggerated the ferocity of the struggle; I have observed that men do when they are attempting to prove their valour. What woke me was a summons, as I thought – a voice calling my name, with considerable urgency. I took it to be Mama's voice, and responded; but I have no clear memory of anything beyond that until Mama took me by the shoulders and shook me.'

We had reached our tent. I got out the extra blankets and made a sort of nest for Ramses beside our sleeping mats, but when I would have settled him on them, he resisted. 'One more thing, Mama. When you saw me searching the ground – '

'I suppose you were playing detective. A very silly habit of yours, Ramses; you are only a little boy, after all. You should have left that to Mama and Papa.'

'It occurred to me that if the assailant had left any clue, he might return and remove it before morning,' said Ramses.

'Criminals are not so careless as to leave incriminating evidence lying about, Ramses. You have been reading too many romances.'

'No doubt that is generally the case, Mama. But this criminal did leave evidence. I presume it was torn from his head in the struggle.'

From the folds of his voluminous white nightgown he produced an object that he offered for my inspection. It was a cap, of a type with which I was very familiar, though this example was a good deal cleaner than most of the ones I had seen on the heads of Egyptians. It was not a popular item of dress in Nubia, where most men preferred a turban.

'Hmph,' said Emerson, inspecting it. 'The pattern resembles some I have seen in Luxor. Could Forthright's assailant have been his own servant? He's an insolent sort of fellow.'

'Reggie would surely have recognised him,' I said, shaking my head. 'None of our men wear such a thing, but a clever malefactor might assume an object of attire as a disguise, or ...'

Here I stopped, and gazed with a wild surmise upon my son, who returned my stare with an expression so limpid-eyed and innocent it was practically tantamount to a confession. The art of disguise was one of Ramses's hobbies. He was somewhat restricted in the practice of it, since his size limited him to imitating only the juvenile portion of the population, but I had a nasty feeling that as his height increased, so would his expertise.

'Ramses,' I began; but before I could proceed, Ramses produced another strange object.

'I also found this near the scene of the crime, Mama. To my mind it is even more provocative than the cap.'

Emerson let out a muffled exclamation and snatched the thing from the boy's hand. At first glance I could see nothing to explain the concentrated attention with which he regarded it. It was a shaft of what appeared to be reed, only a few inches long; the jagged end suggested it had been broken off a longer object. The other extremity ended in a bit of wood, to which was attached a blunt, rounded stone shaped like a miniature club. At the point where the wood joined the reed, a band of pierced decoration ornamented the shaft and, one presumed, helped to hold the two together.

'What on earth?' I exclaimed.

Emerson shook his head, not in denial but in dazed disbelief. 'It is an arrow, or part of one.'

'There is no point,' I objected.

'This is the point, or pile, as it is called in archery.' Emerson's fingernail flicked the rounded stone. 'It is attached to this piece of wood, which is in turn tanged to the shaft. Footed, in other words. The point is blunt because it was designed to stun, not to kill.'

'I see.' I leaned over to examine the object more closely, noting the delicacy of the decoration. 'It reminds me of something but I can't remember where I saw it.'

'No? Then I will refresh your memory.' Emerson's eyes remained fixed on the broken arrow. 'The hunting scenes in the Theban tombs – that is where you saw such an arrow. This is identical with the weapons used by the nobles of ancient Egypt when they hunted fowl in the marshes. Identical, Peabody. Except that it cannot be more than a few years old.'

The Ghost of
a Bowman of Cush

Long after I had sought my couch Emerson sat silent in the lamplight, turning the broken shaft over and over in his hands with the absorbed fascination of a connoisseur inspecting the rarest of gems. He had thrown off his robe; shadows moulded the broad bands of muscles on his breast and arms; shadows sculpted his strong cheekbones and intellectual brow and deepened the dimple (or cleft, as he prefers to call it) in his manly chin. It was a sight to stir the strongest sensations, and since I was forced by circumstances to repress them, they left a lasting imprint upon my heart.

Well, of course I knew what he was thinking, even though he had refused to discuss the matter. For one thing, he was afraid I would remind him of his careless jest concerning Reggie's earlier injury. 'The ghost of one of the Bowmen of Cush,' he had said; and here, before our very eyes, was a fragment of an arrow that might have been carried by one of those very archers. Mayhap the bow had not been used in this area for a thousand years – I was willing to take Emerson's word for that – but one of the ancient names for Cush was 'Land of the Bow,' and 'Commander of the Bowmen of Cush' was a military title of the Late Egyptian Empire.

I fell asleep at last, and when I awoke I was alone. An unnatural silence prevailed. No shouted commands, no sound of the tuneless singing with which the men lightened their labours. . . Then I remembered that it was the day of rest, and that the men were gone. Still, it was strange that Emerson had taken pains not to waken me; stranger still that Ramses had managed to leave the tent without making a racket of some kind. A hideous foreboding seized me, and I hastened to rise.

For once my foreboding portended nothing in particular. I found Emerson seated in a chair before the tent calmly drinking tea. He greeted me with a cheerful good morning and the hope that I had slept well.

'Better than you,' I said, remembering my last glimpse of him the night before, and noting the shadows of sleeplessness that darkened his eye sockets. 'Where is Ramses? How is Reggie getting on? Why didn't you wake me earlier? What – '

'The situation is under control, Peabody. I will make you a cup of tea while you change into more suitable attire.'

'Really, Emerson – '

'Mr Forthright will be joining us shortly. His injury was less severe than you believed. Curious, isn't it, that his injuries always are less severe than you believed them to be? I don't blame you for exposing yourself to him last night in that fetching but flimsy garment – I make all due allowances for your understandable state of agitation – but a repetition of the error might be taken amiss.'

'By you, you mean.'

'By me, my dear Peabody.'

Torn between annoyance and amusement, I retired and followed his suggestion. When I returned I found them all assembled – Ramses squatting on the rug, Reggie seated in a chair next to Emerson. He leapt to his feet with an alacrity that went far to support Emerson's assessment of his condition, and insisted on offering me a chair before he reassumed his own.

'It is a great relief to see you looking so well,' I exclaimed, taking the cup Emerson handed me. 'You had lost a great deal of blood – '

'Obviously the blood was not his,' said Emerson. (Lack of sleep always makes him short-tempered.)

'Quite right,' Reggie agreed. 'As I told you, I grappled with the fellow – '

'A most courageous act,' said Emerson. 'For you were unarmed, were you not? A man going for a peaceful moonlight stroll does not ordinarily carry a weapon.'

'No, not ordinarily. I – er – '

'Is the knife yours, Forthright?' Emerson whipped it out of his pocket and brandished it under Reggie's nose.

'No! That is . . .'

'For heaven's sake, Emerson, stop interrupting him,' I exclaimed. 'How can he explain what happened when you won't let him finish a sentence?

Emerson glowered at me. 'The implications of my questions must be obvious to you, Amelia. And to Mr Forthright. If he – '

'They are indeed obvious, Emerson. It is your tone to which I object. You do not ask, you interrogate, like – '

'Curse it, Amelia – '

A burst of hearty laughter from Reggie ended the discussion. 'Please don't quarrel on my account, my friends. I understand what the professor is getting at, and I don't blame him for having doubts. As he says, a man bent on a peaceful errand does not go armed. I might claim that a sensible man would go armed in this region, but had I feared encountering a wild animal or wilder man, I would have strapped on my revolver or carried a rifle.'

'Precisely,' Emerson growled.

'It did not occur to me to take such a precaution,' Reggie continued. 'It happened just as I told you. Seeing the shadowy figure about to seize the boy, I flung myself upon him. He drew a knife; we struggled for possession of it, and after being wounded slightly I got it away from him. To be honest, I don't remember clearly what happened afterwards, but I have a vague recollection of striking a blow and hearing a muffled cry before unconsciousness overcame me.'

There was a brief silence. Then a voice murmured, '"Yet who would have thought the old man had so much blood in him. . ."'

Emerson nodded. 'Well put, Ramses. Your mama will no

doubt be happy to hear you quote from a more literary source than your favourite thrillers. There was a great deal of blood.'

'And your retainer has disappeared,' said Reggie.

'What?' I exclaimed. 'Kemit has gone?'

'He and both his men,' Emerson said.

Another silence ensued, longer and more fraught with emotion. Finally Emerson squared his shoulders and addressed the group in the voice that never ceased to thrill me – the voice of a leader of men. 'Let us consider this situation coolly and rationally, without prejudice. Something deucedly peculiar is going on.' I started to speak; Emerson turned his burning blue gaze upon me. 'I will invite your comments, my dear Peabody, when I have finished. Until then I beg you – all of you – will permit me to speak without interruption.'

'Certainly, my dear Emerson,' I murmured.

'Hmph,' said Emerson. 'Very well. When Lord Blacktower called upon us with his preposterous story, I reacted as any sensible individual would – with incredulity. That very night an odd incident occurred. You know of it, Mr Forthright. No comment, please, a simple nod will suffice. Thank you. At the time I was unable to see any connection between this incident and Lord Blacktower's proposal, for the reason that no such connection was apparent.

'Nothing else untoward occurred until we reached Nubia. You may recall, Peabody, the curious incident of Ramses walking in his sleep.' He went on hastily, before I could reply. 'One such event might be dismissed as meaningless. A second similar event, such as occurred last night, raises certain doubts. Again Ramses claims to have heard a voice call him. He remembers responding to the call, but has no recollection of anything else.

'Any attempt to concoct a theory that would weave these bizarre events into a connected narrative would be no more than idle fiction.' The blazing blue eyes turned towards me; and such was their hypnotic effect that I made no attempt at rebuttal. 'However,' Emerson went on, 'one of the objects found at the scene of the crime last night is, to say the least, remarkable. This fragment' – he took it from his pocket, with the air of a conjurer pulling a rabbit from his hat, and waved it before us – 'this scrap of broken arrow changes the entire affair. I will stake my reputation – which is not inconsiderable – on the fact that nothing remotely like it is manufactured today by any known tribe of Nubia, Egypt, or the surrounding deserts!'

He paused for effect. This was a mistake, as he immediately realised; before he could resume, Ramses said, 'With all respect, Papa, I believe we all – with the possible exception of Mr Forthright – have followed your reasoning and anticipated your conclusion. If this arrow was not shaped by any known people, then it must have been made by some member of a group hitherto unknown. It is the second such unique artifact you have encountered; the armlet shown you by Mr Forth fourteen years ago was the first.'

'Good heavens!' The words burst from Reggie's throat. 'What are you getting at? You cannot mean –

'Curse it,' Emerson shouted. 'Be still, all of you! You have interrupted the reasoned discourse – '

'Well now, my dear, you were going on at quite unnecessary length,' I said soothingly. 'It is obvious, isn't it? This bit of arrow was broken off during the struggle last night, it must have been carried by Reggie's assailant, who was caught in the very act of luring Ramses out of his bed, for the second time since we arrived in Nubia. Why he wants Ramses I cannot imagine . . . that is to say, I do not know. But one might reasonably conclude that abduction rather than physical assault was his aim, for he had plenty of time to attack the boy on both occasions. As to why he wishes to kidnap Ramses – '

'Excuse me, Amelia,' said Emerson softly. His face was crimson and his voice shook with repressed emotion. 'Did I hear you say something about going on at unnecessary length?'

'You are right to remind me, Emerson. I was about to commit the same error.' I brandished my teacup and raised my voice to a thrilling pitch. 'Let us cut through the cobwebs of speculation with the sharp sword of common sense! The lost civilisation Willoughby Forth set forth to find is a reality! He, and, let us hope, his wife, are prisoners of this mysterious people! One or more of them has pursued us, from the wilds of Kent to the barren deserts of Nubia! Their occult powers, unknown to modern science, have enslaved Ramses, and even now – '

But here my audience cut me short with a chorus of comment. Dominating the other voices was the deep, infectious laughter of my spouse. Not until his whoops of mirth had subsided could any other sound be heard, and that sound, as one might have expected, was the voice of Ramses.

'Mama, I beg your pardon, but I must take exception to the word "enslaved," which is not only exaggerated and unsubstantiated but derogatory, implying as it does – '

'Never mind, Ramses,' said Emerson, wiping the tears of amusement from his eyes with the back of his manly hand. (Emerson never has a clean handkerchief.) 'Your mama did not mean, I am sure, to insult you. Her imagination – '

'I do not see that imagination enters into it,' I said loudly. 'If either of you can come up with a better explanation for the strange events of the past – '

Ramses and Emerson spoke at once, then fell silent; and Reggie remarked, as if to himself, 'Conversation with the Emerson family is stimulating, to say the least. May I say a word?' He went on without giving any of us an opportunity to reply. 'I take it, Professor, that you disagree with Mrs Emerson's conclusions.'

'What?' Emerson stared at him in surprise. 'No, not at all.'

'But, sir – '

'My amusement derived not from Mrs Emerson's deductions but from her manner of expressing them,' Emerson said. 'I can think of other explanations, but hers is certainly the most probable.'

Reggie shook his head dazedly. 'I don't understand.'

'It is difficult for an ordinary intelligence to follow the quickness of Mrs Emerson's thought,' Emerson said kindly. 'And she does – oh, yes, my dear, you do – she does exaggerate. There is no question of occult powers here; Ramses's odd behaviour is easily explained on the grounds of a post-hypnotic suggestion, instilled by the conjurer whom we encountered in Halfa. If we assume, as we now have reason to do, that the message from Willoughby Forth was genuine, it must have been brought to England by a member of the group that holds him prisoner, for otherwise the messenger would have identified himself and explained how the paper came into his hands. That same mysterious messenger may have shed the blood we found at our gate – but if he was wounded, who shot him, and why? Can we conclude that there are two different groups of people involved, one hostile to the other? The conjurer in Halfa and the presence in camp last night of a man carrying an arrow of an antique and unknown pattern indicate that some member of one of the postulated groups has followed us from England for purposes – er – for purposes impossible to explain at this time.'

'Nonsense,' I exclaimed. 'The purpose is obvious. It is to prevent us from setting out to rescue Willoughby Forth and his poor wife.'

'Curse it, Amelia, there you go again,' Emerson cried. 'That purpose would have been more readily achieved by leaving us strictly alone. They, whoever they are, cannot suppose we will sit calmly by while they lure our son into their clutches.'

'You have a point there, Emerson,' I admitted. 'Then may we conclude that they want us to set out to rescue the Forths?'

'Cursed if I know,' said Emerson candidly.

A brief silence followed this noble admission of fallibility; pondering, we sipped our cooling tea. Finally Reggie asked timidly, 'What are you going to do, Professor?'

Emerson set his cup in the saucer with a decisive thump. 'Something must be done.'

'Quite,' I said, with equal decisiveness.

'But what?' Reggie demanded.

'Hmmm.' Emerson fingered the cleft in his chin. 'Well, I am certainly not going to set out on some harebrained expedition into the desert.'

'We might try to hypnotise Ramses again,' I suggested. 'He may know more than he is aware of.'

Ramses uncurled himself from his squatting position and rose to his feet. 'With all respect, Mama, I would rather not be hypnotised again. From my reading on the subject I feel it is a dangerous activity when practised by one who is untrained in its techniques.'

'If you are referring to me, Ramses,' I began.

'Weren't you referring to yourself?' Emerson inquired, his eyes twinkling. He put a friendly hand on Ramses's shoulder. 'Sit down, my son; I won't let Mama hypnotise you.'

'Thank you, Papa.' Ramses sank down, keeping a rather wary eye on me. 'I have given the matter considerable thought, and I can say with some certainty that the voice I thought I heard, and that I assumed to be that of Mama, was no more than my own interpretation of a wordless but urgent demand. I heard it as a single word: "Come."'

'Come . . . where?' Emerson asked softly.

Ramses's narrow shoulders lifted in the ineffable Arabic shrug, but his normally imperturbable countenance showed more than a trace of perturbation. 'There.' His outflung arm indicated the western desert, barren under the steaming sun.

A shudder ran through my limbs. 'Ramses,' I exclaimed. 'I insist that you – '

'No, no,' Emerson said. 'No hypnotism, Amelia. I agree with Ramses that it might do more harm than good. It appears that something must be done, however. We can't have Ramses trotting around the desert, or guard him every second.' His eyes were fixed on the far horizon, where sand faded into sky, and the longing in his mind was as clear to me as if he had shouted it aloud. The lure of the unknown and of discovery – it called to that sensitive and brilliant spirit as strongly as the unknown force called his son. Had he been alone, with no fears for my safety or that of Ramses, he would have set out on the greatest adventure of his life. I remained respectfully silent in the presence of that noble forbearance (and because I was trying to think how best to express my own opinions on the subject).

'An expedition must be mounted,' Emerson said at last. 'But not by me, and not without careful preparation. Unpleasant as the prospect may be, I will consult with Slatin Pasha and the military authorities at the camp.'

'They won't believe you, Emerson,' I cried. 'The evidence is too complex for their limited minds to comprehend. Oh, my dear, they will mock you – think how Budge will laugh – '

Emerson's lips writhed with fury. 'It must be done, Peabody. There is no other course. If it were only a question of searching for our hypothetical lost culture, we could wait a year – plan a proper expedition, gather supplies and sufficient manpower – but Forth and his wife may be in deadly danger. Delay could prove fatal.'

'But – but – ' Reggie gasped. 'Professor, this is a complete volteface! In England you laughed at me, you refused my grandfather's request. . . What has changed your mind?'

'This.' Emerson picked up the broken arrow. 'To you it may seem a fragile reed on which to risk men's lives. It is useless to explain. You would not understand.'

His eyes met mine. It was one of those thrilling moments of absolute communication that so often occurs with my dear Emerson and myself. 'But you,' that silent message said, 'you understand me, Peabody.' And of course I did.

'I see,' Reggie said – though it was evident he did not. 'Well, then . . . You are right, Professor. An expedition must be mounted, and certainly not by you – not while you bear the responsibility for these precious lives. And not by the military authorities, who will never be convinced to act in time, if they act at all'. Rising to his feet, he stood straight and tall, his hair blazing in the sunlight. 'You will assist me with advice, I hope – help me acquire the necessary camels, servants, supplies?'

'Sit down, you young idiot,' Emerson growled. 'What melodrama! You are incapable of leading such an expedition, and in any case you could not set forth this instant.'

I added my entreaties to Emerson's. 'My husband is right, Reggie. We have a great deal to discuss before any action is taken. As Emerson has said, this broken arrow is of paramount importance. Was it snapped off during the struggle between you and your assailant last night? Could you have mistaken some other man of the same height and build for Kemit? I cannot believe it was he, and yet his disappearance does cast doubt upon his – '

A high-pitched cry from Reggie stopped me. He leapt to his feet, eyes popping, and fumbled for the revolver at his belt.

Without stirring from his chair, Emerson stretched out a long arm and clamped his fingers over Reggie's wrist. Reggie let out an oath. I turned. Behind me stood our missing servant.

Kemit folded his arms. 'Why does the white man scream like a woman?'

I could not blame Reggie for being startled by Kemit's sudden reappearance, and my reply was a trifle acerbic. 'The day you hear ME utter a sound like that, Kemit, you will be justified in making such an insulting comparison. Mr Forthright was surprised, and so are we all. We believed you had left us.'

'You see it is not so, Lady.'

'Where are your friends?'

'It is the day of rest,' said Kemit. The corners of his thin lips compressed, as they did when he had said all he intended to say, so I did not ask where and how his friends spent their free time. Besides, as Emerson would have pointed out, it was none of my business.

'Very well,' I said. 'I apologise for my unjust suspicion, Kemit. Go and enjoy your day of rest.'

Kemit bowed and walked away. Ramses rose to his feet and was following when I called him back. 'From now on, young man,' I said sternly, 'you are not to be out of my sight or that of your papa. We have no reason to think that Kemit is involved in our difficulties but until we know who is, you must not go off alone with anyone.'

'Quite right, Peabody,' said Emerson. 'And that prohibition includes you, Mr Forthright. Devil take it, you are far too quick to attack people. If I let loose of your arm will you sit down and behave yourself?'

'Certainly, Professor,' Reggie said. He passed his free hand across his perspiring brow. 'I apologise. The way he appeared, like a genie from a bottle . . . You think me rash, but I swear to you, that man knows more than he is saying. I cannot imagine why you trust him as you do.'

'I don't trust anyone,' said Emerson with a snap of his teeth. 'Now let us stop wasting time and get back to business. I hope you were not serious when you announced your intention of going off to look for your uncle.'

He released Reggie's arm. The young man rubbed it, wincing. 'Quite serious, Professor. I am only ashamed that it took me so long to decide. I intend to leave immediately for the military camp, to ask the advice of Slatin Pasha and begin gathering the necessary supplies.'

Emerson took out his pipe and tobacco pouch. 'It might be wise to ascertain first where you intend to go. You don't even have the purported map your grandfather received; he left it with me, and I never returned it.'

A smile spread across the young man's face. 'My grandfather took a copy of it, Professor – and I in turn took a copy of his. I have it with me. And I rather suspect you have the original here. Am I right?'

Emerson concentrated on filling his pipe. Not until he had completed the exercise and lit the thing did he speak. 'Touché, Mr Forthright. Let's have a look at yours, then.'

Reggie took a folded paper from his pocketbook and spread it out on the packing case that served as a table. The paper was thin but tough onionskin, upon which the newly drawn lines stood out with far greater clarity than they had upon the original. (I append a copy of the map, in order to facilitate the Reader's understanding of the ensuing description; but I feel it necessary to warn said Reader that certain details have been deliberately altered or omitted. The reasons for this will become apparent as my narrative proceeds.)

Along the right-hand edge of the paper a sweeping loop indicated the great bend of the Nile. Two points along the river were labelled with initials only 'G.B.' and 'M.' A dotted line that roughly paralleled the straight northern section of the river had been marked 'Darb el A.,' and another line running south-west from the southernmost part of the loop bore the identification 'Wadi el M.' Near the left-hand margin of the page a roughly shaped arrow accompanied to the word 'Darfur.'

These features were known to me from modern maps. 'G.B.' stood for Gebel Barkal, the great mountain across the river from our present location. 'M.' could only be the ancient Meroë. The Wadi el Melik or Milk, one of the canyon like depressions cut by watercourses long since vanished, struck off from the river into the southwestern desert. The other scrawled set of initials must indicate a portion of the fabled 'Forty Days' Road' (Darb el Arba'in), the caravan route from Egypt followed by the gallant traders of the ancient Egyptian kingdom. And Darfur, of course, was that western province of Nubia which had been the terminus of the caravan route.

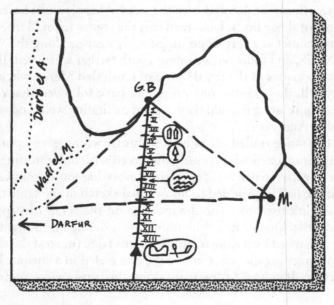

The other lines and markings on the paper could be found on no known map. Some had been traced by Emerson over a decade earlier, and he now proceeded to explain the reasoning that had produced certain of them.

'There must have been an overland route between Napata and Meroë,' he said, indicating the line that connected the dots marked 'M.' and 'G.B.' 'My own excavations at the latter site, hasty though they were, indicate that it was already a city of some importance when Napata was the royal seat. To go between the two by water would take considerable time and necessitate traversing the Fifth Cataract. The country was less arid at that time –'

'Agreed, Emerson, agreed,' I exclaimed. 'You need not justify your reasoning. But what is this line, leading southwest from Meroë towards the Wadi el Melik?'

'Pure hypothesis,' said Emerson sombrely. 'I am convinced that caravans travelled from Meroë, and from Napata, to the fertile oases of Darfur. Traces of ancient remains have been found along certain desert routes, and in Darfur itself. The first part of this line' – he pointed with the stem of his pipe – 'is based on some of those finds. I assumed that the routes from Meroë and Napata met at a certain point, possibly near or along the Wadi el Melik, and followed a common path farther westward. If the last survivors of the royal house of Cush fled Meroë when the city fell, they would, one presumes, have followed that road, since only along it could they depend on finding wells and water holes. And yet . . .'

His voice trailed off as he bent his frowning gaze upon the map. Someone had obviously disagreed with his reasoning, for the line that struck off at an angle, almost due south from Gebel Barkal, had been added to his original sketch in the same thick black ink used to write the message on the scrap of papyrus Lord Blacktower had shown us. It was divided into segments each marked by a Roman numeral, from one (nearest the river) to thirteen, at the point where the line ended in a curious little picture-drawing. At intervals along this route were scrawled numbers, not Roman but the ordinary Arabic numerals in common usage, and several odd little signs that resembled ancient Egyptian hieroglyphs.

I lost no time in proclaiming the obvious conclusions. 'The numbers along the route must indicate travel time, don't you think, Emerson? Thirteen days in all, from Napata to –'

'The Holy Mountain,' said Ramses. 'But that is what Gebel Barkal means. That is where we are now. From the Holy Mountain to the Holy Mountain – '

'You interrupted me, Ramses,' I said. 'And what is more – '

'I beg your pardon, Mama. Excitement overcame me.'

'But why hieroglyphs?' I demanded. 'Not only for the Holy Mountain, but here – this is ancient Egyptian for water – and here again, the sign for ... obelisks, are they? Or towers, perhaps.'

'Or pillars,' said Ramses. 'They are not very expertly drawn. I believe Mr Forth had some knowledge of the hieroglyphs; he may have chosen to employ signs known only to a few, in case his map fell into the wrong hands.'

Emerson brooded over the paper. His pipe had gone out; Reggie took his own from his pocket, filled it, and offered Emerson a match. 'Thank you,' Emerson said abstractedly. 'This is a much clearer copy than the original. You are certain of these Arabic numbers, Forthright? For they appear to be compass readings, and any error in transcribing them could be literally deadly.'

Reggie assured him he had copied the numbers exactly. I will admit to the Reader in confidence that I had not realised the numbers might be compass readings. The excitement that had set my heart pounding earlier was nothing to the thrill I felt at this announcement, for those numbers meant that the map was more than an idle fantasy. Someone had followed that trail; someone had inscribed those numerals. And where one had gone, others could follow.

It took three days to assemble Reggie's expedition. This was a remarkable achievement, and it would have taken much longer had it not been for Emerson's energetic help – and the fact that at the end of that time we had hired every willing man and every healthy camel. The group was small, dangerously small for such a trip, but there were simply no more beasts to be had. Emerson mentioned this depressing fact more than once, but his warnings had no effect on Reggie.

The young man's dedication and courage moved me greatly – and surprised me too, if I must be candid. Evidently it took him a while to make up his mind, but once he had made a decision, he stuck to it. Though Emerson never said so to Reggie, he was also favourably impressed. He admitted as much to me, the night before Reggie's scheduled departure, as we reclined in our tent engaged in conversation. (Conversation being the only thing in which we could engage, since Ramses now shared our sleeping accommodations. Emerson had reacted to this situation more calmly than I had expected; the only sign of perturbation he displayed was to smoke his wretched pipe incessantly.)

'I never thought he'd stick to it' were Emerson's precise words. 'Blasted young idiot! I am tempted to cripple him a little, to keep him from carrying out this harebrained scheme.'

'Is it really very dangerous, Emerson?'

'Don't ask stupid questions, Peabody; you know how it maddens me when you pretend to be an ordinary empty-headed female. Of course it is dangerous.'

A fit of coughing prevented me from replying. Emerson was smoking, and the atmosphere in the tent was rather thick. After a moment Emerson went on, 'Forgive me, Peabody. My temper is a trifle short these days.'

'I know, my dear. I too feel the pangs of remorse. For if we had not forgotten ourselves in the heat of enthusiasm, and had maintained our original scepticism about Mr Forth's quest for the lost civilisation, Reggie might not have decided as he did. One might even say that he is taking this step to prevent us from risking our lives in the attempt. There could be no nobler – '

'Oh, do be quiet, Peabody,' Emerson shouted. 'How dare

you say I feel remorse? I feel none. I did everything I could to dissuade him.'

I put my hand over his lips. 'You will wake Ramses.'

'Ramses is not asleep,' Emerson mumbled. 'I don't think he ever sleeps. Are you asleep, Ramses?'

'No, Papa. The event of the morrow must induce in any thoughtful person the most serious reflections of wonder, doubt, and inquiry. Yet every possible precaution against disaster has been taken, has it not?

Emerson did not reply, for he was occupied in nibbling gently on my fingers. The sensations thus produced were quite remarkable, and indicated how effectively a talented and imaginative individual can overcome the limitations posed by the presence of a small, unsleeping child.

'Yes, indeed, Ramses,' I replied somewhat abstractedly. 'Mr Forthright has sworn to turn back immediately if he does not find the first of the landmarks indicated on the map, and his camels are the best . . . !'

'Is something wrong, Mama?' Ramses asked in alarm.

I will not describe what Emerson was doing; it has no part in this narrative. 'No, Ramses,' I said. 'Quite the contrary. That is . . . stop worrying, and go to sleep.'

But of course he did not, and after Emerson had gone as far as he could go without attracting Ramses's attention, he had to leave off. Long after his steady breathing betokened his surrender to Morpheus, I lay awake staring up at the dark canopy of canvas above me and asking myself the same question Ramses had asked. Had every possible precaution been taken? Only time would tell.

The caravan was supposed to set forth at dawn, but nothing ever happens on schedule in the East; it was nearer midday when Reggie at last mounted his camel. It lurched to its feet in the awkward way these beasts have; Reggie swayed and clutched the pommel with both hands. Emerson, standing beside me, let out a sigh. 'He'll fall off before he has gone a mile.'

'Hush,' I murmured. 'Don't discourage him.'

At least the camel was in good condition. It was one of the prized white racing meharis beloved of the Beduin, and how Emerson had persuaded its owner to part with it I dared not ask. The other beasts were the best of the ones I had been tending. The military authorities had flatly refused to lend any of theirs, but after seeing how effective my medications had proved, several of the local sheikhs had brought their animals to me for attention, and exorbitant payments had induced them to hire the beasts out to Reggie. Four of them were loaded with food and water. The latter, of course, was the most vital commodity; it was carried in goatskins, each containing slightly over two gallons. Four servants accompanied Reggie. Three were local men; the fourth was Daoud, one of Reggie's Nubian servants. He was a singularly unprepossessing fellow, with a huge dirty black beard and a cast in one eye, but I could forgive him his looks because of his loyalty to his master. The other servants had flatly refused to go.

Reggie carefully took one hand from the saddle and lifted his hat. The sunlight cast his features into strong relief and woke golden highlights from the smooth, oiled surface of his auburn hair. 'Farewell, Mrs Emerson – Professor – my young friend Ramses. If we do not meet again – '

I let out a cry of distress. 'Don't harbour such thoughts, Reggie! Keep a stout heart, and faith in the Presence that protects the valiant. I will remember you in my prayers – '

'Fat lot of good that will do,' growled Emerson. 'Don't forget what you promised, Forthright. If the cursed map is accurate, you should find the first landmark – the twin towers – at the end of your third day of travel. You can give it another day if you like – you have food and water enough for at least ten days – but then you must turn back. Failure to find the first landmark will prove the map isn't to be trusted. If you do find it – you won't, but if you do – you will send a messenger back to us at once.'

'Yes, Professor,' Reggie said. 'We've been over that a number of times. I gave you my word, and even if I were inclined to break it, which I would never do, I hope I am sensible enough to know the risks attendant upon – '

'He has been with us too long,' said Emerson to me. 'He is beginning to sound like Ramses. Very well, Forthright; if you are determined to go, why the devil don't you go?'

This speech rather spoiled the emotional tone of our leave-taking, and a further pall was cast upon the occasion by Reggie's Egyptian servant, who broke into a weird keening wail, like a paid mourner at a funeral, as his master rode away. Emerson had to shake him to make him stop. The sun was high overhead and the moving figures cast no visible shadows. Slowly they dwindled until they vanished into a haze of heat and blowing sand.

I had never seen Emerson drive the men as he did during the following days. We were short-handed, thanks to the fact that we had sent two of our most dependable men with Reggie, and the fact that Kemit's friends never returned from their 'day of rest.' When I questioned him about them, Kemit only shook his head. 'They were strangers in a strange land. They have returned to their wives and children. Perhaps they will come again...'

'Oh, bah,' said Emerson, there being very little else to say. It was not uncommon for local workers to tire of labour or fall victim to *Heimweh*, but we had thought Kemit's men to be of stronger mettle.

Ramses began badgering us to let him return to his own tent, claiming that (a), Emerson's snoring kept him awake, and (b), it was unlikely he would be 'called,' as he put it, again. The first claim was untrue (Emerson seldom snored); and the second was utterly without foundation. As a compromise Emerson had Ramses's tent moved near to ours, and occupied it himself. 'I may as well, Peabody,' he remarked gloomily. 'Being in such close proximity to you without being able to act upon my feelings has a deleterious effect on my health.' (This is a paraphrase of

Emerson's speech; the actual words he used were more direct and thus inappropriate for the eyes of the reading public.)

Fortunately for Emerson's health, mental and physical, we made a discovery that distracted him temporarily. It would have been a momentous event in any season and at any site, for the identification of a hitherto anonymous monument is of consuming importance. Here, after days of dull surveying and fruitless digging, it was as exciting as a tomb chamber full of treasure. The object itself was not impressive – only a weathered slab of stone – but Emerson at once identified it as the lintel of a small pylon-gateway. It was buried deep in sand, which had to be cleared away from its surface and its surroundings, for Emerson refused to move it – in fact, he declared his intention of covering it up again as soon as he had finished studying it and recording the position in which it had been found.

Kneeling in the narrow trench, he carefully brushed away the last layer of sand from the surface. The men gathered around, as breathless with anticipation as we. If the worn marks on the stone proved to be hieroglyphs, the discovery would mean a sizable bonus for the lucky finder.

Unable to endure the suspense any longer, I lay flat on the edge of the trench and looked down. This movement sent a shower of sand onto the stone and the bowed, bare head of my husband; he looked up, frowning. 'If you want to bury me alive, Peabody, go right on squirming.'

'I beg your pardon, my dear,' I said. 'I will be careful. Well? Are they ... Is it ... ?'

'They are, and it is – a royal titulary! The curved ends of the cartouches are quite clear.'

He strove to speak calmly, but his voice quivered with emotion and his long, sensitive fingers brushed the stone as tenderly as a caress. 'Congratulations, my dear Emerson,' I exclaimed. 'Can you read the names?' (As I am sure I need not explain to my learned Readers, the kings of Egypt and of Cush had several names and titles; official monuments always carried at least two of them.)

'I'll have to do a rubbing, and wait until the sun is at a better angle, before I can be certain,' Emerson replied. 'This local sandstone is so cursed soft, it has weathered badly. But I think . . .' Leaning close, he blew gently on one section. 'I see an *n* sign with two tall narrow signs below; the first appears to be a reed leaf. Following are two long narrow signs, and then a pair of rush plants. Yes, I think I can hazard a guess. The signs match the ones given by Lepsius for King Nastasen.'

Emotion overcame me. I leapt to my feet and let out a loud 'Hurrah.'

Emerson replied with a volley of bad language (evidently my sudden movement had precipitated some amount of sand into the trench) and the men began to cheer and dance around. I turned to Kemit, who as usual stood aloof from the others, watching their display with an ironic smile.

'Please, Kemit, fetch the thin paper and the magic drawing sticks,' I ordered. 'And one of the lamps.'

Kemit turned his wide dark eyes on me. 'Nastasen,' he repeated.

He pronounced it differently, but I understood. 'Yes, is it not exciting? This is the first pyramid we have been able to identify with its owner – the first anyone has identified.'

Kemit murmured something in his own language. I thought I recognised one of the words from the vocabulary list Ramses had made. It meant 'omen' or 'portent.'

'I hope so,' I said, smiling. 'I hope it is a portent of more such discoveries. Hurry, Kemit, the sand is unstable and I don't like the professor to stay down there any longer than is necessary.'

Well, we managed to clear the stone and record the inscription; it was, as Emerson had thought, the titulary of King Nastasen Ka'ankhre, one of the last rulers of the Meroitic dynasty. A stela belonging to this monarch had been obtained by Lepsius for the Berlin Museum. On it Nastasen claimed he had been given the crown by the god Amon, and described various military operations against an invader from the north, who may have been the Persian king Cambyses.

It was a truly thrilling discovery and kept us busy for several days; but at the end of that time even the hope of further finds could not distract me from my worries about poor Reggie. Emerson's discovery had been made on the sixth day after the young man's departure. It was on that evening we might first have expected to see him if the map proved to be an *ignis fatuus* and he turned back, as he had promised.

Darkness came with no sign of him. We did not mention him that evening, even Ramses displaying a tactful reticence I would not have expected from him. After all, I told myself, this was the earliest moment at which we might have expected him. Any number of causes might have delayed him or his messenger.

But after two more days had passed without word, I began to fear the worst. Emerson put on a good show of unconcern, but every now and then, when he thought I was not looking at him, I saw the bronzed mask of control crack into lines I had never seen on that beloved face.

On the evening of the eighth day I left camp, drawn out into the desert as if by a magnet. The western sky blazed with violent shades of copper and amethyst; the last glowing rim of the sun clung to the horizon as if reluctant to leave the realms of the living for the dark abode of night. The brilliance of the sunset was caused by particles of blowing sand; I thought of the violent storms that could bury men and camels in the space of an hour. The worst of it was we might never know their fate. A rescue expedition would be folly, for if they had wandered off their course by as little as a mile, they might as well be halfway across the globe.

The sunset colours faded – not only because the sun was sinking but because tears dimmed my eyes. I let them fall; their release would relieve my heartache.

I became aware of a presence, not by any sound or movement, but by some more mysterious sense; turning my head, I saw Kemit.

'You weep, Lady,' he said. 'Is it for the fiery-haired youth?'

'For him and the other brave men who may have perished with him,' I replied.

138

'Then spare your tears, Lady. They are safe.'

'Safe!' I exclaimed. 'Then a message has come?'

'No. But I speak the truth.'

'You speak words of kindness, Kemit, and I appreciate your attempt to cheer me. But how can you possibly know their fate?'

'The gods have told me.'

He stood straight as a lance, his stalwart figure limned black against the fiery sky, and his voice and manner carried a conviction that assured me he, at least, believed what he had said. It would have been rude as well as unkind to point out I had heard nothing from MY God, and that I regarded that source as somewhat more reliable than his.

'Thank you, my friend,' I said. 'And render my thanks to your gods for their kind reassurance. I think we had best return now, it is getting . . . Kemit? What is it?'

For he had stiffened like a thoroughbred hound scenting an invisible prey. I sprang to my feet and stood beside him; but though I strained my sight to the utmost, I saw nothing in the direction in which he stared so intently.

'Something comes,' said Kemit.

He was fifty feet away before I could gather my wits and follow him. He could run like a deer. By the time I caught him up he was kneeling beside a prostrate figure. The brief twilight of the desert darkened the air as I too fell to my knees beside the body, but I saw immediately that the fallen form was, for once, not Reggie's. The dark robe and turban were those of an Arab.

Kemit's eyes were better than mine. 'It is the servant of the fire-haired one,' he said.

'Daoud, the Nubian? Help me to turn him over. Is he . . . ?'

'He breathes,' said Kemit briefly.

I unhooked the canteen from my belt and unscrewed the top. In my agitation I spilled more water on his face than into his parted lips, but no doubt the result was all to the good; almost at once the man stirred and moaned and licked his lips. 'More,' he gasped. 'Water, for the love of Allah . . .'

I allowed him only a sip. 'Not too much, it will make you ill. Rest easy, you are safe. Where is your master?'

The only answer was a tremulous whisper, in which I caught only the word 'water.' In my agitation I actually shook the poor fellow. 'You have had enough for now. Does your master follow? Where are the others?'

'They . . .' Black night covered his face and form, but his voice was stronger. I dribbled a little more water into his mouth, and he went on, 'They found us. The wild men of the desert. We fought . . . they were too many.'

Kemit's breath caught in a startled hiss. 'Wild men?' he repeated.

'Too many,' I repeated. 'Yet you escaped, leaving your master to die?'

'He sent me,' the man protested. 'For help. They were too many. Some they killed . . . but not the master. He is a prisoner of the wild men of the desert!'

Lost In
the Sea of Sand

'S lavers,' said Slatin Pasha.

The buzzing of a chorus of flies droned a dismal accompaniment to his words as he went on. 'We have done our best to stop that vile trade, but our efforts have only driven the ghouls who trade in human flesh farther from their customary routes. It must have been some such group who attacked Mr Forthright.'

'What does it matter who they were?' I demanded. 'The question is, what are the authorities going to do about it?'

We were in Slatin Pasha's tukhul at the military camp. Outside a crowd of people squatted patiently on the mats, waiting for his attention, but he had given our problem precedence.

The distinguished soldier coughed and looked away. 'We will, of course, mention the matter to any patrols that go into that region.'

'I told you this was a waste of time, Peabody,' said Emerson, rising.

'Wait, Professor,' Slatin Pasha begged. 'Don't misjudge me; I would do anything within my power to assist this unfortunate young man. But you of all people should understand the difficulties. We are preparing for a major campaign, and we need every man. Mr Forthright was warned that his search was both dangerous and futile, yet he persisted in going. I would not, even if I could, persuade the Sirdar to endanger more lives.'

I administered a gentle kick to the shins of my spouse in order to forestall the contemptuous response I saw hovering upon his lips. Slatin Pasha did not deserve our contempt. No man knew better than he the tortures of slavery among savage people. His distress and his helplessness were equally plain to see.

Once outside the tukhul, we turned towards the market. The flies were particularly bad that day; they clustered like patches of black rot on every piece of fruit and formed a whining cloud around the food stalls.

'I will leave you to make the necessary purchases,' I said to Emerson, 'while I beg an additional supply of camel ointment and other medications from Captain Griffith.'

I started to walk away, but Emerson caught me by the shoulder and spun me around. His eyes sparkled wickedly, and his cheeks were flushed with rising temper. 'Here – wait, Peabody. What the devil are you doing? You have plenty of the cursed medicine, you got a fresh supply last time we came here.'

'Only enough for a week,' I replied. 'It is important to have an adequate amount, Emerson; our lives may depend on the good health of the camels.'

The hand that held me tightened until it felt as if the fingers were digging into the bone. The eyes that looked deep into mine glowed like the purest blue water. Though the crowd of the sûk jostled us on every hand, we might have been alone in the desert waste, no one seeing, no one hearing.

'I won't let you come, Peabody,' said Emerson.

'Your tone lacks conviction, my dear Emerson. You know you can't prevent me.'

Emerson let out a groan so deep and heartfelt that a passing woman robed in dusty black forgot the modesty of her sex and turned a startled look upon the suffering foreigner. 'I know I can't, Peabody. Please, my dearest, I beg you – I implore you. . . Think of Ramses.'

'I trust,' said my son coolly, 'that no such consideration will affect your decision, Mama. I fail to see that we have any other course than the one Papa has evidently decided upon; and it would be as impossible for me to remain behind as for Mama to be parted from Papa. I am sure I need not trouble you with an expression of excessive emotion in order to convince you both that my feelings are as profound and as sincere as – '

I took it upon myself to stop him, since I knew he would go on talking until his breath gave out. 'Pedantic little wretch,' I said, attempting to conceal my own emotion, 'how dare you appeal to affection in order to have your own way? It is out of the question, Ramses; you cannot come with us.'

'Us?' said Emerson. 'Us? Now see here, Peabody – '

'That is settled, Emerson. Whither thou goest, I fully intend to go, and I won't entertain any further debate on the subject. As for young Master Ramses – '

'What alternative do you propose, Mama?' inquired that individual.

I stared at him, at a loss for words. He stared unblinkingly back at me. Never before had he looked so much like his father. His eyes were deep brown instead of brilliant blue, but they held the same saturnine expression I had often seen in Emerson's when he backed me into a verbal corner.

For the alternatives were, to say the least, limited. Ramses could not be left alone at the excavation site, or in the army camp. Even if we could persuade the authorities to send him back to Cairo, via military transport – which was improbable – I did not believe that a full army corps, much less a single officer, could control him. If I could get his solemn promise not to run away ... But even as the idea occurred to me I realised its futility. In a matter as serious as this, Ramses would not equivocate or prevaricate; he would simply refuse to give me his word. And then what? I felt fairly certain the army would not agree to putting him in irons.

'Curse it,' I said.

'Damnation,' said Emerson.

Ramses, wisely, said nothing at all.

A certain amount of equivocation on my part was necessary before we were able to start out. We had to borrow some of the army camels I had been tending, for no others were to be had at any price. This meant that our expedition had to be kept a secret from the military authorities. They might not have attempted to stop us from going, but they certainly would have objected to our unauthorised use of their property.

Manpower too was in short supply. The most reliable of the workers had been sent with Reggie, and their failure to return quite understandably acted as a deterrent to other volunteers.

Yet we persevered, as duty directed us, until we made a discovery that might well have marked the end of our endeavours. When Emerson went to look for Willoughby Forth's map, it was nowhere to be found.

'I tell you, Peabody, I put it in this portfolio,' Emerson roared, scattering the contents of the portfolio all over the tent. 'Don't tell me I am mistaken; I am never mistaken about such things.'

Years spent stumbling through the pitfalls of matrimony had taught me that it would be ill-advised to deny this ridiculous statement. In silence I stooped to pick up the papers, and Emerson continued, 'It must be found, Peabody. Though it is a frail reed upon which to risk our lives, it is better than nothing.'

'Daoud has agreed to guide us,' I said hesitantly.

'He's no more use as a guide than Ramses there. Less, in fact,' Emerson added quickly, as Ramses started to protest. 'If he were a Beduin, familiar with the desert, that would be one thing, but he told me he has lived all his life in Halfa. No, we must have the map. We dare not set forth without it!'

I started to reply, but something stopped me, like an invisible hand placed over my lips. I can truthfully claim that I seldom suffer from indecision. Such, however, was the case now. Before I could make up my mind, Ramses emitted the small cough that usually preceded a statement of whose reception he was not entirely certain.

'Fortunately, Papa, there is a copy of the map at hand. I took the liberty of tracing it before we left England.'

Emerson dropped the papers I had handed him and spun around to face his son. His face shone with delight. 'Splendid, Ramses! Run and fetch it at once. It is the last thing we need; we will set forth at dawn.'

With a sigh, I stooped to collect the papers again. The die was cast, our fate determined – but not by me. I too had a copy of the map.

The night before he left us Reggie had handed me a little packet of papers, requesting me in manly but faltering tones to refrain from mentioning it or opening it until after his departure. I knew what it must contain, and my own voice was a trifle unsteady as I assured him he could trust me to carry out his wishes, in the unhappy event that such action should prove necessary. When I did open the packet I found what I had expected – Reggie's last will and testament, written in his own hand. There were also two letters, one addressed to his grandfather and the other to Slatin Pasha. A copy of the map was attached to this last document; I assumed the letter itself expressed Reggie's hope that the military authorities would carry on his quest if he fell by the way.

Neither of the letters was sealed. I thought this a particularly delicate and gentlemanly touch on Reggie's part. Naturally I would never dream of reading such private communications, but under the present circumstances there was no honourable reason why I should have hesitated to admit I possessed a copy of the map. Why did I hesitate? I knew the answer, as well as the Reader must. Without the map we dared not set forth. To supply the commodity that might doom us all to death was a responsibility I had lacked the fortitude to assume.

The first pale hint of sunrise touched the eastern sky as we prepared for departure. I had anointed the camels' healing sores and forced a dose of cordial – my own invention, compounded of strengthening herbs and a modicum of brandy – down their throats. (Emerson had expressed doubts about the brandy, but the camels seemed to like it.) The baggage, carefully balanced and padded, had been loaded upon their backs. I placed my booted foot upon the foreleg of my kneeling steed and swung myself into the saddle. Ramses was already mounted, perched like a monkey atop a pile of baggage. Emerson followed suit. We were ready.

I turned to survey the little expedition. Little it was; only a dozen camels, only five riders in addition to ourselves. One of them was Kemit. He had been the first to volunteer. In fact, he was the only one to volunteer; the others had only agreed after the payment of extravagant bribes. They were all silent; there was none of the cheerful talk, or song, or laughter with which they were wont to meet the day. The cold grey light cast a corpselike pallor upon their gloomy faces and those of the friends and family members who had come to bid them farewell.

Emerson flung up his hand. His deep voice rolled out across the empty waste. 'We depart with the blessing of God! *Ma' es-salâmeh!*'

The formal answer came in a ragged chorus. '*Nishûf wishshak fi kheir* – May you be fortunate at our next meeting.' I detected a certain lack of conviction in the voices, however, and a woman's voice broke into soprano lamentation.

Emerson drowned her out with a sonorous rendition of an Arabic song, and urged his camel to a trot. Gritting my teeth – for the motion of a trotting camel is the most painful thing on this earth – I followed his lead. In a cloud of sand, accompanied by song, we thundered away.

As soon as we were out of sight of the others, Emerson allowed his camel to slow to a walk. I drew up beside him. 'Are we going in the right direction, Emerson?'

'No.' Emerson glanced at the compass and turned his beast slightly to the right. 'That was purely for effect, Peabody. A stirring departure, wasn't it?'

'Yes, indeed, my dear, and it has had the desired effect.' One of the men had continued the song ('When will she say to me, "Young man, come and let us intoxicate ourselves?"') and the others were humming along.

The cool of morning gave way to warmth and then to excessive heat. We paused to rest during the hottest part of the day in the shade of a rock outcropping. Deserts vary as people do. The great sand sea of the Sahara, with its sterile golden dunes, was far to the north. Here the underlying skin of the planet was sandstone, not limestone, and the flat surface was broken by rocks and gullies that marked the course of ancient waterways. Late in the afternoon we set out again. Only when approaching darkness made travel impossible did we stop to make camp. We had seen no sign of anyone who might have preceded us, not even the bones of fallen men and camels that form grisly guideposts along such well-travelled routes as the Darb el Arba'in.

'We are off all the known caravan routes,' Emerson said, when I mentioned this later as we sat around the campfire. 'The nearest part of the Darb el Arba'in is hundreds of miles west of here; there is no known route between it and this part of Nubia. Still, I had hoped to find some sign of Forthright's passage – the dead ashes of a fire, discarded tins, or even the tracks of the camels.'

The stars blazed like gems in a sky as cold as airless space, a chill breeze ruffled my hair. We sat in reflective silence until the moon rose, casting strange shadows across the silvered sands.

The next day was a repetition of the first except that the terrain became even more arid and forbidding. In that waste any object would have stood out like a beacon; tracks, which Emerson identified as those of an antelope, were as plain as if they had been printed on the sand. But we saw no signs of man. That evening one of the camels showed signs of distress, so I gave it an extra dose of my cordial. In spite of this, it died during the night. I was not surprised; it had been the weakest of the lot. Leaving the poor creature lying where it had fallen, we pushed on.

By the afternoon of the third day the uncomfortable temperature changes, from unbearable heat by day to freezing cold by night, and our failure to find any traces of Reggie's caravan, were beginning to tell on even the hardiest. Sifting sand had rubbed our skins raw; those unaccustomed to riding were stiff and sore. The men rode in sullen silence. An ugly haze veiling the sun did not lessen the heat, but awoke dire forebodings of sandstorm. I found myself falling into a kind of stupor as the camel plodded onward; it was hard to tell which ached more, my head or certain portions of my abused anatomy.

I was aroused from my semi-slumber by a shout. Dazed and dizzy, I echoed it in fainter tones. 'What? What is it?'

Emerson was too elated to note my enfeebled state. 'Look, Peabody. There they are! By heaven, the lunatic was right after all!'

At first the objects he indicated seemed only another mirage quivering as if viewed through water. They took on solider dimensions as we urged our beasts to a faster gait, and before long we had reached them: a pair of tall, rocky columns, like the twin obelisks marked on Mr Forth's map. They formed part of a larger group of tumbled stones, rising above their lesser fellows like crudely shaped pillars, or the gateposts of a ruined doorway.

'It was a structure of some kind,' Emerson declared, a short time later. The discovery had enlivened him; he looked as fresh and cheerful as if he had spent the day roaming English meadows. 'I can't find any traces of reliefs or inscriptions, but they may have been worn away by blowing sand. We'll make camp here, Peabody, though it is early. I want to do a bit of digging.'

In this activity he got scant help from the men. Groaning and protesting, they demanded an extra ration of water before they would consent to do anything at all, and they worked slowly and reluctantly. Only Kemit, looking more than ever like a bronze statue, pitched in with his usual zeal. At the end of an hour Emerson was rewarded by a few scraps of stone and pottery, and another shapeless ugly lump that brought a cry of rapture to his lips. 'Iron, Peabody – an iron knife blade. It is Meroitic, beyond a doubt. They were here – they passed this way. Good Gad, this is incredible!'

I inspected the corroded lump doubtfully. 'How do you know it wasn't lost by a modern explorer or wandering Beduin?'

'There are occasional rains in this region, in summer; but it would take centuries, nay, millennia, to reduce cold iron to this state. The Cushites worked iron; I have seen the black slag heaps around Meroë, like the ones at Birmingham and Sheffield.' Turning to the men, who squatted on the sand looking like piles of dirty laundry, he shouted cheerfully, 'Rest, my friends; we must make an early start.'

He appeared not to notice the sullen looks with which they obeyed him, it would never have occurred to Emerson that he could not command any group who worked for him. Nor, under ordinary circumstances, would any such doubt have entered my mind. But these circumstances were far from normal, and the discovery that had enraptured Emerson had precisely the opposite effect on the men. We had water for only about ten days. According to the map, seven or eight days of travel would bring us to a source of that vital fluid; but if the map had proved to be untrustworthy, common sense would decree that we turn back while we still had a sufficient supply for the return journey. The men had hoped we would not find the first landmark, and decide to give up. Well, I could sympathise with their point of view, but I felt a stirring of unease as I saw the ugly look one of them gave my unconscious husband. Daoud's willingness to return into the desert that had almost cost him his life had surprised and pleased me; he was a man of considerable stamina, for his recovery from his ordeal had been quicker than I had expected. However, he had turned sullen when Emerson rejected his advice on the route we should follow, and after repeated criticism from Daoud, Emerson had lost his temper. 'I am guided by the marks on the paper and the needle of the magic clock [i.e., the compass]. If your master followed your lead, it is no wonder we have found no trace of him!'

He added a few well-chosen expletives that put an end to Daoud's complaints. At least he did not complain to Emerson, but I had an uneasy feeling that he was undermining the confidence of the other men.

Still, we had two more days before we reached the point of no return, and there were no overt signs of rebellion when we set out the next morning, even though during the night another camel had passed on to wherever camels go. There were enough left to mount all the men, and I took care to renew their medication.

The fifth day dawned hazy and still. The rising sun resembled a swollen, blood-red balloon. The sandstorm passed to the south of our path, but the outlying skirts of it filled the air with fine grit that rubbed skin raw and clogged breathing. One of the camels collapsed shortly after we set forth after the midday rest period. Less than an hour later, a second dropped. If there had been a particle of shade to be found, I expect the men would have insisted on stopping, but they went on in the hope of finding a better place. Towards evening the wind turned to the north and the gritty air cleared, giving us some relief; and as the sun sank lower I saw a stark outline limned against the brilliance of sunset. It was not so much a tree as the skeleton of one, leafless and scoured bone-white by wind-driven sand. But it was unquestionably Forth's second landmark.

We camped in what might have been its shade if it had possessed any leaves. Bathing was out of the question, of course, but we spared a scant cupful of water to sponge off the sand that had formed a crust on our perspiring faces and limbs. A change of clothing, as well, afforded great relief. As the chill of the desert night closed around us, Emerson and I sat by the small fire on which our meagre evening meal was cooking. He had lit his pipe. Ramses was seated some distance away, talking to Kemit. Beyond them crouched our riding camels, grotesque shapes in the cold moonlight.

The men had placed their camp farther from us each night –
a gesture whose significance did not escape me, but which I
considered it best not to mention to them. When I mentioned it
to Emerson, he shrugged his broad shoulders. 'They were the
pick of a poor lot, Peabody. If I had had the time to send
messengers to my friends among the Beduin . . . I don't know
what they're complaining about, thus far matters have gone very
well.'

'Except for the camels dying.'

'The weak have been winnowed out,' said Emerson
sententiously. 'They were the weakest. The others appear
healthy enough.'

'I saw Daoud haranguing the men this evening. They were
gathered around him like conspirators, and he broke off when
he saw me coming.'

'He was probably telling them a vulgar story,' Emerson said.
'Good Gad, Peabody, these womanish qualms are not like you.
Are you feeling well?'

He reached for my hand.

Within it – figuratively speaking – lay the means of altering
Emerson's set purpose. I was not feeling well. All I had to do
was admit to the feverish malady that had afflicted me since the
previous afternoon, and we would be on our way back to
civilisation and a doctor as fast as Emerson could take me. But
such a course was unthinkable. No one understood better than
I the passion that drove him on into the unknown. Not only
had Forth's map proved accurate, but the discovery of ancient
remains substantiated the theory that along that hitherto
unknown and unsuspected road had passed the merchants and
messengers and the fleeing royalty of ancient Cush. I was as
eager as Emerson to discover what lay at the end of that road.
At least I would have been, if my head had not ached so much.

'Of course I am well,' I replied crossly.

'Your hand is warm,' said Emerson. 'You brought your
medical kit, of course; have you taken your temperature?'

'I don't need a thermometer to tell me when I have a fever,

and I know as well as any doctor what to do about it if I have. Don't fuss, Emerson.'

'Peabody.'

'Yes, Emerson.'

Emerson took my face between his hands and looked into my eyes. 'Take some quinine and go to bed, my dear. I'll dose the da – the cursed camels and bed them down for the night. If I am not entirely satisfied in the morning that you are in perfect health, I will tie you on a camel and take you back.'

Tears flooded my eyes at this demonstration of affection, one of the noblest ever made by man for the sake of woman. But my gallant Emerson was not forced to that agonising decision. Fortunately the men abandoned us during the night, taking with them the camels that carried most of our remaining food and water.

The effect of this admittedly disconcerting discovery made me forget my discomfort, and when our greatly reduced party gathered to discuss the situation, I felt almost as alert as usual. Kemit, whom Ramses had discovered lying unconscious amid the trampled sand and camel dung that marked the men's former camp, had refused to let me treat his wound. It was only a bump on the head, he said, and his sole regret was that the blow had prevented him from raising the alarm.

'It wouldn't have mattered,' I reassured him. 'We could not have forced them to go on; we do not use chains and whips, like the slavers.'

'No, but we might have – er – persuaded them to leave us food and water,' Emerson said. 'Not that I blame you, Kemit, you are a true man and you did your best. It is my cursed stupidity that is to blame for our plight; I should have kept one of the supply camels with us, instead of trusting the men with them.'

'There is nothing so futile as regret for what cannot be mended,' I remarked. 'If a mistake was made we all share the blame.'

'True,' Emerson said, cheering up. 'Precisely what do we have left, Peabody?'

'Our personal possessions, changes of clothing, notebooks and papers, a few tools. Two waterskins – but both are less than half-full. A few tins, a tin opener, two tents, blankets . . .'

'Hmph,' said Emerson when I had finished. 'It could be worse, but it could certainly be better. Well, my dears – and my friend Kemit – what shall we do? There are only two possibilities, for we obviously can't remain here. Either we go on or we turn back – try to overtake those villains and force them to share the supplies – '

A general chorus of disapproval greeted this last suggestion. 'They have several hours' start on us and they will travel as fast as they are able,' I remarked.

'The ugly man has a fire stick,' said Kemit.

'Daoud?' Emerson gave him a startled look. 'Are you certain?'

'He struck me with it,' Kemit said briefly.

'It seems to me that we have no choice,' said Ramses. 'According to the map, which has hitherto proved accurate, there is a source of water less than three days' journey from here. It would take twice that length of time to return to the river. We must go on.'

'Quite right,' said Emerson, jumping to his feet. 'And the sooner we start the better.'

We camped that night in a wilderness of rock and sand, without even a dead shrub to suggest there had ever been a drop of water available. In order to spare the camels, we had abandoned all our nonessential baggage, including the tents, but as the long hot day wore on, all the beasts showed ominous signs of weakness. Sheer willpower, of which I have a considerable amount, prevented me from admitting even to myself that I was in little better case. There was nothing with which to make a fire, so we dined on cold tinned peas and a sip of water, rolled ourselves in our blankets and sought what relief we could find in sleep.

I will not dwell on the misery of the night or in our sensations the following morning when we found two of the three camels dead. My malady was of such a nature that it seemed to be relatively quiescent in the morning and grow worse as the day went on, so I had been able to conceal it from Emerson. He had, I am bound to admit, other things on his mind. So we went on, until the event occurred which I have described, when the last camel dropped gently to its knees and – in a word – died.

I daresay most individuals would have been speechless with horror at this catastrophe; but that condition has never affected the Emerson-Peabodys. Adversity only strengthens us; disaster stimulates and inspires us. I found myself considerably refreshed by our discussion, and as we proceeded on foot, after a brief rest in the shade of the camel, I dared to hope my illness had been overcome by quinine and determination. (Mostly the latter.)

We had gone through the saddlebags and discarded most of their contents, since we could carry only the barest of necessities: the clothing on our backs, the remaining water-skins, with their sadly depleted and evil-tasting contents, and a blanket apiece. The latter were essential, for the night air was bitter cold, and they could be arranged to offer some shade during the hottest part of the day. Ramses insisted on carrying his little knapsack, and of course my parasol could not be left behind. Kemit carefully buried the rest of our goods, though I attempted to dissuade him from expending effort on such trivial things as changes of linen and a few books – for I never travel without a copy of Holy Writ and something to read. After he had finished covering the hole, we started walking. I confess to considerable pride in Ramses. He had not voiced a word of complaint or alarm, and he trotted briskly across the burning sands. Kemit, ever near him, slowed his steps to match the boy's.

My initial optimism proved false. The breeze that rose towards evening did not suffice to cool my burning brow. The terrain became ever more rough and broken, making walking difficult. Some distance ahead a range of low hills, as arid and hard as the desert floor, crossed the route the compass indicated.

They promised some illusion of shelter, and I kept telling myself that when I reached them I could rest. But a sudden stagger betrayed me; the ever-watchful eye of my devoted spouse saw me falter and his stalwart arms broke my fall. The soft sound of muted curses came like music to my ears as he lifted me, and such was the relief of resting against that broad breast, I let myself sink into a swoon.

The blessed trickle of water between my parched lips roused me. It was blood-warm and tasted like goat, but no draft of icy spring water has ever been more refreshing. I sucked greedily until reason returned; then sat up with a cry, striking the container from my lips.

'Good Gad, Emerson, what are you thinking of? You have given me far more than my share.'

'Mama is feeling better,' said Ramses.

They were gathered around me in an anxious circle. I lay in the shadow of a great rock, wrapped in a blanket.

'There are dead trees on the slope,' said Kemit, rising. 'I will make a fire.'

It was welcome; the night air was intensely cold. After consultation we agreed to pass around the brandy I carried for medicinal purposes. It lessened my headache, but made me uncommonly sleepy, so that I drowsed and woke and drowsed again. During one of these periods of wakefulness I overheard the others talking.

It was Kemit's voice that woke me. He spoke more loudly than was his habit. 'There is water, I know it. I have – I have heard the desert men say so.'

'Hmph,' said Emerson. 'We made slow progress today. At this rate it will take two more days.'

'Half a day for a running man.'

Emerson's snort of scepticism was even more emphatic. 'None of us can run at that speed, Kemit. And Mrs Emerson...' He had to pause to clear his throat, poor man.

'She has the heart of a lion,' Kemit said gravely. 'But I fear the demons are winning over her.'

I heard Emerson blow his nose vigorously. I wondered, vaguely, what he was using for a handkerchief.

A small, hard hand touched my forehead. 'Mama is awake,' said Ramses, bending over me. 'Shall I give her a drink, Papa?'

'Not under any circumstances,' I said firmly, and drowsed off again.

It seemed to me that I lay in that state, half-waking, half-sleeping, for the rest of the night, but I must have sunk into deeper slumber, for I woke with a start to find myself clasped close to Emerson's body. He was snoring loud enough to rattle my eardrums. I felt light-headed and weak, but comparatively better, and as the light strengthened I found great comfort in contemplation of the dear face so close to mine. Not that it was looking its best. A prickly stubble of black beard blurred the contours of his jaw, and his firm lips were blistered and cracked. I was about to press my own lips against them when a shrill voice broke the silence.

'Mama? Papa? I hope you will forgive me for waking you, but I feel I must inform you that Kemit is gone. He has taken the waterskin with him.'

Half a day to water, for a running man. That was what Kemit had said, and apparently he had decided to act upon it. By abandoning us he had a chance at saving himself. I did not doubt that those long legs of his could eat up the distance as quickly as he had claimed, especially when he had water to replenish the moisture lost through perspiration.

'I am sadly disappointed in Kemit,' I declared, as we passed round my canteen. Each of us took a sip; there was enough left, I surmised, for one more such indulgence. Fastening it onto my belt, I went on, 'I am seldom mistaken in my judgment of people; apparently this was one of my few errors.'

There was no need to discuss what we would do. We would go on, refusing to admit defeat, until we could go no farther. That is the way of the Emersons.

But we were a sorry crew. Bearded and gaunt, Emerson led the way. Except for his bright eyes, Ramses looked like a miniature mummy, thin as a bundle of sticks, brown as any sun-dried corpse. I was only glad I could not see myself. We plodded doggedly on until the cool of morning passed and the sun beat down with hammer blows of heat. I began to see strange objects in the glimmer of furnace-hot air – mirages of palm trees and minarets, gleaming white-walled cities, a towering cliff of black rock topped by fantastic ruins. They blended into a grey mist like that of evening. My knees gave way. It was an odd sensation, for I was fully conscious; I simply had no control over my limbs.

Emerson bent over me. 'We may as well finish the water, Peabody. It will only evaporate.'

'You drink first,' I croaked. 'Then Ramses.'

Emerson's lips cracked as they stretched in a smile. 'Very well.'

He raised the canteen. I focused my hazed eyes on his throat and saw him swallow. He passed it to Ramses, who did the same, and then gave it to me. I had finished the last of the water, two long, delicious swallows, before the truth dawned on me. 'You didn't – Ramses, I told you – '

'Talking only dries the throat, Mama,' said my son. 'Papa, I believe we can use one of the blankets as a litter. I will carry one end, and you – '

The harsh cackle that emerged from Emerson's throat was a travesty of his hearty laugh. 'Ramses, I am honoured to have sired you, but I don't think that idea is practicable.' Stooping, he lifted me in his arms and started walking.

I was too weak to protest. If there had been any liquid left in my body, I would have wept – with pride.

Only a man like Emerson, with the physique of a hero of old and the moral strength of England's finest, could have gone on as long as he did. As my senses swam in and out of consciousness I felt his arms holding me fast and the slow steady stride that carried us forward. But even that mighty frame had its limits.

When he stopped he had just enough strength left to lay me gently upon the ground before he crumpled and dropped at my side – and his last act was to stretch out his hand so that it rested on mine. I was too weak to turn my head, but I managed to move my other hand a scant inch, and felt another, smaller hand grasp it. As my senses faded into the merciful oblivion of approaching death, I thanked the Almighty that we were all together at the end, and that He had spared me the torture of watching those I loved pass on before me.

BOOK TWO

The City of
the Holy Mountain

T he Hereafter was not nearly so comfortable a place as I
had been led to expect.

Not that I had possessed precise ideas of what lay Beyond,
for, to be honest, the conventional images of angels and halos,
harps and heavenly choirs had always seemed to me a little silly.
(Not just a little silly, if I am to be entirely honest. Preposterous
would be more like it.) At worst, I believed, there would be
quiet sleep; at best, a reunion with those loved ones who had
gone on before. I looked forward to meeting my mother, whom
I had never known but who, I felt sure, must have been a remarkable individual, and to finding my dear papa in some
celestial reading room pursuing his endless researches. I
wondered if he would know me. In his earthly existence he was
sometimes rather vague on that point.

Delirium takes strange forms. If I had not been so confident
of having lived a thoroughly virtuous life, I might have thought
myself translated to Some Other Place, for I felt as if I were
being broiled on a huge griddle. Quantities of water were poured
down my throat without assuaging my burning thirst. Worst
of all, my demands for my husband went unanswered. I ran
down endless corridors walled in mist following a shadowy form
that ever retreated before me. Could my estimation of my moral

worth be mistaken after all, I wondered? The worst punishment an offended Deity could visit upon me was vainly to seek my dear Emerson through the limitless halls of Eternity.

After eons of searching, I found myself no longer running, but walking with dragging steps down a long, sloping passageway where walls and floor were of a flat dull grey. Far ahead a flicker of light appeared, and as I proceeded it strengthened to a golden glow. I began to hear voices. Laughter rippled through them, and the sounds of sweet music; but despite the welcome they promised, my steps dragged and I fought the force that drew me remorselessly forward. To no avail! At last the passageway ended in a beautiful chamber filled with flowers and fresh greenery and suffused with a brilliance brighter than sunlight. A throng of people awaited me. Foremost among them was a beautiful woman whose heavy black tresses were wreathed with roses. With arms outstretched she beckoned me to her embrace. Behind her I saw a face I knew – that of my dear old nanny, framed by the starched white frills of her cap. A venerable couple stood nearby, dressed in the antique styles of the early part of the century; I recognised them from the portraits that had hung in Papa's study. The other faces were unfamiliar, yet I knew, with a certainty transcending mortal experience, that in past lives they had been as dear to me as I was to them. All faces were wreathed in smiles, all voices cried out in welcome. (My papa was not present, but then I had not expected he would be; no doubt he had become involved in some bit of fascinating research and forgot the appointment.)

There were children among them, but none had swarthy complexions and features a trifle too big for their faces. There were stalwart, handsome men – but none had eyes that blazed with blue brilliance, or dimples in their chin.

Summoning all my forces, I screamed that beloved name like an invocation. At last – at last! I was answered. 'Peabody,' the well-known voice thundered, 'come back from there this instant!'

The light vanished, the music and laughter faded into a long sigh and I fell through limitless night into the peace of nothingness.

When I opened my eyes, the vision before them bore a distinct resemblance to the Christian version of heaven. A cloudlike veil of gauzy white formed a canopy over the couch on which I lay and hung in soft folds around it. The curtains stirred in a gentle breeze.

When I attempted to rise, I found I could do no more than raise my head, and that not for long; but the thud with which it struck the mattress convinced me that I was not dreaming, or even dead. I tried to call for Emerson. The sound that came from my throat was scarcely louder than a whimper, but it brought immediate results. The footsteps that approached were steps I knew; and when he thrust the draperies aside and bent over me I found the strength to fling myself into his arms.

I will draw a veil over the scene that followed, not because I am at all ashamed of the strength of the mutual devotion that unites me with Emerson, or the ways in which it is manifested, but because mere words cannot describe the intense emotion of that reunion. When my narrative resumes, then, you may picture me in the affectionate grasp of my husband, and in a state sufficiently composed to take note of my surroundings.

First, of course, I asked about Ramses. 'Fully recovered and inquisitive as ever,' Emerson replied. 'He is somewhere about.'

With ever increasing astonishment I gazed about the room. It was of considerable size, the walls painted with bright patterns in blue, green, and orange, and interrupted, at intervals, by woven hangings. A pair of columns supported the ceiling; they had been painted to imitate palm trees, with the fretted leaves forming the capitals. The bed stood on legs carved like those of lions. There was no headboard; the panel at the foot of the bed was gilded and inlaid with formalised flower shapes. Beside the bed was a low table with an assortment of bottles, bowls, and pots, some of translucent white stone, some of earthenware. There was little more furniture in the room, only a few chests and baskets, and a chair whose seat was covered with the skin of some unknown animal. It was deep brown with irregular patches of white.

'So it is true,' I said, on a breath of wonder. 'I can scarcely believe it, even though I see it with my own eyes. Tell me everything, Emerson. How long have I been ill? To what miracle do we owe our survival? Have you seen Mr Forth and his wife? What is this place, and how has it gone undiscovered through all the years that – '

Emerson stopped my questions in a particularly pleasant manner, and then remarked, 'You shouldn't tire yourself, Peabody. Why don't you rest and take some nourishment, and then – '

'No, no, I feel quite well and I am not hungry. The danger is that my brain will burst with curiosity if it is not satisfied instantly.'

Emerson settled himself more comfortably. 'Perhaps you aren't hungry. I must have poured a gallon of broth into you since last night, when you first showed signs of returning consciousness. You were like a little bird, my dearest, swallowing obediently when I pressed the spoon to your lips, but never opening your eyes. . .' His voice deepened, and he had to clear his throat before going on. 'Well, well, that terrible time is over, thank Heaven, and I certainly don't want to risk the bursting of that remarkable brain of yours. We may as well take advantage of this time alone while it lasts.'

There was a strange note in his voice when he pronounced the last words; so anxious was I to hear his story, however, that I did not question it. 'Begin, then,' I urged. 'The last thing I remember is being laid gently upon the sand, and seeing you collapse at my side – '

'Collapse? Not at all, my dear Peabody. I was merely taking a little rest before going on. I must have dozed off for a bit; when I opened my eyes I could scarcely believe what they saw – a cloud of sand, rapidly approaching, raised by the hooves of galloping camels. I got to my feet; for whether they were friend or foe, demon or human, I meant to demand assistance from them. They saw me, the troop swerved, and one rider drew out in front of the others. He was practically upon me before I recognised him, and I verily believe it was sheer astonishment that made me – er – lose control of myself for a brief time. When I awoke I was surrounded by robed and hooded forms, one of which was pouring water over my face. I need not say, Peabody, that I turned from him to make certain you and Ramses were being attended to. It was Kemit himself who held a cup to your lips.

'He was soon pushed aside by another attendant, veiled in snowy white, who worked over you with an air of authority I had no wish to deny. Though my brain boiled with questions, I restrained them for the time; the most important consideration was your survival, my darling Peabody. After an anxious consultation it was decided to proceed at the quickest possible pace, for you were in need of attention that could not be rendered under those conditions. Ramses, too, was in poor shape, though not as serious as yours. I saw him lifted into the grasp of one of the riders, and helped place you on a remarkably clever sort of litter that had been rigged up, and then we set out. I rode beside Kemit and was able to satisfy some of my curiosity.

'He had not abandoned us; he had taken the only possible means of saving us. His first words were an apology for having been long. Living in the outer world, as he put it, had softened him; he was only able to run five miles at a stretch! The reception party he expected was waiting at the oasis – for that is what the water sign signified, a veritable oasis with a deep well. He led them back along the trail at full speed, and if ever there was a rescue in the nick of time . . .

'But after we left the oasis and set out on the last stage of our journey there were times, my dearest Peabody, when I feared rescue had come too late. Your medical adviser, if I may use that term, kept bathing and anointing you, and pouring peculiar substances down your throat. You were in such dire straits, I dared not interfere; I had nothing better to offer. The only thing I could do was sample the bloo – blooming stuff myself before – '

'Oh, my dear Emerson!' Moved beyond words, I clung to him. 'What if it had been poison?'

'It wasn't.' Emerson squeezed me tight. 'But it was not until last night that I was sure you were out of danger. And you will be ill again, Peabody, if you don't rest. I have satisfied your curiosity – '

'You have scarcely begun,' I cried. 'How did Kemit know there was a rescue party at the oasis? Are these people the descendants of the nobility and royalty of ancient Meroë? What is this place – how has it remained unknown?'

'Answers to your questions would take days, not minutes,' said Emerson. 'But I will try to give you a brief summary. As you know, there are many isolated peaks and larger massifs in the western desert. This place – the Holy Mountain, as it is called – is a massif hitherto unknown. We approached it in darkness, after riding through several miles of outlying foothills. The cliffs must be a thousand feet high, but they looked even higher, towering against the moonlit sky like the ruins of an enormous temple. Vertical erosion has carved them into a maze of natural pillars, with winding passages between. And that fantastic vision, my dear Peabody, was all I saw. As soon as we reached the foot of the cliffs, Ramses and I were blindfolded. I protested, of course, but to no avail; Kemit was very polite but very firm. There is only one way through the cliffs, and it is a closely guarded secret. I tried to keep track of the windings and turnings of the path, but I doubt I could retrace my steps. After some time my camel stopped; still blindfolded, I was helped to dismount and assisted into a carrying chair. I had given Kemit my word I would not remove the blindfold. Otherwise, he politely but firmly informed me, he would have had me bound hand and foot.'

'Did you keep your word, Emerson?' I asked.

Emerson grinned. His face was as tanned and fit as ever, if a trifle thinner, and I was pleased to see he was clean-shaven. 'How can you doubt it, Peabody? Anyhow, the chair was curtained all around; I couldn't see a thing. It was not difficult to deduce that the mode of power was not horses or camels, but human bearers; but I never saw them, because my blindfold was not removed until after we had reached this house and they had departed. Nor, to be honest, was I concerned about anything except seeing you properly cared for.'

He paused in his narrative to administer a few demonstrations of that concern before resuming. 'The precautions taken by Kemit in my case explain one of the reasons why this place has remained unknown. I fancy the unfortunate Beduin who happened to stumble on the secret entrance would not return to tell the tale. In fact, it is unlikely he would get so far; groups of armed men, who use the oasis as one of their bases, constantly patrol the surrounding areas. As I observed, they disguise themselves as ordinary Beduin, wearing the usual robes and headcloths. No doubt they have inspired some of the bizarre legends about raiders like the Tebu, whose camels are said to leave no tracks and who purportedly drink the liquid from the bellies of those beasts. They probably also account for many of the stories about stolen camels and looted caravans. As for our friend Kemit – '

He broke off. 'Brace yourself, Peabody,' he remarked with a laugh; and Ramses was upon us.

As a young child he had been given to extravagant displays of affection, but in the last year or two these had become infrequent, owing, I suppose, to his notion that he was getting too old for such things. On this occasion he quite forgot his dignity, and rushed at me with such impetuosity that Emerson was forced to remonstrate. 'Gently, Ramses, if you please; your mama is still weak.'

'Never mind, Emerson,' I said, speaking with some difficulty because Ramses had a stranglehold around my neck. In obedience to his father's order he relaxed his hold and stood back, his hands clasped behind him. His lean little body was bare to the waist and brown as any Egyptian's; a short kilt or skirt of white linen reached to mid-thigh and was belted with a wide sash of vivid scarlet. But the most remarkable change was his coiffure. His hair, which was one of his best features, being black and soft like his father's, had grown rather long during our journey. Now it was all gone, except for a single lock on one side, which had been braided and bound with ribbons. The rest of his head was as bare as an egg.

A cry of maternal anguish burst from my lips. 'Ramses! Your hair – your beautiful hair!'

'There is a reason for the alteration, Mama,' said Ramses. 'It is very good – very, very good indeed – to see you better, Mama.'

His countenance did not echo the warmth of his words, but I, who knew that countenance well, saw the quiver of his lips and the moisture in his eyes.

Before I could return to the subject of Ramses's missing hair, one of the hangings at the end of the room was lifted, and two men entered. They wore the same simple short kilt Ramses was wearing, but their military bearing and the tall iron spears they carried designated their profession as definitely as any uniform. They separated and turned to face one another, stepping as smartly as any royal guardsmen, and grounded the spears with a muted clash. Next came a pair of individuals eerily veiled in white that covered them from head to foot. Like the soldiers, they took up positions on either side of the doorway. Two more men followed the mysterious veiled persons; they too wore short kilts, but the richness of their ornaments suggested high rank. One of them was considerably older than the other. His hair was snow-white and he had a long mantle draped about his bony shoulders. His face was scored with wrinkles but his eyes were bright, and he focused them on me with avid yet childishly innocent curiosity.

A brief pause ensued; then all six of them – soldiers, nobles, and swaddled forms – bowed low as a single individual entered with stately stride.

It was Kemit – but how incredibly changed! His strong, keen features were the same, his frame as tall and well-formed. Indeed I had not realised how well-formed until then, for like the other men he wore only a short kilt. His was finely pleated, and the belt that confined his narrow waist was inlaid with gold and gleaming stones. A collar of the same precious substances lay across his broad shoulders, and a narrow band of gold shone against the black of his hair.

'Kemit!' I exclaimed, gaping at this apparition from the distant past – for I am sure the Reader, like myself, recognises the costume as that worn by nobles of imperial Egypt.

Still holding me, Emerson rose to his feet. 'That was his nom de guerre, Peabody. Permit me to present His Highness Prince Tarekenidal.'

The title seemed entirely appropriate. His bearing had always been royal, and I could only wonder why it had taken me so long to realise that he was no common tribesman. I was keenly aware of my own lack of dignity, cradled like an infant in Emerson's arms and clad informally. I did the best I could under the circumstances, inclining my head and repeating, 'Your Highness. I am deeply grateful to you for saving my life and those of my husband and child.'

Tarekenidal raised his hands in the gesture with which he had always greeted me and which I now recognised (how could I have failed to do so!) as one depicted in innumerable ancient reliefs. 'My heart is happy, Lady, to see you well again. Here is my brother the Count Amenislo, son of the Lady Bartare' – he indicated the younger man, a chubby-cheeked smiling chap wearing long golden earrings – 'and the Royal Councillor, High Priest of Isis, First Prophet of Osiris, Murtek.'

The elderly gentleman's mouth stretched in a broad smile that displayed gums almost entirely without teeth. Only two remained, and they were brown and worn. Despite the sinister appearance of his dental apparatus, there was no mistaking his goodwill, for he bowed repeatedly and kept raising and lowering his hands in salutation. Then he cleared his throat and said, 'Good morning, sir and madam.'

'Good gracious,' I exclaimed. 'Does everyone here speak English?'

The prince smiled. 'Some among us speak a little and understand a little. My uncle the high priest wished to see you and be sure your sickness was ended.'

His uncle was seeing more of me than I would have preferred, for my linen robe was sleeveless and sheer as the finest lawn. I have never been studied with such intense fascination (by another than my husband), and it was clear, to me at least, that the old gentleman had not lost all the interests and instincts of youth. Oddly enough, I did not find his survey of my person insulting. It approved without offending, if I may put it that way.

Emerson did not appreciate these subtle distinctions. He folded me up, knees to chest, in an attempt to conceal as much of me as possible. 'If you will permit me, Your Highness, I will return Mrs Emerson to her bed.'

He proceeded to do so, covering me to my chin with a linen sheet. Murtek gestured; one of the white-veiled figures glided fowards and approached the bed. Its feet must have been bare, for it made no sound whatever, and the effect was so uncanny I could not help shrinking back when it bent over me. The veils were thinner over the face; I saw a gleam of eyes regarding me.

'It is all right, Peabody,' said Emerson, ever-watchful. 'This is the medical person I mentioned.'

A hand appeared from amid the filmy draperies. With the brisk assurance of any Western physician, it drew the sheet aside, opened my robe, and pressed down upon my exposed bosom. It was not the professionalism of the gesture that surprised me – one of the ancient medical papyri had proved that the Egyptians knew of 'the voice of the heart' and where upon the body it could be 'heard' – but the fact that the hand was slim and small, with tapering nails.

'I forgot to mention,' Emerson went on, 'that the medical person was a woman.'

'How do you know it's the same one?' I demanded.
'I beg your pardon?' said Emerson.

The visitors had departed, except for the 'medical person,' whose duties appeared to include several a Western doctor would have considered beneath him. After performing those services only a woman can properly render to another female, she was now occupied in heating something over a brazier at the far side of the room. I deduced that it was soup of some kind; the smell was most appetising.

'I said, how do you know she is the same person who nursed me on the journey?' I said. 'Those veils render her effectively anonymous, and since I have seen two people so attired, I assume it is a kind of uniform or costume. Or do all the women here go veiled?'

'Your wits are as keen as ever, my dear,' said Emerson, who had pulled up a chair to the side of the bed. 'The costume appears to be peculiar to one group of women, who are known as the Handmaidens of the Goddess. The goddess in question is Isis, and it seems that here she has become the patroness of medicine, instead of Thoth, who held that role in Egypt. Isis makes better sense, when you come to think about it; she brought her husband Osiris back from the dead, and a physician can't do better than that. As for the Handmaidens, one of them has always been here with you, but to be truthful I can't tell one from the other and I have no idea how many of them there are.'

'Why are you whispering, Emerson? She can't understand what we are saying.'

It was Ramses who replied. At my invitation he had seated himself on the foot of the bed; he looked so like a lad of ancient Egypt that it was rather a shock to hear him speak English.

'As Tarek just told you, Mama, some of them do speak and understand our language.'

'How did they . . . Good heavens, of course!' I clapped my hand to my brow. 'Mr Forth. I am ashamed that I neglected to ask about him. Have you seen him? Is Mrs Forth here as well?'

'You did ask, Peabody, and the reason why you did not receive an answer is twofold,' said Emerson. 'Firstly, you asked too many questions without giving me an opportunity to reply. Secondly . . . well, er, to be frank – I don't know the answer.'

'Far be it from me to be critical, Emerson, but it seems to me you haven't made good use of your time. I would have insisted upon seeing and speaking with the Forths.'

Ramses said quietly, 'Papa has sat by your side since we arrived here, Mama. He would not have left you even to sleep if I had not insisted.'

Tears filled my eyes. The truth is, I was weaker than I had thought, and that made me cross. 'My dear Emerson,' I said. 'Forgive me.'

'Certainly, my dear Peabody.' Emerson had to stop to clear his throat. He had taken the hand I had offered him; he held it like some fragile flower, as if the slightest pressure would bruise it.

Was I moved? Yes. Was I annoyed? Very. I was not accustomed to being handled like a delicate flower. I wanted Ramses to go away. I wanted the Handmaiden to go away. I wanted Emerson to seize me in his arms and squeeze the breath out of me, and . . . and tell me all the things I was dying to know.

Emerson read my mind. He can do that. The corners of his mouth twitched, and he said affectionately, 'I have the better of you just now, my dear, and I mean to take full advantage. You are not yet fit for prolonged activity, or even conversation. Apply yourself with your usual determination to recovering your strength, and then I will be delighted to supply – er – supply answers to all your questions.'

He was right, of course. Even the brief interlude with Tarek (for so we agreed to call him, his full name being something of a mouthful) had tired me. I forced myself to eat the bowl of soup the Handmaiden gave me; it was hearty and nourishing, thick with lentils and onions and bits of meat. 'Not chicken,' I said, after tasting it. 'Duck, perhaps?'

'Or goose. We have been served roast fowl on several occasions. They also raise cattle of some kind. The meat tastes strange; I have not been able to identify it.'

I forced myself to finish the soup to the last drop. Soon afterwards Ramses and Emerson took their leave.

'We sleep in the adjoining room,' Emerson explained, when I protested. 'I am, and have always been, within reach of your voice, Peabody.'

Blue-veiled twilight crept into the room. I watched drowsily as the ghostly form of the Handmaiden glided to and fro on her duties of mercy. As the darkness deepened, she lit the lamps – small earthenware vessels filled with oil and provided with wicks of twisted cloth. Such lamps are still used in Egypt and Nubia; they are of immemorial antiquity. They gave a soft, limited light, and the oil was scented with herbs.

I was almost asleep when the woman approached my couch and seated herself on a low stool. She raised her hands to her face. Was she about to unveil? I forced myself to breathe slowly and evenly, feigning slumber, but my heart pounded with anticipation. What would I see? A face as frighteningly lovely as that of Mr Haggard's immortal She? The withered countenance of an aged crone? Or even – for my imagination had fully recovered, if my body had not – a fair face crowned with silvery-golden hair, that of Mrs Willoughby Forth?

She did unveil, throwing the folds of linen back with a very human sigh of relief. The face thus disclosed was neither fair-skinned nor terrifyingly lovely, though it had a beauty of sorts. Like Prince Tarek's, her features were finely cut, with high cheekbones and a strong, chiselled nose. A net of gold mesh confined the masses of her dark hair. I enjoyed the display of girlish vanity in her use of cosmetics on a face that was not meant to be seen – kohl that emphasised her dark eyes and long lashes, some reddish substance on lips and cheeks. She seemed so gentle and ordinary, in contrast to the enigmatic figure she had presented while veiled, that I debated as to whether I should speak to her, but before I could make up my mind I fell asleep.

For the next few days I did little except sleep and eat. The food was surprisingly well prepared – roasted goose and duck served with different sauces, mutton in a variety of forms, fresh vegetables such as beans, radishes, and onions, and several kinds of bread, some shaped into little cakes that were sticky-sweet with honey. The fruit was particularly tasty – grapes, figs, and dates as sweet as the incomparable fruits of Sukkôt. To drink we were offered wine (rather thin and sour but refreshing), a thick, dark beer, and goat milk. Water was not offered and I did not ask for it, since I suspected it would not be safe to drink unless it was boiled, and I had abandoned my tea with the rest of our supplies.

At Emerson's suggestion we made use of our forced inactivity to study the local dialect. I had hoped our knowledge of Egyptian would assist us, but except for certain titles and proper names, and a few common words, the language of the Holy Mountain was a different tongue entirely. Nevertheless we made excellent progress, not only because of certain mental attributes modesty prevents me from naming, but because Ramses had already picked up a good deal from Tarek-alias-Kemit even before we arrived. Needless to say he took full advantage of his position of instructor to his elders, and on several occasions I was sorely tempted to send him to his room.

One night I decided to try my burgeoning linguistic skill on my attendant. I let her finish her tasks and relax with face unveiled before I spoke. 'Greetings, maiden. I thank you for your good heart.'

She almost fell off the stool. I could not help laughing; recovering herself, she glared at me like any young person whose dignity has been damaged. In stumbling Meroitic I attempted to apologise.

She let out a flood of speech which I could not follow; then, visibly pleased at my lack of comprehension, she said slowly, 'You speak our tongue poorly.'

'Let us speak English, then,' I said in that language – making mental note of the adverbial form, whose meaning was quite clear.

She hesitated, biting her lip, and then said in Meroitic, 'I do not understand.'

'I think you do, a little. Do not all the high-born people of your land learn English? I can see that you are of the high-born.'

The compliment lowered her guard. 'I speak . . . a small. Not many words.'

'Ah, I knew it. You speak very well. What is your name?'

Again she hesitated, looking at me askance from under her long lashes. Finally she said, 'I am Amenitere, First Handmaiden to the Goddess.'

'How did you learn English?' I asked. 'Was it from the white man who came here?'

Her face went blank and she shook her head. None of my attempts to rephrase the question or render it in my stumbling version of her language brought an answer.

I learned a few things from her, however. She had never unveiled or spoken while Ramses or Emerson was present, but this was not as I initially supposed, because of their sex. Only 'the goddess' and her fellow handmaidens were supposed to see her face. She was unable or unwilling to explain why she made an exception in my case; I came to the conclusion that she found me so very unusual that she was not quite certain how to treat me.

We got to the point where we could chat in a friendly fashion about cosmetics and food and particularly about that subject dear to feminine hearts, clothing. My travel-stained garments had been carefully laundered and returned to me; she never tired of fingering the fabric, exploring the pockets, and laughing at the cut and style. She would have laughed even louder, I daresay, if she had known about corsets.

Since I only had the one set of garments, I was forced to assume native attire. It was extremely comfortable but rather lacking in variety, for all the women's clothes were nothing more than variations on a simple unshaped robe of linen or cotton. The most elegant of them – to judge by the fineness of the weave – were pure white, but some were brightly embroidered or woven with coloured threads. Possessing neither buttons nor clasps, they were open all the way down the front, and were meant to be kept closed by means of girdles or belts. Having not much confidence in such doubtful expedients, I made a strategic use of pins and wore my combinations under the skimpier garments.

Emerson was as deficient in the haberdashery line as I, and often wore one of the long masculine versions of the loose robe, or a linen shirt of local manufacture, but he steadfastly refused to appear in a kilt like the one Tarek had worn. At first I could not understand his modesty, for as a rule I had a hard time making him keep his clothes on.

Let me rephrase that. When on a dig, Emerson was only too prone to stripping off coat and shirt, and of course his hat. I objected to this because it struck me as undignified, even when there was no one to see except the workers, but I must confess that aesthetically the effect was extremely pleasing, and I suspected that Emerson was fully aware of my reaction to the sight of his bronzed muscular frame. Yet now that he had a valid excuse to induce that reaction, he refrained. Finally, after what he was pleased to term 'your incessant nagging, Peabody,' he agreed to change into an elegant set of garments that had been supplied, and let me judge for myself.

Since Amenit was present – as she always was – he retired into his chamber to change. When he appeared, flinging back the curtain with a passionate gesture, I could not repress a cry of admiration. His hair was almost shoulder-length by now; the thick, shining tresses were held back from his noble brow by a crimson fillet studded with gold flowers. The rich colours of turquoise and coral and deep lapis-blue in the broad collar upon his breast glowed against his deeply tanned skin. Armlets of gold and gemstones circled his wrist; a wide girdle of the same precious materials supported the pleated kilt that bared his knees and . . .

I managed to transform my laugh into a cough, but Emerson's face turned a pretty shade of mahogany and he hastily retreated behind the bed curtains.

'I told you, Peabody, curse it! My legs!'

'They are very handsome legs, Emerson. And your knees are quite . . .'

'They are white!' shouted Emerson from behind the curtains. 'Snow-white! They look ridiculous!'

They did, rather. It was a pity, for from the crown of his head to the hem of his kilt he was a picture of barbaric, manly beauty. After that I said no more about changing clothes, but I sometimes saw Emerson in the garden, behind a tree, exposing his shins to the sunlight.

We were never alone. When Amenit slept I do not know; she was always in the room, or leaving the room, or entering it, and when she was not present, one of the servants was. They were shy, silent little people, several shades darker in colour than Amenit and Tarek, and if they were not mute they pretended to be, communicating among themselves and with Amenit by means of gestures. The more my strength increased, the more I resented the lack of privacy, for I felt sure that was what prevented Emerson from taking his rightful place at my side by night as well as by day. He was rather shy about such things.

Our suite of rooms surrounded a delightful little garden with a pool in its centre. They consisted of several bedchambers, a formal reception room with exquisitely carved lotus columns, and a bath chamber, with a stone slab on which the bather stood while servants poured water over him. The furniture was simple but elegant – beds with springs of woven leather, chests and beautifully woven baskets that served for storage of linen and clothing, a few chairs, several small tables. Only our rooms were furnished; the rest of the building had been abandoned. It was very large, with innumerable rooms and passageways and several empty courtyards, and part of it had been cut out of the cliff against which it apparently stood. These back rooms had probably been designed for storage; they were small and windowless and looked very eerie in the dim light of the lamps we carried when we explored them.

The walls of many of the larger chambers were handsomely decorated with scenes in the ancient style, depicting long-past battles and long-dead dignitaries, both male and female. The inscriptions accompanying these paintings were in the hiero-glyphic script familiar to us from our study of Meroitic remains. Ramses at once announced his intention of copying them – 'to take back to Uncle Walter.' I encouraged him in this; it kept him busy and out of mischief.

The only windows were high up under the roof, clerestory-style. There were no inner doors; woven draperies and matting provided a modicum of privacy.

A particularly heavy set of draperies covered one end of our reception room. Emerson had unobtrusively steered me away from them when we explored (for he was always at my side), but one day, after we had thoroughly examined the rest of the place, I resisted his attempt to lead me towards the garden.

'I don't want to go into the garden, I want to go through that door – for I presume there is one, behind the hangings. Is there a pit full of venomous snakes or a den of lions beyond, that you are so determined to prevent me?'

Emerson grinned. 'It is a pleasure to hear you sound like your old crotchety self, my dear. By all means go ahead, if you are so set on it. You won't like what you find, but I think you are now strong enough to deal with it.'

He politely parted the draperies for me, and I passed through them into a corridor whose walls were painted with scenes of battle. With Emerson close on my heels, I marched the length of the passage towards what appeared to be a blank wall. An opening on the left led into an extension of the passageway; after several more turns and jogs I emerged abruptly into an antechamber, lit by a row of narrow windows high up under the beamed ceiling, and found myself facing a file of men standing at stiff attention. They must have heard the slap of my sandals as I approached, for I felt certain they did not stand around in that uncomfortable pose all the time.

They were a fine-looking set of men, all quite young, all at least six feet tall. In addition to the usual kilt, each man wore a wide leather belt supporting a dagger long enough to be called a short sword, and carried a shield pointed at the top like a Gothic arch. Some held huge iron spears and wore a sort of helmet, fashioned of leather and fitting closely to their heads. Others were armed with bows and quivers bristling with arrows; their heads were bare except for a narrow band of braided grass from the back of which arose a single crimson feather. When I examined them more closely I saw that, though the shields were identical in shape, some were covered with brownish-fawn hide while others – the ones held by the archers – had white patches on a red-brown background. Holding these shields before them, the men formed a living wall across the room from one side to the other. Nor did they give way as I approached them. I stopped, perforce, when my eyes were a scant inch from the well-formed chin of the young man who seemed to be in charge. He continued to stare straight ahead.

I turned to Emerson, who was watching with evident amusement. 'Tell them to let me pass,' I exclaimed.

'Use your parasol,' Emerson suggested. 'I doubt they have ever faced such a terrible weapon as that.'

'You know I didn't bring it with me,' I snapped. 'What is the meaning of this? Are we prisoners, then?'

Emerson sobered. 'The situation is not so simple, Peabody. I let you see this for yourself because you would have insisted on it anyway. Come away; we must talk about this.'

I let him take my arm and lead me back along the corridor. 'Rather cleverly constructed, this,' he remarked. 'The turning of the passage gives the occupants privacy and makes it easier to defend against an attacking force. It makes one suspect that the ruling classes don't enjoy the loyalty of all their subjects.'

'I don't want to hear suggestions and deductions and surmises,' I said. 'I want to hear facts. How much have you kept from me, Emerson?'

'Come into the garden, Peabody.' We circled a group of the little servants who were scouring the floor of the reception room with sand and water, and sat down on a carved bench next to the pool. Lilies and lotus blooms covered its surface; the leaves of the giant lotus, some of them a good three feet in diameter, lay on the water like carved jade platters. A soft breeze whispered through the tamarisk and persea trees that shaded the bench, with a chorus of birdsong forming a musical counterpoint. Birds haunted the garden – sparrows and hoopoes and a variety of brilliantly feathered flyers I could not identify. It was indeed Zerzura – the place of the little birds.

'Beautiful, isn't it?' Emerson took his pipe from the pouch that hung at the belt of his robe, serving as a substitute for pockets. He had smoked the last of his tobacco the day before, but apparently even an empty pipe was better than none. 'Some people might think themselves fortunate to spend the rest of their lives in such peace and tranquillity.'

'Some people,' I said.

'But not you? You needn't answer, my dear; we are, as always, in complete agreement. Never fear, when we are ready to leave, we'll find a means of doing so. I didn't want to make a move of any kind until you were yourself again. We may have to fight our way out of here, Peabody. I hope we do not; but if we do, I need you at my side, parasol at the ready.'

Has ever woman received a more touching tribute from her spouse? Speechless with pride, I could only gaze at him with eyes brimming with emotion.

'Blow your nose, Peabody,' said Emerson, offering me a singularly dirty rag which had once been a good pocket handkerchief.

'Thank you, I will use my own.' From my own pocket pouch I took one of the squares of linen that had been cut, at my direction, to replace my own lost handkerchiefs.

'We've never been in a situation quite like this, Peabody,' Emerson went on, sucking reflectively on his empty pipe. 'Always, before, we were familiar with the local customs, the manners and habits of the people with whom we were dealing. Based on what little I have seen and heard, I have developed a few theories about this place; it seems to be a peculiar mixture of several different cultural strains. Originally, like the oasis of

Siwa in northern Africa, it may have been sacred to the god Amon. I believe that some of the priests who left Egypt after the Twenty-Second Dynasty came here and gave new life to the old traditions. After the fall of the Meroitic kingdom the Sacred Mountain became a refuge for the Cushite nobles. There is a third strain of native peoples, the original occupants, whom we have seen acting as servants. Add to all these factors the changes wrought by the passage of time and by centuries of virtual isolation, and you end up with a culture far more alien than any we have encountered. We can make informed guesses about how things are done here, but we would be taking an awful risk if we acted on those guesses. Do you agree with me so far?'

'Certainly, my dear, and without wishing to appear critical of your lecture – which was well-reasoned and eloquently expressed – it was quite unnecessary to go into such elaborate detail, since I had already arrived at the same conclusions. Facts, Emerson. Give me facts!'

'Hmph,' said Emerson. 'The fact is, Peabody, that I haven't spoken to Tarek alone since we got here. He visited you every day, but he only stayed for a few minutes, and there was always someone with him. Besides, I wasn't in the mood for anthropological discussions.'

'Yes, my dear, I understand, and I am deeply appreciative of your concern. But now – '

'Tarek hasn't been back since you recovered consciousness,' Emerson replied somewhat snappishly. 'I couldn't question him if he wasn't here, could I? I discovered early on that there were armed guards in the antechamber, and that they were disinclined to let me pass. But curse it, Peabody, we don't know why they are there. They may be protecting us from dangers we know nothing about. Let me remind you that Tarek's title is that of king's son. He is not the king. We haven't seen the king – or the queen. The royal women of Meroë seem to have held considerable political power. The same may be true here.'

'That would be splendid,' I exclaimed. 'What an example – '

'Curse it, Peabody, that is just what I was afraid of – that you would start jumping to conclusions. The point I am endeavouring to make is that until we know who is in control here, and how they feel about uninvited visitors like ourselves, we must walk warily.'

'Why, certainly, Emerson. And the point I am endeavouring to make is that it is time we made an effort to learn these things. I am fully recovered and ready to take that place at your side you so kindly offered me.'

'I believe you are,' said Emerson, without the wholehearted enthusiasm I had expected. 'All right, then. The first step is to get in touch with Tarek. Do you suppose that omnipresent column of white swaddling will carry a message to him? If you can convince her that you have made a full recovery, we may be able to dispense with her services,' he added, brightening visibly at the idea. 'The confounded girl is getting on my nerves, gliding around like a ghost.'

Amenit made it clear that carrying a message was beneath her dignity, but she agreed to find someone to take it. She admitted I was no longer in need of her medical attention. This did not have the effect Emerson (and I) had hoped, however; when I suggested, as tactfully as my still limited command of the language allowed, that her services could now be dispensed with, she pretended not to understand.

We had made our move; it remained only to await a response. After luncheon we retired for the brief rest that is customary in warm climes. Not for the first time, I regretted the loss of my little library. I would as soon think of travelling without my trousers as my books – cheap paperbound editions of my favourite novels and works of philosophy – for I preferred to spend my resting time reading, my normally vigorous health making extra sleep unnecessary. The books had, of course, been among the unnecessary luxuries discarded after the mutiny of our servants. With nothing better to do, I did sleep for a few hours. When I awoke I went into the reception room to find

Ramses and Emerson already there, hard at work on a language lesson.

'No, no, Papa,' Ramses was saying in an insufferably patronising voice. 'The imperative form is *abadamu,* not *abadmunt*'

'Bah,' said Emerson. 'Hello, Peabody; did you have a good rest?'

'Yes, thank you. Has there been any word from Tarek?'

'Apparently not. I can't get a word out of that wretched girl. She just squirms and grunts and scuttles off when I speak to her.'

'Yet it appears we are about to have guests,' I remarked, taking a seat next to him.

'Why do you say that?'

I indicated Amenit, who was hopping around the room like a flea on a griddle, as my old North Country nurse would have put it, her hands flying as she directed the servants.

'I have never seen her move so briskly. The room was already spotless (as indeed it always is), but she has made them clean it again, and now they are setting up those little light tables and chairs. I recognise the actions of a nervous hostess.'

'I do believe you are correct, Peabody.' With an obvious air of relief, Emerson pushed his lesson aside and rose. 'I had better change. These loose robes are quite comfortable, but I feel at a disadvantage in skirts.'

I felt the same. I hastened to assume not only my trousers but my belt. Thus accoutred, and with my parasol ready at hand, I felt ready for anything that might ensue.

It was a good thing I had noticed Amenit's behaviour, for we were given no other warning. The curtains at the entrance were suddenly flung aside. This time Tarek's entourage was more extensive and impressive. There were six soldiers instead of two and four of the veiled maidens. They were followed by a number of men, all of them richly dressed, and by several young women who were hardly dressed at all. (A few strings of beads, however strategically placed, do not in my opinion constitute clothing.)

183

These damsels carried musical instruments – small harps, pipes, and drums – on which they began to play, enthusiastically if not euphoniously. All fanned out as they entered and took up positions on both sides of the door. An expectant pause ensued; then came Tarek – and his twin.

There were two of them at any rate, almost equal in height and dressed identically; but a second glance told me that the resemblance was not as exact as I had thought. The second man was a trifle shorter and more heavily built, with shoulders almost as massive as those of my formidable spouse. By Western standards (which are, if I may remind the Reader, as arbitrary as those of any other culture) he was even better-looking than Tarek, with finely chiselled features and a delicate, almost feminine mouth. Yet there was something repellent about him. Tarek's bearing had the dignity of a true nobleman; the other man carried himself with the arrogance of a tyrant.

(Emerson maintains that I am reinterpreting my reaction in the light of later experience. I stick to my statement.)

After a moment one of the courtiers stepped fowards. It was Murtek, the old High Priest of Isis. Clearing his throat, he spoke in a sonorous voice, 'Sir and madam. And small worthy son. Here are the king's sons of his body, the two Horus, carrying the bow to the destruction of the enemies of His Majesty, the defenders of Osiris, the Prince Tarekenidal Meraset, son of the king's wife Shanakdakhete; the Prince his brother Nastasen Nemareh, son of the king's wife Amanishakhete.'

His pleasure at getting through the long address with what he believed utter success was evident in his broad if toothless smile. It was certainly a remarkable speech, fraught with intriguing implications, but I fear I was too busy struggling to preserve my gravity to take them all in, or to reply in kind.

Emerson claims to have comprehended better than I. Be that as it may, he was obviously the proper person to reply, and he was never at a loss for words.

'Your Royal Highnesses, gentlemen and – er – ladies. Allow me to introduce myself. Professor Radcliffe Archibald Emerson, M.A.

Ox., Fellow of the Royal Society, Fellow of the Royal Geographical Society, Member of the American Philosophical Society. My honoured chief wife, the Lady Doctor Amelia Peabody Emerson, et cetera et cetera, et cetera; the noble youth, heir to his father, born of the chief wife, Walter Ramses Peabody Emerson.'

Beaming, the old gentleman proceeded to present the others. It took quite a long time, since they each had a string of impressive titles – priest and prophets, courtiers and counts, fanbearers and carriers of the sandals of His Majesty. Their names have no bearing on this narrative, except for one – Pesaker, royal vizier and High Priest of Aminreh. All our visitors were finely dressed, with gold glittering on every limb, but Pesaker fairly clanked with bracelets, armlets, massive pectorals, and a broad jewelled collar. His ornately dressed hair was obviously a wig; the stiff little black curls formed an incongruous frame for his weathered, scowling face. I suspected he was a blood relative of the two princes, for his features were an older, harsher version of theirs.

We had got more than we bargained for – not only Tarek, but representatives of the highest in the land. I would have taken this as a good omen had it not been for the hot hostile stare of Prince Nastasen (who bore the same name as that of the remote ancestor whose tomb we had found at Nuri) and the unsmiling regard of the High Priest of Aminreh.

Rising to the occasion, as a good hostess must, I indicated the tables, where the servants stood ready with jars of wine and platters of food. There was a certain amount of rude scuffling to determine who sat next to whom; I had hoped to get Tarek as a dinner partner, but his brother fairly pushed me into a chair and took the one next to me, beckoning to Murtek to join us. Apparently his services as translator were required; Prince Nastasen did not speak English.

His grave face lightening in a smile, Tarek elected to favour Ramses, which left Emerson to the High Priest of Aminreh – he and the two princes being the three highest in rank. The others took their places at different tables, each of which seated only two or three people.

The musicians, who had stopped playing while the old man spoke, now struck up a jingling tune, punctuated by thumps on the drum, and one of the young women began to gyrate around the room. She was extremely limber.

Nastasen was not much of a conversationalist. He applied himself to his food, and Murtek, though obviously dying to show off his English, confined himself to smiles and nods. Something warned me to follow his example, which was wise, for as I later learned, one does not speak until the person of highest status present has deigned to do so.

After demolishing a roast duck (and throwing the bones over his shoulder), Nastasen fixed his fine dark eyes on my face. Even when he pronounced the guttural sounds of his native tongue his voice was beautiful, a deep, mellow baritone. I understood only a few words, and deemed it best to admit not even to that, so I turned an inquiring smile on Murtek.

'The king's son asks how old you are,' said that worthy.

'Oh, dear,' I said, in some confusion. 'In our country it is not polite . . . Tell him we do not count the years as he does. Tell him . . . I am as old as his mother.'

A voice not far distant murmured, 'Well done, Peabody,' and the old man translated what I had said.

Nastasen proceeded to ask me a series of questions that would have been deemed highly impertinent in civilised society, having to do with my personal habits, my family, and my relations with my husband. For all I knew, such questions might have been rude in this culture as well, but I was in no position to object, so I fended them off as well as I could. Emerson, seated at an adjoining table, was not so controlled as I; I could hear him gurgling and gasping with rage as the inquisition continued. The dear fellow assumed that the prince's intimate questions betokened a personal interest in my humble self. I doubted this; though to be sure I also doubted that my claiming to be the age of his mother would deter him from adding me to his collection should he care to do so.

Having answered a good dozen or more questions, I decided

I might venture upon a few of my own. 'I hope your honoured father the king is well?' seemed safe, but Nastasen did not seem to like it; his face darkened and he replied with a short, curt sentence.

The old gentleman took some liberties in the translation. 'His Majesty is Osiris. He had flied to the sky. He is king of the western peoples.'

'He is dead?' I asked, surprised.

'Dead, yes, dead.' Murtek smiled broadly.

'But then who is king? Does His Highness have an older brother?'

The old man turned to the prince. The answer was a curt nod, and I realised that he had asked for permission to explain the situation, which he proceeded to do at some length and with a striking absence of grammar.

The king had only been dead a few months. ('The Horus flied in the season of harvest.') In many other societies the eldest surviving prince automatically assumes the crown, but here the succession depended on a number of factors, the most important of which was the rank of the mother. The king had had a great number of wives, but only two of them had been royal princesses – the late king's half-sisters, in fact. The survival of this particular custom, which was practised in ancient Egypt as well as in the Cushite kingdom, did not surprise me. It made a certain amount of sense in terms of dogma as well as practical politics; for by marrying his sisters the king kept them out of the clutches of ambitious nobles who might be tempted to claim the throne by right of their wives' royal birth, and also insured that the divine blood of the pharaohs would be undiluted. The children of lesser wives and concubines held noble rank, like the young count whom Tarek had introduced as his brother; but the sons of the royal princesses had first claim on the crown. For the first time in the annals of the kingdom, each of these ladies had one surviving son – who were exactly the same age.

When I questioned this remarkable statement, the old man shrugged. Not the same moment, the same hour, no; in fact, the noble Prince Tarek was somewhat the elder. But both had been born in the same year of His Majesty, and whenever there was a question – as, for instance, in the case of twins – the final decision was left to the gods. Or to the God, Aminreh himself. When He came forth from the sanctuary on the occasion of His yearly circuit of the city, He would choose the next king. This was due to occur within a few weeks. In the meantime, the noble Prince Nastasen had acted as regent, in the absence of his brother, and with the assistance of the vizier, the high priests, the councillors. . .

'And Uncle Tom Cobley and all,' I murmured.

'No,' said old Murtek seriously. 'He lives not in this place.'

To say I was fascinated is a vast understatement. My life's work had been the study of ancient Egypt; to find actual living examples of rituals I had known only from weathered tomb walls and desiccated papyri was an indescribable thrill. Aminreh was obviously Amon-Re, and he held the same high position here as in Egypt. From an obscure godling of Thebes he had risen to be king of the gods, taking on their names and attributes even as his ambitious priests gathered land and wealth into the treasuries of their temples. This would not be the first time Amon-Re had selected a king. Over three thousand years ago the nod of the god had gone to a humble young priest who had, as Thutmose III, become one of Egypt's mightiest warrior pharaohs. And had not the stela of the first Nastasen, found by Lepsius, mentioned his selection by Amon? Murtek's words had also confirmed Emerson's theories about the importance of the royal women. How far did their power extend? I wondered. Could they only convey the right to rule, or did they wield real power? I was about to demand additional details when His Royal Highness barked out a brusque comment. It was evident that he was bored, and perhaps suspicious as well; poor old Murtek swallowed convulsively and did not speak again.

More wine was poured, and the formal entertainment began – dancers, acrobats, and a juggler. The juggler may have been nervous – I would have been, with Nastasen glowering upon me – for he ended by dropping one of the blazing torches, which rolled dangerously close to the foot of His Highness before someone stamped it out. Nastasen rose in his wrath, shouting; the juggler fled, pursued by two soldiers.

It appeared the entertainment was over, and the banquet as well. One of his attendants, bowing obsequiously handed Nastasen his gold-bordered mantle, which he flung about his shoulders. I breathed a sigh of relief, for as courtesy seemed to demand, I had drunk quite a lot of wine.

It may have been the wine that emboldened me to ask one final question, though I believe I would have done it anyway. There were hundreds of things I wanted to know, but this was the most vital. I turned to Murtek. 'Ask His Highness what has happened to the white man, Willoughby Forth, and his wife.'

The old man's jaw dropped. He glanced uneasily at his prince. But no translation was necessary; either Nastasen understood more English than he admitted, or Mr Forth's name itself made my meaning clear. For the first time that evening his delicate lips curved in a smile. Slowly and deliberately he pronounced a single word.

I knew the word. Shock and comprehension must have registered upon my countenance, for Nastasen's smile broadened, baring his strong white teeth. Tossing the end of his scarf over his head, he turned on his heel and strode from the room.

'Touch This Mother
at Your Peril!'

'Dead!' I exclaimed. 'They are dead, Emerson! I feared it, I feared it, and yet I hoped . . . Did you see how that dreadful young man smiled when he told me? He knew the news would distress me, I am sure he did – '

'Hush, Peabody.' Emerson put his arm around me. We were alone; the others had hastened out after the prince, whose abrupt departure had obviously taken them by surprise. They had left the room in a shambles; puddles of spilled wine, bones, scraps of bread, and shards of broken crockery littered the floor.

A group of servants were already at work, under the direction of the handmaiden, cleaning up the mess. I leaned against my husband's strong shoulder and struggled to compose myself. Your behaviour is absurd, I told myself sternly. You were not acquainted with Mr Forth or his wife, and you are carrying on as if you had lost some close relation.

Emerson offered me his handkerchief. I found my own and wiped my eyes.

'I believe your assessment of the prince's character is correct, Mama,' said Ramses. 'I am sorry you gave him the satisfaction of distressing you, for I had already learned the truth from Tarek, and would have broken it to you more gently.'

'I seem to detect a note of criticism in your remarks, Ramses,'

I said. 'And I take strong exception to it. Er – what did Tarek say?'

Ramses looked around for something to sit on, his lips curling as he surveyed the mess on the floor. Though his personal habits left a great deal to be desired, in some ways he was as fastidious as a cat. (That is, he was intolerant of all messes except the ones he made.) 'May we go into your sleeping room, Mama? We can converse more comfortably there.'

We did as he suggested – Emerson stepping absently over the servants, who were crawling around picking up the scraps. Darkness had fallen but it was still early, by our standards; like other peoples who lack efficient means of artificial lighting, the citizens of the Holy Mountain rose at sunrise and went early to bed. I was a little tired myself, so I was glad to recline. Emerson drew up a chair and Ramses curled up at the foot of the bed, cleared his throat, and began.

'Mrs Forth did not long survive her arrival here. "She went to the god," as Tarek put it, quite delicately, I thought. Mr Forth lived for many years. Tarek assured me he was happy here and did not want to leave.'

'Ha,' I exclaimed. 'We may take that with a grain of salt, I think!'

'Not necessarily,' Ramses argued. 'It may be that his appeal for help was written early in his captivity.'

'And took over a decade to be delivered?'

'Stranger things have happened,' Emerson said thoughtfully. 'The message must have been composed while Mrs Forth yet lived. Forth may have changed his mind.'

'He did,' said Ramses. 'If you will permit me to finish – '

'How did Mr Forth die?' I demanded.

Ramses spoke in a rush. 'Of purely natural causes, if Tarek is to be believed, and I see no reason why we should doubt him, for he went on to say that Mr Forth had risen to the rank of Counsellor and Tutor of the Royal Children; it was from him that Tarek and certain others learned English, and Tarek spoke of him with great affection and respect.'

He paused and inhaled deeply.

'That doesn't explain the message, or the map,' I said critically. 'Or why Tarek came to work for us, or his reasons for doing so, or who is responsible for our being here.'

Ramses's eyes narrowed in exasperation. 'Tarek could not speak freely. Not all those present tonight were loyal to him. He warned me to be careful of what we said by quoting the precept, "A man may be ruined because of his tongue – "'

'Ah – the Papyrus of Ani!' exclaimed Emerson. 'To think that ancient book of wisdom has survived so long! It must have been carried to Cush by the priests of Amon who fled Thebes at the beginning of the Twenty-Second Dynasty. Peabody, you remember the rest of the passage – "Do not open your heart to a stranger – "'

'I do remember it. It is excellent advice, but I think Ramses is giving way to his love of the theatrical when he interprets it as a warning.'

Ramses looked indignant, but before he could protest, his father came to his defence. 'I am inclined to think it was meant as Ramses interpreted it, Peabody. We seem to find ourselves in the middle of a political struggle for power. Tarek and his brother are competing for the kingship – '

'The god will decide,' I broke in. 'I presume you overheard what Murtek told me; you heard him mention the ceremony of coming-forth.'

'Yes. But I hope you are not so naive as to believe that the god is incorruptible. Behind the pious platitudes of inscriptions like those of Thutmose the Third lies the same ugly truth that controls modern struggles for power and prestige. In Egypt the High Priests of Amon were the *eminences grises* behind the throne; eventually they seized the crown itself.'

'Then you think – '

'I think Nastasen and Tarek both want to be king,' Emerson said. 'And that the High Priest of Aminreh – ' He broke off with a muttered curse as the handmaiden appeared in the open doorway. 'Confound it, what does she want? Tell her to go away.'

'She wants to put me to bed, I think,' I said, stifling a yawn. 'You tell her to go away.'

'Never mind.' Emerson rose with a sigh. 'You must be tired, Peabody. It has been an interesting day.'

'I am not that tired,' I said, meeting his eyes.

'Oh? Yes, but . . .' Emerson cleared his throat. 'Well. Er. Come, Ramses. Good night, Peabody.'

'*Au revoir*, my dear Emerson.'

I was a trifle tired, but I was not at all sleepy. My busy brain teemed with questions I yearned to discuss with Emerson. As the handmaiden bustled about the room, dimming the lamps, straightening the bedclothes, and helping me into my night robe, I wished Kemit had been more direct instead of so confounded literary. It was all very well to warn us not to open our hearts to strangers – but they were all strangers here, even Kemit. What did he want from us – whom could we trust?

After tucking me into bed, the handmaiden proceeded to 'listen to the voice of the heart.' I looked at the slender fingers resting on my breast, and suspicion blossomed into certainty. 'You are not Amenit,' I said. 'Your fingers are longer than hers and you move quite differently. Who are you?'

I was prepared to repeat the question in Meroitic, but there was no need. Drawing my robe into place, she said softly, 'My name is Mentarit.'

Her voice was higher in pitch than Amenit's – soprano rather than contralto. 'May I see your face?' I asked; and, as she hesitated, I went on, 'Amenit unveiled for me. We were friends.'

'Friends,' she repeated.

'That means – '

'I know.' With a sudden movement she flung back the veil.

It was a lovely face, rounder and softer than that of her fellow-priestess, with great dark eyes and a delicate mouth. In outline the last-named feature strongly resembled that of Nastasen. It suited the girl far better than it did the prince, but it rather prejudiced me against her.

'You are very pretty,' I said.

She ducked her head shyly, like any modest English maiden, but she watched me from under her long lashes and her eyes were bright and wary. 'You must sleep now,' she said. 'You have been very ill.'

'But I am not ill now. Thanks to your excellent nursing, I am fully recovered. Didn't Amenit tell you I was better?'

Her smooth forehead crinkled in a frown, and I repeated the question in my stumbling Meroitic. Unlike Amenit she did not smile at my mistakes. 'I did not speak with my sister,' she said, speaking slowly and clearly. 'Her time of – was over, my time began(?) today.'

I questioned her about the words I had not understood; she explained that the first meant 'service' or 'duty,' and that my interpretation of the second had been correct. When I attempted to continue the conversation, however, she placed her fingers on my lips. 'You sleep now,' she repeated. 'It is not good to talk.'

She retreated to a corner of the room, where she sat down on a low stool. A few moments later the curtain to the next chamber was drawn aside. Emerson stood there. He was attired in a particularly handsome robe woven with stripes of bright blue and saffron and he carried one of the pottery lamps. It may have been the light that cast a rosy flush upon his face, but I suspected not.

'Go, Handmaiden,' he said in stumbling Meroitic. 'Tonight I am with my woman. It is the time – er – I wish – er ...' Here his native modesty overcame him, and his speech failed, for his study of the language had not gone so far as to include euphemisms for the activity he had in mind. Resorting instead to sign language, he blew out the lamp and advanced on Mentarit, pointing towards the door and flapping his hand at her.

I think she caught his meaning. A muffled sound that might have been a gasp or a giggle came from her, and she backed towards the door. I watched, choking with laughter and another emotion I am sure I need not specify. The expression of placid satisfaction on Emerson's face after he had shooed her out and was advancing with long strides towards the bed where I lay was almost too much for me, but amusement was soon overcome by other sensations even more powerful. It had been a long time. I will say no more.

Thereafter, as we reclined in the pleasurable aftermath of fulfilled connubial affection, Emerson hissed, 'Now we can converse freely without fear of being overheard.'

I shifted position slightly, for he had spoken directly into my ear, which produced a not-unpleasant but distracting effect. Emerson tightened his grasp. 'That was not my only motive for joining you, Peabody.'

'You have demonstrated your primary motive most effectively, my dear Emerson, but we may as well take advantage of the situation. I presume you have in mind some brilliant scheme of escape?'

'Escape? From what? Devil take it, Peabody, getting out of this building is not the problem. We could manage that, I expect; but then what? Without camels, water, and supplies we wouldn't stand a chance of escaping from this place, even assuming I could locate the entrance to the tunnel by which we entered, which I could not.'

'What do you propose then? For I presume you have not arranged this romantic rendezvous solely in order to point out the things we can't do.'

Emerson chuckled. 'My darling girl, it is wonderful to hear you scolding me again. In case you have forgotten my real reason for arranging this rendezvous – '

'Now, Emerson, stop that. Or rather – please postpone what you are doing until after we have arrived at a solution to our difficulty, for I can't think while you are . . .'

After a further interval Emerson remarked breathlessly, 'You talk too much, Peabody, but it is a pleasure to stop your mouth in that particular fashion. What I was about to say, when your presence distracted me, was that I have yet to have it demonstrated to me that there is any need for escape. We haven't even begun to explore this remarkable place. The opportunities for scholarly research are endless!'

'I am sure I needn't tell you I share your enthusiasm, my dear. Yet I have seen a few ominous signs – '

'You are always seeing ominous signs,' Emerson grumbled.

'And you are in the habit of ignoring them when they conflict with what you want to do. Mr Forth may or may not have wanted to leave this place; the one indisputable fact is that he did not. I am not urging a precipitate departure; I only want to make certain that when we are ready to go, we will be permitted to do so. You don't want to spend the rest of your life here, I suppose? Even if they do make you a councillor and tutor to the royal children.'

'With no tobacco for my pipe and those swaddled females constantly hovering over us? Hardly.'

'It pleases you to be frivolous, Emerson. Another of the ominous – or, if you prefer, significant – signs I mentioned is the conflict between the two princes. You were quite right' – (I thought it time to apply a little flattery) – 'when you pointed out that political struggles of this sort are pretty much alike. "He who is not for me is against me" is a saying which I am sure applies just as forcibly here as in our part of the world. It can hardly be supposed that we will be allowed to remain neutral, and in a society like this one, political opposition is apt to take the form of violent attack.'

'It is a pleasure,' said Emerson, with several little demonstrations of that pleasure, 'to deal with a mind as quick and logical as yours, my dear Peabody. I admit the force of your argument. We should anticipate the worst in order to be prepared for it. Almost certainly there will be a party, or parties, who will not want us to leave. Therefore we will require allies who can supply us with the necessities for a desert journey.'

'You propose we offer to assist one of the princely candidates in return for his promise to help us get away?'

'Nothing quite so Machiavellian. I am already inclined towards our friend Tarek.'

'So am I. I grew quite fond of him while he was Kemit, and I don't like Nastasen's mouth.'

Emerson let out a roar of laughter, which I stifled promptly and efficiently. While he was trying to catch his breath I said

severely, 'Physiognomy is a science, Emerson, and I have always
been a keen student of it. So we throw our weight to Tarek?'

'Such as it is. I find it difficult to understand why we were
lured here – for we were, Peabody, I am convinced of that – or
why our presence is so important.'

'We must know more,' I agreed. 'Not from what people tell
us, but from our own observation. I have now made it clear
that my health is fully restored, so they can't use that as an
excuse to keep us confined.'

We discussed this matter a while longer, considering various
alternatives. Then I started to yawn, and Emerson said that if I
was bored, he had an idea that might relieve my ennui.

It did.

We were awakened rather late the following morning by
Mentarit pulling back the curtains Emerson had drawn around
the bed. Veiled though she was, she managed to convey interest
and curiosity by the very tilt of her head. Fortunately, the nights
being quite cool, we had ample covering, but still Emerson did
not like it and swore a good deal. After considerable thrashing
about under the covers he managed to get into his robe and
stalked off, still muttering, to his own chamber.

We had decided to try two methods of winning freedom from
the building and I put the first one into effect immediately,
picking at my breakfast and trying to look limp and depressed
– not an easy task, for I was as hungry as a lioness and had
never felt more alert. Mentarit observed my behaviour and asked
what was the matter.

'She fades and droops in this room,' Emerson answered. 'The
women of our country are accustomed to walk abroad freely,
to go wherever they wish.'

He had deliberately spoken English. The girl did not pretend
she had not understood; she pointed to the garden.

'That is not enough,' I said. 'I need to walk, exercise, go far.
Tell the prince.'

A brusque nod was the only response, but before long she left the room and I hoped she had gone to pass on my request. Emerson followed her through the curtain.

While he was gone I reclined on a bench or divan covered with soft cushions, to carry out my claim of weakness, and watched the servants. A new idea had come into my head.

In any society (save the Utopian inventions of imaginative writers), there are at least two classes: those who serve and those who are served. Human nature makes it inevitable that there should be conflict between these groups; the history of mankind holds innumerable examples of the horrors that may ensue when the downtrodden working class rises up in resentment of those who oppress them. Could we, I wondered, make use of this well-known social phenomenon? Could we, in short, foment a revolution?

The servants I had seen certainly appeared to have been trod upon. They might have been a different race from the rulers, being on the average four to six inches shorter, and far darker in colour. They wore only loincloths or lengths of coarse, un-bleached fabric wound about their waists. They might not be servants at all, but serfs or even slaves. The more I thought about it, the more convinced I became that slaves was probably the proper word. The utter silence in which they carried out their duties confirmed this theory; the poor things were not even free to chat among themselves, or sing a merry tune. A slave uprising! My spirit thrilled at the thought of leading a fight for freedom!

Acting upon my impulses has always been one of my charac-teristics. One of the women, a stocky individual whose waving hair showed a piebald blend of brown and grey, was on her knees sweeping under the bed. I stretched out my hand and touched her shoulder.

She reacted as violently as if I had struck her. Fortunately she hit her head on the bedframe and let out an involuntary yelp of pain, which enabled me to kneel down beside her and offer assistance. At least that was what I meant to do, but perhaps she misunderstood my gesture, for instead of responding she scuttled backwards on hands and knees like a scarab beetle.

My vision of myself as Joan of Arc, waving the banner of freedom, faded. If a mere touch could terrify these little people, they were not likely candidates for an army of liberation. I reminded myself to ask Ramses what the Meroitic word for 'freedom' was.

Emerson returned at that moment, and stood staring in surprise. 'What the devil are you doing, Peabody? Playing a local version of tag?'

I got to my feet. The woman snatched up her broom and resumed her sweeping, at some distance from me.

'I was merely attempting to establish communication with one of these unfortunate slaves, Emerson. It occurred to me – '

'You don't know that they are slaves,' Emerson interrupted, twisting his handsome features into an extraordinary grimace. 'Lie down, Peabody. You are weak and faint.'

'I am not . . .' Then I saw Mentarit had returned. 'Oh, yes. Thank you, Emerson.'

I resumed my position. Emerson sat down beside me, taking my hand in his. 'Do control your socialistic impulses, my dear,' he said in a low voice, and then, louder, 'Are you feeling better?'

'No. I need fresh air, freedom. . .' I let out a heartfelt groan.

'You are overdoing it, Peabody,' said Emerson, his lips barely moving. 'Take heart, my dear; I spoke with the guards, and they have assured me our messages will be delivered.'

When the midday meal was served I again forced myself to pick at my food, though by then I could have eaten everything on the table and fought Ramses for his share. Emerson put on a great show of concern, feeling my forehead and shaking his head sadly. 'You are no better, Peabody. Indeed, I think you are weaker.'

'Inanition has that effect,' I said, feeling sure Mentarit would not know the word.

Emerson grinned and sank his teeth into a chunk of bread dripping with honey.

We were still eating – Ramses and Emerson were, at any rate – when there was a commotion outside the door and the hangings were drawn aside. Evidently the rank of the individual governed the number of his attendants. Murtek – for it was he – rated one spearman, one archer, and no handmaiden. His sandals scraped along the floor as he hurried towards me, grinning from ear to ear and trying to bow as he walked.

'You wish to go out, Lady?'

'Why, yes,' I replied.

'You go, then.'

'What, now?' Emerson exclaimed.

'Now, anytime. Why you not say?'

'Curse it,' Emerson began. 'That is not – '

'Emerson,' I murmured.

'Oh, yes, to be sure. We thank you, noble one. We are ready.'

'Now?'

'Now,' Emerson said firmly.

'It is good. We go.'

There was a little delay, however, for I thought it prudent to assume my own clothing, including my belt with its invaluable accoutrements. When I emerged from my room the old man burst into cries of admiration. 'How beautiful is the lady! How beautiful her ornaments of shiny iron! How beautiful her foots and her leg in the boot! How beautiful her – '

I deemed it advisable to cut off the catalogue of my charms at this point, so I bowed and thanked him.

The corridor beyond our rooms was only wide enough for two to walk abreast. Murtek led the way, with Emerson and me following and Ramses bringing up the rear. This time, instead of barring the way, the guards lined up in two rows next to the exit. After we had passed through, one of the groups, consisting of three spearmen and the like number of archers, fell in behind us.

Emerson stopped. 'Why are they following, Murtek? We don't need them.'

'They honour you,' Murtek hastened to explain. 'All great ones of the Holy Mountain have guard. To be safe.'

'Hmph,' said Emerson. 'Well, tell them to keep their distance. Especially from Mrs Emerson.'

After passing through several rooms of considerable size and handsome decoration we emerged into a wide entrance hall with two rows of columns down its length. Straight ahead were the first doors we had seen, constructed of wood heavily bound with iron and wide enough to admit an elephant. Emerson marched straight towards them without breaking stride. Two of the guards dashed ahead and shoved the panels open.

The brilliance of sunlight dazzled my eyes, and for a moment I was blinded. When vision returned, I saw that we stood on a broad landing or terrace. There was no balustrade between the level space and the sharp drop below, only a row of life-sized statues in the ancient Egyptian style. Later I had the opportunity to identify some of them: the cat-headed goddess Bastet and her more ferocious counterpart Sekhmet, who wears a lion's head; Thoth, the god of wisdom and writing, in the form of a baboon; Isis, suckling the infant Horus; and others; but at that time I was more interested in what lay beyond the terrace. It was my first view of the City of the Holy Mountain. I was bitterly disappointed.

It was my own fault, or rather, that of my finely honed imagination. Unconsciously I had expected to see the fairy-tale city of the legends – white marble walls and domes of shining gold, lacy minarets and towers, majestic temples. What I saw instead was a valley shaped like an elongated and irregular ellipse. Rugged cliffs enclosed it, not like protecting hands but like taloned paws, with protruding spurs of rock forming the claws.

The building we had just left was situated on a steep hillside which had been cut into level terraces; as I had thought, it backed up against the cliff and extended into it. Trees and gardens filled the spaces below, with the flat roofs of other structures showing between them. To the right and left, as far as the eye could see, the terraced slopes were similarly occupied. Some of the buildings appeared to be (comparatively) modest in size, others were as large and sprawling as our own house. My attention was caught and held by one particular building that occupied a wide plateau

201

midway up the steep cliffside. It was impossible to make out the details of its construction, but its size proclaimed it a structure of some importance, possibly a temple.

But when I looked down at what lay immediately below me, on the valley floor, I saw what appeared to be a typical African village. A few of the houses were built of mud brick, with enclosed gardens, but the majority were rounded huts of reeds and sticks, like the Nubian tukhuls. The village occupied only a small part of the enclosed ellipse. A body of water surrounded by marshy areas filled the central section. The rest was laid out in fields and pastures. Every inch of land was in use; even the lower slopes had been terraced and planted.

'Oh, dear,' I said. 'It is not the fabled city of Zerzura, is it?'

Emerson shaded his eyes with his hand. 'Just so must large sections of ancient Meroë and Napata have appeared, Peabody. You don't suppose the working class lived in palaces, do you? What an astonishing place! You see how intensive is the cultivation; they may get two or three crops a year. Even so, I don't understand how they can feed themselves. They must trade for foodstuffs with other peoples farther west. And perhaps limit their population by means of – '

'One method or another,' I interrupted – for I preferred not to think of certain of those methods. 'Where does the water come from?'

'Deep springs or wells. I imagine the valley floor is considerably lower than the desert beyond. You'll find the same thing at Kharga and Siwa and the other northern oases, except, of course, for the surrounding cliffs. Not the healthiest of climates, Peabody; you observe that the huts of the humble are down below, while the homes of the upper classes are on the slopes, above the miasmatic air of the swamp.' He turned to Murtek, whose amiable countenance was set in a frown of concentration as he attempted to follow our conversation. 'Where is your house, Murtek?'

The old man extended his arm. 'There, honoured sir. You see its roof.'

He went on to point out other spots of interest. The dwellings of the two princes were widely separated; they were located on the slopes to our right and left, as were the dwellings of other nobles. 'And that?' Emerson asked, indicating the massive structure across the valley.

I had been right. The building was a temple – the house of the gods and those who served them, as Murtek put it. 'Will you go there?' he asked. 'Or stay in this place; here is air, a space to walk oneself in.'

There was no need for consultation on that point; having got so far, we were determined to go on. I was about to cast my vote for a visit to the temple when Murtek spoke again. 'To the house of the Prince Nastasen, to the house of the Prince Tarek, to the house of the Candace (the Meroitic title of the Queen)? All, all is free to you, honoured sir and madam. All good, all beautiful places where the honoured persons wish to go.'

'All good, all beautiful places,' Emerson repeated, fingering the cleft in his chin. 'Hmmm. But that is not a good, beautiful place, is it?'

He pointed to the village.

'No, no, it is not the place for the honoured persons,' Murtek exclaimed, visibly agitated. 'You do not go there.'

'I think we will, though,' said Emerson. 'Peabody?'

'Whatever you say, Emerson.'

I was not really sure why Emerson was so determined to visit the nastiest, least-interesting part of the city, but I knew – as Murtek apparently did not – that opposition was the surest way of strengthening my husband's resolve. Murtek did everything he could to dissuade him, to no avail. He lost a second argument when he tried to order litters for us, but when Emerson demanded the guards be dismissed, Murtek dug in his heels. That, no. That was forbidden. If any harm or offence came to the honoured guests, he would be held responsible.

Emerson gave in with a great show of disgust, but there was a gleam of satisfaction in his blue eyes. He had gained more than he had hoped – more than I had expected.

Stairs descended steeply to a landing from which other
stairways and paths led off, some to the other houses on the
hillside, some to the valley below. A broad roadway led, by
winding and elevated ways, towards the temple. Murtek made
one last attempt to persuade us to take this path, but when
Emerson refused he threw up his hands in despair and gave in.
Preceded and followed by our guards, we descended the stairs
to the valley floor.

The heat and humidity increased with every downward step,
and so did a strong unpleasant smell. Its main component was
that of rotting vegetation, but there were interesting undercurrents of cattle and human excrement and unwashed bodies
of various species. Seeing me wrinkle my nose, Murtek reached
into the breast of his robe and produced a little bundle of flowering herbs, which he presented to me with a bow. He pressed
another such bouquet to his own prominent nasal appendage,
but Emerson and Ramses refused the ones he offered them. Mine
certainly did very little to overcome the stench.

At the bottom of the stairs we found ourselves in what was
apparently the High Street of the village. The paths leading off
to right and left were as narrow and winding as animal trails,
paved with mud and puddles of stagnant water. The main
thoroughfare was wide enough for the three of us to walk
abreast, but I was glad I had changed into boots. The surface
squelched underfoot. It was comical to see Murtek mincing
along, holding his long skirts up with one hand and pressing
the nosegay to his face with the other.

'You see they live like rats,' he said around the flowers.

'Quite,' said Emerson. 'But where are they?'

There was not even a rat to be seen. Every window and door
was closed by shutters or hangings of woven grass.

'They work,' said Murtek, spitting out a leaf from his
bouquet.

'All of them? The women and children too?'

'They work.'

'The women and children too, I expect,' said Emerson. 'But

not all in the fields, surely? Where are the craftsmen – the potters, the weavers, the wood carvers?'

But he knew the answer, and so did I. I had been in many such villages. The inhabitants spent most of the daylight hours out of doors, and always the advent of strangers attracted a crowd of the curious. Either these people were abnormally timid, or they had been ordered to stay away from us. Perhaps the mere appearance of armed guards sent them scuttling into their huts. Every now and then there would be a flicker of movement at one of the darkened windows, where some inhabitant more daring than the rest risked heaven only knew what terrible punishment to snatch a glimpse of the strangers.

Finally the street opened out into a central space with a stone-rimmed well and a few palm trees. The houses around it were a little larger and better built than the ones we had passed; some had the appearance of shops. Woven mattings had been dropped to cover the entrances.

'We go back now,' said Murtek. 'All is like what you see. It is nothing.'

'We may as well, Peabody,' Emerson said. 'We have seen enough, I think.'

I was about to agree when the hangings before one of the shops lifted and a small form wriggled under it. It was no bigger than a year-old English infant, but when it scampered towards us, the dexterity of its movements informed me that it must be two or three years old. He, I should say, instead of it; there was no mistaking his gender, for his small brown body was unclothed except for a string of beads. His head had been shaved, leaving a single lock on the left side.

Murtek sucked in his breath. The child stopped. His finger went to his mouth. One of the spearmen stepped forward, lifting his weapon, and a woman burst out of the shop. Snatching up the child, she crouched and turned, shielding him with her body.

With a mighty crack Emerson's fist struck the would-be assassin square in the nose, sending him reeling back. I kicked the soldier in front of me in the shin, slid past him, and ran to stand before the mother and child. So great was my anger and agitation that my speech, I fear, was not entirely appropriate.

'Shoot if you must this old grey head,' I shouted. 'But touch this mother at your peril!'

'Very nice, Peabody,' said Emerson breathlessly. 'Though I have yet to see a grey hair on your head. I expect you pluck them out, eh?'

'Oh, Emerson,' I cried. 'Oh, curse it! Oh, good Gad... Murtek! What the devil do you mean by this?'

It was necessary for someone to take command, for Murtek had covered his eyes with his hands and the soldiers were milling around in a shocking display of military disorder. One of them bent over the fallen form of his comrade, whose face was drenched in blood; another waved his spear uncertainly at Emerson, who ignored him with magnificent aplomb.

Murtek peered out from between his fingers. 'You live,' he exclaimed.

'Yes, and mean to go on doing so,' said Emerson. 'Now, then, get along with you,' he added, pushing aside the spear that menaced him and giving the fellow a sharp shove.

Murtek rolled his eyes heavenward. By now I knew enough Meroitic to understand his comments, which consisted mainly of heartfelt prayers of gratitude towards various gods. It was clear that he had not been lying when he told us he had been made responsible for our safety. 'But who would have thought they would risk themselves for one of the rekkit?' he ended.

No one answered. Perhaps Murtek was rehearsing the explanation he would have to render to his superiors.

Impressed by Emerson's air of command, the soldiers straggled sheepishly back into line. The man Emerson had struck was back on his feet. He had suffered nothing more serious than a nosebleed.

Feeling a tug at my trousers, I turned to find the young mother clutching me around the knees. Ramses had taken the child from her; he was pulling at Ramses's nose, and the expression on my son's face compensated for a good many of the indignities he had inflicted on me.

'Cast the shadow of your protection(?) upon me, great lady,' the little woman gasped. 'Wrap me in the — of your garments(?).'

'Certainly, certainly,' I replied, trying to raise her to her feet. Murtek came tottering towards us.

The Great Pylon of the Temple.

'Come, honoured madam. Come quickly. You have done a thing not permitted, very dangerous – '

'Not until you give this woman your word she will be safe. I hold you responsible, Murtek. Be sure I will find out, by my magic, if anything happens to her.'

Murtek groaned. 'I think you would, honoured madam I will swear by Aminreh.'

He repeated the words to the woman. She glanced up; her face was streaked with tears, but the dawning light of hope that transformed it assured me that this was indeed a solemn oath. Still she did not rise, but showered innumerable kisses upon my dusty boots and tried to do the same to the sandals of Murtek. He jumped back as if she had been a leper – as, in social terms, she probably was. The strangest thing, though, was the way she behaved towards Emerson. She had knelt to me and kissed my boots; when Emerson approached, she flattened herself out like a doormat, face down in the dirt.

Emerson retreated, blushing furiously. 'I say, Peabody, this is cursed embarrassing. What the devil is wrong with her?'

I bent over the little woman but she refused to move until Emerson spoke to her. He was so flustered he had a hard time finding the proper words. 'Arise, honoured lady – er – woman – oh, curse it! Fear not. You are well. Er – the young male child is well. Oh, come along, Peabody, I can't stand this sort of thing.'

This last in English, of course. The woman must have understood something, for she hoisted herself to her knees. Covering her face as a sign of great respect, she addressed a brief speech to Emerson and, finally, indicated she was ready to retire

We had to detach the baby from the nose of Ramses, which made him yell lustily – the baby, I mean, not Ramses. The roars went on until they were muffled by the door hanging falling back into place.

Murtek was not inclined towards conversation during the return trip, and for some time we also were silent, as we considered the dramatic incident and its possible ramifications. Finally Ramses (it would, of course, be Ramses) spoke.

'Did you understand what she said to you, Papa?'

Emerson would like to have claimed he had, but he is at heart an honest man. 'Did she call me her friend?'

'That was one of the words she used,' said Ramses with insufferable assurance. 'The entire phrase was something like "friend of the rekkit." The word "rekkit" appears to be derived from the ancient Egyptian for "common people."'

'Hmmm, yes,' said Emerson. 'Like other words in the speech of the nobility. The little woman appeared to be speaking a different form of the language. I confess I could hardly understand her.'

'She and the servants we have seen are also different physically,' Ramses said. 'They might belong to another race.'

'They don't, though,' Emerson replied. Imprecision of speech always irritates him. 'That word is often misused, Ramses, even by scholars. However, there are subdivisions within races, and it may well be . . . Hi, Murtek.'

He poked the high priest, who was trotting along ahead of us muttering under his breath. Murtek jumped. 'Honoured sir?'

'Do your people mate with the rekkit?'

Murtek pursed up his lips as if about to spit. 'They are rats. People do not mate with rats.'

'Yet some of the women are not ugly,' said Emerson, giving the priest a man-to-man smirk.

Murtek brightened. 'Does the honoured sir wish the woman? I will fetch her – '

'No, no,' said Emerson, trying to conceal his disgust and giving me a sharp poke in the ribs to keep me quiet. 'I want no woman except the honoured madam.'

Murtek's face fell. Shoulders bowed, he tottered on up the stairs.

'Well, really,' I exclaimed indignantly. 'Apparently your interference would have been condoned, even approved, if you had wanted the woman for a concubine! To think that old reprobate would offer her to you like a pet cat! And in front of me, too.'

'Monogamy is not universal, Peabody,' said Emerson, taking my arm as we began to ascend the steps. 'And I believe that in many societies women welcome additional wives, for companionship and help with domestic duties.'

'That would not be my attitude, Emerson.'

'I am not surprised to hear that, Peabody.' Emerson sobered. 'It appears you were right, though; the rekkit are little better than slaves. They may have been the original inhabitants of this oasis; the present ruling class is descended from Egyptian and Meroitic emigrants, and marriage between the two groups is forbidden, or at least discouraged. I don't doubt that there has been a certain amount of interbreeding, however.'

'Men being what they are, I don't doubt it either,' I said sharply.

'Peabody, you know I never have and never will – '

'Present company excepted, of course,' I conceded.

Murtek took leave of us with the forlorn air of one bidding a final farewell to a dying friend – or a dying man bidding a final farewell to his friends. He had aged ten years since we set out; two of the guards had to lift him into his litter.

'Do you suppose we have really endangered him by our actions?' I asked, as we preceded the remaining members of the escort towards our rooms.

Emerson replied with another question. 'Do you really care?'

'Well, yes, rather. He is a pleasant old gentleman, and one can hardly blame him for failing to rise above the mistaken standards of his society.'

'You should rather be concerned with whether we endangered ourselves.'

'I suppose we did, didn't we?'

'We didn't do ourselves any good,' said Emerson calmly.

'We had no choice in the matter,' remarked Ramses in his most dignified manner. 'There was nothing else we could have done.'

'Quite right, my son.' Emerson clapped him on the back. 'That being the case, we can only wait and see what consequences ensue. I have no doubt Murtek will report our adventure; he knows that if he doesn't, one of the guards will.'

Mentarit pounced on me, clucking and shaking her head, and insisted I change my clothing, especially my boots, which were encrusted with various noxious substances. I made no objection, since I was all in a glow from excitement, exertion, and the horrid hot climate of the village. I was trying to mend a rent in my trousers – an exasperating task, for though I always carry needle and thread, I have absolutely no skill in sewing – when Ramses came in from the garden. Cradled in his arms was a huge brindled cat.

I stuck myself in the thumb. 'Where on earth . . .' I began.

'It came over the wall,' said Ramses, an expression of almost normal childish pleasure on his face. 'It might be the sister or brother of the cat Bastet, don't you think, Mama?'

The creature did bear a resemblance to Ramses's pet, who had adopted us during an earlier expedition to Egypt. But though this feline had the same tawny coat as Bastet, it was at least twice her size – and Bastet is not a small animal.

'Would you like to hold it, Mama?' Ramses offered me the cat. I appreciated his willingness to share his pleasure, but decided to decline. Though the cat blinked its huge golden eyes at me, I noticed its claws were out.

Ramses folded his legs and sat down, murmuring to the cat, which seemed to enjoy the attention. 'Curious,' I said, watching them with a smile. 'We saw no cats in the village, did we?'

'It is likely that they enjoy superior status, as they did in ancient times,' replied Ramses, tickling the cat under its chin. A rasping purr accompanied Ramses's next words. 'This one is wearing a collar.'

And indeed it was – a collar of finely woven straw or reeds. I had not observed it until the cat lifted its head, for its fur was extremely thick and plushy.

Ramses amused himself with the cat for some time – if 'amuse' is the right word. It was uncanny to watch them, heads together, exchanging murmurs and purrs and, on the part of the cat, an occasional hoarse mew, for all the world like a reply to a question. Finally, however, it rolled off Ramses's lap, picked itself up and stalked away. Ramses followed it out into the garden.

Night seemed slow in coming. Such is often the case, I have observed, with something eagerly desired. But at last I reclined upon my couch and Emerson emerged from his room.

From his lordly stride, and the peremptory gesture that sent Mentarit giggling away, I got the distinct impression he was beginning to enjoy this procedure. My impression was further strengthened by certain actions on his part, which admittedly lent a new and piquant interest to the proceedings.

Sometime later we got to talking about assassination.

'Highly unlikely,' Emerson declared, still in his masterful mood.

'I disagree. Anyone could climb that garden wall. I could do it myself.'

'You would tumble into the waiting arms of several guards, Peabody.'

'How do you know? Have you seen them?'

'No, but I have heard them. I assumed they would be there, for the garden is, as you suggested, a vulnerable point. Listening carefully, I could hear an occasional rattle of weaponry or a murmured comment. As for the windows, a man might squeeze through, but not without making a noise; they are too narrow and too high.'

'Ah,' I said. 'So you have considered the possibility too.'

Emerson stirred restlessly. 'What has put you in such a morbid frame of mind tonight, Peabody?'

'Can you ask?'

'I just did,' Emerson retorted. 'And please don't mention dire forebodings or feelings of incipient disaster. Here – what are you doing?'

'Listening to the voice of your heart,' I replied. 'It is a trifle quick, I think.'

'I wouldn't be at all surprised,' said Emerson. 'How is yours?' Sometime later, however, Emerson announced his intention of retiring to his own room. 'Do you mind, Peabody? That wretched girl keeps flitting back and forth across the doorway. I can't concentrate on . . . on what I was doing.'

I thought he had concentrated quite nicely, but I did not argue with him. He would not admit it, but he felt the same sense of incipient disaster that lay heavy on my heart. I was armed and ready; Ramses was neither – and twice before he had been lured from his bed by forces mysterious and unknown. So I bade Emerson an affectionate good night, and the last sounds I heard before slumber claimed me were his muted curses as he stumbled over a stool on his way to the door.

I would not like to claim that I am often awakened in the middle of the night by burglars, murderers, and other intruders. 'Often' would be an exaggeration. However, it has happened often enough to hone my senses so that my sleeping mind is almost as alert as its waking counterpart. There was, I believe, no sound at all on this occasion; but I burst from sleep, propelled by that trained sixth sense, to find a dark figure bending over me. No lamps burned; the faint glow of moonlight from the garden did not reach to my bedside. But I did not require light to realise it was not the handmaiden who stood there. As I stirred, trying to roll away and off the other side of the bed, a heavy hand clamped over my mouth and an arm like steel pinned my body to the mattress.

Assaulted
at Midnight!

I am not one of your weak, swooning females. I even know a few tricks of wrestling, thanks to assiduous study of ancient Egyptian reliefs and the assistance of my parlourmaid Rose, who amiably allows me to practise on her. Neither strength nor skill availed against this opponent. When I raised my knee in an unladylike but shrewd blow, he twisted lithely aside and then lowered his body onto mine so that every limb was pinioned.

It was a hard, lean body, banded with muscles like leather straps. I could feel it only too well through the thin linen gown that was my only covering, and my own muscles began to weaken.

Warm lips slid across my brow, down my cheek . . . to my ear. 'I come to help, not harm, Lady.' The whisper was hardly more than a warm, moist breath. 'Trust me.'

Well, I had very little choice, did I? He went on in Meroitic, speaking very slowly and distinctly. 'If you cry out it will mean my death. Hear me first. I put my life in your hands to prove my good (faith, intentions?).'

Indeed, the argument was persuasive. When he took his hand away I gulped a great breath of air. His body was tense and ready but he did not cover my mouth again. 'Who are you?' I whispered.

'You will not call the guards?'

'No. Unless . . . Are you alone?'

He caught my meaning at once. The weight that pressed me down lifted, but he kept his mouth close to my ear as he said softly, 'I am alone. Your man, your child are safe. They sleep.'

'Why are you here? Who are you?'

'I come to . . .' The word was unfamiliar to me, but his next sentence made its meaning clear. 'There is danger. You must (escape, get away?) from this place.'

'We need camels, water,' I began.

'They will be found.'

'When?'

'After . . .' He paused.

Aha, I thought; I rather suspected there would be an 'after.'

'What do you want from us?' I asked.

'Today you save two of my people. They die, they suffer. You help them to be – ?'

'I do not know that word.'

'To go, to come, to do what they wish.'

'Ah!' In my excitement I had spoken too loudly. His hand clapped over my mouth. When he took it away, I breathed, 'I understand. Yes, we will help. What can we do?'

'Wait. A messenger will come, carrying the – . Trust only the one who carries the – .'

'The *what?*'

'Ssssh!'

'I do not know that word! It is important,' I added – an understatement if ever I made one.

His breath came quick and uneven. After an interval he said in English, 'Book.'

'*Book?*'

'Book!' The exasperation in the muted whisper sounded so like Emerson I almost smiled. 'Book. English book.'

'Oh. Which –'

'I go.' He spoke in Meroitic.

'Wait! I have questions, many questions –'

'They will be answered. I go. The guards change(?) at the turning of the night.'

'What is your name? How can I find you?'

'No one can find me. I live only because no one knows my name.' He rose lithely to his feet, featureless as a carved column in the darkness. Then he bent to my ear again, and there was a hint of what might have been laughter in his voice when he whispered, 'They call me the Friend of the Rekkit.'

'B – H – !' said Emerson.

I did not remonstrate, though Ramses sat cross-legged at our feet, his ears pricked like those of the huge cat that overflowed his lap. Emerson's outrage was so vast that the effort to contain it in a whisper made him quiver like a teakettle on the boil. To exasperate him further would have been dangerous to his health.

'First I find myself dropped into a plot that might have been concocted by your favourite author Rider Haggard,' Emerson went on in the same hoarse whisper. 'Now I must contend with another character out of fiction – or, what is worse, English fairy tales. Robin Hood! Defending the poor against the oppression of the nobles – '

'I don't know what you are complaining about,' I replied. 'That is exactly what you did yesterday, and now we understand what the little woman meant. No wonder she was awed; she must have taken you for the valiant and mysterious defender of her people. You see what that implies, don't you, Emerson? No one knows who he is, or even what he looks like. It is a very romantic – '

'Rrrrr,' growled Emerson. (The cat flattened its ears and growled back at him.) 'Why did you wait until this morning to tell me this, Peabody? Why didn't you come to me at once?'

Here, of course, was the true cause of his discontent. Emerson knows better, but he continues to cling to the forlorn hope that I will turn into one of those swooning females who unfortunately typify our society, and fling myself squealing at him whenever anything happens. He really would not care for it, but like all men he clings to his illusions.

'Because, my dear, the guard changed at midnight,' I replied.

'Midnight? There is no such – '

'I translate freely. Whatever time he meant, it was imminent, and his haste to depart suggested that the replacements were not sympathetic to him. I did not want to alert possible spies by doing anything out of the ordinary.'

'But you got out of bed and went looking for Amenit – Mentarit – whichever cursed female it was. . .'

'My getting out of bed, for one reason or another, was not out of the ordinary. I could hardly help finding Mentarit – for it was she – since I fell over her on my way to the – er. She was sleeping so soundly that she did not even stir.'

'Drugged,' Emerson muttered.

'She must have been. When I say I fell over her, I mean that I literally fell on top of her. She woke at the usual time, though, and seems quite normal.'

Emerson fingered his chin thoughtfully. Ramses fingered his. The cat rose with oiled grace and stood alert, tail twitching and eyes fixed on a bird that swung, singing, from a branch.

The air was still cool and sweet; the lilies in the pond folded modest petals about their hearts, awaiting the wooing of the sun. All was peace and beauty here. I thought of the foul streets of the village, the closed and shuttered houses, the almost palpable stench of fear.

'We cannot leave here without trying to help those poor people,' I whispered.

'Apparently we cannot leave unless we do' was my husband's sour reply. 'Try we may, but curse it, Peabody, I don't believe the poor devils have a chance.'

'Surely there are more of them than of the ruling class.'

'They are not allowed weapons,' said Ramses.

He had somehow acquired – I did not like to ask where or from whom – the knack of speaking without moving his lips, almost in the fashion of a ventriloquist.

'They must have tools,' I argued. 'Spades, ploughs – '

'One cannot beat a stone plough into a sword, Mama,' said Ramses. 'The ruling class has iron weapons. It is death for a commoner to possess iron in any form.'

'How do you know that?' I demanded.

'From the guards, I presume,' said Emerson. 'He has become something of a pet with them.'

'These people are very fond of children,' said Ramses, with a callous cynicism that chilled my blood. 'The captain (his name is Harsetef) laughed and patted me on the head when I asked to hold his big iron spear. He said he hoped his son would grow up to be a brave boy like me.'

During the course of the morning I watched the slaves closely, wondering if they had heard of our noble efforts on behalf of one of their number. If anything, they avoided me more assiduously; my smiles and attempts at conversation brought no response. Finally Mentarit said curiously, 'Why do you talk to the rekkit? They will not answer. They are like animals.'

I gave her a little lecture on the Rights of Man and the principles of democratic government. My command of her language was not great enough to do justice to those noble ideals, but I feared her incomprehension was due more to her prejudices than to my verbal inadequacies. So I gave up – for that time.

As the hours passed I became prey to increasing uneasiness. That our actions would be ignored or overlooked I could not believe; Mentarit's question had proved, if further proof was needed, how strange our behaviour must have seemed to these lordly aristocrats. I remembered the reaction of our neighbour Sir Harold Carrington and the members of his hunting party when Emerson charged into their midst and beat the dogs off the cornered fox. Not anger so much as utter disbelief had marked every face, and one of the men said something about a thrashing. (Needless to say, that suggestion was not repeated.) So must the nobles of this society have felt at seeing us interfere to protect creatures they regarded as mere animals.

We might not have improved our situation by interfering, but on the other hand, we might not have worsened it – for the simple reason that it could not be any worse. The real intentions of our captors were still unknown. We had been treated with courtesy and supplied with every comfort; but the Aztecs of ancient America, among others, pampered captives scheduled for sacrifice and no doubt would have been seriously annoyed if one of them had been carelessly destroyed before the ceremony. To the best of my knowledge, human sacrifice was not practised by the ancient Egyptians, but times had changed – quite a lot of time had changed, in fact.

Emerson's increasing restlessness showed he shared my uneasiness. After the midday meal he paced the floor for some time, muttering under his breath, before retiring to his sleeping chamber. I assumed he had sought relief with his journal, so I returned to mine – for of course we were all keeping copious notes on this remarkable adventure, and I felt confident that my feminine viewpoint would provide valuable insights. I was scribbling busily away when the sounds of an altercation sent me flying to the doorway. One of the voices (the most audible) was that of Emerson.

I found him in the antechamber, expostulating with the guards. Their great spears barred the doorway like a cross of iron, and their faces remained averted even when Emerson shook his fist under each nose in turn.

'Come away, Emerson,' I begged, seizing him by the arm. 'Don't lower your dignity by screaming. They are only obeying orders.'

'Curse it,' said Emerson; but the force of my argument prevailed, and he allowed me to lead him away. 'I was not screaming, Peabody,' he added, mopping his perspiring brow.

'The word was ill-chosen, Emerson. What were you trying to do?'

'Why, go out, of course. I don't understand why we have had no official reaction to our unorthodox activities in the village. Murtek's consternation made it obvious that we must have committed a gross social error, if nothing worse. I cannot believe it will be passed over without so much as a reprimand. The suspense is preying on my mind. Better a confrontation, even of a physical nature, than this uncertainty.'

'I would much prefer uncertainty to a physical confrontation, my dear. These people are not so unsophisticated as to be unaware of the effect of delay on characters such as ours. They may take several days to respond.'

'They are already responding,' Emerson said grimly. 'The guards refused even to answer me when I demanded they take a message to Murtek. And look here' – his gesture took in the reception room and the garden beyond – 'they have all disappeared. Not a soul around. Not even the handmaiden.'

He was quite correct. Absorbed in my writing, I had not observed the servants leave. We were alone.

It is difficult to defend oneself against the unknown, but we did what we could. Emerson had already changed into his civilised garments and I followed suit, buckling the belt around my waist and placing my parasol conveniently at hand. At my insistence Emerson put my little pistol and a box of ammunition in his coat pocket. He dislikes firearms – and indeed manages quite well without them – but on this occasion he did not argue, and the grim look on his face assured me that in the final extremity I could count on him to use the last bullet as I would myself.

In addition to my useful parasol, I had my knife and a pair of scissors. Not a great armament with which to combat an entire city; but it was comforting to realise that express rifles or even Gatling guns would have been little more use, with only two of us to wield them.

So we sat waiting as the shadows lengthened and the blue dusk crept in. I occupied the time by bringing my journal up to date. I had just reached the line 'only two of us' when a sudden recollection made me drop my pen. 'Where the devil is Ramses?' I asked.

'Language, Peabody, language,' said Emerson, grinning. 'He is in the garden with the cat.'

'Well, get him in here at once. We must stand together.'

Ramses, sans cat, came into the room. 'I am here, Mama. But I do not believe – '

'Never mind what you believe. Go and change into your suit.'

'There is not time,' said Ramses calmly.

'What do you – '

'Peabody.' Emerson held up his hand. 'Listen.'

Ramses had heard them first, of course. The murmur of sound quickly grew into a full-fledged . . . chorus? They were singing, certainly, and the twang and tootle of musical instruments accompanied the voices. Before I could decide whether this was a good omen or the reverse, the curtains were drawn aside and the musicians trotted in, singing or wailing at the tops of their voices and strumming enthusiastically. They were followed by a band of officials – I recognised two who had attended the banquet – and three women. I stared at the latter with unabashed curiosity, for they were the first females I had seen who were neither handmaidens nor slaves.

I was given no time to study them, for the whole group advanced upon us, waving various objects. I took them to be weapons of assault and reached for my belt. A flame wavered and brightened, followed by others. Mentarit – one of the handmaidens, at any rate – was gliding around the room lighting the lamps. In their glow I saw that the faces of the newcomers were friendly and smiling and that they held not weapons but combs, brushes, pots and vases, and piles of linen.

The women gathered around me; the men surrounded Ramses and Emerson. 'Now see here,' Emerson said indignantly.

'I believe they only want us to tidy up, Emerson,' I said. One of the women had uncorked a pot and thrust it under my nose; it smelled powerfully of some aromatic herb. Another displayed a filmy linen robe.

'That is precisely what I am objecting – ' A sneeze interrupted the speech; I could not see my husband, for he was surrounded, but I deduced he too had been offered a sniff at the sweet-scented oil. Realising the futility of a struggle, he allowed himself to be led away, but I could hear him long after I lost sight of him.

The women escorted me to the bath, where several of the slaves awaited us. One of them was a young man; when busy hands began to pluck at my garments, preparatory to removing them, I objected, but it was not until Mentarit joined us and translated that the women understood. With giggles and tolerant smiles they dismissed the youth. I needed no translation to comprehend their attitude. To them he was not a man at all, only an animal.

Yet their faces and forms indicated that Emerson had been right when he spoke of interbreeding between the two peoples. They were handsome enough, but so would the rekkit have been with proper food and a good deal of washing. Their linen robes and their ornaments were of the same style, but not the same quality, as the ones they had brought for me; instead of gold they had bedecked themselves with copper bracelets and strings of beads. I deduced that they were of the lower nobility, perhaps personal attendants to the women of the princely ranks. Certainly they were skilled at their job. They doused me and dried me and rubbed me with fragrant oils; one of them wove my hair into an elaborate coiffure of braids and waves, fastening it in place with gold-headed pins.

I have seldom been so distracted. Part of my mind was taking it all in, making detailed notes about the toilette. Another part wondered whether this elaborate ceremony might be the prelude to another, far less comfortable; and a third speculated on how poor Emerson was taking it, for I did not doubt he and Ramses were undergoing similar attentions.

When the ladies started draping me in the filmy white robe I waved them back. They watched with bemused smiles while I located my combinations and put them on. The effect was a trifle odd, I suppose, but I absolutely refused to appear in public wearing only sheer linen that showed everything underneath.

When I was ready, complete with a dainty little golden diadem and bracelets, necklaces, and armlets of heavy gold, sandals were strapped upon my feet. The soles were of leather, but the upper portion consisted only of narrow bands encrusted with the same blue and red-brown stones that covered the jewellery. I had dire forebodings about my ability to walk in the cursed things, and indeed, when they led me back into the reception chamber I had to shuffle to keep from tripping.

Emerson and Ramses were waiting. Ramses looked little different, except for the richness of his ornaments, which were, like mine, of heavy gold. But Emerson! I bitterly regretted that he had not allowed me to bring along a photographic device – but even that would not have captured the full effect of barbaric splendour, the rich glow of gold, the gleam of lapis and turquoise against his skin, which had been oiled till it shone like burnished bronze. His expression suited the costume, for it was that of a warrior prince – dark brows lowering, lips set in a lordly sneer. I risked a quick look at his lower extremities. They were a trifle paler than his arms and breast, but not nearly as white as they had been. Those hours baring his shins to the sun had borne fruit.

'I can't walk in these cursed things, Peabody,' he said, observing the direction of my gaze. He referred to his sandals, which appeared to be of beaten gold with curled-up toes.

'But you look superb, Emerson.'

'Hmph. Well, so do you, Peabody, though I prefer that garment you are, I am happy to observe, wearing under your robe.'

'Please, Emerson,' I said, blushing.

The difficulty about the sandals was soon removed by the appearance of a number of curtained litters, complete with stalwart bearers. I expected Emerson to balk at this, which of course he did; but his remark, as he stood staring at the dark-skinned, heavily muscled men, came straight from his noble heart. 'Bred for this,' he murmured. 'Bred like cattle. Curse it, Peabody. . .'

'Say no more, Emerson. I am with you heart and soul. But this is not the time to object.'

Emerson climbed awkwardly into one of the litters. Ramses hopped nimbly into another, followed by one of the attendants. I had one of the ladies with me, which was deuced annoying because in her effort to display great respect she refused to sit down, and she kept falling from her knees into my lap. I observed, from peeping between the curtains, that the bearers' legs were moving in perfect unison; still, it was not the most comfortable means of transportation I have ever experienced.

As I had expected, we were being borne along the elevated roadway that led from the quarter of the nobles towards the temple. Darkness was almost complete; stars lay pinned like diamond ornaments upon the bosom of the night. A few lights showed from the fine houses on the hillsides above; but the village looked as if a thick black veil had been dropped over it. Curls of mist crossed it like gauzy scarves on a velvet wrap.

I placed my fingers on my wrist and noted, without surprise, that my pulse was a trifle quick. Never mind, I thought; a rapid heartbeat will send the blood rushing more strongly through my veins. We had been treated with great honour and respect, but that was no guarantee that we would survive the night. Again I found myself remembering the ancient Aztecs of America. I shifted position slightly, for the point of my knife was pricking my skin. I had seized the opportunity of secreting it upon my person when I assumed my combinations.

As we went on I resisted my companion's timid attempts to pull me back into seemly seclusion; from the litter ahead of mine I could see Emerson's head protruding through the curtains. The moon had lifted over the cliffs; it was not yet at the full, but in that cold, dry air its light was strong enough to cast a silvery patina over the scene, and it was one no scholar could resist. Moonlight over ancient Thebes! Not the mighty ruins that survive, but the hundred-gated city in its proud prime, with its palaces and monuments untouched by time. A pyloned gateway glided past; a row of Hathor-headed columns formed the portico to some great mansion. Now, on the right, came a broad staircase with couchant sphinxes lining the balustrades;

above it towered walls carved with monumental figures. A brighter, ruddier glow brightened the road ahead. I craned my neck to see better, but the litters ahead of mine obscured my view until we were almost upon it: twin pylons soaring high into the heavens, their painted facades lit by flaring torches. Without breaking stride the bearers trotted through them into a court filled with columns like the Hypostyle Hall of Karnak.

At that point my attendant's remonstrations reached the point of hysteria, and since we passed dangerously close to some of the columns I reluctantly withdrew my head. When I next ventured to peek out I realised that the moonlight had disappeared. We were deep in the heart of the mountain, and as we moved on through room after room and passage after passage, I marvelled at the magnitude of the achievement. What multitudes of slaves, what countless centuries had been necessary to achieve such a mighty work?

At last the procession halted and the bearers lowered the litters to the ground. I managed to scramble out, though my trailing draperies got in the way.

Compared to some of the others I had seen, this room was fairly small. Woven hangings covered the walls; a stone-cut bench heaped with cushions ran along one side. The bearers picked up the litters and trotted out the way they had come. The women pounced on me and began straightening my skirts and poking the pins more securely into my hair, like lady's maids preparing their mistress for a state occasion.

I pushed them away and went to Emerson, who stood with one hand on Ramses's shoulder. He held out the other to me. 'Your little hand is frozen, my dear,' he remarked poetically.

'The air is chill.'

'Hmmm, yes. I wonder if – ' He broke off as a brazen booming sound reverberated through the room. The chatter and laughter stopped. Our attendants formed into ranks, some before, some behind us. The hangings at one end of the room were lifted by invisible hands. Another great stroke of brass sounded, and the procession started forwards.

'We're for it now, whatever it may be,' Emerson remarked cheerfully. 'I only hope these cursed sandals don't trip me up.'

I squeezed his hand.

The corridor we entered was broad but short, no longer than ten or twelve feet. At its farther end were other hangings, of such fine linen that the light shone through them, bringing out the rich patterns of embroidery that adorned them. They parted as we approached. Emerson tripped, but caught himself and went on. 'Good Gad,' I heard him mutter.

They were my sentiments exactly. We were in the innermost sanctuary of the temple – a vast, high chamber of noble dimensions. Columns divided the area into three aisles; down the widest, central aisle we marched in solemn silence, staring in wonderment at what lay ahead.

Strange as the sight was, it was not completely unfamiliar, for the temple was laid out on the same plan as those in Egypt. After passing through the pyloned gateway and columned courtyard, we were now in the sanctuary – the abode of the gods to whom the temple was dedicated. Quite often there were three of them, constituting a divine family – Osiris and Isis and their son Horus; or Amon, his consort Mut, and their son Khonsu. There were three statues in the niches at the end of this sanctuary, but they were not one of the usual triads. On the left was the seated form of a woman crowned with curving horns and holding a naked infant to her breast – Isis, suckling the young Horus. The statue must have been quite old, for the features of the divine mother were delicately carved, with none of the crudeness typical of Meroitic or Late Egyptian work.

The right-hand niche contained another familiar form, the rigid, mummiform shape of Osiris, ruler of the Westerners (i.e., the dead) whose death and resurrection offered hope of immortality to his worshippers. But the third member of the group, who occupied the central position of greatest importance, had no place in that divine family. It stood a good twenty feet high. Its tall, twin-plumed crown and the sceptre it held in its raised hand were of gold gleaming with enamel and precious stones.

'By heaven, it's our old friend Amon-Re,' said Emerson, as coolly as if he were studying a statue he had dug up from a four-thousand-year-old grave. 'Or Aminreh, as they call him here. Not in his usual form, but showing the attributes of Min, who is the one with the enormous – '

'Quite,' I replied. 'Oh, Emerson – I am not at all comfortable about this. I believe we are about to be sacrificed. Sun worshippers have a habit of sacrificing people, and Amon – '

'Don't be absurd, Peabody. Those trashy novels you read are weakening your brain.'

So vast were the dimensions of the temple that it required this length of time to reach the space before the high altar – for an altar was there, ominously stained with dark streaks. The procession stopped; our attendants retreated, fading into the ranks of the priests who filled both of the side aisles.

I had just observed the chairs that stood on either side of the altar when two men entered and took possession of them. One was Tarek, the other his brother. I tried to catch Tarek's eye, but he stared stonily ahead. Nastasen was scowling; he looked like a sulky child.

A long silence followed. Emerson began to fidget; he dislikes formal ceremonies of any kind, and he was itching to break ranks and have a closer look at the carvings on the walls and the altar. As for me, I found enough of interest in the scene to prevent me from growing impatient. None of the divine statues from ancient Egypt had survived in their original condition; these were all brightly painted, and certain elements, such as the beard on the chin of Amon and the crook and flail held by Osiris, were separate pieces of wood or precious metal. Now that my eyes had adjusted, I saw the wall behind the statues was not blank, as I had supposed, but pierced by several doorways. The niche in which Amon stood was deeper and darker than the other two. As I stared, narrowing my eyes, I seemed to see a hint of movement there.

At last the distant sound of music broke the silence. The shrill piping of flutes mingled with the mournful mooing of oboes;

the ripple of harp strings was punctuated by the soft throbbing of drums. From an entrance at the back of the sanctuary the musicians entered, followed by priests robed in pure white, their shaven skulls shining in the lamplight. Murtek and Pesaker walked side by side, and although Pesaker's stride was longer and firmer, the older man managed to keep pace with him, though he had to break into a trot every few steps to do so. A veritable cloud of white draperies followed – the handmaidens, whirling in a solemn dance. I tried to count them, but I kept losing track as they circled and crossed in complex patterns. Their movements were dizzying; it was not until they stopped before the altar in a final whirl of fabric that I realised the pattern of the dance had circled around one individual, which now seated itself upon a low stool. Like the others, it was swathed entirely in white, but these draperies glittered with threads of gold.

I have described the ceremony that followed in a scholarly article (whose publication, I regret to say, must be delayed for reasons that will become apparent as I proceed), so I will not bore the lay reader with details. In some ways (unfortunately including the sacrifice of a pair of poor geese) it was reminiscent of what little we knew of similar ceremonies in the ancient world. Emerson gripped Ramses tightly when the geese were brought in, but I give the lad credit; he saw the futility of protesting. However, if he had stared at me as he stared at Pesaker, who wielded the sacrificial knife with obvious relish, I would have hired extra guards.

Following the sacrifice a group of priests trotted out with a huge linen sheet, elaborately embroidered, which they proceeded to drape over the stony shoulders of Amon. I did not see how they managed it, for they worked from behind the statue; one had to postulate scaffolding or ladders. When they came back into view they were leading a woman garbed more richly than any female I had yet seen, in a gown of sheer pleated linen, and crowned like a queen. Pesaker advanced to meet her and escorted her to the front of the statue, where she proceeded to embrace the feet and certain other parts of it, and to make a number of gestures whose import was only too plain but which it is not necessary to describe. Pesaker then took her hand and led her behind the statue, and she was seen no more.

Amon having received his due, it was the turn of Osiris and Isis. The veiled figure before the altar rose, lifting her hands. I had not recognised the implements they held; hearing the sounds that came forth as they were gently shaken, I knew they were sistra, the curious rattle-like instruments sacred to the goddess Hathor. Beads of crystal and bronze strung on wires produced a soft, musical murmur, like water flowing over stone. She shook them at Osiris, singing as she did so, then did the same before the statue of Isis; flowers were heaped at the feet of both statues by the handmaidens, and then she returned to her chair.

How, you may ask, do I know that the veiled form was female? Despite the muffling veils I could see that she was slight and graceful, and when she spoke, as she eventually did, her voice left no doubt as to her sex.

In fact, we first heard her voice when she addressed the god in song. It was a high, clear voice, and would have been quite pretty, I thought, if it were properly trained. The quavering ululations that passed for song here did not do it justice, but Ramses appeared quite struck by it; I saw him lean forwards, his face intent.

The priests scampered up the ladder again and removed Amon's robe; they folded it carefully, like housemaids folding a sheet. Pesaker made a final, almost perfunctory gesture of respect towards the statue . . . and then, with a suddenness that made me start, he whirled around and pointed at us.

I could not make out what he said, but from his impassioned tones and the expression on his face I got the distinct impression that he was not suggesting that we be raised to the rank of royal councillors. My hand stole to the breast of my robe.

'Calm yourself, Peabody,' hissed Emerson out of the corner of his mouth. 'There is no danger. Trust me.'

If I had trusted the Nubian Robin Hood, I could hardly do less for my husband. My hand dropped to my side.

When Pesaker had finished, Nastasen rose, as if to comment further; but before he could speak, the high, sweet, and now fairly shrill voice of the mysterious veiled lady was heard. She spoke for some time, waving her arms like graceful white wings. When she finished, there was no rebuttal. Biting his lip in obvious vexation Pesaker bowed, and the whole group began to file out.

'Well!' I exclaimed, turning to Emerson. 'We are still honoured guests, it seems. I really expected Pesaker to demand we be put to death.'

'Quite the contrary. He invited us to come and stay here in the sacred temple area.'

'Yes,' said Ramses eagerly. 'And she – Mama, did you hear – '

'Certainly, Ramses, my hearing is perfectly good. But I confess I did not understand all she said.'

Our attendants, chattering among themselves, began leading us to the exit. Scuffling carefully along in the detested sandals, Emerson replied, 'The language of religious ritual often preserves archaic forms. The survival of Coptic, which has not been spoken for hundreds of years, in the Egyptian Christian Church – curse it!'

He was not referring to the Church (at least not on that occasion) but to his sandal, which had come off. 'But Mama,' said Ramses, fairly prancing with excitement. 'She – '

'Ah, yes,' I said. The litter bearers were waiting, grumbling, Emerson climbed into his. 'She-Who-Must-Be-Obeyed – as this mysterious lady was. Veiled all in white lest her incredible beauty arouse the passions of all who behold her – '

Emerson's head popped out between the curtains of his litter. He was scowling horribly. 'You are speaking of a figment of some cursed writer's imagination, Peabody. Get in your litter.'

'But Papa!' Ramses's voice rose to a near shriek. 'She – '

'Do as your papa told you, Ramses,' I ordered, and took my place in the litter.

The return journey seemed to last longer than the trip to the temple, perhaps because I was so impatient to discuss the remarkable events of the evening with Emerson. We might even snatch a few moments alone; for surely Mentarit (or Amenit, as the case might be) would have duties to perform for her mistress before returning to us.

However, this expectation was doomed to disappointment. After delivering us to our rooms, the litter bearers departed. Not so our attendants. Emerson, who had removed his sandals and was carrying them in his hand, turned to the hovering group and bade them a pointed 'Good night.' They replied with smiles and nods, and continued to hover.

'Curse it,' said Emerson. 'Why don't they go away?' He gestured forcibly at the door.

The gesture was misinterpreted. One of the men took the sandals from Emerson's hand; two others darted at him and began removing his ornaments.

'They are preparing you for bed, I think,' I called, as Emerson retreated like a cornered lion harassed by snapping jackals. 'It is a sign of respect, Emerson.'

'Respect be – ' said Emerson, backing through the doorway into his room, followed closely by his attentive servants.

I resigned myself to receive similar attentions from the ladies. As their hands moved deftly and deferentially to divest me of my ceremonial attire, loosen my hair, and wrap me in the softest of linen robes, I told myself that one must adjust gracefully to different customs, however painful the experience may be. When they tucked me into bed I was reminded of the rituals of medieval days, when the newly married couple was escorted to the nuptial couch by hordes of well-wishers – many of them intoxicated and all of them making rude jokes. The ladies were not intoxicated, I believe, but they giggled a great deal; and when one of them

Elizabeth Peters

indicated the door to Emerson's room, with a roll of her eyes and a series of extremely graphic gestures, they let out little screams and giggled again.

There was no sound from behind that door; the curtains remained closed. The ladies settled down by my couch and stared expectantly at me.

It had all been rather amusing, but something had to be done; my poor Emerson would never come out while they were present. I raised myself up and called to the white-veiled figure that sat in its accustomed place by the wall. 'Mentarit. Tell them to go away.'

It broke their hearts to obey, but obey they did. Mentarit left with them. After a moment the curtain quivered and was drawn aside just enough to allow Emerson's head to emerge. His eyes moved on a slow, suspicious survey of the entire room; then, pausing only to extinguish the one remaining lamp, he came to my side.

'How did you get rid of them, Peabody?'

'I asked Mentarit to send them away. She is also one who must be obeyed, it seems. How did you – '

'I sent them away myself,' said Emerson with an evil chuckle.

'They are a nuisance, I agree, but I believe they are a sign of our improved status. It's astonishing, isn't it? I thought we would be punished, or at least reprimanded for interfering with the discipline of the rekkit; instead we are even more respected.'

'Or feared,' said Emerson. 'Though that seems unlikely. Fascinating ceremony, wasn't it?'

'Yes, indeed, I believe it is safe to assume this was one of the religious rituals performed at set intervals to honour the gods. We were privileged to be able to observe it.'

'Privileged in more than one way,' Emerson replied thoughtfully. 'Professionally it was a remarkable experience, but even more remarkable, in my opinion, is the fact that we were invited to attend.'

'Oh, I imagine there were sinister undercurrents of which we were unaware,' I said cheerfully. 'Perhaps the High Priest of Amon hoped by this means to get his hands on us and subject us to imprisonment and hideous tortures. Or perhaps the High Priestess of Isis had similar designs on our humble persons. Who was that other female, the richly dressed individual who made such – such unladylike advances to the statue of Amon?'

'Obviously she represented the god's concubine,' Emerson said. 'I couldn't quite make out her title, though Pesaker addressed her by it several times.' He took me in his arms and kissed the top of my head.

'High Priestess of Amon?' I tilted my head back. Emerson's lips moved to my temple.

'It didn't sound like it. The other lady, the one with all the swaddling, was certainly the High Priestess of Isis. Both may be king's daughters, which raises the question of how much real political power, as opposed to religious rank, they actually have. I mean to do a paper on that subject one day. . .'

'I have already begun a paper on that subject,' I murmured.

'Mama! Papa!'

It was not a cry for help from the adjoining room. It was a penetrating whisper from only too close at hand.

Every muscle in Emerson's body convulsed. Every muscle in mine cracked painfully as his arms contracted like bands of steel. I let out a gasp of protest.

'I beg your pardon, Peabody,' said Emerson, relaxing his grip but not his teeth. I could feel most of them, clenched and grinding, against my cheek.

I was unable to reply. Emerson patted my back and rolled over. 'Ramses,' he said very softly. 'Where are you?'

'Under the bed. I am very sorry, Mama and Papa, but you would not listen to me before and it is absolutely imperative that you – '

The bedsprings (straps of woven leather) creaked as Emerson lifted himself and propped his chin on his hand. 'I have never given you a sound thrashing, Ramses, have I?'

'No, Papa. Should you feel my present behaviour merits such punishment, I would accept it without resentment. I would never have stooped to such a trick had I not felt – '

233

'Be quiet until I give you leave to speak.'

Ramses obeyed; but in the silence that followed I could hear him breathing fast. He sounded as if he were on the verge of choking and I sincerely wished he would.

'Peabody,' said Emerson.

'Yes, my dear?'

'Remind me, when we return to Cairo, to have a word with the headmaster of the Academy for Young Gentlemen.'

'I will go with you, Emerson.' Now that the first shock had passed I was beginning to see the humour of the situation. (I am known for my sense of humour; my ability to make little jokes has got me and my friends through several tight spots.) 'So long as he is here, however, shall we let him stay awhile? He may be able to contribute something to our evaluation of the ceremony.'

'He may as well stay,' Emerson remarked gloomily. 'Conversation is the only activity in which I am able to engage at the moment. Very well, Ramses. You presumably overheard our discussion about the priestesses.'

'Yes, Papa. But – '

'It was the Priestesss of Isis who decided that we should remain in our present quarters instead of moving to the temple area. The High Priest of Amon, who suggested the latter course, was visibly displeased, but he didn't argue the matter. Now can we conclude that he wished to get us into the hands of the priests, and that she countermanded the order because she felt we would be safer here?'

'Pa – ' said the voice under the bed.

'The reverse might be argued, Emerson,' I said. 'We would be more closely protected in the temple. And perhaps closer to the tunnel through which we must escape.'

'Mama – '

'We agree, however, do we not, that two different, opposing factions are in contention for control of our humble selves?'

'At least two. Even if we assume that the High Priestess of Isis and Pesaker favour different princes, don't forget my visitor. He must represent a third party – that of the people.'

'Not necessarily,' Emerson argued. 'The theory of government by the people is alien to a culture such as this. The best the rekkit can hope for is a king sympathetic to their needs.'

'Democratic government may be an alien concept, but the seizure of power by an adventurer is not.'

'True. The next time you are visited by Robert of Locksley, you might ask him what his intentions are. I think we might have a little chat with the Priestess of Isis. That is a suitable task for you, Peabody; it would be only courteous to pay your respects. She may have been hinting at just such a visit when she said – '

'"From Greenland's icy mountains!"' Ramses's whisper was as forcible as a shout. '"From India's coral strand!"'

'I beg your pardon?' said Emerson.

The words tumbled out. 'She did not say it, Papa, Mama, she sang it. The hymn. When she sang to the god. Mixed in with the other words. "Hail Amon-Re great progenitor from Greenland's icy mountains, It is thou who wakens the child in the womb from India's coral strand." Mama, Papa – *she sang it in English.*'

'Another Pair of Confounded Young Lovers!'

O ur response to Ramses's announcement was – quite without malicious intent – the most deflating we could have made. I stifled my laughter against Emerson's broad shoulder, and he said with kindly tolerance, 'Did she, my boy? Well, that is not surprising; the priestesses are all of noble birth, and as we know, many of them learned a bit of English from Forth. She may have intended a delicate compliment to her god by singing the hymn of another faith. Or even . . . I say, Peabody! Could it have been meant as a delicate compliment to us – a sign that she means us well?'

'I don't believe for a moment that she sang anything of the kind,' I replied. 'Ramses's imagination has run away with him. One could find any tune one wanted in the weird ululations of this music.'

'I assure you, Mama – '

'Oh, I am sure you thought you heard it, Ramses. Hang it all,' I added in mounting irritation – for Emerson's amusement had improved his mood and resulted in certain surreptitious gestures that belied his earlier fears – 'your papa and I have been amazingly tolerant of your outrageous behaviour. Off to bed with you this instant.'

From under the couch came a faint grinding sound. Ramses was trying to grit his teeth – one of the rather touching ways in which he strove to emulate his sire. He made no other objection, however, and his retreat was as silent as his approach had been. Only when the faint rustle of the hangings indicated that he had passed into the next room did Emerson continue with what he had been doing.

Our attendants reappeared the following morning, to Emerson's extreme annoyance. As soon as we had finished breakfast he declared his intention of paying a few social calls, first on Murtek and then, if it was permitted, on the princes.

If he had hoped to elude his attendants, the trick did not work. The gentlemen of the bedchamber were close on his heels. He did not return, so I concluded he had been permitted to leave the building, and I determined to do the same.

When I suggested I might call on the High Priestess, the shocked reactions of my ladies-in-waiting made it clear that I had committed a social error by even suggesting such a thing. The Priestess did not entertain visitors or leave her chambers except to participate in religious ceremonies. I felt very sorry for the poor creature; even Moslem women had greater freedom, for they could walk in their gardens and go out if properly veiled and attended.

'Is it the same for all the noble women?' I asked. 'Are they also prisoners?'

They hastened to assure me that, first, the Priestess was not a prisoner and, second, that priestesses were subject to different rules. Other women came and went as they pleased. And where did they go? I asked. Oh – to the temple, to one another's houses, to wait on the queen and the royal children. . .

That gave me my opening. I announced that I would also attend Her Majesty, to whom they had referred by her ancient title of Candace. 'In my country,' I added, 'all visitors pay their respects [literally, go and bow down] to our Queen. It would be rude [literally, bad conduct] not to do it.'

After some discussion, the ladies agreed I had struck on an excellent idea. It turned out to be a much more complicated procedure than I had anticipated; every step had to be argued and discussed. Should someone be sent ahead to announce our coming? (Yes, she should.) What should I wear? (We were unanimous on that point; I was determined to go armed and accoutred, and the ladies seemed to think Her Majesty would like to see my peculiar clothing.) How should we go? (A compromise was finally reached; the ladies took the litters, I walked.) Should Ramses accompany us?

Ramses was nowhere to be found, which settled that question. The ladies seemed to think it was a game, something like hide and seek, and would have gone on looking for him all day if I had not announced my intention of proceeding without him. I was not concerned about his safety, since he could not get out of the house, and it had already occurred to me that the visit might go more smoothly without him. One never knew what he might say. So finally we set out. The sun was high and the temperature extremely warm, but I did not mind; it was such a pleasure to stride freely, breathing deeply and taking in the sights along the way. I fancy the litter bearers were pleased too, for they were obliged to match my pace, and although that pace was brisk it was a good deal less tiring than their usual trot.

The stone-paved causeway was in excellent condition. A group of the little dark people was engaged in making repairs on one section; they knelt at the sight of the guards, and remained in that position until after we had passed. I caught glimpses of others working in the gardens along the way. Parts of the hillside were beautifully terraced and landscaped, but others had been given up to weeds and brambles, among which fragments of the broken walls stood up like rotting teeth. I wondered whether the ruins were signs of a past civil war or of declining population and resources. Some decline was inevitable; it was a wonder this curious culture had survived as long as it had. The days of its isolation were numbered, I thought with a curious sense of regret. Sooner or later it would be discovered, not by solitary wanderers like ourselves and Willoughby Forth, but by the advancing tide of civilisation armed with weapons against which the spears and bows of the guardsmen could not avail. And then what would be its fate?

The residence of the Candace adjoined the temple on the western side; it was the impressive building I had noticed the night before and was, in fact, the royal palace. Owing to the uncertainty regarding the succession, Her Majesty was at present the only occupant, except for the usual clutter of concubines, servants, attendants, and hangers-on. I had learned from my ladies that she was the mother of Prince Nastasen, Tarek's mother having died when he was a child.

After the usual tedious ceremonies of welcome, I was escorted through a series of courtyards and entrance halls to a magnificently decorated reception room, where the queen awaited me; and I am sorry to admit that the sight of her – and her ladies-in-waiting – was such a shock that I forgot my manners and stood gaping rudely.

Her Majesty had dressed in her finest to do me honour. On her head was a cunning little cap surmounted by a bejewelled falcon whose wings curved down towards her cheeks. She wore heavy necklaces and gold bracelets; braided tassels adorned her gown, which was of the sheerest linen gauze with wide, pleated sleeves. It showed a great deal of the lady, and there was a great deal to show. She was incredibly obese, almost as wide as she was tall. Rolls of fat circled her body; her round, smiling face appeared to rest directly on her shoulders with no sign of a neck. The face itself was quite pretty, with delicate features strongly resembling those of her son. Though her rounded cheeks dwarfed them, they suited her better than they did Nastasen, and her little dark eyes twinkled with amiable curiosity. Her ladies were also elegantly dressed and several of them were almost as large, though none equalled the imposing dimensions of the queen.

She did not rise to greet me – I imagine it would have taken two or more strong men to hoist her to her feet – but she welcomed me in a high, chirping voice and indicated a nest of cushions that had been placed at her side. Conquering my amazement with my customary savoir faire, I bowed politely and sat down.

Mentarit had not accompanied us, so I had to make do without an interpreter. This proved to be an asset rather than a handicap, for my blunders and peculiar accent delighted the ladies – Her Majesty most of all – and laughter broke the social ice. The laughter was good-natured; the queen chuckled just as merrily at her own attempts at an English greeting. I could not resist asking her age. After considerable discussion and counting on the fingers, of herself and her ladies, she informed me that she was thirty-two. I was incredulous at first, but upon reconsideration I realised she might have become a mother at the tender age of fourteen, as some unfortunate girls do in Egypt and Nubia even today. That would make Nastasen, and Tarek, who had been born in the same year, eighteen years of age – mere youths by English standards, but not by the standards of this society. They had probably 'cut off the sidelock of youth' before they reached their teens.

Her Majesty's innocent curiosity and her excessive hospitality foiled further attempts to question her. Vast amounts of food and drink were pressed upon me. Though I did my best, for fear of seeming discourteous, I could not begin to emulate the consumption of the queen and her ladies, and my lack of appetite distressed Her Majesty. Pinching my arm and shoulder, she shook her head sympathetically. What sort of — was my husband, that he starved me?

I could not think of an answer that would exonerate Emerson without insulting Her Majesty, so I flexed my muscles and smiled to show I enjoyed perfect health and happiness. This provided a useful distraction in turning the queen's attention to my attire. I had to display and explain the use of every object on my belt. The ladies of the court edged closer and all hung breathless on my words. My parasol was a great attraction; they understood its function, for they possessed sunshades of various kinds, but the mechanism fascinated them, and I had to raise and lower it a dozen times before they tired of it.

I considered giving it to the queen, but decided I dared not part with any potential weapon. Instead, when she indicated that the audience was over by presenting me with an elaborate gold bracelet from her own wrist (it slid up clear to my shoulder and was loose even then), I gave her my mending kit. It was no great loss to me, and it proved an enormous success. The slim shining needles, the fine, coloured threads had already been admired, and as I bowed myself out I saw one of the ladies squinting desperately at a needle as she tried to thread it, while the beaming queen forced the silver thimble onto the tip of her little finger.

The walk back relieved some of the distress resulting from my overindulgence in sweetmeats, but the sight of the table spread for the midday meal would not have stirred my appetite even had I not found a more attractive distraction in the presence of my husband. He scolded me for having been gone so long in such a cheerful voice that I realised he must have learned something of interest. He was in no hurry to enlighten me, however. Instead he held a chair for me and inquired how I had spent the morning.

'Eating,' I replied, repressing an unseemly sound of repletion. 'I don't think I can force down another morsel.'

'Nor I.' Emerson eyed the bowls of stew and fresh fruit with loathing. 'Murtek was an assiduous host. Was it the High Priestess who entertained you, Peabody?'

I explained. 'Emerson, you should see the queen,' I went on 'except for being prettier, she looks exactly like the Queen of Punt in the reliefs from Hatshepsut's temple! You remember her, a great rotund figure standing next to her tiny donkey?'

'One of the many indications that the ancient Egyptians had a sense of humour,' Emerson agreed with a grin. 'The royal ladies of Meroë were constructed on similar lines. So you don't believe Her Majesty is another Agrippina or Roxelana?'

His reference to the ambitious royal mothers of Rome and Turkey meant nothing to our attendants, but of course I understood what he was driving at. 'No. I managed to get in a few questions about her son and the succession; she replied simply that the god would decide, and I would swear she meant it. You know I am an excellent judge of character – '

'Hmph,' said Emerson.

'Furthermore, her extreme corpulence must make mental as well as physical exertion difficult. I wonder,' I went on, struck by a new idea, 'if that explains the size of the royal ladies of Meroë. Stuffing them like geese would be one way of keeping the women from interfering in affairs of state – and, I must confess, a more humanitarian method than assassination or imprisonment.'

Emerson studied me speculatively. Then he shook his head with a certain air of regret. 'You and I both know obese individuals who are as energetic as anyone. And some of the Meroitic reliefs depict the queens spearing captives with girlish vigour and enthusiasm.'

'True.' I forced myself to take a bite of stew. 'I doubt that adding a stone or two to my weight would change my character.'

'I don't have any doubts on the subject,' Emerson declared. 'And I hope you will not be tempted to try the experiment. Did you learn anything more of interest from the lady?'

'Not really. What about you?'

'I cannot even look at food,' Emerson announced, pushing his chair away from the table. 'If you have finished, Peabody, come walk in the garden with me.'

Thus far we had said nothing that was not already known to our attendants, but I could see he had matters of a private nature to discuss, and I tried to think of a tactful manner of escaping our entourage An invitation to partake of the food which we had scarcely touched distracted the men; when the ladies would have followed us, I sent them to look for Ramses. He had been missing the entire morning, so my maternal concern was not entirely feigned.

'Well?' I demanded, as we strolled by the pool. 'Did you see Tarek?'

'No. I was informed that both princes were busy with affairs of state. However, Murtek received me cordially and kept me the entire morning. I like the old fellow, Peabody; his is the mind of a true scholar. He was the only adult who had the intellectual curiosity to learn English from Forth, and question him about life in the outside world.'

'Murtek's English is not as good as Tarek's.'

'Murtek was handicapped by learning the language late in life. A youthful tongue twists itself around strange sounds more readily. Tarek's intelligence is certainly of a high order; according to Murtek he was Forth's prize pupil, going on with his studies after many of the other young people had lost interest and dropped away. Murtek did the same, and he spoke of Forth with what sounded like genuine affection. He possesses that rare and admirable quality of intellectual curiosity – love of knowledge for its own sake. You should have heard some of the questions he asked me, about our government, our history, even our literature. At one point I actually found myself trying to explain Hamlet's "too solid flesh" soliloquy.'

'Shakespeare?' I cried. 'Emerson! Do you realise what this means? Did Murtek show you the book?'

'No, why should he? He . . .' Emerson stopped and stared at me. 'Good Gad, Peabody, you must think me a complete idiot. I was so fascinated by encountering a mind of that calibre, the connection never occurred to me. Forth must have had a copy of Shakespeare with him; how else would Murtek know of it?'

'There are other possibilities, I suppose,' I admitted. 'The Bard has been in print, in various editions, for a good many years, and Mr Forth can't be the first outsider to have come here. This may have been a coincidence. Murtek did not actually show you the volume in question, and my nocturnal visitor told me to await a messenger.'

'Yes, but circumstances may have changed,' said Emerson, looking chagrined. 'I don't know how the devil Robin Hood managed to get in here the first time; he may not be able to do it again. I learned quite a lot more about the political situation from Murtek. He said nothing that could be viewed as treasonable – his attendants and mine were hanging on every word – but I feel sure he expected me to have sufficient intelligence to understand the implications. You know, of course, that in ancient Egypt the distinctions we make between politics and religion were meaningless. The king was a god and the priests were also state officials.'

'What has that to do with the situation here?'

'It has everything to do with it. Over the centuries, as was the case in Egypt, Amon took over the powers and attributes of other gods – Re, Atum, Min – the one with the enormous – '

'Yes, Emerson, I am familiar with the process. It is called syncretism.'

'Correct. Well, Osiris is the one god Amon could never quite manage to assimilate. The two are so completely different – Amon-Re the great and powerful king of the gods, remote and awe-inspiring; Osiris the suffering redeemer, who died as ordinary mortals do, and who lived again. His devoted wife Isis, the divine mother, also has great popular appeal.

'The other gods – Bes, Bastet, Apedemak, the old lion god of Cush – have their followers here, but only two cults really matter – that of Amon-Re, as represented by that sour-faced old villain Pesaker, and that of Osiris and Isis – whose high priest is our friend Murtek.'

'I see. That explains the strange configuration of the images we saw last night – Aminreh, Isis and Osiris, instead of one of the usual divine families.'

'It also explains the disagreement between Pesaker and the Priestess of Isis over our humble selves.' Emerson stretched, sending muscles rippling under his thin linen shirt. 'Flattering, isn't it, to be fought over by a pair of gods?'

'You mean by their mortal representatives, Pesaker and Murtek – for the High Priestess of Isis undoubtedly spoke for the latter. It is the same old humdrum power struggle, Emerson; do we assume that Amon supports one of the princes and Osiris the other?'

'I wish it were that simple. Both princes must want the support of Amon; it is his priests who determine the choice of the god. Both priests want a prince they can control. I expect there is a good deal of bargaining, bribery, blackmail, and intimidation going on behind the scenes. But that was not the most interesting information I gained today, Peabody. Murtek is a sly old fox – he would not have survived in this hotbed of intrigue if he were not – but as he walked me to the door he dropped a remark that went through me like a jolt of electric current.'

'Well?' I demanded.

The curtain of green vines behind us rustled. It was only a breeze, which caressed my cheeks gently, but Emerson took my hand and raised me to my feet. 'Let us stroll, Peabody.'

'It is unworthy of you to prolong the suspense this way, Emerson!'

'I don't want to be overheard.' Emerson put his arm around my waist and drew me closer. 'Peabody – there is another white man here!'

Emerson had to stifle my questions by drawing me behind a flowering shrub and placing his lips firmly on mine. It was a refreshing interlude in every sense, and when at last I was free to speak I was able to appreciate why he had acted as he had.

'You didn't pursue the matter – ask who the man was, and where he lives?' I whispered.

Emerson shook his head. 'Murtek went on talking, with scarcely a pause, and the cursed courtiers gathered around us. It was very craftily done, a casual reference to something the "other white man" had told him recently; even if it had been overheard, it might have been no more than a slip of the tongue.'

'Could it be Willoughby Forth after all? If they lied about his death – '

Emerson cut off my voice by squeezing the breath out of me. 'Keep calm, Peabody, I beg you. I believe that to be highly unlikely. You have forgotten another candidate.'

'Of course,' I breathed.

I had not forgotten poor Reggie Forthright, and I trust the Reader has not. We had discussed his sad fate on several occasions, but had been forced to trust in Fate, the Good Lord, and the military (not necessarily in that order) for his deliverance, since there was nothing we could do. Now the truth burst upon me like a blinding revelation and I wondered why the possibility had not occurred to me earlier.

'The wild men of the desert,' I said. 'The same "wild men" who succoured us, perhaps? But we saw no trace of him along the way.'

'He could have been off course by as little as fifty yards and we would have missed those traces. Inept as he was in all other ways, I would not be surprised to learn that he could not read a compass. Don't count on its being your friend, though, Peabody. Many people were reported killed or missing during the Mahdist rebellion.'

'No matter who it is, we must see him. I think you are right, Emerson; dear old Murtek meant us to know this, and to act upon it. But how?'

One of the ladies appeared at the entrance to the garden. Emerson directed such a hideous scowl at her that she squealed and retreated. 'Thus far fortune seems to favour the bold. In other words, I shall simply demand to be taken to "the other white man." We'll see what comes of it.'

The lady had come to tell us Ramses had been found – or rather, had returned of his own accord. He was seated at the table finishing off the food left from luncheon and feeding scraps to the cat. The cat was sleek and clean as ever; the boy was covered with dust and cobwebs. When I ordered him to go and wash, he protested that he had washed – his hands. Upon inspection they proved to be several degrees cleaner than the rest of him, so I did not insist.

'Where have you been?' I asked. 'We have been looking all over for you.'

Ramses stuffed a huge piece of bread in his mouth and waved a hand towards the back part of the building. I took this to mean that he had been engaged in his self-appointed project of copying the wall paintings and inscriptions. I gave him a stern lecture on table manners – for his had deteriorated markedly under the influence of our attendants – and on the rudeness of hiding from people who were searching for him.

Emerson had gone at once to the guards to put his plan into effect. He returned, scowling and muttering.

'They prevented you from leaving?' I asked.

'Not at all.' Emerson dropped heavily onto a chair. 'They professed not to understand what I was talking about.'

'Perhaps they did not, Emerson. The poor fellow may be a closely guarded prisoner.'

'Or a figment of my imagination,' Emerson muttered, fingering the cleft in his chin. 'No; no, confound it, the words were perfectly clear. Now what do we do?'

Ramses requested elucidation, and his father obliged. 'Most interesting,' said Ramses, fingering his own chin. 'It would seem to me that one might now request – or demand – information from someone higher in authority.'

'Precisely what I was about to suggest,' I said. 'One of the princes?'

'Both of them,' said Ramses.

So we put our heads together and composed a miniature Rosetta Stone, with the message in both English and Meroitic. Once we had settled the phraseology to our mutual satisfaction, I made a copy, and Emerson carried both of them to the guards.

'No difficulty about that, at any rate,' he said upon returning. 'I was assured they would be promptly delivered. Now all we can do is wait.'

'I am getting very tired of saying and doing that,' I declared. 'Waiting is not our style, Emerson. I yearn to act. A bold stroke, a coup d'état –'

'I suppose you could march into the village waving your parasol and call the rekkit to arms,' Emerson replied, reaching for his pipe.

'Sarcasm does not become you, Emerson. I am quite serious. There must be some way we can increase our prestige, inspire awe and terror. . . Emerson! Is there by chance an eclipse of the sun imminent?'

Emerson took his pipe out of his mouth and stared at me. 'How the devil should I know, Peabody? An almanac is not standard equipment on an African expedition.'

'I should have thought of it,' I said regretfully. 'From now on I will make certain I carry one. It would be so convenient – an eclipse, I mean.'

'So would the arrival of the Camel Corps with pennons flying,' remarked Emerson, upon whose sense of humour delay seemed to have a deleterious effect. 'Curse it, Peabody, astronomical effects don't occur so conveniently, and total eclipses of the sun are fairly uncommon. What put such a fool notion into your head?'

Twice during the afternoon I went to the anteroom to ask if there had been a message for us. I was assured that when such a thing arrived it would be promptly delivered. Emerson's calm, as he wrote busily in his journal, only increased my impatience, and I was pacing the floor, hands behind my back, when finally I heard the slap of sandals and ringing of weapons that betokened the approach of the guards – not one, but several, to judge by the sounds.

'At last!' I cried. 'The message!'

Emerson rose to his feet, his eyes narrowing. 'Not a single messenger, by the sound of it. Perhaps Tarek has come himself.'

The curtain was thrust aside by the blade of a spear and two soldiers entered, dragging a third person between them. A cruel shove sent the prisoner staggering forwards. Unable to break his fall because his hands were bound behind his back, he dropped to his knees and toppled forwards, collapsing at my feet.

The prisoner was, of course, Reggie Forthright. His suit was crumpled and faded, and he was now the possessor of a heavy beard. Except for paler skin, which spoke of a long period of close confinement, he appeared healthy enough; indeed, if anything, his face was rather full. Lack of exercise might be responsible, but again I was reminded of the hideous rites of the ancient Americans, who fattened their prisoners for sacrifice. Emerson rolled his eyes heavenward and sat down again. I knelt by the fallen man and . . . But a description of my actions would, I fear, be repetitious. Before long Reggie was seated and partaking of some wine to restore his strength.

Questions poured from my lips, only to be met by an equal flood of questions from Reggie. It was some time before we could attain a degree of calm that permitted coherent statements.

Reggie insisted that first I describe our journey and what had befallen us since. Emerson showed signs of increasing impatience as my narrative proceeded; after I had described our visit to the village, and the rescue of the woman and child, he cut me off. 'You are getting hoarse, Peabody. Let Mr Forthright tell us his story.'

Reggie admitted, in his engaging way, that he had promptly got lost. 'At least I must have done, Mrs Amelia, for I never saw the landmarks you described. I thought nothing of it at the time, for like the professor here I always doubted the accuracy of my poor uncle's map. But after hearing of your journey . . . It is unaccountable! I am not so stupid as to misread a compass.'

'Not so unaccountable, perhaps,' I said thoughtfully. 'Your copy of the map may have been in error.'

'I assure you,' Reggie began.

'Never mind that,' said Emerson. 'If you failed to find the first of the landmarks, why didn't you turn back?'

'Well, you see, we did find water on the fourth day out, at which time we still had ample supplies for the return trip. It was only an abandoned well, which required considerable clearing before it was usable; but it gave us more time, you see. We had none of the misadventures you experienced, the camels were healthy and the men cheerful and willing. I determined, therefore, to continue for another day or two. I felt I could leave no stone unturned.'

'Very admirable,' I said warmly. 'So when was it that you were attacked?'

Reggie shook his head. 'It is all a blur, Mrs Amelia. I was ill afterwards. . . They struck at dawn. I remember only being roused from sleep by shouts and groans, and rushing out of my tent to see my men in full flight. I can't blame them; they were armed only with knives, and the fiends who pursued them had great iron spears, and bows and arrows.'

'You had a rifle, I believe,' said Emerson, chewing on his pipe.

'Yes, and I managed to dispatch a few of the devils before they overwhelmed me,' said Reggie, a look of grim satisfaction hardening his affable face. 'I fought all the more fiercely when I realised they were bent on capturing rather than killing me. A quick death would have been preferable to slavery. But 'twas in vain. A blow on the head struck me down, and I must have been unconscious for days. I remember nothing of the journey here.'

'Nor what happened to your men?' Emerson asked.

Reggie shrugged. 'Some of them may have got away – only to die miserably of thirst, I suppose. But now it is your turn again, Mrs Amelia – how long have you been captives here? What plans have you made for escape? For knowing you and the professor, I cannot believe that you would accept imprisonment meekly.'

'You have a rather theatrical way of putting things, Mr Forthright,' said Emerson. 'This place is an archaeologist's dream; I would be reluctant to tear myself away before I had made a thorough study of the fascinating survivals of Meroitic culture. We have not been treated like prisoners, but like honoured guests. And then, you see there is the little matter of our primary reason for coming – to discover the fate of your uncle and his wife.'

'They are dead,' said Reggie quietly. 'God rest them.'

'How do you know?'

'He told me.' Reggie tried to control his voice, but anger and grief distorted his face. 'Laughing like the fiend he is as he described their lingering, painful deaths by torture. . .'

'Nastasen?' I cried.

'Who?' Reggie stared at me. 'No. It was your friend Kemit – who is known here as Prince Tarekenidal, and in whose dungeons I have been imprisoned all these long terrible weeks.'

The interruption of Reggie's story was not occasioned by his overwhelming emotions or by any literary trick of mine, but rather by the reappearance of the servants, who began preparing the evening meal. Emerson ordered them to find quarters for the newcomer and went along to interpret, for Reggie admitted he had learned very little of the language. Shortly afterwards one of the guards came in carrying a knapsack, which I recognised as Reggie's; I sent one of the servants to take it to him.

Ramses had gone with his father and Reggie, but the cat had declined to accompany them, preferring to curl up on a pile of cushions. I sat down beside it. It opened one golden eye and uttered a peremptory comment. I stroked its head. The feel of the sleek fur was soothing and helped calm my turbulent thoughts

I had always considered myself a good judge of character, but it appeared that I could not be right about both the characters in question. Either Reggie was a liar or Tarek was a villain of the deepest dye – and also a liar. But were these the only alternatives? Was another explanation possible?

Several occurred to me, in fact. Reggie had been ill, perhaps delirious. He might have imagined the whole thing, or mistaken one prince for the other. Like many ignorant white men he had difficulty distinguishing one 'native' from another, and the two men were superficially alike in appearance, especially in semidarkness. (It was a safe assumption that his cell was dark and dank; all of them are.)

Alternatively, Tarek may have deliberately deceived Reggie, for reasons that had yet to be determined.

I felt a great deal more cheerful after I had arrived at these theories.

In honour of our guest I decided to change my trousers for a robe. I had finished my bath and the ladies were drying me off when Emerson poked his head into the room. His scowl changed to a much more attractive expression when he saw what was going on.

'Send them away,' he said.

'But Emerson, they are – '

'I can see what they are doing.' He barked out an order that sent the ladies scuttling off, and picked up a fresh linen towel.

'Upon my word, Peabody,' he remarked, in the course of the activities that followed, 'you are becoming quite a sybarite. Will I have to supply you with obsequious slaves after we return to Kent?'

'I have no complaints about the service I am presently receiving,' I replied humorously.

'I should think not,' muttered Emerson. 'Why are we always getting into situations like this, Peabody? Why can't I conduct a simple archaeological excavation?'

'You cannot blame this situation on me, Emerson. And it is not at all like our other investigations.'

'It has some features in common with them,' Emerson argued. 'Your unfortunate habit of attracting members of the aristocracy for instance. Not just British aristocrats this time, but a whole extra set of nobility.'

The concomitant attentions he bestowed as he spoke made it impossible for me to resent the criticism. Good-humouredly I replied 'At least there are no young lovers this time, my dear.'

'I give you that,' said Emerson, giving me something else as well. 'It is a distinct improvement, Peabody, for which I am grateful. As I hope you are for this . . . and this . . .'

I expressed my appreciation in a proper fashion, but finally was forced to say reluctantly, 'My dear, I think I should get dressed now. We have a guest. You found proper quarters for him, I assume?'

'They suited me,' Emerson replied enigmatically. 'What did you make of his story?'

I assumed he referred to the startling revelation concerning Tarek and explained my theories.

'Hmph,' said Emerson, even more enigmatically. 'I would not be too forthcoming with Forthright if I were you, Peabody. Don't mention your midnight visitor or insist upon Tarek's virtues.'

The enigma was resolved. 'You never liked Reggie,' I said, allowing Emerson to wrap me in my robe and fasten my girdle.

'That has nothing to do with the case,' said Emerson. 'There are still a number of things he has not explained to my satisfaction.'

As it turned out, there were a number of things we had not explained to Reggie's satisfaction. When he joined us in the reception room the improvement in his appearance was considerable. The snowy robes set off his ruddy complexion and fiery hair, and his beard had been laundered till it shone like the setting sun. However a new constraint shadowed his frank face, and instead of resuming his narrative he chatted about the food and the objects on the table like a curious tourist. It occurred to me at last that the presence of the attendants might explain his reticence, so I dismissed them.

'Now you can speak freely,' I said. 'You were right to be careful; I believe we have become so accustomed to the servants we forget they are here.'

'Yes, I observed that,' said Reggie, avoiding my eyes. 'You seem quite at home here. Quite comfortable.'

Emerson, always sensitive to possible insult, caught the implication before I did. Dropping his carved horn spoon with a clatter, he snarled, 'What are you getting at, Forthright?'

'You wish me to speak candidly?' A flush warmed the young man's cheeks. 'I will do so; I have never learned the arts of trickery and deception. In the flush of relief at my release and the joy of seeing you alive and well, I forgot caution, but now I have had time to think things over, and I tell you frankly,

Professor, that there are a number of things you have not explained to my satisfaction. My map was faulty; yours was accurate. I was captured and beaten; you were rescued and nursed. I have spent the past weeks in a dank, dark cell while you have enjoyed these handsome rooms, with food and wine and splendid raiment, servants obeying your every command – '

'Say no more,' I exclaimed. 'I understand your doubts, Reggie. You suspect our motives. But, poor boy, you are wrong. I cannot account for the difference in the treatment we have received, but we would never betray a fellow Englishman or -woman. If your aunt and uncle still live, we will never leave this place without them.'

'I – I beg your pardon?' said Reggie, gaping.

'It is given,' I replied graciously.

'Just a moment,' said Emerson, grasping his hair with both hands and tugging at it. 'I believe I have lost the thread of the discussion. Am I to understand, Mr Forthright, that you believe your aunt and uncle have survived after all? We too were told they had died – though not in the grisly fashion you mentioned.'

'I don't believe they are alive,' said Reggie. 'I only meant to ask – to suggest . . . I don't know what I meant.'

'That often happens in the course of conversations with Mrs Emerson,' said my husband soothingly. 'Get a grip on yourself, Forthright, and try to use a little common sense. I see your difficulty, but you surely cannot believe we want to spend the rest of our lives lolling around this palace.'

'Then – then you do mean to escape?'

'We mean to leave, yes. Sooner or later, by one means or another. It may be,' Emerson said thoughtfully, 'that we have only to ask. We haven't tried that.'

Reggie shook his head. 'No one leaves the Holy Mountain. How do you suppose it has remained hidden all these years? We are not the first wanderers to stumble upon the city, or be captured by the patrols that guard the approaches to it. The penalty for attempted escape, by stranger or citizen, is death.'

'Ah.' Emerson pushed his chair back and bent a penetrating look upon the young man. 'You have learned more than you told us earlier.'

'Of course. We were interrupted, if you remember.'

'Then please continue, from the point where we were interrupted. If you have decided to trust us, that is.'

'I don't know what came over me,' Reggie muttered. 'I apologise. But if you knew what I have been through ...'

'We will take your sufferings as given,' said Emerson dryly. 'Go on.'

'Well, then. You must understand that we have fallen into the midst of a struggle for power...'

Most of what he told us was already known to us – the death of the king, the conflict between the two heirs to the throne. I would have said so, had not a peremptory gesture from Emerson forbidden speech; and indeed Reggie presented us with a new and quite different interpretation of those facts. 'Kemit, or Tarek, as I must call him, more or less admitted his brother is the legitimate heir. He referred to a rumour that his mother ... that his father was really ... that he is not ...'

'Ah, yes, the old illegitimacy rumour,' said Emerson. 'Very popular with European usurpers. Tarek admitted it was true?'

'Oh, not in so many words; in fact, he denounced it as a vile slander. He protested a bit too much, though. And if he were the true heir, why would he need help from strangers?'

'Was it your help he wanted?' Emerson asked. 'A peculiar way of winning a man's allegiance, shutting him up in ... a dank, dark cell, I believe you said?'

'The cell came about after I had refused,' Reggie said wryly. 'He wanted me to assassinate his brother. What else could I have said but no?'

'You could have said yes, and then warned Nastasen,' said Emerson. 'Forthright in name and forthright in manner, eh?'

'Why you?' I inquired. 'With so many methods of murder to choose from and so many loyal men about him – '

'Ah, but his brother has loyal supporters too. Assassination

Elizabeth Peters

is an old custom here, the nobles all employ food tasters and bodyguards. But they don't have firearms. I am a crack shot, and could pick Nastasen off at a distance.'

I was loath to abandon my favourable opinion of Tarek, but this story made terrible sense. 'What are we to do?' I murmured. 'It is impossible to know whom to trust.'

Reggie pulled his chair close to mine and spoke in a whisper. 'We must escape, and soon. The festival of the god is approaching. Tarek must kill his brother before then if he is to win the kingship, for the god will choose the rightful heir. If we do not get away, we will be faced with the horrible choice of killing or being killed.'

'Not much of a choice,' muttered Emerson. 'I doubt the assassin would enjoy a long life span. You are very well informed, Forthright, and Tarek is incredibly indiscreet. Did he tell you all this?'

The sun was sinking in the west; a mellow dusky light warmed the chamber. Reggie's lips parted in a smile. 'No. My informant was quite another person. Had it not been for her tender nursing, I would have died of my wounds. When we escape, she will go with us, for I will never love another.'

Emerson's fist came down on the table with a crash that made the crockery rattle. 'Damnation! I knew it! Another pair of confounded young lovers!'

After Emerson had calmed himself, Reggie went on with his story – and quite a touching tale it was. It seems that initially his treatment had been similar to ours. Waking, in a fresh, airy, sunlit chamber, he had found himself tended by one of the white-robed maidens, who, as I have said, acted as physicians in this society. Women are very susceptible to handsome, wounded young men; it was not long before the lady was prevailed upon to unveil, and, as Reggie expressed it (rather tritely, I thought), to see her was to love her. The absence of a common language is never a barrier to love and the handmaiden spoke some English – enough to warn him of his danger and enlighten him as to the desperate situation he faced. 'She risked her life in telling me,' Reggie whispered, tears suffusing his eyes. 'And she would have done more, but soon afterwards I had my final confrontation with the prince, and he ordered me thrown into the dungeon. Now that I am free – ' He broke off with a hiss of breath as a white-veiled form materialised in the shadows.

'Not your ladyfriend?' Emerson inquired, turning to inspect the girl curiously.

Reggie shook his head. 'Cursed if I know how you can tell,' Emerson said. 'Swaddled to the eyebrows as they all are.'

'The eyes of love can pierce the thickest veil, Emerson,' I remarked.

'I don't know about that, Peabody. I can think of at least one occasion when your eyes failed to pierce the mask I wore.'*

'I was too intent upon avoiding recognition myself,' I replied. 'You knew me, though, in spite of my own mask.'

'My dear Peabody, you are unmistakable.'

Reggie made agitated gestures for silence. 'Watch what you say in the presence of the handmaiden. Many of them understand English, and if they discovered my beloved's treachery – for so they would view it – it would mean her death. Not to mention ours!'

'Surely they would not betray a friend, a sister,' I whispered.

'You don't understand the effect of superstition on the minds of primitive people,' Reggie said – a glaring underestimation of our talents, which wrung a snort of disgust from Emerson. 'These girls have been raised from infancy to believe in their pagan gods and in their own status. They are virgins. . .'

He broke off, as Mentarit (I recognised her by her walk) approached to light the lamp. After she had withdrawn, Reggie went on, 'The handmaidens are all of noble birth; some are princesses of the royal house. After they have served a designated

Deeds of the Disturber

257

time, they are given in marriage to men selected by the king for that honour.'

'How appalling,' I exclaimed. 'Given in marriage, like prize cattle. . . They have no choice in the matter?'

'Naturally not,' said Emerson. 'If the right to the throne passes through the female line, as we surmised, the marriage of a princess becomes a matter of state. Hmmm. I wonder which –'

'Sssh!' Reggie leaned forwards, an anxious frown wrinkling his brow. 'You are about to venture onto dangerous ground, Professor. I will explain at another time; too many ears are listening.'

Indeed they were. The lamps had been lighted, preparations for the evening meal were under way, and our attendants had begun to take their places. Emerson took Ramses off to be washed.

'See if you can discover her name,' Reggie whispered, indicating Mentarit. 'A few of the girls are sympathetic to us.'

'I know her name. So far only two of them have waited upon us, and I have talked with both. That is Mentarit.'

A deep groan escaped the lips of the young man. 'I feared as much. In the name of heaven, Mrs Amelia, take care! Of all the handmaidens, she is the most dangerous.'

'Why?' His fear was infectious; my breath quickened.

'She didn't tell you who she is? But then she would take care to avoid the subject. She is one of the royal heiresses – and Tarek's sister.'

'When I Speak the Dead Hear and Obey!'

Emerson took a sip of beer and made a horrible face. 'If I had any inclination to remain here, beer for breakfast would change my mind. What I wouldn't give for a decent cup of tea!'

'You could have goat's milk,' I said, sipping mine.

'It tastes worse than the beer.'

Reggie had finished his beer. He held out his cup and one of the attendants rushed up to refill it. Though he had retired early the night before, he had been late joining us for the morning meal, and he was looking rather seedy. He refused my offer of medication, however, saying that he was only feeling the delayed effects of his imprisonment.

'Have some of this porridge stuff, Forthright,' Emerson said solicitously. 'It's not half bad if you pour a pint of honey over it. Some variety of dura, do you think, Peabody?'

Reggie pushed the bowl away with a grimace of distaste. 'I can't eat a mouthful. I wonder that you can.'

'We need to keep our strength up,' Emerson declared, spooning up the last of his porridge. 'Perhaps you ought to have a rest, Forthright. Mrs Emerson and I are going out for a while.'

Reggie looked up in alarm. 'Where are you going?'

'Oh – here and there, around and about. I would hate to miss any opportunity of studying this fascinating culture.'

'Your nonchalance astonishes me, Professor,' Reggie exclaimed. 'I don't think you fully realise the peril of your situation. A wrong word here, a thoughtless action there – '

'Your concern touches me,' said Emerson, patting his lips with the linen squares that had been (at my insistence) supplied us in lieu of serviettes. Such articles were unknown here, and it pleased me to think that I had contributed in some small measure to the development of civilisation in this backwards culture.

Reggie offered to go with us, but was easily dissuaded by Emerson, who flatly refused to entertain such a notion. Somewhat to my surprise Ramses also decided to remain behind. I assumed he was hoping to find his friend the cat, for he went into the garden as soon as he had finished eating.

The guards made no difficulty about our leaving the building, but we had to accept an escort. Emerson fussed about it until I reminded him they were only following orders. 'Furthermore,' I added, 'Reggie's story must inspire a certain degree of caution even if one assumes, as I do, that his view of the situation is unduly pessimistic.'

'Oh, bah,' said Emerson, thereby admitting the truth of my argument.

The soldiers took up their positions, two marching ahead of us, two bringing up the rear. Emerson set a brisk pace, bounding down the staircase like a mountain goat and turning immediately onto the causeway. I looked down at the village below; I fancied I could smell it, even from this distance. 'What are we going to do, Emerson? There has been no word from . . . you know who. If Reggie really can make arrangements for . . . you know what, shall we – er – you know?'

'I don't see how we can decide yet,' Emerson said. 'There are too many unknowns in that equation.'

'Then we ought to resolve them, Emerson.'

'Precisely what I am doing, Peabody.'

'Where are we going, then?'

Emerson slowed his pace and took my arm. 'You sound a trifle breathless, my dear; was I going too fast for you? We are going to look for Willie Forth's tomb.'

As we walked on, Emerson explained what he had learned from Murtek concerning the mortuary customs of this society. The tombs were all of the rock-cut variety, for with cultivable land so scarce it would have been impractical to build pyramids. 'It's a wonder these cliffs haven't collapsed,' Emerson said. 'They are honeycombed with tombs and temples and storerooms. The cemeteries are reserved for kings and nobles, of course.'

'What do the rekkit – '

'Don't ask, Peabody.'

'Oh.'

'There are several such cemeteries,' Emerson went on. 'A few generations ago a new one was begun on this side of the valley. Forth should be there, if he is anywhere. As a royal councillor he would rate a fairly handsome tomb. If we don't find it, we will have reason to question the veracity of our informants.'

'Very clever, Emerson,' I said approvingly. 'And while we are searching for the tomb in question, we can make observations about burial customs. I am glad I brought notebook and pencil.'

There was no difficulty in locating the entrance to the cemetery. It was marked by the monumental pyloned gateway I had noticed during our journey to the temple. The sloping sides and flat lintel had been carved with figures of the mortuary deities – Anubis, the jackal-headed god of cemeteries, Osiris, ruler of the dead, Ma'at, goddess of truth and justice, against whose feather symbol the heart of the deceased is weighed at the final judgment. The traditional conventions had been accurately, even slavishly, followed, but the crudeness of the carving indicated how much of the old artistic skill had been lost.

While we examined and discussed the reliefs, our escort stood watching us uneasily, but they did not interfere until we started up the stairs beyond the pylon. Then the young captain sprang forwards, barring the way. His speech was exceedingly agitated, but I caught the words 'forbidden,' and 'sacred,' repeated over and over. Emerson settled the matter by pushing him out of the way and going on. When I looked back I saw the four men were huddled together as if for protection, staring fearfully after us and making agitated gestures.

Despite the bright sunlight and sweltering heat the place had an air of brooding desolation. We met no one until we reached a stone-paved landing from which paths led out on either side, winding up and down and along the cliff.

Our booted feet thudding upon the stone of the stairs must have made the guardian priest doubt the evidence of his own ears. When he emerged, in stumbling haste, from the open doorway of the little shrine at the back of the platform, his eyes and mouth opened wide at the sight of us. Presumably he had been at his prayers, for his long white skirt was crumpled and dusty. His head had been shaved; sunlight striking off the stubble of grey hair made it glow like a saint's halo.

Emerson gave him no time to recover from his surprise. 'It is good that you are here,' he announced. 'We have come to pay our respects [lit. make offering] to our friend and countryman, the Royal Councillor Forth. Where is his tomb [lit. House of Eternity]?'

'Well done, my dear,' I remarked, as we followed the path the astonished religious person had indicated.

'If you take a man by surprise, Peabody, and behave with sufficient arrogance, he will generally do what you ask. But I expect that as soon as the fellow gets his wits back, he will rush off to ask for advice and assistance. We had best make haste.'

The path was wide, but on the left hand there was no parapet, only a sheer drop to a tumble of jagged rocks twenty feet below. On the right-hand side were the tombs, some on the same level as the path, some reached by flights of stairs. I had to fight the impression that I was looking at models or reconstructions, for although the plans were similar to many such tombs we had excavated in Egypt, I had never seen one in its original condition. Before each tomb the cliff had been cut back to form a shallow forecourt with a columned portico behind and a quaint miniature pyramid above. The white-plastered walls and painted reliefs shone bright in the sunlight. The doors leading into the rock-cut chambers of the tomb were closed with blocks of stone and flanked on either side by statues of the occupant. On each shady porch stood a large stela on which had been painted a portrait of the deceased, with his name and titles and the conventional offering formulas.

We hurried along, pausing at each tomb to read the hieroglyphic inscriptions on the stelae. 'Most of them seem to be high priests and councillors, and their families,' Emerson said, lingering to admire an attractive painting of the Last Judgment – Osiris enthroned, watching the weighing of the dead man's heart against the feather of justice. The deceased did not appear to be incapacitated by the absence of this organ; looking quite sprightly and dressed in his finest, he raised his hands in adoration to the god. His elegantly attired wife stood by his side. 'Curse it, Peabody,' Emerson went on, glaring at the blocked doorway of the tomb proper, 'I would give ten years of my life to get a look inside. What the devil, haven't these people enough gumption to rob tombs and leave them open for visitors?'

'Language, Emerson,' I said. 'I share your sentiments but I don't suppose tomb robbing is a very popular profession here. Where would a thief spend his ill-gotten gains? Oh, curse it, where is the cursed place? Here's another confounded Cushite, and his wife and four of his children.'

'Language, Peabody,' said Emerson. 'I think – ah! Look here!'

The tomb entrance was the last on that section of the path. In size and in the richness of the decoration it was at least the equal of the others we had seen.

'Yes,' Emerson murmured, tracing a line of hieroglyphs with his finger. 'Not the way I would have transliterated the name, but poor Forth's knowledge of the hieroglyphs was somewhat superficial. No doubt about it, though.'

'You think he composed his own funerary inscriptions?' I asked.

'I would have done. Oh, damnation – I hear someone coming. Hold them off, can you? I need more time here.'

The guardian priest had sought instructions and had returned with reinforcements – two of his fellows and a more impressive figure carrying a long gilded staff and wearing a leopard skin slung over his white robe. I stationed myself squarely in the middle of the path, arranged a smile on my face, and opened my parasol.

It was quite a large parasol. Without pushing rudely past it, and me, the delegation could not proceed. They stopped. I explained that we had come to honour our friend, expressed innocent surprise when I was told that no one was allowed near the tombs unless he had undergone the proper ritual purification, apologised for our inadvertent error, and asked for details of the ritual. The higher-ranking priest sputtered and brandished his staff, but that was all the action he took. He was still sputtering when Emerson joined me.

'Thank you, my dear,' he said. 'We may now retreat with honour.'

So we did. The priest followed us partway, wearing the same expression I have seen on the face of our former butler when he was required to escort some of our more unconventional visitors to the door.

'Well?' I demanded, as we descended the stairs. 'Did Mr Forth leave a message for us?'

Emerson stumbled, but caught himself. 'Upon my word, Peabody, you have the most remarkable imagination! How could he have managed that? The texts are as formularized as The Lord's Prayer; any deviation would be noted and questioned.'

'What kept you so long, then? I thought our purpose was to learn whether or not Mr Forth had a tomb in the necropolis. It appears he did, and its size and location prove that he had attained high rank. It does not rule out the possibility that he met a sticky end, however. If he fell into disfavour – '

'You asked a question some time ago,' said Emerson. 'Would you like to know the answer, or would you prefer to go on speculating indefinitely?'

Our escort fell into place, before and behind, as we began to retrace our steps. I thought they looked a little gloomy.

'What else could you have discovered, if the texts were only conventional mortuary formulae?' I demanded, a trifle nettled at his critical tone.

'In this society,' said Emerson, 'a man's wives, and sometimes his children, are buried in the same tomb. You noted that, I believe.'

'Yes; their titles and figures appear on the . . . Emerson! Do you mean – '

'She isn't there, Peabody. The only name is that of Forth himself.'

The sun was high and hot. From a persea tree on the hillside above, a small bird soared up, its feathers glittering bright as emeralds. A sand-coloured lizard, alarmed by our approach, slid over the edge of the parapet and disappeared. The rhythmic slap of the guards' sandals sounded like muffled drumbeats.

After a time Emerson remarked, 'You are uncharacteristically silent, Peabody. I hope that means you are considering all the possibilities before you make one of your dogmatic pronouncements.'

'I cannot imagine what you mean, Emerson,' I replied. 'I always weigh the facts dispassionately before reaching a conclusion. In this case we have not enough information about funerary customs to assert unequivocally that Mrs Forth must have been interred in the tomb of her husband. If our informant was correct, she passed on long before he did. She may have insisted upon Christian burial instead of succumbing, as I am sorry to see her husband did, to the influence of pagan ceremonial.'

Emerson gave me a suspicious look. 'Quite,' he said.

Despite the shade of my parasol (which Emerson irritably refused to share) I was bathed in perspiration by the time we reached our temporary abode. I was quite looking forwards to a bath and a cool drink, and the opportunity to discuss the conclusions I had reached with the others. However, there was a brief delay. Instead of dispersing, as they usually did, our guards formed up in a row. The leader, a handsome chap who appeared to be no more than twenty years old, barked out an order. With mechanical precision the quartet raised their spears and clashed them together, then flung them away. The weapons clattered and rang on the stone. The men dropped to their knees in a deep obeisance, then rose and began to march away, leaving their spears on the floor.

'What the devil,' I exclaimed, forgetting myself in my surprise.

Emerson stroked his chin. 'I wonder if this could be a Meroitic version of *"morituri vos salutamus."* Hi, there – halt! Come back here! *Abadamu,* curse it!'

His shout made the metal blades of the spears ring, and brought the marching men to a stop. None of them turned or answered, however. Emerson strode forwards. Taking the leader by the shoulder, he whirled him around. 'Why do you not obey?'

The young man swallowed convulsively. His face was dusky pale and his lips scarcely moved when he replied. 'O Father of Curses, we are dead men. The dead do not hear.'

It was the first time I had heard him address Emerson directly and I noted that the Meroitic words were a literal translation of the affectionate title by which Emerson was commonly known in Egypt. Tarek and his two lieutenants who had worked for us at Napata were the only ones who could have known of it; one of them must have mentioned it and the word had spread – together, I felt sure, with tales of the well-nigh supernatural awe in which my remarkable spouse was held by those who knew him.

'Damnation,' said Emerson. 'I should have anticipated this. . . You heard me, though,' he added in Meroitic.

The young man winced. 'The voice of the Father of Curses rolls like the thunder, and his hand is heavy as the hand of the god.'

'Good Gad, Emerson, what are we to do?' I exclaimed. 'We cannot let these poor fellows be punished on our account. Is it because they were unable to prevent us from visiting the cemetery?'

Emerson repeated the question in Meroitic. The young man nodded. 'We failed in our duty. The penalty is death. Now I will die the second death for hearing, for speaking. Will the Father of Curses take his hand from me so that I may die with my men?'

'I think you are hurting him, Emerson,' I said. 'His arm is turning blue.'

'If I let him go he will bolt,' Emerson said abstractedly. 'Discipline is certainly tight in these parts. Hmmm.'

The young officer stood passive in Emerson's grasp, his face as expressionless as that of the dead man he claimed to be. After a moment Emerson said, 'Stand back a bit, my dear Peabody.'

I did so, and as an additional precaution I clapped my hands over my ears.

'I am the Father of Curses,' Emerson bellowed, shaking the young man like a doll. 'When I speak the dead hear and obey! When I command, the gods tremble! The power of my voice troubles the heavens and makes the ground shake!'

He went on for some time in this vein. By the time he reached his peroration he had attracted quite an audience, a dozen or more soldiers, including several officers; a few of the attendants; and, unobtrusive as curious mice, some of the little servants. Ramses and Reggie came trotting in, and behind them was the white-robed form of the handmaiden – whichever one it was.

Emerson pretended not to notice them, but his voice rose to an even more penetrating pitch and his sparkling orbs betrayed his enjoyment. He is always at his best in the presence of a large audience.

'I forbid you to die!' he shouted. 'You are my men, you belong to the Father of Curses! Pick up your spears!' And, with a gesture as graceful as it was powerful, he sent the young officer staggering towards his fallen weapon.

I must say it was one of Emerson's most impressive performances. I felt an overpowering urge to rush off and pick up a spear myself.

One of the officers made a vague gesture of protest as the doomed men, looking a good deal more cheerful, hastened to obey. Quick as a cat, Emerson wheeled on him. 'The men of the Father of Curses are sacred! No man dares touch them.'

Turning, he offered me his arm. As we proceeded towards our apartments the audience melted away, leaving only Ramses and Reggie to greet us. 'Upon my word, Professor,' Reggie exclaimed, 'that was – that was certainly . . . Er – what was it all about?'

Emerson deigned to explain.

'It was a brilliant performance, my dear,' I said. 'And it has, I trust, gained us a few loyal adherents. Those men owe you their lives.'

'Don't count on it, Peabody. Old superstitions die hard. And it may backfire. Successful demagogues are not popular in tyrannical societies.' Emerson's frown cleared and he shrugged his broad shoulders. 'Ah, well, I had no choice in the matter. Now I want my bath. Where are those abominable attendants? Never around when you need them!'

After bathing and changing we sat down to an excellent meal and Emerson and I at least did it justice. I was forced to speak to Ramses about eating with his fingers and putting his elbows on the table. 'You are turning into a perfect little Cushite, Ramses,' I scolded. 'And your head is still bare as an egg. I told you not to let them continue shaving it.'

'They were quite insistent, Mama,' said Ramses.

'Then you must be more insistent. I won't have you going back to civilised society with your hair in that state.'

When the table had been cleared and the crumbs swept up, Reggie suggested we go into the garden. 'I must speak to Mentarit about Ramses's hair,' I said. 'I will not have . . . Where is she? I didn't see her leave.'

Reggie took my arm. 'That is what I wanted to tell you,' he

whispered. 'She has gone back to the temple. It will be Amenit who returns.'

'Mrs Emerson is quite capable of walking without your assistance, Forthright,' said Emerson, scowling. 'Hands off my wife, if you please.'

Reggie jumped away from me as if he had been stung, and we proceeded into the garden. As we walked along the pool, the vines along the far wall swayed violently. A face peered down at us. It was covered with tan fur.

Ramses went to greet the cat with one of his peculiar murmuring noises. It replied in kind, but instead of jumping down, it began pacing along the top of the wall. Ramses trailed it, eyes lifted and arms extended, like a miniature Romeo in pursuit of a furry, ambulatory Juliet.

'One of the temple cats – here?' Reggie exclaimed.

'How do you know it is a temple cat?' Emerson asked, as I simultaneously inquired, 'The temple of Bastet?'

As courtesy demanded, Reggie answered me first. 'Bastet, Isis, Mut – all these heathen goddesses are the same. Her cats are of a particular breed, larger than the common kind and held to be sacred.'

'She won't come down,' exclaimed Ramses, sounding as pettish as any ordinary child. 'Mama, can you – '

'No, I cannot,' I replied firmly. 'Cats are not susceptible to the sort of persuasion one uses on human beings, and what is more, they are eccentric individualists – '

'Who possess extremely keen hearing,' Emerson said. 'I believe we are about to have a visitor, Amelia.'

Moved by an indefinable instinct, we moved closer together. The cat vanished and Ramses came to stand beside me. When the visitor appeared, following an escort of archers and white-garbed maidens, Reggie let out an oath and retreated to the far side of the pool.

Tarek – for it was he – seated himself in the chair a servant hastily placed behind him. His broad golden armlets glistened in the sunlight as he gestured; other chairs were brought, for us and for the men who had accompanied him. One was Pesaker, the High Priest of Aminreh. He did not appear to be in a pleasant frame of mind.

Neither was Tarek. The eyes he fixed upon us lacked the kindly look they had always held before, and instead of uttering the formal greetings he burst into angry speech. 'What manner of people are you, that you lack courtesy and gratitude towards those who have rescued you? Have you no respect for our customs? You violate one of our strict laws; we show you mercy, we restore your friend to you. Now you have committed sacrilege. If one of our people had acted in such a way he would die!'

'But we are not of your people,' said Emerson calmly. 'If we have offended we did so in ignorance, and we deeply regret having done so. We will make whatever reparation you think proper.'

'It is true that you are ignorant barbarians,' Tarek said thoughtfully.

The corners of Emerson's mouth twitched. 'True,' he said, with equal gravity. 'It is the duty of the wise to educate the ignorant, not punish them. Is not that also true?'

Tarek considered the idea. Pesaker's face darkened. He may not have understood all that was said, but he could see the prince's mood had softened and he was not pleased. 'What do they say?' he barked. 'Do not listen to them. There is no excuse(?) for their crime. I order – '

Tarek turned on him. 'You dare to order me? You do not speak for the god here. I will decide the fate of these offenders.'

I have sometimes been accused of being precipitate and of acting upon impulse. Such was not the case now. I had carefully considered what I meant to do, and in fact Emerson himself had made a similar suggestion. (Though of course he claimed afterwards he never intended it to be taken seriously.)

'We are most grateful for Your Highness's kindness,' I said. 'And as my husband has said, we deeply regret any inadvertent rudeness. Perhaps the best thing would be for us to leave. We will need camels – a dozen or so should be sufficient – and an escort as far as the oasis.'

Emerson choked and muttered something. The word might have been 'incorrigible.'

Tarek leaned back in his chair and studied me unsmilingly. 'What, would you leave us? Perhaps what you say is true; we should teach, not punish you. You could also teach us, and win great honour and high position.'

'Yes, well, that is very good of you, but I am afraid we must be going.'

Emerson had enjoyed a hearty if muffled laugh during the conversation. Now he sobered and spoke slowly and emphatically. 'You know why we came, Tarek. Our friend is found, as you see. You tell me that the others we sought are with the gods. We have accomplished our task. It is time for us to return to our own place, our own country.'

The High Priest followed that speech, or part of it. (Was that why Emerson had used simple words and spoken slowly? I wondered.) Hands clenched on the arms of his chair, he burst out, 'No! It is forbidden! What, will you allow these strangers, these – , to defy the laws of – '

Tarek caught his eye, and he stopped.

'My friends,' said Tarek. 'For you are my friends; can my heart deny those whom I have loved, even when they love me not? If you must go, you will have your way, though I will mourn you as I would those who have gone to the god.'

'Somehow I don't like the sound of that,' murmured Emerson. Aloud he said, 'You will help us, then?'

Tarek nodded.

'When?' Emerson asked.

'Soon, my friends.'

'Tomorrow?' I asked.

'Oh, but such a journey cannot be arranged so quickly,' said Tarek, whose English had improved noticeably. 'A fitting escort, gifts . . . Ceremonies of honour and farewell.'

I didn't like the sound of *that*. 'Ceremonies,' I repeated.

'You wish to observe our customs,' said Tarek. 'Our strange, primitive ceremonies. That is your interest, is it not? That is one reason why you came. Yes. You will observe the greatest ceremony of all before you . . . depart. It is soon, very soon. And then, my friends . . . your departure.'

'Oh, dear,' I said. 'I fear I was sadly mistaken in our friend Tarek.'

'For one thing,' said Emerson, 'he speaks English much better than he led us to believe. A credit to his teacher, eh, Peabody?'

'Yes, although personally I found his style of speaking rather florid. He sounded exactly like – '

'How can you be so calm?' Reggie burst out. 'Didn't you understand the threat behind those suave words?'

'Why, I suppose they were meant to convey a threat,' said Emerson. He took out his pipe and gazed sadly at it. 'But what threat precisely? We have seen no indication that these people practice human sacrifice.'

'They do, though,' Reggie said, biting his lip. 'Tarek described in grisly detail . . .'

He broke off, shuddering. Ramses said interestedly, 'How is it done, Mr Forthright? In the old Egyptian style, by smashing the victim's head with a club, or – '

'Never mind, Ramses,' I said. 'If Mr Forthright is correct, we may have a firsthand opportunity to find out.'

'You astonish me, Mrs Emerson,' Reggie exclaimed. 'You are not taking this seriously. I assure you – '

'Let me assure you that we take it very seriously,' said Emerson, sucking on his empty pipe. 'But look on the bright side, Mr Forthright. If we have been chosen for the star roles in the performance they will take very good care of us in the meantime. I wonder . . .' He made a face and removed the pipe from his mouth. 'I wonder if Tarek could get me some tobacco. Obviously these people trade with some of the Nubian tribes.'

'Well, Professor, I must say you are a credit to the British nation,' said Reggie admiringly. 'Stiff upper lip, eh? If it's tobacco you want, I can supply you. I brought along an extra tin.'

'You did?' Emerson clapped him on the back. 'I will be in your debt, my dear chap. A nasty, dirty habit, as Mrs Emerson is always telling me, but I find it assists the process of ratiocination.'

One of the servants was sent to fetch Reggie's knapsack. After rummaging in its depths he produced a tin of tobacco, upon which Emerson fell like a starving man on a thick beefsteak. He filled his pipe, lit it, and blew out a great cloud of smoke. A look of blissful satisfaction transformed his face.

Reggie smiled, like an indulgent parent enjoying the pleasure of a child. 'Well, sir, are you now capable of ratiocination? We have no time to lose. Tarek's threats should have convinced you that I was right when I said we must escape before the ceremony.'

'I never disagreed with your conclusion,' said Emerson mildly. 'I only wondered how you hoped to accomplish it.'

Reggie leaned closer and lowered his voice to a whisper. 'The arrangements were made before I was imprisoned. Camels, guides, supplies – all will be ready. We can leave as soon as – '

'As soon as we are certain Mrs Forth is no more,' I said.

Reggie's mouth hung ajar. Emerson looked at me with a smile; Ramses nodded vigorously. Having got the floor, I proceeded. 'We have only the statements of people whose veracity is questionable to prove that the Forths are not alive. We came here in haste, risking much, because we feared they were in imminent danger.'

Reggie closed his mouth. Then he opened it.

'Don't waste your breath arguing with her,' said Emerson, smoking placidly. 'It never has the slightest effect. Continue, my dear Peabody.'

I told Reggie and Ramses of our discovery that morning. 'I have been accused,' I went on, 'of jumping to conclusions. I do not believe anyone can accuse me of doing so if I state that we are still uncertain as to the fate of Mrs Forth. Would you agree with that, Emerson?'

'Oh, certainly,' said Emerson, grinning around the stem of his pipe.

'But – ' Reggie began.

'Let me finish, please, Reggie. In the light of what we learned today, several other points take on new significance. We were told that Mrs Forth had "gone to the god." We took it to mean that she had died; but here, as in ancient Egypt, it might have quite another meaning. Now during the ceremony at the temple, the High Priestess of Isis recited, or sang, certain English verses. Put all these details together, and what do we have?'

'Are you asking me?' Reggie's eyes were wide. 'I fail to see what you are driving at. You cannot mean – '

'His wits are a trifle slow,' said Emerson to me. 'It's an interesting idea, Peabody. I had a strange feeling you were thinking along those lines.'

'I endeavoured to suggest that possibility, Mama,' said Ramses in an injured voice. 'And you and Papa implied I was imagining things.'

'We have acquired additional information since then, Ramses. I would be the first to agree that the sum total of it is inconclusive, but I must insist that we cannot depart without making absolutely certain that Mrs Forth is not a prisoner of the priests.'

'But,' Reggie stuttered. 'But Mrs Amelia – '

'I told you not to waste your breath arguing with her,' said Emerson. 'In this case I must say that I am in complete agreement. It is probable that Mrs Forth is dead, but we can't take the word of sinister savages, can we?'

'She is no savage,' Reggie said hotly. 'And she swore – '

'She may have been deceived,' said Emerson. 'You refer to your – er – fiancée, I presume.'

'Er – yes. I cannot believe. . .' Reggie appeared dazed. Then he reached into his knapsack. 'She gave me this.'

The object he withdrew was a small book bound in shabby brown cloth.

'The Book,' I cried. 'Of course! Emerson – '

Emerson's teeth lost their grip on his pipe, which fell onto my lap. He leapt at me and began beating out the smouldering patches.

'I do beg your pardon, Peabody. I was caught quite by surprise.'

'So I see. Curse it, I shan't be able to mend these holes; I gave my sewing kit to Her Majesty.'

'It is certainly a book,' Emerson went on, taking it from Reggie. '*The Moonstone,* by Wilkie Collins. I am not at all surprised; it is precisely the sort of literature I would have expected Willie Forth to enjoy. Yes, here is his name on the inside cover.'

'He gave it to her,' Reggie said. 'Upon his deathbed. She was his favourite pupil.'

'She,' Emerson repeated thoughtfully. 'Are you telling us that she – your friend – confound it, what is the girl's name?'

'She is Princess Amenit – the daughter of the former king.' Reggie smiled at our looks of surprise. 'You see now why I am so confident she can arrange for our escape.'

'Can she also arrange for us to see the High Priestess of Isis?' I asked.

'I don't think. . .' Reggie's face brightened. 'That won't be necessary; all we need do is ask her. She must know whether the woman she serves is – '

'I do not wish to question the veracity of your sweetheart, Reggie but you must see that her mere word would not be sufficient. She may be deceived; she may be so concerned with your safety that she would conceal the truth if it meant further risk to you.'

'I can't believe she would lie to me,' Reggie muttered.

'Mrs Emerson can,' said Emerson, knocking out his pipe. 'And so can I. We must see the High Priestess unveiled!'

'I could not have put it better myself, Emerson,' I said approvingly.

'Hmph,' said Emerson. 'It's a rather tall order, though. If she doesn't receive visitors, and dwells in the most remote areas of the temple . . . I doubt the high-handed methods we employed this morning would work, Peabody.'

'We can but try, Emerson. We must make the attempt.'

'Let me talk with Amenit,' Reggie said urgently. 'Promise me you won't do anything until I have consulted her. She may be able to arrange something, but if you go blundering in ... Excuse me! I meant to say –'

'I will pretend I didn't hear it,' said Emerson, rising in awful majesty and scowling like Jove. '"Blundering"! Come along, Peabody it is time for your rest.'

We left Reggie frowning at his feet, deep in thought. 'You were a little hard on him, my dear,' I said 'And I really don't see how Amenit can get us admitted to the presence of the High Priestess.'

'There's no harm in asking, is there?' Emerson sat down beside me on the edge of my bed. 'Curse it, Peabody, I've got to the point where even a tombstone would fail to convince me. All we have is a series of unproven and contradictory statements; I don't know what to believe or whom to trust.'

'I quite agree, Emerson. By the way, thank you for setting my trousers on fire. I keep forgetting that Reggie has no more sense than a lizard. He certainly can't be the messenger promised us by my nocturnal visitor. But that little book of Mr Forth's was a strange coincidence. Could Princess Amenit be the messenger?'

'If so, she has taken a dangerously roundabout method of approaching us,' said Emerson. 'It may be no more than a coincidence after all; we don't know the size of Willie's library, or how many books he gave his friends and students. I recommend discretion on the subject of the rekkit with both young lovers, Peabody. People of that sort seldom give a curse about anything except their own precious skins.'

'I would not go so far as to say that. However, they are inclined to be gullible when they fancy themselves in love. Reggie may be deceived by this young woman.'

'Quite so. Confound it, Peabody, I hate to sneak away without having done something for those poor devils in the village. We'll have to mount a second expedition.'

'Of course. But I haven't given up hope of hearing from my mysterious visitor, one way or another.'

I looked forwards with great anticipation to the lovers' first meeting after so many days of separation and uncertainty. My sympathetic imagination visualised Amenit's tears of anguish as she contemplated her sweetheart's danger, her tears of joy when she learned of his deliverance. I pictured them flying into one another's arms – their embraces – their murmured endearments. And then they would wander off, hand in hand, to the seclusion of the garden, where, soothed by the humming of bees and the cooing of doves in the mimosa trees, they would lose themselves in the rapture of love restored and hope renewed.

I pictured it, but of course I knew it was romantic nonsense. Any open expression of affection would have to wait until after they had succeeded in their plan of escaping from the valley, for the latter hope would be doomed if the former were known. It was Amenit who came later, I knew that gliding walk of hers, but she paid no more attention to Reggie than she did to the rest of us, and he scarcely glanced at her. However, he soon excused himself and went to his rooms; and a short time later Amenit quietly vanished.

They were gone for quite some time. Amenit was the first to return. She went about her duties, imperturbably as ever (it is very easy to look imperturbable when one is completely swaddled in veils). My anticipation had risen to fever pitch before Reggie entered, yawning and stretching and declaring that he had had a most refreshing nap.

'I seem to have lost a button off my shirt, though,' he added gazing at his chest with an expression of chagrin that would not have fooled an infant. 'Could I impose on you, Mrs Amelia?'

I followed him into my sleeping chamber. 'You silly young man,' I hissed. 'I gave my sewing kit to the queen; every woman in the city must know of it by now.'

'Well, how could I have known?' Reggie asked, looking injured. 'I wanted an excuse to speak with you alone.'

'You have no talent for intrigue, Reggie. You had better . . . Well what is it, Ramses?' For he had entered, followed by his father.

'Here is your needle and thread, Mama,' said Ramses. 'I borrowed it. I hope you do not mind.'

It was not my needle and thread. The dirty grey colour of the latter (not its original shade) betrayed its real ownership. I was afraid to ask why Ramses had needle and thread. Too many hideous possibilities came to mind.

'Thank you,' I said, advancing upon Reggie. Seizing cloth and button firmly, I plunged the threaded needle into the hole.

'Ouch,' cried Reggie.

'Talk quickly,' I ordered. 'I can't prolong this indefinitely. We look ridiculous.' For Emerson and Ramses were pretending to watch intently, as if the sewing on of a button were a rare and remarkable event.

'Everything is prepared,' Reggie hissed. 'Tomorrow night Amenit will lead us to the waiting caravan.'

'What about Mrs Forth?' I asked. Reggie sucked in his breath. 'I am sorry,' I said. 'I am no needlewoman.'

'You are determined on this?' Reggie inquired.

'Yes, certainly, of course,' came our united replies.

'Very well. Amenit will try. She laughed when I told her of your theory, but if you cannot be convinced otherwise . . . Be ready tonight.'

'When?' we chorused.

'At whatever time she can manage it,' was the grim reply. 'It will be very dangerous. Don't sleep; await her summons.'

'That should do the trick,' I said aloud, as one of the attendants appeared in the doorway, bright-eyed with curiosity.

'Thank you,' said Reggie, staring at his shirtfront.

'I think you have sewn the button to his undervest, Mama,' said Ramses.

How long I lay waiting in the dark I cannot say; it seemed an eternity. I did not have to fight sleep, for I had never been more wakeful. After a rather acrimonious discussion with Reggie I had reluctantly agreed to leave my belt and its accoutrements behind. Not so unexpectedly, Emerson supported him. 'You jingle, Peabody. You always say you won't and you always do, so don't say you won't. Besides, if we are surprised along the way we might be able to pass for natives if we wear native attire.'

I was deep in thought – not slumber – when a hand brushed mine. Silently I rose from the bed and stood beside the white-veiled figure.

After the other three had joined us, Amenit glided away, not towards the garden or the outer door, as I had expected, but towards the rock-cut chambers at the back of the palace. Farther back and farther we went, through narrow doorways and rooms dusty with disuse. The darkness pressed in on us like something actively malevolent that had fed on centuries of lightlessness. The tiny flame of Amenit's lamp flickered like a will-o'-the-wisp. Her white robes might have enclosed empty air.

At last she stopped in a small windowless chamber. I could see very little, but there appeared to be no furniture except for a stone bench or ledge, approximately two feet high and barely wide enough to support a reclining form. The ghostly form of the handmaiden bent over it. There was a click and a murmuring sound, and the top of the bench rose, as on a spring. Hoisting her skirts with a curiously modern gesture, she climbed nimbly over the edge and sank out of sight.

At his insistence, Emerson was the first to follow her. I went next, and found myself on a flight of narrow stone-cut steps. They were so steep I was forced to descend them like a ladder, holding on with both hands, but my dear Emerson's arm steadied me and offered assurance of rescue should I miss my footing. Ramses managed to step on my hand several times but eventually we reached the bottom of the steps and paused to count noses and catch our breaths.

'All right, Mrs Amelia?' Reggie asked.

Amenit had already started off down the tunnel that led

straight ahead. 'Yes, certainly,' I said. 'Hurry or we shall lose our guide.'

It would have been dangerous to do so, for the tunnel began to bend and turn, and other passages opened up on either side. I have been in pyramids whose inner structures were as complex and in far worse repair; but it did occur to me as we went on that if I wanted to rid myself of unwelcome guests I could hardly find a more convenient place. Amenit must know the way by memory, for the walls were unmarked. If we ever lost her, we could never find our way back. The place was a regular maze.

Emerson, close on Amenit's heels, kept staring at the rough stone surfaces that pressed so close upon us. 'I wish we had more light,' he muttered. 'From what I can see . . . Yes, that would explain a good many things.'

'What do you mean?' I asked.

'Remember the famous gold of Cush, Peabody? Most scholars believe the mines were in the eastern desert – but if this maze was not begun as a mining project, I miss my guess. The vein is exhausted now, and the tunnels have been adapted to serve other purposes, but there is still gold in these hills – there must be. Where else would our hosts get the metal they use for their ornaments, and what other commodity could they trade for the foodstuffs they import?'

'I am sure you are right, Papa,' said Ramses, behind me. 'And have you observed the small openings that occasionally break the surface of the walls? No doubt there are shafts leading to the surface, as was the case in some of the Egyptian pyramids. The air here is remarkably fresh, considering we must be deep underground.'

The air was only relatively fresh. It was very dry, and my throat was beginning to ache. I poked Emerson in the back. 'Ask her how much farther.'

'Curse it, Peabody, have you got that cursed parasol? I told you – '

'You said I must not jingle, Emerson. My parasol does not jingle. Ask her – '

Amenit interrupted me with a vehement demand for silence. 'Not far now. They will hear. Be still!'

After a few more minutes of walking, the tunnel opened into a larger space. Another hiss from Amenit brought us to her side before what seemed to be a blank wall. 'Be still,' she breathed. 'Be still!' Then she blew out the lamp.

I had no idea darkness could be that intense.

Then came light, like a benediction. A small square had opened in the wall before us. The light came from it – faint, yellow, and flickering, but more welcome than the sun's most brilliant beam. I took Ramses firmly by the arm and moved him off my left foot; he was crowding me, trying to see through the opening, but it was above his eye level. Emerson's cheek pressed against mine as together we gazed into the chamber beyond.

Archaeological fever! There is no passion like it, few that equal it in intensity. It gripped me even as it gripped my remarkable spouse. There could be no question as to the function of the chamber that lay beyond. Rich furnishings – carved chests, great jars of wine and oil, statues adorned with gilt and faience – were illumined by several alabaster lamps. The pièce de résistance lay upon a low bed in the centre of the room – a mouldering corpse, reduced by time and the natural processes of decay to a semi-skeleton. The yellowing teeth were bared in a hideous grin, and the bones of one arm protruded through the withered flesh.

'They don't practice mummification,' exclaimed Emerson. 'Hard to get natron, I – oof!'

I do not know whether it was Reggie or Amenit who had reminded him, somewhat forcibly, that silence was imperative, but the gesture had the desired effect. And it was just in time. The light strengthened. It came from lamps carried by a pair of figures whose contours we knew well – two of the handmaidens, swaddled from crown to heel. I did not think either was Mentarit, however.

The High Priestess followed them.

The Queen of Meroë spearing captives with girlish enthusiasm.

Only her gold-embroidered draperies differentiated her from the others. She gestured. Her attendants placed the lamps on a chest and joined her, one on either side, as she took up a position before the grisly remains. Three voices blended in a soft chant. Amenit had done what we asked. Before us stood the High Priestess. But unless she unveiled, the long, tortuous, dangerous journey would have been in vain. Fortunately for my nerves the ceremony was brief, almost, one might say, perfunctory. After a short chorus, the three figures knelt and rose and knelt again. The two on either side remained kneeling. The central figure rose and lifted its hands to its face. The draperies quivered and fell. Then – I confess it with some shame – I closed my eyes. The reason she had unveiled was so that she might kiss the corpse's withered brow.

She was not Mrs Forth. Her jetty locks and smooth brown cheeks were those of a high-bred Cushite maiden.

'I Would as Soon
Leave Ramses'

I moved away from the window so that Emerson could lift Ramses, who had, by increasingly peremptory tugs and pokes, indicated his wish to see too. A few moments later the light within the chamber dimmed but did not yield to utter darkness. The lamps that had been left to light the dead would burn on until the oil was consumed – an ironic commentary on the brevity of human life. We too go out into darkness when our light is consumed.

So wrapped was I in philosophic and other musings that Reggie's whisper sounded like a shout. 'Well? Was it . . . ?'

Only then did it occur to me that he had not been given a chance to look for himself. 'No,' I whispered.

The return trip was made in silence. I should have been speculating on the meaning of the grisly ceremony and making mental notes of the contents of the burial chamber for future publication, but I was in the grip of a foolish depression. I had never really believed in Ramses's theory that Mrs Forth was the High Priestess, but I had allowed myself to hope. The fate of the poor young bride had always seemed to me more tragic than that of her husband. He at least had known what he was getting into, while she had followed him, loyally and without question, trusting in his judgment and in his protective strength.

It may have been stupid, but it was noble. I felt an affinity with her – not with her stupidity, but with her courage.

We gained our apartments without incident, finding them dark and deserted as they had been when we left them. 'I would like to bathe,' I said softly to Emerson, 'but I suppose it would be ill-advised to risk waking one of the attendants. I say, Emerson, what about the clothes we are wearing? The dust and cobwebs clinging to them may alert a spy.'

Amenit understood this, or part of it. She giggled. 'I will hide. Give them me.'

'What, now?' said Emerson, outraged.

'This is no time for jokes, Professor,' said Reggie. 'Get to bed at once. The guard changes at midnight.'

He took his own advice, hastening towards his room. Amenit went with him. I could not see clearly in the dark, but their two forms were so close together I assumed his arm must have been around her. A soft giggle floated back to us as they melted into the shadows.

'Did you hear, Emerson?' I whispered. 'The guard changes at midnight!'

'Hmmm, yes. Presumably the first shift is loyal to the lady and the second is not. She seems an efficient sort of girl; if only she wouldn't giggle! Hurry, Peabody, we had better follow Forthright's advice.'

There seemed to be an endless supply of the fine linen robes. I bundled the soiled ones up and hid them under the bed, hoping Amenit would deal with them in the morning. She apparently had other plans for the remainder of the night.

It was not long before Emerson joined me. 'I won't stay if you are sleepy, Peabody,' he whispered.

'I doubt if I will sleep at all. What are we to do, Emerson? Is that young woman true to poor Reggie, do you think?'

'If she isn't in love with him she is putting on a convincing show. No woman could do more for a man.'

I sat up in bed. 'Emerson! You didn't!'

'Certainly I did. Our lives may hang on the genuineness of

her affection. I had to find out.' He put his arms around me and pulled me down beside him before continuing, 'There remains a more serious doubt. Has she the power to do what she has promised? It won't be easy to equip an expedition of that size, in absolute secrecy, even for a princess of the royal house.'

'That is certainly a consideration,' I replied. 'And there are others that suggest we ought not be in any particular hurry to rush off. We should at least hear what the promised messenger has to say.'

'I don't know why you're so set on that fellow and his vague promises,' Emerson said suspiciously. 'What sort of man was he? Old and feeble, did you tell me?'

I smiled in the darkness. 'I told you I never saw his face. He certainly was not old and feeble, though. Quite the contrary.'

'Hmph,' said Emerson. 'It has been several days. He may have been captured.'

'I don't think so.'

'Curse it, Peabody – '

He broke off with a sound that, in a lesser man, I might have taken for a muffled cry of alarm. I should explain that we were lying on our sides facing one another; in the heat of argument Emerson had raised himself on his elbow, so he could see past my recumbent body. Hastily I rolled over. A white-swathed form bent over me, its hand outstretched.

'Good Gad,' I hissed. 'What is it, Amenit? Why do you disturb us?'

With a brusque gesture the girl tore the veil from her face. I could not make out her features clearly; it was the movement itself that betrayed her identity. 'Mentarit,' I exclaimed.

Her hand covered my lips. The other hand reached into the breast of her robe and came out with . . .

'Emerson,' I whispered. 'It is a book, I believe.'

'Another one?' said Emerson dubiously.

'Come,' Mentarit said softly. 'Will you trust me? I bring the sign he promised you. There is little time and great danger. You must come now.'

'Emerson?'

'Are you asking me, Peabody? Remarkable. Well, why not? If you can persuade the lady to turn her back while I . . .'

'I will fetch the young one,' said Mentarit tactfully.

'He is probably under the bed,' I remarked, reaching for my robe. 'What do you suppose she wants him for?'

'Ours not to reason why,' said Emerson. 'Where the devil is my sash? Ah, here it is. Ours but to – '

The reappearance of Mentarit with Ramses in tow mercifully prevented him from completing the depressing quotation. 'Ah, there you are, my boy,' he said pleasantly. 'Sorry to knock you up; it was the lady's idea.'

'I was not asleep,' said Ramses. 'Where are we going, Papa?'

'Cursed if I know,' said Emerson.

'Sssh,' said Mentarit.

I wondered at her assurance, for although she had cautioned us to silence, she seemed not to fear being discovered. One part of the mystery was explained when we reached the anteroom. There were four guards, motionless as statues, their great spears reflecting the lamplight. They did not move even their eyes as Mentarit led us past them.

'Hypnotised, perhaps,' I breathed.

'By my eloquence,' said Emerson. 'Hem. Didn't you recognise them?'

The great wooden doors were closed and bolted. Mentarit ignored them, directing us through a series of corridors that grew ever narrower and plainer, and then down a flight of stairs that ended in a small door covered with coarse matting. Mentarit thrust it aside; we filed through, to find ourselves in a walled courtyard. I let out a stifled exclamation, for the sight was a horrid one – row upon row of motionless bodies, stretched out like corpses in the pale light of the waning moon.

We had to pick a path among them. As I stepped carefully over one prostrate body I caught a gleam of eyes, open and alert, and I knew the truth. This was the sleeping place of the servant-slaves; the sky their only roof, a thin mat their only bed. But they were not sleeping. Wherever we stepped, those wide, watching eyes were upon us. Call me fanciful if you will, but I felt the thoughts they dared not express aloud – hope and encouragement and goodwill – guiding my steps like warm, helping hands.

A gate opened out onto the hillside and a pile of vile-smelling refuse. Mentarit picked up her skirts and started to run, following a narrow path of beaten earth. She was as fleet as a hare, and I was quite breathless when she finally came to a stop. Looking down at the causeway far below, I saw just ahead a familiar pyloned gateway. We were on the edge of the cemetery.

When I looked back, Mentarit had disappeared. Emerson took my hand. 'Another tunnel, Peabody. There is a hole here, behind the rock.'

There were a good many holes, fissures, and cracks. The one Emerson indicated did not look promising, but I squeezed through and felt Mentarit's hand clasp mine. Emerson's broad shoulders stuck but he got through at the expense of a few inches of skin.

Mentarit struck a light. She seemed more at ease now that we were under cover, but she went even more quickly. The tunnels looked exactly like the ones we had traversed earlier, narrow and dark and unadorned. For all I knew they might be part of the same network.

We must have travelled for a good twenty minutes through this maze. At last we came to a steep stairway, lit by a glow from an opening above. I followed Mentarit, with Ramses close on my heels and Emerson bringing up the rear. Soft though the lamplight was, it blinded me after the relative darkness of the tunnel. Mentarit guided me through the opening and I found myself standing upon a bare stone floor.

The chamber was small and so low Emerson's head brushed the ceiling as he climbed up to join me. A dark rectangle on the far wall indicated a more conventional entrance to the room, which was unfurnished except for another of the low stone benches. Someone was sitting on it – not the stalwart male figure I had expected, but a veiled female. Another swaddled form stood by her, holding a lamp. Mentarit went to stand on the other side of the seated woman, whose gold-embroidered veils glittered in the light.

'Oh, good Gad,' exclaimed Emerson. 'Not another one!'

For the figure had risen, and he saw at once, as did I, that it was not the same woman who had kissed the grisly brow of the dead man. This form was slighter and its movements more graceful. A long shiver passed through her; her diaphanous draperies fluttered like the wings of a frightened bird. Then, with a sudden gesture, like a bird taking flight, she flung them back and they drifted to the ground.

Her slim body, scarcely concealed by the flimsy garment beneath the veils, was that of a girl on the threshold of womanhood. Her face was heart-shaped, curving gently from rounded cheeks to a delicate pointed chin. Her skin had the translucent lustre of a pearl. The faintest tinge of rose warmed its pallor. Her eyes were blue – not the blazing sapphire of Emerson's, but the tender azure of forget-me-nots. Delicate brows arched above them, long lashes framed them. And from her broad white brow the crowning glory of her hair fell over her shoulders and down her back, a flood of molten gold bright with coppery highlights.

The first sound that broke the stillness came from somewhere in the region of my left shoulder blade. It resembled the last drops of water gurgling from a hose.

Emerson, on my right, let out his breath in a great sigh. The girl's lips trembled and her eyes swam with tears. I knew I ought to say something – do something – but for perhaps the first time in my life I was literally incapable of speech.

Straightening, she squared her little shoulders and tried to smile. 'Professor and Mrs Emerson, I presume?' she said.

Her voice was soft and sweet, with a quaint little accent. There was another gurgle from Ramses, and a choking sound from Emerson, who is very sentimental under his brusque exterior.

I ran to her and threw my arms around her. I cannot remember what I said. It is safe to assume that I said something.

She clung to me for a moment, and I felt a few hot tears dampen my shoulder. They were quickly controlled, however. 'I beg your pardon,' she said, drawing away. 'I had quite given up hope. You cannot know what it means to me. . . But we are in desperate danger, and we dare not waste time. You are – you will – you won't leave me here?'

Emerson cleared his throat noisily and stepped forwards, holding out his hand. She gave him hers; his big brown fingers closed over it. 'I would as soon leave Ramses,' he declared.

'Ramses.' She glanced at him and smiled. 'Forgive me for failing to greet you. I have heard a great deal about you from – from a friend of mine.'

'You must forgive *us*, my dear,' I said. 'For staring so rudely and behaving as if we had lost our wits. The truth is, we had no idea you were here.'

'The truth is we had no idea you existed,' said Emerson. 'Good Gad! I have not recovered my wits yet. You can only be Willoughby Forth's daughter, but you seem so . . . How old are you, child?'

'I was thirteen years of age on April 15,' was the reply. 'My father taught me to reckon time as the English do, and impressed upon me the importance of remembering that date – and many other details, so that I would not forget my heritage. But please forgive me if I do not answer your other questions – you must have many, and, oh! so do I. I must return at once; my loyal handmaidens – of whom, alas! there are only a few – will suffer a hideous fate if my absence is discovered. This meeting had to be arranged in haste, without the precautions I would have preferred. We learned only a short time ago that you had been shown an impostor. I was afraid – so afraid! – you would believe in her, and leave without me.'

'Wait, my dear,' I exclaimed. 'Questions that serve only to satisfy our curiosity must wait, but there are others of burning importance. How are we to communicate with you? Whom can we trust? This place appears to be a hotbed of intrigue.'

'You are quite right, Mrs Emerson.' Mentarit touched her

shoulder and whispered in her ear, and she nodded. 'Yes, we must hurry. Fear not, those questions and others will be answered, by the person who will take you back to your house.'

'Mentarit?'

'No, she must return with me. But your guide is someone you know – the friend of whom I spoke. My dearest friend.' She turned; and from the passageway behind her came a man. He wore the short coarse kilt of a commoner; a hood or mask of the same loosely woven fabric covered his head and the upper part of his face. Feet, breast, and arms were bare, with no distinguishing marks of rank or rich ornaments. I knew him, though, even before he pushed the hood back from his brow.

'Prince Tarek,' I said. 'So you are the Friend of the Rekkit. I thought so.'

'Your eyes are keen as an eagle's, Lady,' said Tarek with a smile. 'I came to you in darkness because I knew that you would recognise your servant even when he was masked and in the dress of a commoner. Now we must hasten. And you, little sister – '

She threw her arms around him. It was the innocent embrace of a child; her shining head barely reached his shoulder. 'Take care, dear brother. I will be ready when you summon me.'

And with a last radiant smile at us she wrapped the veils around her and vanished into the opening from which Tarek had come. Mentarit and the other girl followed. Tarek stood looking after her until the glow of the lamp died into darkness.

'Come,' he said in sonorous tones. 'You shall know all; but there is no time to lose. You must be back in your accustomed place before dawn tiptoes into the eastern sky.'

Emerson descended the stairs first while Tarek held the lamp. I was about to follow my husband when I realised that Ramses was still standing, rigid as a block of wood, in the exact spot he had occupied throughout the interview.

'Ramses!' I said sharply. 'What the dev – Come here at once!'

Ramses jumped. When he turned I saw that his face was as blank and withdrawn as that of a sleepwalker. I seized him and shook him briskly. 'Get down there!' I ordered.

He obeyed without so much as a 'Yes, Mama.' A hideous foreboding gripped me.

Tarek was the last to descend, drawing the trapdoor back into place as he did so. As we hastened along the path by which we had come he told us, not all but a good deal.

'I was still in the Women's House [i.e., he was less than six years of age, at which time boys left the care of their mothers] when the strangers came. It was a great wonder to me. I had never seen people like them, especially the lady, with her strange white face and her hair like a moonlit stream. My Uncle Pesaker, who had just become High Priest of Aminreh, feared the white man and would have slain him; but my mother quoted from the old books of wisdom that tell us the gods love those who give water to the thirsty and clothing to the naked. The lady was ill, and she was soon to have a child.

'My mother's words moved my father, who was a kindly man; and soon he came to love the white man, who gave him good counsel and taught him many things. I too grew to love the stranger; I drank in his words about the great world beyond this place.

'After the child was born, her mother sought the god. The child was given to my mother's women to nurse, for her father denied her. Later, though, he came to love her and found happiness in her care. He named her Nefret, the beautiful maiden, and she was ... But you have seen her. She was like a white lotus, and when I first saw her she curled her fingers around my hand and smiled at me.'

He was silent for a time. Then he said, 'I must be brief, for soon we must go in silence. The sage, as we called him, had sworn to stay with us forever; he hated the world outside and we were his children. But one day he sickened and he felt the cold breath of the Gatherer of Souls, and he opened his eyes and saw his child would soon be a child no longer but a woman grown. My mother had died, my father was old – and my brother, my brother Nastasen had also seen Nefret blossom with the promise of womanhood. For who could see her and not desire her...'

'I think you love her too,' I said softly. 'Yet you are willing to help her escape.'

Tarek sighed. 'The day does not mate with the darkness, or the black with the white.'

'Bah,' said Emerson. 'Of all the silly twaddle!'

'Hush, Emerson,' I said. 'You are a noble man, Tarek.'

'She must go back to her own people, that was the desire of her father,' Tarek said. Again he sighed. 'I will wed Mentarit, whom I also love, and she will be my Chief Wife, Queen of the Holy Mountain.'

He stopped, holding the lamp high. 'From now on we creep like lizards, under the open sky. Hear me. From Forth I also learned that all men are brothers under the law. When he sent me to find Nefret's people, I saw the world of the white man. There is cruelty and suffering there, but some among you strive for justice. I would bring that justice to my people. I saw that another thing of which Forth had warned me was true. The soldiers of the English queen gather like locusts along the great river. Someday they will find this place and we will be like mice in the claws of the sacred cats of Bastet. I alone can prepare my people for that time. I alone can lift the sufferings of the rekkit. Because of these beliefs, and because I would keep Nefret from him, my brother hates me. He wants the kingship and will do anything to get it. He will kill you if he can, for you have shown kindness to my people and defied his orders. Be wary! Stay in your house! An assassin's arrow can strike from afar! Trust only Mentarit. Even the men wearing my colours may be my brother's spies.'

He gave us no time to ask further questions, but hastened on. After we had squeezed through the hole in the hillside he increased his pace. The moon was down. The breeze that cooled our perspiring faces had the fresh smell of morning.

When Tarek stopped we were still some distance from our abode but I could see its outlines; the sky had lightened that much. 'I talked too long, the hour is late,' he whispered urgently. 'Can you find your way from here? You must be in your rooms before the sun lifts over the mountain, and so must I.'

'Yes,' I answered. 'But what about Amenit? She is – '

'My brother's spy,' said Tarek. 'But the wine she and her lover drank tonight was drugged. Tell him nothing of this! He believes the lies she told him, and he . . . There is no time! Begone!'

He followed his own advice, melting into the darkness like a shadow. The sound of his passage was no louder than the rustle of dry grass in the wind.

We were not as skilled as he; it sounded to me as if we made enough noise for an army as we scrambled along the path. Speed seemed more important than silence, however. The stench from the rotting trash guided us to the gate, which we found open, and as we trotted across the courtyard, a path miraculously opened for us, as bodies turned, as a sleeper may turn, away from our feet. Emerson's men were at their posts, but as we ran down the passage towards our sitting room I heard in the distance the sound of marching men.

'That was a near thing,' muttered Emerson, mopping his brow. 'Quick, Ramses.'

Ramses did not utter a word or break stride, even when Emerson snatched his kilt off him and thrust it at me. 'What did you do with the other clothing?' he snapped, stripping off his dusty, wrinkled robe.

'Under the bed. But I hardly think it would be wise – '

'Quite right. Here – ' He caught hold of the edge of my garment and gave it a sharp tug, sending me twirling in a circle as it unwound. Emerson bundled up the clothing, pitched them into one of the baskets, pushed me onto the bed, and dropped down next to me.

'Whew,' he said, on a long expiration of breath.

'I could not agree more, my dear. What a revelation – what an astonishing development! Confess, Emerson; you were as amazed as I, weren't you?'

'Thunderstruck, my dear Peabody. Mrs Forth must have been already in the family way when I met her, but of course no such idea entered my head – nor, I would hope, that of her husband. No man worthy of the name would take a lady in her delicate condition on such a journey.'

'It must have entered her head, though,' I said. 'Why on earth didn't she tell him?'

'Would you have told me, Peabody?' Having recovered his breath, Emerson proceeded to squeeze mine out of me.

'Well . . . I hope I would have had sense enough. But she was very young and, I suppose, madly in love. Poor girl, she paid a terrible price for her misplaced loyalty, but at least she was spared the knowledge of the fate that threatens her child.'

'We'll get the girl safely away, Peabody.'

'Of course. We . . . good Gad, Emerson! We are supposed to make our escape tomorrow – no, by heaven, tonight! With the treacherous Amenit!'

'Curse it, that's right. I had forgotten.' Emerson rolled over onto his back. 'We'll have to invent some excuse, Peabody. If we told Forthright that his ladylove was a liar and a spy he wouldn't believe us.'

'He would insist on confronting her,' I agreed. 'I am beginning to share your opinion of young lovers, Emerson; they can be a frightful nuisance. It is a pity we had not time to ask Tarek's advice.'

Emerson yawned. 'It is a pity we had not time to ask him a good many things. I must say he has a confoundedly long-winded, literary way of talking. It reminded me of those –'

'Perhaps he knows about Amenit's plan, Emerson, and will take steps to prevent it.'

'Perhaps. Everybody spying on everybody else. . .' Another great yawn interrupted him. 'I refuse to worry about it now. We'll think of some way out; we always do.'

'Certainly, my dear. I am not at all concerned.'

'Good night, my dear Peabody.'

'Good night, my dear Emerson. Or rather, good morning.'

My eyelids felt as if they were made of lead. Sleep crept upon me; I was going, going. . .

'Peabody!'

'Curse it, Emerson, I was almost asleep. What is it?'

'You didn't know the Friend of the Rekkit was Tarek until he took off his mask. Confess, you only claimed you knew beforehand in order to annoy me.'

'Oh, for . . . Do you think me capable of such duplicity, Emerson?'

'Yes.'

'I did know, however. Through the ratiocinative process.'

'Indeed. Would you care to explain it to your slow-witted spouse?'

I moved closer to him, but he stayed stiff as a stick and did not respond in the slightest. 'Oh, very well,' I said, turning over in my turn and clasping my hands. We must have looked ridiculous, lying side by side like a pair of mummies, with our arms folded across our breasts.

I began, 'I have always believed it was Tarek who carried Mr Forth's message to London. He was Mr Forth's favourite pupil, with a good command of English. Who would be a more likely candidate? And only a man high in favour with the king could have risked breaking the law of the Holy Mountain with relative impunity. He risked more than he knew, however, for his father died while he was gone ("The Horus flied in the season of harvest," if you remember) and when he returned he found his position seriously undermined.'

'Likely, if unproven,' said Emerson, forgetting his pique in the interest of my exposition. 'But you still haven't connected Tarek with the Friend of the Rekkit.'

'It is proven,' I replied calmly. 'Tarek admitted tonight that it was he who journeyed to England. We did not meet him until we arrived in Nubia, so he must have followed us from England, or, what is more likely, preceded us once he had ascertained that we intended to work at Gebel Barkal. He must have been the old magician who hypnotised Ramses – '

'Hmph,' said Emerson. 'His aim being, I suppose, to carry Ramses off. We would follow him, of course – all the way to the Holy Mountain. We had refused to seize the bait of the message, so Tarek must have concluded that was the only way to get us here. And now we know why he wanted us – to help get Nefret away.'

'It is a pleasure to deal with a mind as quick and responsive as yours, my dear,' I said demurely.

Emerson chuckled. 'Touché, Peabody. But you still haven't explained how – '

'Have you ever read *The Moonstone*, Emerson?'

'You know I don't share your trashy taste in literature, Peabody. What does that book have to do with it?'

When he refers, as he often does, to what he is pleased to call my reprehensible literary tastes, Emerson is only making one of his little jokes. I knew perfectly well that he read thrillers on the sly and had done so even before he met me. However, I had learned that husbands do not care to be contradicted (indeed, I do not know anyone who does), so I only do it when it is absolutely necessary. It was not necessary on this occasion.

'In *The Moonstone*,' I said, 'there is a scene describing the performance of three mysterious Indian priests who are seeking the gem stolen from the sacred statue of their god. They pour liquid into the hand of their acolyte, a young child – '

'Curse it,' Emerson muttered.

'As soon as I saw that interesting work of fiction I knew it must have been given, not to Amenit – whose English is extremely poor and whose intellectual capacity, I fear, is limited – but to Tarek. How Amenit came into possession of it I don't know; but she must have given it to Reggie to convince him of his uncle's death. Now – follow me closely, Emerson – '

'Oh, I will try, Peabody. It strains my inferior intellect, but I will make the attempt.'

'It is a simple equation, my dear. Tarek had read *The Moonstone*. The talisman sent by the Friend of the Rekkit was another English book and his messenger was Mentarit, who, as we had learned, is Tarek's sister. I was not absolutely certain,' I admitted handsomely, 'but all the evidence pointed in the same direction.'

In fact, I had known my visitor was Tarek as soon as he . . . Well let me put it this way. I had known the young man whose frame was in such intimate contact with my own was not one of the little undernourished slaves. While Tarek was masquerading as Kemit I had had occasion to admire, in a purely aesthetic fashion, his admirable musculature. There is a certain aura. . . The Reader will understand why I chose not to mention this clue to my dear husband.

'Hmph,' said the husband in question. 'Touché again, Peabody and well done.'

'Good night, Emerson.'

'Good night, my dear.'

Sleep, beneficent sleep, that ravels up the tattered sleeve of care. . .

'Peabody.'

'Good Gad, Emerson! What is it now?'

'Is this the book Mentarit brought you?'

'If you found it on or under the bed, I suppose it must be,' I said irritably. 'I should have hidden it, I admit; I was so surprised I just dropped it.'

'Do you know what book it is?'

'No, how could I? It was dark; I didn't read the title.'

In silence Emerson offered it to me. The sickly grey light of dawn gave his face a corpselike pallor.

'*King Solomon's Mines*,' I read. 'By H. Rider Haggard.'

'I should have known,' Emerson said in a hollow voice.

'Known what?'

'Where Tarek got his high-flown style of talking and his sentimental notions. He sounds exactly like one of the confounded natives in those confounded books.' Emerson collapsed with a heartfelt groan. 'Forth has a great deal to answer for.'

'You can't blame him for this,' I said.

'What do you mean?'

'This book was not published until after Mr Forth disappeared. I brought a copy along this year because it is one of my favourite . . . yes, here is my name. I left it behind when we were forced to lighten our baggage. Tarek must have taken it.'

The light had strengthened. Emerson turned his haggard face towards mine. 'Why?' he asked in faltering tones. 'Why would he do such a da – such a fool thing?'

'Well, it was clever of him to have used this particular book as his talisman. If it were found, it would be assumed to be one I had brought with me. But I am afraid. . .'

'What?'

'I am afraid he took it for the simplest possible reason,' I said. 'He wanted to read it. It is quite touching, Emerson, when you think about it. Having been introduced by his teacher to the joy of reading and the beauties of literature, this intelligent and sensitive young man . . .'

I will not reproduce Emerson's remark. It did not do him justice.

I had hoped Amenit would sleep late and let us do the same, but she was on duty bright and early. Though I could not read her countenance, nothing in her manner or her movements would have led an observer to suspect that she had been drugged. If anything, she was livelier than ever. However, Reggie did not leave his room until the morning was well advanced and his first words made my heart leap into my throat. 'What the deuce do these savages put in their wine? I haven't felt like this since my undergraduate days.'

'I have heard similar excuses from other young men who drank too much,' I said severely. 'I suppose you were celebrating your reunion with your sweetheart, but if you will permit me to say so, that increases rather than mitigates your offence.'

Reggie took his head between his hands and groaned. 'Don't lecture me, Mrs Amelia, I am already in a delicate condition. But' – his voice dropped to a thrilling whisper – 'the arrangements are complete. It will be tonight.'

I looked at Emerson. The slightest sideways movement of his head conveyed his meaning, for the mental bond that unites us is so strong, words are scarcely necessary. 'Wait,' was the message he sent me. 'Do not protest. Something may yet turn up.'

I certainly hoped it would, for we had not been able to invent a convincing yet innocent excuse for declining to escape. If nothing occurred to us before the actual moment of departure, we would have to resort to sudden illness or incapacity, or (it was my idea and a rather clever one, I thought) Ramses could hide and refuse to be found. When I had asked him if he could manage it, he gave me a look of kindly contempt and nodded.

Emerson was his normal self that morning, if rather more silent than usual. His only sign of perturbation was to smoke a great deal. I envied him the cursed tobacco; it seemed to soothe his nerves, and mine could certainly have used assistance. I do not believe in the supernatural – that is forbidden by Scripture – but I do firmly believe that certain individuals are sensitive to subtle currents of thought and emotion. I am one of them, and that morning I could not seem to draw a deep breath. The very air was heavy with foreboding.

They say that a condemned man suffers more in the waiting than in the actual execution. I have some doubts about that, but I felt something amounting to relief when the metaphorical axe finally fell. Reggie was grumbling about his headache and complaining that the powders I had given him had not lessened it when we heard the tread of marching feet. It sounded like a troop of soldiers rather than the usual princely escort.

The room emptied as if by magic; a rekkit scuttled for cover and the attendants who were close to an exit fled through it, leaving only a few who were delayed by repletion or slow wits. They promptly fell to their knees. I rose to my feet. With one swift stride Emerson was beside me, his face alert as that of a hunting cat. The hangings were thrust aside and the men filed in – six, eight – ten spearmen in their leather helmets, followed by Prince Nastasen. He was accompanied by Pesaker and Murtek; but I looked in vain for Tarek, and my heart began to sink towards my boots.

Nastasen stood looking us over, his thumbs hooked in his belt. I suppose he was trying to intimidate us with the ferocity of his glare; it certainly was an ugly sight, but Emerson returned his scowl with one twice as fierce, and Nastasen was the first to give way.

He levelled an accusing finger. 'You are traitors,' he cried. 'You have conspired(?) with my enemies.'

Murtek began to gabble out a translation, but the prince stopped him with what was obviously an oath; it made reference to the improbable habits of a particular rodent. 'Let them answer in our tongue. Well?' He jabbed his finger at Emerson. 'You hear me.'

'I hear your words, but they do not make sense (lit. contain wisdom),' said Emerson calmly. 'We are strangers. How can we be your enemies when we do not know you? Curse it,' he added in English, 'I'm not sure I made my point. My knowledge of the language is too limited to express fine legal distinctions.'

Ramses cleared his throat. 'If you would allow me, Papa – '

'Certainly not,' I exclaimed. 'How would that look, a little boy presuming to speak for his parents? I doubt His Highness would recognise those legal distinctions in any case.'

Nastasen's face swelled with fury. 'Stop talking! Why do you not show fear? You are in my hands. Fall to the ground and beg for mercy.'

'We fear no man,' I said in Meroitic. 'We kneel only to God.'

The High Priest of Aminreh let out a harsh bark of laughter. 'Soon you will kneel to him and the hand of the Heneshem(?) will – '

'It is I who will say what will happen,' Nastasen shouted, turning on his ally.

'Yes, yes, great one, great prince. Forgive your servant.'

Really, I thought (for I deemed it prudent not to speak just then), Prince Nastasen was nothing more than a nasty, spoiled little boy. He would make a very poor ruler, and it would not be long before Pesaker was the real power in the land.

However, nasty little boys can be dangerous when they command a lot of men armed with big sharp spears, and Nastasen proceeded to demonstrate that he was not so stupid as I had believed. His breathing slowed, his muscles relaxed, and a slow, evil smile replaced his frown.

'You are strangers,' he said. 'You have no friends here? But you had a friend before you came. You are the friends of a traitor.'

'Guilt by association,' I remarked to Emerson.

'Let him finish,' Emerson said. 'I have an unpleasant feeling about this. . .'

'He is a traitor to his people,' said Nastasen. 'He would betray his own kind and raise up the (obviously a pejorative term of some kind) to rule over them.' He struck himself on his chest with the flat of his hand. 'But I, the great prince, the defender of the people, cast my all-seeing eyes upon the land! I saw this scum; I knew him, I knew his name! And now – '

He clapped his hands sharply and turned. Two soldiers entered, gripping a prisoner. Roughly they forced him to his knees. His arms were bound behind him, not at the wrists, but at the elbows, a particularly uncomfortable position familiar to me from ancient Egyptian depictions of captives. The hood still covered his face, and the coarsely woven kilt was the one he had worn the night before. They must have taken him shortly after he left us. We had delayed too long – or someone had laid a trap for him. I looked around for Amenit. She had disappeared, and so had Reggie.

Nastasen stood gloating over his brother like a stage villain. 'He has quite a talent for melodrama,' Emerson muttered. 'I wonder if they still perform the old religious plays here? Get ready for the next scene, Peabody.'

I moved closer to Emerson. He slipped his arm around my waist. There was a slithering sound behind me as Ramses moved; whither, I could not tell.

Nastasen was enjoying his triumph and his theatrics too much to heed us. 'He hides his face like a coward, but I know him! My eye sees all, knows all. Your eyes are weak; perhaps you do not know him. Look then!'

He snatched the hood off. I was relieved to see that except

for a few scratches Tarek appeared to be unharmed. He was a trifle paler than usual, but there was no sign of fear on his face, only contempt, as he looked steadily at his brother. Nastasen gripped him roughly by the hair and pulled his head back. Whipping a knife from his belt, he laid the sharp blade against the beating vein in Tarek's throat.

A faint moaning sound, like a sad winter wind, echoed through the room. The little people were watching; they mourned the death of their hope with the capture of their hero.

A thin trickle of blood slid down Tarek's bronzed throat. He made no sound, nor did his expression change. Emerson's fingers moved along the leather of my belt, as if he were tightening his grasp. I felt a small body press against my back in apparent terror; extending my hand towards my son I felt, not trembling flesh but a hard metal shaft. I closed my fingers around it and waited.

With a sudden movement, Nastasen sheathed his knife. 'The king does not kill except in war,' he declared. 'This death would be too merciful.'

I had anticipated some such conclusion, but I was immensely relieved all the same, for weak, unbalanced personalities do not always behave predictably, and Nastasen's hatred of his brother distorted every feature of his face.

He pushed Tarek into the grasp of the soldiers, who dragged him to his feet. 'Now,' he said, turning to us. 'Here is your friend, the traitor. You will share his fate, but not until after you have witnessed the failure of your plans and the crowning of the rightful king. Do you wish to say farewell to your friend the traitor? You will not see him again until you meet before the altar of the god. And then ... then, I think, he will have no tongue with which to speak.'

'What an unpleasant little swine he is,' said Emerson in a conversational tone. 'Now, Peabody.'

I had planned to burst into tears and fling myself at Nastasen's feet, but I simply could not make myself do it. The shriek I emitted instead proved equally effective; Nastasen started back, but he was not nimble enough to avoid me as I rushed at him, waving my arms in feigned agitation and screaming at the top of my lungs. A carefully calculated stumble and a failed recovery brought my lowered head into painful contact with the prince's midsection. He took one of the soldiers down with him as he fell; another dropped when my parasol got tangled in his legs.

I rolled over in time to see Tarek dash towards the back of the room with one of the soldiers hot on his heels. The great spear was raised, it was about to leave the pursuer's hand, when a wicker basket loaded with linens shot across his path with the fine accuracy of a pitch to the wicket. The spear clattered to the floor, the soldier fell on top of it, and Ramses prudently skuttled back behind a huge jar of wine. Running like the wind, Tarek vanished through the doorway. It was several seconds before another soldier followed.

Tarek was safe – at least I hoped he was. But what of my gallant, my courageous spouse? I could not move, since Nastasen had me by the throat and was trying to throttle me and bang my head against the floor. It was a fairly ineffectual performance and just went to prove what I was always telling Ramses – that it is difficult to do two things at the same time unless one is equipped with superior mental and physical qualities.

A hand plucked the prince from me and tossed him away like a rag doll. 'All right, Peabody?' Emerson inquired, helping me to my feet.

The knife he had taken from my belt was not in his hand. I concluded he had managed to slip it into his pocket after cutting Tarek's bonds.

Nastasen was pounding the floor and screaming, Murtek had taken refuge behind a very tall soldier and was wringing his hands as only he could do. Pesaker was the only one who kept his head. He shouted out an order. It was the one I (or any sensible person) would have given. The soldiers left off waving their spears at me and Emerson and hastened towards the doorway through which Tarek had gone.

'I believe I feel a trifle faint, Emerson,' I said.

'That might be an excellent idea, my dear.'

So I rolled my eyes up as far as they would go and sagged at the knees. Emerson lifted me with a cry of distress; I reclined comfortably in his arms and listened with interest to the ensuing discussion.

Emerson demanded medical assistance for me. Nastasen, in a voice so choked with fury it was scarcely recognisable, replied that he would do anything possible to ensure my survival since he hoped to have the pleasure of killing me with his own hands. He began describing some of the methods he had in mind. The High Priest of Aminreh broke into this tirade with an accusation Emerson indignantly denied. His poor wife had become hysterical, as women will; hastening to her assistance, he had been attacked by the prisoner, who had struck him down along with several of the soldiers. He had no idea how the prisoner had got his arms free. One of the soldiers must be a traitor.

Everyone began shouting at once. The first sound to be heard when the tumult died was the timid but high-pitched voice of Murtek. 'To kill these strangers now would be a mistake. First, they are the god's; he will be angry if another drinks their blood. Second while you talked, the traitor has escaped. If the strangers helped him, he will be grateful. He will return to help them.'

'Huh,' said Nastasen. 'That would be – foolish. I would not take such a risk'

'No, my prince. But Prince Tarek would. Even as a child he was weak and soft of heart, listening to the stories of Forth.'

'As did you,' said Pesaker in a grating voice. 'Your own loyalty is doubtful, Murtek. What did you do to prevent Tarek's escape?'

'I am an old man,' Murtek said pitifully. 'I help as I can – by giving good advice, words of wisdom. The god must not be robbed of his sacrifice.'

'That at least is true,' said the High Priest of Aminreh. 'And the other, it may be, is also true. We will take the strangers to the darkest cells in the prison – '

Murtek coughed deprecatingly. 'You wish to set a trap for Prince Tarek? Then leave the strangers here in this place, where Tarek lived as a child, and whose hidden ways are known to him. He cannot reach Prince Nastasen's cells. He will not try.'

There was a long thoughtful silence. I knew our fate hung in the balance and I decided I would face it standing, as a true Briton should. 'Put me down, Emerson,' I muttered.

'Good, she wakes,' said Nastasen, as Emerson set me on my feet. 'She will hear her doom from the lips of the king.'

'You aren't king yet, you young villain,' said Emerson between his teeth. Aloud he said in Meroitic, 'Come, wife. We go to the house of Prince Nastasen.'

'Wait!' The High Priest of Aminreh raised his hand. 'You are ready to go? You do not ask to remain here?'

Emerson shrugged. 'One place is as good as another. We are ready.'

'This is – ,' said Pesaker, studying us with narrowed eyes and an expression that made the meaning of the word clear. 'They are too willing. I have a better plan. They will stay. We will take the child.'

Into the Bowels
of the Earth

I bit my lip to repress an exclamation of dismay. Things had
been working so nicely up to that point! In considerable
agitation of mind I looked about me in search of inspiration.
Ramses was nowhere to be seen, but I did not think he had had
a chance to leave the room, and the most cursory of searches
would reveal his hiding place behind the wine jars. Then I saw
a pale face peering out from the doorway to my sleeping
chamber. Had Reggie been there all along, skulking behind the
draperies – and a woman's skirts? I felt a slight qualm about
throwing him to the wolves but less than I would have felt had
he played the man.

'Reggie!' I cried. 'Save him! Save Ramses!'

He had no opportunity to withdraw; one of the soldiers saw
him and dragged him out of hiding. Perhaps he hoped that
presenting this little bird to his master would sweeten his failure,
for, as he was forced to report, the eagle had escaped him.

'Shall we continue to search, great prince?' he asked.

'Yes,' snapped Nastasen. 'You will search without food or
drink until you find him. If you do not . . .'

'I have found this one, great prince,' the soldier said,
swallowing nervously.

Nastasen turned to his advisers. 'What shall we do with this vermin? Perhaps he would like to taste the pleasures of my cells.'

Neither of the reverend gentlemen appeared to have an opinion. Reggie drew himself up. There was mettle in the lad after all; perhaps it had been a paucity, not of courage but of intelligence that had made him hesitate before. 'I will go,' he said. 'Take me instead of the boy. Leave him with his mother.'

Nastasen nodded. 'One hostage is as good as another,' he said, or words to that effect. He shot a malignant glance at me. 'Later, I may bring this one back and take the boy. Or I may not. Amuse yourself, Lady, in trying to think what I will do.'

He turned on his heel and marched out. Pesaker made us a mocking bow. 'Until we meet before the god, strangers.'

Held fast in the grip of his guards, Reggie smiled bravely. 'I don't blame you, Mrs Amelia. Don't give up hope. There is still a chance – ' He was dragged away. Murtek followed; he did not speak or look at us.

Then we were alone – except for a dozen or so soldiers bumbling around and Amenit, who had followed Reggie out of my room and was now staring at the row of wine jars.

I ran to her and put my arm around her. 'Poor girl! How well you conceal your anxiety for your lover! Is there nothing we can do to help him?'

Lithely as a snake she slithered out of my grasp. Her anger and frustration – which I had felt in the quivering tension of her body – were so great she could hardly bear for me to touch her. 'What have you done? You let him go free. . .'

Recollecting herself, she stopped speaking. I deemed it wiser to pretend I had misunderstood her meaning. 'I am a mother,' I said in her own tongue. 'Could I see my child taken from me? Your lover is a man, strong and brave. And you will hasten to his side and find how best to help him.'

Goodness, but the girl was slow! I had prevented her from betraying herself and practically spelled out what her next move should be, but it took her forever to think it through.

'Yes,' she said at last. 'I must hasten to him and find out . . . Stay here. Do not try to escape. Do nothing until I bring you word.'

She glided from the room. I waited a moment and then looked behind the wine jars. 'You can come out now, Ramses. It was clever of you to remain hidden; if they had been able to lay hands on you, they might not have accepted Reggie as your substitute.'

'It was clever of you, Mama, to distract Amenit,' said Ramses, emerging. 'When she said she would consult "him," it was not Mr Forthright she meant, was it?'

'What the devil did I do with my pipe?' Emerson demanded, rummaging through my notes and papers. 'If ever a man deserved a quiet smoke . . . Ah, here it is. And here, my dear Peabody, is your little knife. I commend you for keeping it well-sharpened. Tarek's bonds were not rope, they were rawhide.'

'I wish I had a dozen pipes and a sack of tobacco for you, my dear Emerson,' I replied. 'They didn't hurt you?'

'Only a few bruises.' Emerson began filling his pipe. 'I felt certain we risked nothing worse; these polytheists do take their sacrifices, and lingering tortures, and that sort of thing so seriously. The only really ugly moment was when Nastasen threatened to pop us into his dungeon.'

'That was Pesaker's idea, I believe,' I said.

'Same thing. The young swine hasn't a brain in his head; Pesaker will find him a perfect tool, which is no doubt the reason he supports Nastasen rather than Tarek. Now we have a reprieve until the moment of the ceremony, and with Tarek on the loose we ought to be able to work something out – if we can keep out of Nastasen's dungeon.'

'We owe our escape from them to Murtek,' I said, taking a date from the bowl on the table. 'Whose side is he on, anyhow?'

'His own, I fancy,' said Emerson cynically. 'Politicians are all the same, in the Halls of Parliament or darkest Africa, and he is a clever man. I would guess that his sympathies lie with us and with Tarek – the triumph of Nastasen means the triumph of Amon and his high priest over Osiris and Murtek – but he is too careful of his wrinkled hide to commit himself until victory is certain.'

I expelled the seed of the date daintily into my hand and reached for another. 'I'm starved. All that exercise, and the noon meal delayed . . . Where have the servants gone?'

'Into hiding, like sensible people.' Emerson cocked his head, listening. From the back regions of the house came distant echoes of thuds, crashes, and exclamations of (I felt certain) a profane nature. Emerson grinned. 'Nastasen's soldiers remind me of the pirates of Messieurs Gilbert and Sullivan. "With catlike tread – *thud*! – upon our prey we steal. In silence dread – *crash*! – our cautious way we feel. . ."'

Smiling, I joined my voice to his. There is nothing like a song, I always say, to lift the spirits. '"No sound at all – "' We brought our fists down on the table and Ramses, joining in the spirit of the thing, shouted, 'Bang!' at the top of his lungs.

We finished the verse in fine style, and burst into the chorus with Ramses's piping voice providing an unharmonious treble. 'Come, friends, who plough the sea,' and so on to the end.

Emerson mopped his brow and burst out laughing. 'Every man thinks he is a critic, eh, Peabody? We can't have been that bad.' And he gestured at the doorway, where two of the soldiers stood staring, spears poised.

'Western music must sound strange to them,' I replied. 'Perhaps they mistook the sound for that of struggle. We were making quite a lot of noise.'

Looking sheepish, the men lowered their spears. 'I am a trifle peckish myself,' Emerson said. 'Let's see if we can get the servants back.' He clapped his hands sharply.

It took a while, but eventually the servants reappeared and began serving our luncheon. The presence of the two soldiers, who lingered, looking hungrily at the food, obviously disturbed them, so Emerson dismissed the two with a pointed reminder of Nastasen's orders.

'They don't seem very enthusiastic, do they?' I said as the men shuffled off, dragging their spears.

'They are doomed men,' said Emerson placidly. 'If they have not found Tarek by now, he has got clean away.' He set his strong white teeth into a piece of bread and ripped off a chunk. 'And it may be –'

'Emerson, excuse me, but you are talking with your mouth full. It sets Ramses a bad example.'

'Sorry,' mumbled Emerson. He swallowed, grimacing. 'No wonder Murtek has lost most of his teeth. They must be grinding grain in the old way, between two stones; there is as much grit in this wretched bread as there is flour. One would have supposed Forth would have introduced them to modern methods of manufacture instead of teaching political theory and romantic twaddle. . . I was about to say that from the start I detected a certain lack of enthusiasm among the guards. There were more of them stumbling and staggering and falling over one another's feet than we three could have accounted for, and the pursuit of the fugitive was singularly inept.'

'I thought that myself,' I said. 'The men who attended Nastasen this time all wore leather helmets and carried spears; that must mean (and I ought to have noticed it before) that the archers, who wear the feather, are Tarek's men. He told us not all those who wore his insignia were loyal to him, and it appears the reverse is true. I don't suppose you observed which of the guards was especially clumsy?'

'No, curse it, I was too busy tripping people up.' Emerson scowled. 'That's the trouble with these conspiracies, they don't give one time for leisurely discussion. If Tarek had taken the trouble to tell us whom we can trust . . .'

He took a savage bite of the bread. I looked at the little woman who was filling my cup. Had there been a murmur, soft as a buzzing bee or purring cat, when Tarek's name was mentioned? I had no doubt of her sympathies, but I would not have endangered her by trying to speak to her. No doubt there were spies among the rekkit too. It would be so pitifully easy to bribe

Elizabeth Peters

the weaker ones to betray their own people. To a starving man, a loaf of bread is riches beyond belief.

'I am glad we were able to enjoy that refreshing little tussle this morning,' I remarked to Emerson as we strolled arm in arm around the lotus pond. 'For it appears our opportunity for healthful exercise will be very limited hereafter.'

Amenit had returned, bringing with her a fresh supply of little servants. The latter looked even more miserable and depressed than the first lot; I did not doubt they and their families had been threatened with unspeakable punishments if they attempted to render us aid.

Emerson had immediately tested the new security system by marching to the front entrance and demanding to be let out. He returned with the not unexpected news that the stratagem had failed, and 'his men' were no longer on duty. 'I only hope they have not been harmed, Peabody. That disgusting young swine is quite capable of slaughtering anyone he believes sympathetic to us.'

'My dear, you don't understand Nastasen's psychology,' I said. 'He is in – what is the phrase? – the catbird seat now and able to indulge without restraint in his favourite hobby of tormenting people. I expect that as a child he pulled the wings off butterflies. He won't slaughter any of our friends without making sure we are there to watch. And you may be certain we will be the first to know if Tarek is recaptured.'

'I don't hold with this newfangled fad of psychology,' Emerson grumbled. 'At worst it is fiddle-faddle and at best it is plain old common sense. You haven't had an opportunity to chat with Amenit since she got back, I suppose.'

'Not yet. The girl is not very intelligent, Emerson; I certainly would not allow her to participate in any conspiracy I was directing. She would have given herself away if I hadn't stopped her. I thought it was best to pretend ignorance of her role.'

'Quite. It was she who betrayed Tarek, I suppose.'

'It was she, I feel certain, who discovered we were not in our rooms last night. She was suspiciously alert today for someone who was supposed to have drunk drugged wine. She must have warned Nastasen or Pesaker – probably the latter, since he is the only one who would have sense enough to draw the obvious conclusion – that we were gadding about with some member of the opposition party. If I had been managing the affair I would have set ambushes outside the quarters of all those I suspected of being in league with Tarek, and of course the palace of Tarek himself. The fact that we were not waylaid on our way back here gives me hope that they don't know how we got out of our rooms.'

'Or where we went?'

'Heaven grant that it is so.' I wiped away a tear. 'That poor, brave child! What a terrible blow this news will be to her – how lonely and frightened she must be! If we could only communicate – tell her to keep up her courage, have faith in God and in us.'

'Not necessarily in that order,' said Emerson, with one of his irrepressible smiles. 'Keep a stiff upper lip, Peabody; we may be able to send her a message when Mentarit returns to us.'

'If she returns. Thank goodness she didn't come back with us last night; it is possible that her part in this is unsuspected. Emerson, I do think it likely that Nastasen doesn't know we saw Nefret. He would have thrown that in our faces too.'

'A good point, Peabody. How long are the handmaidens' tours of duty?'

'Five days. I kept careful count. And tonight is Amenit's second day. I don't think I can stand the suspense, but I suppose I must. Unless . . .'

Emerson came to a stop. 'Unless,' he repeated.

A little bird burst into song on a branch above. We gazed at each other – two great minds with but a single thought.

'Can you manage it, Peabody?' Emerson asked.

'Insofar as the means are concerned – yes, certainly. I have an ample supply of laudanum, but we don't want to put her to sleep, we want to render her unfit to carry out her duties. Ipecacuanha perhaps,' I said musingly. 'Doan's pills – tincture of arsenic. . .'

Emerson looked at me uneasily. 'Upon my word, Peabody, there are times when you give me the cold shivers. I am afraid to ask why you are carrying around several deadly poisons.'

'Arsenic clears the skin and makes the hair smooth and shining, my dear – in small doses, of course. I don't use it as a cosmetic, but it is very useful for getting rid of rats and other vermin such as often infest our expedition quarters. Fear not, I will be careful. Her illness must appear to be natural. Otherwise suspicion would fall on us.'

Emerson did not appear to be wholly convinced. He urged me not only to be careful with the dosage but to wait for a suitable opportunity – 'instead of bunging the stuff into her wine this afternoon,' as he put it. I assured him I had no intention of acting precipitately. It would take a while to overcome Amenit's ill-concealed dislike of me and find a suitable vehicle for the medicine.

This last question – that of opportunity, as criminal experts would say – presented some difficulty. Amenit did not dine with us, nor had she partaken of food or drink in our presence. Still, she had to eat sometime, someplace.

My task was made easier by the fact that Amenit was as eager to converse with me as I was with her. I knew, as certainly as if I had been present at their meeting, that she had gone off to confer with Nastasen and the High Priest of Aminreh. Perhaps she had also pleaded for Reggie (I had not yet made up my mind about the sincerity of her feelings for him), but her primary purpose must have been to ask how she should proceed now that the situation had changed so drastically. Before Tarek's exposure and capture, his influence had assured us of kindly treatment. Now the velvet glove was removed, and the iron hand of Nastasen held us in a cruel grip. So long as Tarek remained at liberty, those deadly fingers would not crush us, but I felt certain that if he were taken we would soon join him in his brother's dank, dark cells, to endure heaven only knew what hideous torments before an equally hideous death released us.

My efforts to get Amenit alone, and hers to speak with me, were frustrated by an unexpectedly comic situation. The soldiers searching the house refused to leave. I could hardly blame them, for I knew as well as they the alternative that awaited them, but they became more and more frantic as the afternoon wore on and got in everyone's way, searching places they had already searched a dozen times, and investigating such ridiculous hiding places as Reggie's knapsack and the lotus pond, which they swept from end to end with their spears. When one of them turned over a chest of linens the servants had repacked three times, Amenit lost her temper and began shouting at them. They refused to heed her orders, so she stormed out and was gone for some little time. It was while she was gone that one of the men made a sudden dash for the garden and climbed over the wall. I daresay some of the others would have emulated him had they not heard the extremely unpleasant sounds that followed. If I had had any doubts that the outside of the place was well-guarded, those doubts were now removed.

Turning to the nearest man, whose face had gone a sickly greenish-brown when he heard the screams, thuds, and groans from beyond the wall, I said softly, 'Is this how your master rewards faithful service? Is this the practice of justice (ma'at; lit. truth, right conduct)? What will he do to your wives and children when you are – '

At this point Emerson gripped me by the arm and dragged me away. 'Good Gad, Peabody, aren't we in enough trouble without you spouting sedition?'

'A little seed of sedition may bear rich fruit,' I replied. 'It was worth a try.'

When Amenit returned she was accompanied by a troop of soldiers who, by dint of proddings and blows, persuaded their brothers-in-arms to retire. The soldier to whom I had spoken shot me a piteous glance, to which I responded with a nod and a smile and a 'thumbs-up' gesture. It seemed to surprise him a

315

great deal; I only hoped that I had not inadvertently done something rude in Meroitic.

By the time the last stragglers had been retrieved from the remote chambers where they were hiding, the shadows of evening had stolen into the room. Ramses was in the garden conversing with the cat, whose coming and going appeared to be unaffected by the presence of the guards beyond the wall. Amenit brooded like any normal housewife over the linens the soldiers had crumpled (a happy bit of serendipity for us, since the robes we had worn on our second nocturnal expedition were among them). Her mood seemed pensive, the moment propitious. I sidled up to her.

'What news?' I whispered.

She dropped the crumpled garments back into the chest and shrugged. 'How would I know? I am as much a prisoner as you. He does not trust me.'

'Your brother Nastasen?'

The muffled head moved up and down, signifying affirmation, and I smiled to myself. She had made her first slip by admitting a relationship I had only suspected until then. It had been a logical deduction, however. Mentarit and Amenit, Tarek and Nastasen, were all children of the late king and were therefore brothers and sisters, half or full. As Emerson had once jestingly remarked, it was a close-knit family. To be sure, certain of them failed to display the affectionate loyalty siblings are supposed to exhibit towards one another, but I have known so-called civilised families in which similar deficiencies are to be found.

'What have they done with Reggie?' I asked. 'Were you able to see him?'

'How could I ask, or plead for him? If my brother learned I planned to help him escape, I would die.'

I cursed the muffling veils that hid her features, for they often betray (to a keen student of physiognomy like myself) emotions that spoken words conceal. Her voice certainly failed to carry conviction; she spoke as flatly and unemotionally as if she were reciting by rote.

'It is a pity,' I said. 'You would have been happy with him, in the great outside world.'

It was a random shot, but it struck home. Impetuously she turned towards me, clasping her hands. 'He said that in your world women are the rulers. They wear wonderful garments, crimson and gold and blue; soft as a bird's feathers and covered with shining jewels.'

'Oh, yes,' I said.

A hand emerged from the swaddling and plucked disdainfully at my sleeve. 'Your garments are not soft and shining.'

'I have such garments at home, though. Would you wear your fine robes and ornaments on a long, hard journey?'

'No . . . And is it true, as he said, that the women ride in chariots drawn smoothly along wide roads? That they eat rich foods, as much as they desire, and some of it is so cold it hurts the mouth, and the beds are so soft it is like lying on the air, and frozen water falls from the sky?'

'All those things are true,' I said, as she paused for breath, shaken by an agitation she had certainly not displayed on Reggie's account. Honesty compelled me to add, 'For the rich.'

'He is rich. And a great one among you.'

'Er – yes,' I said, wondering what Lord Blacktower would think of the arrangement.

'He said he would take me with him,' Amenit muttered. 'He swore by his god. Can I believe him?'

'An Englishman's word is his – er – truth,' I said, finding translation somewhat difficult, especially since in this case I was not entirely convinced myself.

'But I am not like the women of his country. My skin is dark, my hair has not the golden brightness of hers – '

She stopped with a snap of her teeth – one word too late.

'Mrs Forth's, you mean?' I said casually.

'And his,' Amenit said. 'It is like red gold. He is very beautiful.'

My heart thudded with excitement. She did not know we had seen Nefret; that had been a genuine slip of the tongue which she had, with my assistance, managed to cover up. More than that – the difficulty of opportunity was solved! I saw the way clear before me.

'Would you like to be beautiful too, Amenit? The women of my country have ways to change the colour of their hair, lighten their skin – '

'And their eyes? I would want mine to be blue, the colour of the sky.'

I frowned. 'That is more difficult. It takes a long time and is sometimes painful, at least in the beginning.'

'We could start now! Then I would be beautiful by the time we get to your country.'

'I don't know. . .'

'You will help me! I order you!'

'Well,' I said, 'if you put it that way. . .'

Plots within plots! Even Machiavelli would have been out of his depth. But not I; the conversation had resolved several hitherto unsettled questions. The girl's desire to escape with her lover was entirely sincere, thanks to Reggie's cleverness in seducing her not only with his charms but with the promise of wonders that must sound like magic to a primitive and ambitious young woman. I could believe in her desire for these things much more readily than I could in her love for Reggie.

I said as much to Emerson that night after we had sought the privacy of our connubial couch.

'I had no idea you were such a cynic about young love, Peabody,' was his reply.

'I am only cynical about Amenit. Not all women are like that, Emerson, as you ought to know.'

'You will have to convince me, Peabody.'

So I did – a procedure that has no part in this story. When he confessed that he was thoroughly convinced, I finished reporting my conversation with Amenit. 'She wanted me to begin at once, but I put her off by demanding certain ingredients – oil, herbs,

and the like – which she had not at hand. I had not quite decided
what method to use – '

'Don't tell me,' Emerson said nervously.

'You will have your little joke, Emerson. I also felt it advisable
to wait another day, in case something develops.'

'It is likely to be something unpleasant,' muttered Emerson.
'I have suggested to Ramses that he stay on the alert and be
ready to bolt into hiding if Nastasen pays us another call. I am
a man of iron control, Peabody, as you know, but I fear my
control would snap if someone laid violent hands on my son.
And you – I well remember what you did on an earlier occasion,
when you believed Ramses had been seriously injured.'*

'You keep referring to that occasion and I keep telling you I
have not the slightest recollection of behaving in such an ill-bred
fashion. It is a good thought, though; getting Ramses out of a
dungeon might present some difficulty.'

'You may get away, Peabody – as Amenit's beauty consultant
and personal maid.'

'Your humour is decidedly macabre tonight, Emerson. She
is probably planning to take the magic potions I concoct and
then do away with me. Now let us be serious. This is how I see
it. Nastasen believes Amenit is loyal to him – he has probably
promised to marry her and make her queen. She supports him
against Tarek, but unbeknownst to either she plans to flee the
country with Reggie. She is desperately jealous of Nefret – '

'It sounds like the plot of one of those absurd novels you
women read,' Emerson muttered. 'What makes you think she
is jealous?'

'Oh, Emerson, it is obvious. Being a man you would not
understand, so you will have to take my word for it. Amenit
does not give a curse about us, she only agreed to take us along
because Reggie insisted. She will not lift a finger to save us from
Nastasen; in fact, her mission would be a good deal simpler if
we were out of the picture.'

The Mummy Case

'Wouldn't it be ironic if she attempted to poison us while you are in the process of poisoning her? Bodies everywhere, like the last act of *Hamlet*.'

'Emerson, if you don't stop that – '

'Sorry, my dear. Continue; your exposition is quite clear and logical.'

'I . . . Where was I? Oh, yes. If Nastasen does decide to commit murder, he will make a clean sweep of it – all three of us and Reggie as well. So far as he is concerned, we are equally expendable, and she can hardly explain to him why Reggie should be treated differently.'

'Yes, that's fine as far as it goes,' said Emerson, who seemed determined to look on the gloomy side. 'But there are other complications. Pesaker – '

'Seeks power for his god and, thereby, for himself. He will insist we be saved for the sacrifice. Bread and circuses, you know – the method by which tyrants control the mob. Murtek is another complication; in my equation he is represented by an x, for unknown. I have not abandoned all hope of his assistance, however.'

'I have,' said Emerson. 'What about Tarek?'

'We have to assume he spoke only the truth, Emerson. Nefret trusts him, and we have no reason not to. There is something about his role I don't understand, though. He is now discredited, a fugitive – why is it so important that he be recaptured before the ceremony, at which Nastasen will certainly receive the nod of the god, since the High Priest of Amon is one of his supporters? They are even willing to take the risk of leaving us here, in relative freedom, in the hope of trapping Tarek. Unless Murtek, devious old man that he is, is secretly on Tarek's side and thinks Tarek can still rescue us. . .'

'I wouldn't count on Tarek,' said Emerson, sighing deeply. 'He'll do well to avoid recapture.'

'Oh, I am not counting on anyone, Emerson. Except ourselves. If all else fails, we will simply have to drug our attendants, overpower the guards, raise the rekkit to arms, and take over the government.'

'Peabody, Peabody!' Emerson seized me tightly in his arms and muffled his laughter against my hair. 'You are the light of my life and the joy of my existence and – and all that. Have I mentioned lately that I adore you?'

I was pleased to have put him in a more cheerful mood.

We needed all the good cheer we could summon, for the following day proved to be full of unpleasant surprises.

The first occurred in the morning. I was inspecting my medical chest trying to decide what to use on Amenit when the now-too-familiar tread of marching feet heralded a new danger.

My first thought was for Ramses. Turning, I was just in time to catch the flutter of his little kilt as he scuttled into the next room One anxiety being relieved – for I had often had occasion to search for my son and knew he could elude pursuit indefinitely – I braced myself for the next.

The guards did have a prisoner, but it was not Tarek. I had not realised I was holding my breath until it burst explosively from my lungs. Reggie – for it was he – smiled at me and waved his hand in greeting He was a trifle pale but appeared to be unharmed.

After a brief delay Nastasen entered, accompanied by more soldiers and the two High Priests. He did not appear to be in a pleasant state of mind – which augured well, I thought, for Tarek. 'This one has confessed,' he announced, gesturing at Reggie. 'You are all guilty – you tried to kill me and steal my crown.'

'Don't believe him,' Reggie cried. 'I – '

One of the guards gave him a shove that sent him staggering. 'I have no use for him now,' Nastasen went on. 'Where is the boy?'

Before long not a single article of furniture remained upright and every hanging had been torn down. Early in the proceedings Nastasen lost his temper and began throwing the furniture around with his own royal hands. It would have been humorous had I been less worried; at one point he overturned a large wine jar, whose contents splashed his beautiful sandals, and then put his head in to make sure Ramses had not been submerged within. Finally Pesaker approached his infuriated prince and began murmuring into his ear.

He had probably learned, through constant practice, how to deal with the royal temper tantrums. The end result was that Nastasen got himself under control and strode away to direct the search in person. The High Priest of Amon followed him. Murtek hesitated, but only briefly, before creaking after the others.

Reggie dropped onto a pile of cushions and hid his face in his hands. 'Forgive me,' he murmured. 'The strain of the past hours . . .'

Amenit went to him and stroked his hair. He looked up at her with a smile. 'I am better now. But poor little Ramses . . . Where has he gone? Is he safe?'

'Safer than he would be in Nastasen's dungeon,' said Emerson, reaching for his pipe.

'Are you certain? He is so young, he may have got into some trouble.'

'I don't know where he is, if that is what you are asking,' Emerson replied.

'They have searched every corner,' Reggie muttered. 'There is only one place he can be.'

'Why don't you trot off and tell Nastasen?' Emerson inquired sarcastically.

Reggie gave him a reproachful look and was silent.

The truth is I was not as easy as Emerson about Ramses, and I suspected he was not as easy as he pretended. There was only one place – the tunnel through which Amenit had led us to observe the false High Priestess. I had not seen how she opened the trapdoor, but Ramses was an expert at finding out things he was not supposed to know. Was Nastasen aware of the hidden passage? If he was not, would Amenit tell him? She might have reasons of her own for keeping quiet – or she might not. How long could Ramses stay there in the dark, without food or water? Even worse – would he be foolish enough to search for another way out of the maze? Knowing my son's monstrous self-confidence, I feared the answer to that question was yes.

At last the sounds of activity in the back chambers stopped, leaving an ominous silence. I could stand the suspense no longer. 'I am going to see what they are doing,' I announced, checking to make certain my belt was firmly buckled. 'I can stand the suspense no longer.'

With a rueful smile Emerson took my arm. 'I was wondering which of us would be first to admit it.'

Reggie and Amenit trailed after us. We found the search party gathered in the room where I had feared they would be. The High Priest of Amon had Nastasen by the arm and was speaking vehemently. He broke off when he saw us.

'No luck?' Emerson inquired. Then he translated 'Good fortune has not attended your efforts?'

'Not yet,' said Nastasen. 'But soon it will. I am glad you are here to see.' Turning, he indicated the stone slab. 'This is a secret place, known to only a few. I did not think the boy could know of it. When I find him, I will ask how he found out.'

He pressed the heels of both hands into shallow indentations under the edge of the slab. Pesaker rolled his eyes and started to expostulate, but he was too late; the slab started to rise and the secret place was secret no longer – not from us, nor from the staring guards.

Nastasen snatched a lamp from one of the men and leaned over the hole. His voice echoed hollowly. 'He is not here.'

'He has retreated into the passage out of sight,' said Pesaker. 'Let the men go and look for him, my prince – since now they know the secret.'

The men were more intelligent than their prince. The implications of that ominous remark were not lost upon them, and it was with extremely dour expressions that they descended, one by one, into a dark maze from which they might or might not come out.

I reached for Emerson's hand. It gripped mine with bruising force. My heart was thudding against my ribs. There was a good chance that Ramses could elude them, but I didn't know whether to hope they would find him or that they would not.

A voice boomed hollowly from the bottom of the stairs. 'He is not here, my prince.'

'Search farther back,' Nastasen shouted.

'How far, my prince?'

'Until you find him, you stupid (a small rodent of unsanitary habits).'

Murtek cleared his throat. 'My prince – forgive this low person – but he is only a child, and too young to know fear of dark places. If this leads to the tunnels, he can avoid large clumsy men forever. Would it not be better to (entice, persuade, lure) him to come out?'

Nastasen considered this novel idea. The light of the single remaining lamp reflected from his eyeballs. 'Yes,' he said finally. 'It is my judgment that we should entice him to come out. You – woman – call your son.'

So distraught was I that I might actually have done so, had not the High Priest of Amon intervened. He was shaking with exasperation. 'My prince, the boy will not come out if he knows we are here. It may be he is too far away to hear his mother's voice. If you will let me speak . . .' He drew Nastasen aside and muttered at him.

It ended with Nastasen doing what any sensible person would have done at the beginning – closing the trapdoor and withdrawing, leaving two men on watch. Pesaker had to explain to him why guards were necessary – to keep us from escaping the same way – and there was some argument as to whether the men down below should be shut in with the fugitive. Nastasen was all in favour, but Murtek finally convinced him that they would only drive Ramses farther from the stairs and perhaps cause him to lose his way.

That was now my greatest fear. Almost I would have preferred the dungeons. The thought of Ramses wandering alone and in utter darkness, his throat parched for lack of water – losing hope, crying out for help, dashing himself against the stony walls as he ran panic-stricken through the endless night of the tunnels – falling, at last, to perish in lingering torment . . . I tried to banish the hideous sights from my mind, but I failed; and when at last the intruders left us, I had no difficulty at all in bursting into tears.

'Don't worry, ma'am, we'll find him,' Reggie exclaimed, patting my hand.

'Come and lie down, my dear,' said Emerson, leading me into my sleeping chamber.

Having thus attained the degree of privacy we required, I attempted to stop crying and was surprised to find I could not. Emerson took me in his arms and I muffled my sobs against his manly bosom. 'He'll be all right, Peabody.'

'In the dark, all alone, lost . . .'

'Hush, my dear. I'll lay you odds he is not lost, but could retrace his steps at any time. And he is not in the dark.'

'What?' I raised my head. Emerson pressed it firmly back against his breast. 'Sssh! I saw it when Nasty held his lamp over the opening – a burned matchstick, deliberately placed on the topmost step.'

After checking the accoutrements on my belt I discovered that a candle and a considerable quantity of matches were missing from the waterproof tin in which I kept them. Since Ramses could not have taken them that morning, he must have stowed them away the night before in the expectation of some such emergency arising, and therefore it was quite possible he had also supplied himself with food and water and whatever other commodities he deemed necessary.

'He might at least have had the courtesy to inform me of what he was planning,' I said crossly, replacing the matches and the two remaining candles. 'I never heard of anything so inconsiderate and ill-considered. What the devil does he think he is doing? He can't stay down there forever. And how are we supposed to find him when – '

'He was considerate enough to leave the burned match,' said Emerson.

'He probably dropped it accidentally.'

'He must have lit his candle or his lamp *before* he opened the trapdoor, Peabody. There are no windows in those back rooms; he could not have found his way, or located the spring that opens the trap, without light. No, I am sure the match was a sign, meant for our eyes only and intended to convey precisely what it did – that he has taken every possible precaution and will re-establish communication when it is safe to do so.'

He was trying to comfort me, and he succeeded – for a while. The situation was not as dire as I had first believed, but it was bad enough. Knowing that he suffered too, I put on a cheerful face and apologised for my momentary weakness, to which he responded with his customary graciousness. 'Feel free to break down again anytime Peabody. I rather enjoyed it.'

Nagging worry about Ramses made me all the more anxious to get on with my plan for rendering Amenit hors de combat. Reggie was a complication I had not expected, and I wished with all my heart that Nasty, as Emerson had taken to calling him, had not returned the young man. A few days more in the dungeon would not have hurt him.

As soon as I was able, I took Amenit aside and warned her not to mention our scheme to her lover. 'If you tell him, he will say what all men do, that he loves you as you are. He believes that, but it is not true. Let it be a surprise when you show yourself in all your new beauty.'

She agreed that this was an excellent plan.

Leaving Emerson to distract Reggie with far-fetched suggestions for escape, I retired with Amenit to my room, where the supplies I had requested had been brought. I made quite a performance of it, crooning 'incantations' in Latin and Hebrew as I mixed and stirred and blended.

I had been teasing my dear Emerson when I claimed to be carrying arsenic and other poisons (though it might not be a bad idea to have something of the sort on hand in the future).

Had I been in dear old England, I could have gleaned numerous deadly substances from the fields and hedgerows. No such richness was available to me here, and the purgatives, of which I always carried an ample supply, acted too quickly for my purposes. I did not want the girl to blame her illness on my ministrations.

I had one thing on hand that would have done the trick – a necklace given me by one of my ladies-in-waiting after I had admired the pretty mottled black-and-brown beads. They were castor beans, from which castor oil is extracted. Cooking destroys the poison, so castor oil was perfectly safe, but these beans had not been cooked before being strung, only dried. There was enough poison in my necklace to dispatch Amenit and half a dozen of the guards.

But did I dare administer it? I had crushed the seeds and set them to soak in cold water. I could probably persuade Amenit to drink some of it under the pretext that it would beautify her from the inside out, but I had not the faintest idea how potent the brew might be. It might have no effect at all, it might induce the cramps and digestive distress I wanted – or it might put an end to her.

I am a Christian woman. I set the liquid aside.

I had washed her hair and plastered her face and arms with a paste of my own invention when the second intrusion of the day occurred – the familiar noises of marching feet and clashing weapons. It was getting monotonous.

Amenit reacted as any woman would when the intimate secrets of the toilette are in danger of being exposed. In other words, she squealed and shrieked and looked around for a place in which to hide. She really was a dreadful sight; I had added some pounded herbs to the mess, for colour, and she looked as if she were wearing a copper mask suffering severely from verdigris. 'Don't wash it off,' I warned, handing her her veils. 'You will spoil the magic.'

I heard Emerson call my name. Wiping a few flecks of the green paste from my forearms (I had taken care to apply it with a cloth), I hurried into the reception room.

Nastasen had not honoured us with his personal attention this time. In command of the troop of soldiers was one of the nobles who had attended our impromptu dinner party.

I greeted him with a bow and a polite 'Good afternoon,' which seemed to fluster him. He started to reply in kind, and got as far as, 'The gods favour – ' before he recollected himself. 'You come,' he said, scowling.

'I really am rather busy,' I replied. 'Can't this wait?'

'Don't push him too far, Peabody,' said Emerson, repressing a smile. 'We seem to be wanted; it would be more dignified to go of our own accord instead of being forced.'

'Oh, certainly, Emerson. Is Reggie also invited?'

Reggie was. Since the dramatic change in our status we had taken to wearing our regular clothing all the time in order to be prepared for unexpected visits, so we were properly attired, and I managed to snatch up my parasol as we were led to the door. This time no litters were provided; we walked, entirely surrounded by guards. I observed, however, that our escort kept a respectful distance; in fact, they seemed wary of so much as touching Emerson. He noticed too, and amused himself by wandering suddenly to one side or the other and watching the men skip quickly out of his way.

'Professor, are you mad?' demanded Reggie, who was walking behind us. 'Don't provoke them. We are walking on a sword's edge as it is.'

'Do you know what this is all about?' Emerson asked.

'No. No, I have no idea. It can't be the crowning ceremony, it is still several days off.'

'So I thought,' said Emerson. 'This is probably another of Nasty's little tricks to unnerve us. I refuse to be unnerved.'

'You have had your fun, though, my dear,' I said, taking his arm. 'Behave yourself. And brace yourself. Nastasen's little tricks may live up to his nickname.'

Brisk exercise and fresh air did us good, though the weather was not salubrious. A haze of sand dimmed the sun, without diminishing its fiery heat. I was short of breath – with anxious anticipation as much as fatigue – by the time we reached our destination – the great gates of the palace, where I had once gone to visit the dowager queen.

Her apartments had been in the open, with courtyards and pretty gardens surrounding them. We went nowhere near this part of the structure, but marched on through increasing gloom into the rock-cut chambers at the rear of the structure. They were no less imposing; in fact, the shadows lent them an eerie majesty suited to their purpose, for they were obviously the state apartments of the ruling monarch, adorned with statues, hangings, and painted walls. Here were none of the gentle scenes of birds and flowering plants and running animals that had decorated the palaces of Amarna which Emerson and I had excavated, only representations of the king's majesty and martial prowess. The iron-bound wheels of his chariot crushed the enemies who had fallen before his arrows; his upraised club dashed out the brains of a kneeling captive.

Finally we entered a room of greater size than any we had seen. Dozens of torches and lamps served only to illumine the central portion; the far-off ceiling was a canopy of shadows, and darkness formed the side walls. On a platform straight ahead stood a chair covered with gold foil. The legs were those of a lion; lions' heads formed the front of the armrests. It was empty except for an object that rested on the cushioned seat. A smooth, bulbous white shape, cradled in a frame of stiffened blood-red reeds – the ancient Double Crown, which had signified the unification of the two lands of Upper and Lower Egypt but which in this forlorn and dying oasis recalled only a memory of vanished glory.

The room was full of people. They stood still as statues, but eyes glittered from the shadows, and I saw that they represented all the classes of this strange society. Rank on rank of armed soldiers; courtiers and nobles, men and women alike, in their rich garb; even a group of the rekkit, herded into a separate enclosure and closely guarded.

At the foot of the steps leading up to the throne and at right angles to it was another chair, also carved and gilded but less ornate. Facing it were three plain wooden chairs, with seats of woven reeds. To these we were led.

'We are to be spectators rather than performers, it seems,' remarked Emerson. He spoke in a normal voice, but echoes amplified the sound, and the watching eyes flashed, as if they had rolled towards us and then rolled back.

After we had seated ourselves, nothing happened for a long time, and I occupied myself by studying the room and its furnishings. There is a trick of adjusting the eyes to comparative darkness; by focusing on the most shadowy portions of the chamber and avoiding looking at the lamps, I began to make out details that had eluded me before. A row of squat, stubby columns ran the length of the room, approximately one-third of the way across; I assumed another such row was behind me. Behind the throne platform was a doorway, discernible only as a square of deeper blackness. To the right of the door another, wider opening appeared. . .

A cold chill rippled through me. The opening was not a doorway. It was a recess, an alcove, deep and wide; and it was not empty. What in heaven's name was the – thing – within? Not lifeless stone, though it bulked as large as a carved boulder. It lived; I sensed, rather than saw, movement. I heard – was it the echo of my own agitated breath or the harsh breathing of some huge beast? I saw a faint glimmer of reflected light. . .

Then I saw no more therein, for torchlight brightened the rectangle of the doorway. The torchbearers took up positions behind the chair at the foot of the dais. A group of priests followed, led by Pesaker; they turned to their left and lined up shoulder to shoulder before the opening of the recess. I had the odd impression that they were not so much protecting what lay within as preventing it from coming out.

Was it a beast after all? The pharaohs of Egypt hunted lions, and although the lordly creatures had vanished from Egypt proper, they were still to be found in Nubia. A captive lion, fed on human flesh trained to mangle and kill the enemies of the king . . . I would greatly dislike being eaten by a lion. I would dislike even more being forced to watch Ramseş eaten by one.

'Oh, dear,' I murmured.

'Peabody?' Emerson glanced questioningly at me.

'I think perhaps you were right, my dear, when you said my imagination was too well developed.'

Further discussion was ended by the appearance of Nastasen, in full regalia. His pleated linen robe, his golden sandals and heavy jewelled collar, were those of a pharaoh; the sword at his belt had a hilt of rock crystal set in gold. The only thing missing was the crown, and oh! what a lustful glance he cast upon it as he passed the throne and seated himself in the chair below it.

Another heavy silence ensued. How theatrical these people were! The delay was, and was intended to be, unnerving – at least it would have unnerved persons who were not trained, as we were, in the traditions of British pluck. Emerson stifled a yawn, I let my eyelids droop as if in boredom, and Nastasen decided to get on with it. He raised the gilded staff he carried and called out, 'Bring them in! Bring the guilty to cower before the vengeance of the god!'

Half-expecting to see Ramses and Tarek, I was momentarily relieved to behold instead a little group of people wearing native garb. My relief was short-lived when I recognised the men, and realised that there were several women and small children in the group. Emerson uttered an oath (which was quite justified, but which I will not record) and started to rise. He was pulled back into his seat by a noose that was dropped over his head and pulled tight across his chest. I felt a similar constraint bind my shoulders and arms to the chair; a swift glance to my right assured me Reggie had been treated the same.

'These men are twice traitors,' Nastasen announced. 'First for failing in their duty. Twice for giving their souls to the white magician. They will die, together with their families. But because they fought bravely in the service of my father the king, and because the magician cast his spell upon them, they will receive the honour of dying at the hand of the Heneshem(?).'

The ranks of priests before the alcove parted and a man emerged from it. He was no taller than the shortest of the priests, but he bulked twice as large, and all of his bulk was muscle. He wore only a loincloth; his entire body, including his head, had been shaved in accordance with the requirements of ritual purity. Heavy supra-orbital ridges and bulging cheeks reduced his eyes to small black circles, cold and polished as obsidian beads. His mouth was a wide lipless line, like a cut in dead flesh. So thick was his neck that his head appeared to rest directly on his massive shoulders. He looked as if he could crush a normal human body with his bare arms, but he carried a weapon – a spear whose blade was dark with old stains except for its point and edges, which gleamed like polished silver.

As he advanced, the torchlight turned his oiled skin the colour of fresh blood. He made a deep obeisance to Nastasen and a deeper one to the dark alcove, then braced his feet and stood waiting.

Thus far there had been no sound from the ranks of the doomed. Rigid and grey-faced, they stared with empty eyes at their executioner. In the front rank was the young officer. He had not looked at us, and he seemed oblivious of the woman who pressed close to him. She was hardly more than a girl, and in her arms she clasped an infant. Her face remained fixed, but her arms must have tightened, for the child began to cry.

The executioner's lipless mouth split. 'The babe weeps? I will stop its tears. And because the Heneshem is merciful, I will not leave its mother to grieve. Stand forth, woman, and hold the babe close.'

He raised the heavy spear as effortlessly as if it had been a twig. The crimson light slid along the bulging muscles of his arms. The young father groaned and raised his hands to cover his eyes.

Dry-mouthed with horror, I struggled to move my arms and reach my little pistol. I knew I could never do it in time.

When he is slightly irritated, Emerson bellows like a bull. When he is really angry, he is as silent and swift as a charging

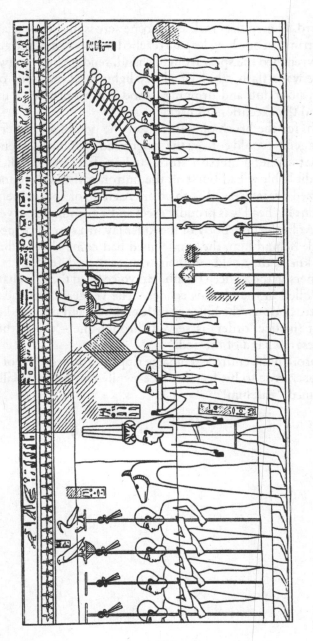

The God comes forth.

leopard. I heard the crack as the rope across his breast snapped like string. In one long leap he reached the nearest of the guards and wrenched the spear from his hand, sending him sprawling. There was a flash, a bolt of silvery light – and the blade of the spear, now dull and dripping, stood out a full twelve inches behind the executioner's back.

Oh, for the brush of a Turner, or the pen of a Homer! No lesser genius could convey the superb and passionate splendour of that scene! Emerson stood at bay, fists clenched. That incredible blow had burst all the buttons off his shirt and his bronzed breast heaved with effort A circle of spears menaced him but his head was proudly erect and a grim smile curved his lips. At his feet the body of the killer lay in a spreading pool of blood. Behind him, the condemned had come alive; falling to their knees, they held out their arms to their defender.

Emerson took a deep breath. His voice filled the vast chamber and rolled in thunderous echoes. 'The vengeance of the gods has struck down the killer of little children and unarmed men! Ma'at (justice, order) is served through me – the Father of Curses, the hand of the god!'

Through the entire assemblage rippled a united gasp of awe. Nastasen rose to his feet, his face swollen with fury. 'Kill!' he screamed. 'Kill him!'

'The God Has Spoken'

My throat was too constricted, my heart too full for speech. My eyes clung to those of my heroic spouse, and in the brilliant blue of their gaze I read undimmed courage, undying affection, and the acknowledgment of the admiration I would have expressed had I been able. His smiling lips shaped words.

'Don't look, Peabody.'

'Never fear me,' I cried. 'I will be with you to the end, my dear, and after. But I will not follow till I have avenged you!'

Nastasen let out a wordless shriek of fury. His order had not been obeyed. The men hesitated, none wishing to be the first to brave the mighty white magician's wrath. Gibbering and frothing at the mouth, the prince pulled the ceremonial sword from his belt and ran towards Emerson.

A voice rose over the murmur of the spectators. 'Stop! The Heneshem speaks. Heed the voice of the Heneshem.'

It was a woman's voice, high and sweet, and it stopped Nastasen as if he had run into an invisible wall. The voice went on, 'The ceremony is ended. Return the strangers to their place. The Heneshem has spoken.'

'But – but – ' Nastasen stuttered, waving his sword. 'The guilty men must die. They and their families.'

Emerson folded his arms. 'You will have to kill me first.'

'Take them back to their places,' said the high clear voice.

'All of them. Await the judgment of the Heneshem. The ceremony is ended. The voice of the Heneshem has spoken.'

The guards obeyed this order as they had not obeyed Nastasen. The rope that had held me fell away. I got to my feet, finding to my chagrin that my knees were a trifle unsteady.

Emerson pushed a pair of spears aside and hurried to me. 'What an anticlimax,' he remarked. 'Here, Peabody, don't faint or anything of that sort. We must continue to keep up appearances.'

'I have no intention of doing anything so absurd,' I assured him.

'Then stop mumbling into my collarbone and let go my shirt.'

I wiped my eyes on the remains of that garment before I complied. 'Another shirt ruined, Emerson! You are so hard on them.'

'That's my Peabody,' said Emerson fondly. 'Come along, my dear – step smartly. Forthright, on your feet, man.'

I had forgotten Reggie, and I expect the Reader will understand why. He too had been freed, but he was still sitting in the chair, staring like a dead fish. The room was almost empty. A shuffle of sandalled feet from the shadows indicated the departure of the last of the spectators. Nastasen had gone, leaving his sword on the floor where he had flung it in a fit of childish pique.

Walking like a somnambulist, Reggie joined us and we started for the exit, surrounded by a decidedly nervous escort. As we passed the little group of prisoners, the young officer flung himself at Emerson's feet. 'We are your men, Father of Curses. To death.'

'Not to death, but to life,' retorted Emerson, never at a loss for the *mot juste*. 'Stand up like men and fight for the right (ma'at).'

'A pity they don't understand English,' I remarked, as we proceeded on our way. 'It lost a bit in the translation.'

Emerson chuckled. 'I resent your criticism, Peabody. I thought it sounded quite well, given my imperfect command of the language.'

'Oh, I meant no criticism, my dear. You understand the language better than I; what was that strange title?'

'I have no idea,' said Emerson placidly. 'Whoever he or she may be, the Heneshem is clearly a power to be reckoned with.'

'It was a woman's voice, Emerson.'

'The Voice was a woman's; the Hand was a man's. Titles, Peabody, don't you think?'

'Good gracious. I hadn't thought of it, but I expect you are right. Emerson – did you see something – someone – in the alcove?'

'The Hand of the Heneshem emerged from it.'

'And the voice was there too. But what I saw – felt – sensed – was something more.'

'Monstrous,' Reggie mumbled. 'Horrible.'

'Ah, so you are with us in spirit as well as in body,' said Emerson, shading his eyes as we came out into an open courtyard. 'Cheer up, man, we aren't dead yet.'

'You were on the brink,' said Reggie. 'And your wife and I were a step behind you.'

'Balderdash,' said Emerson. 'I keep telling you, they are saving us for a more impressive ceremony. Here, take my arm, Peabody, these fellows are practically running.' He gave the soldier ahead of him a sharp smack on the back. 'Slow down, curse you [lit. Anubis take you].'

'They are anxious to get us off their hands, I expect,' I said. 'For fear they will fall victim to the magic of the great Father of Curses.'

Emerson grinned. 'Yes. Nastasen's little trick backfired on him this time; our mana is higher than ever.'

'Your mana, my dear,' I said, squeezing his arm.

Strolling now at a more moderate pace, we continued to speculate on the identity and powers of the Heneshem. Emerson insisted it was a man, I insisted it was a woman, but we agreed that his or her authority was probably limited to religious matters. However, in this society the distinction was by no means so clear as in our own. The dispensation of justice (if it could be so called) was primarily a religious function, since the divine pantheon was the final judge. What effect this would have on our own proposed sacrifice we were unable to determine though we argued the matter for some time.

'Well,' said Emerson at last, 'we can only wait and see. At least we have learned that there is another player in this little game, who seems, for the moment at least, to be disposed in our favour.'

'Hmmm,' I said.

'What is that supposed to mean, Peabody?'

'I think I know why she favours us. You, rather.'

'See here, Peabody – '

'Emerson, just listen and follow my logic. The Hand of the Heneshem uses a spear to execute his victims. Meroitic reliefs depict the queen dispatching prisoners with a spear. There are similar scenes from Egyptian temples showing pharaohs smashing the heads of captives with a huge club. But surely the god-king did not commit this bloody deed himself; we know that priests and officials performed many of the duties that were nominally the responsibility of the monarch. In this case as well, he must have had a deputy who wielded the actual club. It is even more likely that a woman, however muscular and bloodthirsty, would delegate an official – the Hand of Her Majesty – to do the killing.'

'Are you suggesting the unknown power is the queen?' Emerson exclaimed. 'That pleasant plump lady, to whom you presented your needle and thread, ordering the murder of a girl and her infant?'

'One may smile and be a villain, Emerson. One may be pleasingly plump and domestically inclined and still see nothing wrong with murdering babies. And a pleasingly plump, youngish widow may be favourably disposed towards a man of whose physical and moral endowments she has just beheld such an impressive display.'

Emerson blushed. 'Balderdash,' he mumbled.

'Hmmm,' I said again.

In deference to Emerson's modesty, I had understated the case. Any female who had watched him in action that day must have fallen instantly in love with him. I myself had been deeply moved. The sight of my husband's splendid muscular development was familiar to me, but to see it displayed in circumstances of struggle and violence, in the defence of the helpless, had an extremely powerful effect on me. I will not pretend my appreciation was entirely aesthetic. There was another element involved, and this was now increasing in intensity. The phrase 'fever pitch' may not be entirely inappropriate.

'You are trembling, my dear,' said Emerson solicitously. 'Delayed shock, I expect. Lean on me.'

'It is not shock,' I said.

'Ah,' said Emerson. He poked the soldier ahead of him. 'You creep like a snail. Go faster.'

It was with visible relief that our guard handed us over to the soldiers on duty at the entrance to our quarters. Pressing my arm close to his side, Emerson paused only long enough to make sure Reggie was not following before he led me towards my sleeping chamber.

The sight we beheld was dreadful enough to make us forget the purpose for which we had come. I had assumed Amenit would go about her business and that my business with her could be delayed for a few minutes – or longer, as the case might prove. But she was still there, huddled on a mat by my bed. At the sight of her face Emerson let out a cry of horror.

'Good Gad, Peabody! What have you done?'

Her skin was not only blistered and peeling, it was green – the nasty livid shade of a decomposing corpse. It looked particularly gruesome next to her purple hair.

I own I was a trifle taken aback. The substance I had applied was only lye soap, softened and made into a paste. She must have had a particular sensitivity to it. Nor had I really expected the herbs would produce such a pronounced shade of green.

Her expression, as she glowered at me, did nothing to improve her appearance. 'You set my skin afire, you [several epithets whose precise meaning was obscure but whose general intent was plain]. I will kill you! I will tear your tongue from your mouth, your hair from your head, your – ' She broke off with a yelp of agony and doubled up, clutching her stomach.

Emerson swallowed. 'Not – not the arsenic, Peabody?'

'No, of course not. She does appear to be in some digestive distress, though. The soap could not . . . Oh, good Gad!' I had seen the bowl on the floor beside Amenit's writhing form. It was the one in which I had steeped the castor beans – and it was empty.

I dropped to my knees beside the girl and took her by the shoulders. 'Amenit! Did you drink this potion? Answer me at once!'

The cramp had subsided; she lay limp and sweating in my grasp. 'Yes, I drank it. It was powerful magic, you said many spells over it. Ooooh! Now I am ugly, and I die . . . but first I will kill you!'

I struck her hand aside. 'Stupid girl! You took too much. That is why your face has swelled and broken. The gods have punished you for stealing my magic potion.'

'What was in the stuff?' Emerson asked anxiously. 'Really, Peabody, if it was dangerous you shouldn't have left it lying about.'

This from a man who had just driven a spear through a living body, on behalf of a woman who had betrayed her brother to torture and death and who was probably capable of doing the same to us. Sometimes I do not understand the male sex.

'She has rid herself of most of it,' I said, with a look of disgust at the mess on the floor. 'I don't think she is in danger of dying. To be on the safe side, I will give her a stiff dose of ipecacuanha. Hold her head, Emerson – but first get that bowl.'

Amenit let out a piercing shriek. I thought another cramp had gripped her until I saw Reggie in the doorway. 'Don't let him see!' Amenit howled, rolling herself into a ball. 'Tell him to go away.'

'What is wrong?' Reggie asked. 'I heard screams – '

'She has drunk some – some beauty preparation of mine,' I replied. 'It was not meant to be taken internally.'

When the litter I had requested finally arrived, it was accompanied by one of the swaddled maidens. I hoped she had come to attend her stricken sister, but her examination was cursory in the extreme, and after directing the litter bearers to carry Amenit away, she remained, taking over the duties the latter had performed. While she was supervising the servants in cleaning my sleeping chamber, I drew Emerson aside.

'It is not Mentarit!'

'How can you tell?'

'I have my methods. Oh, dear, this is most distressing. Dare I ask about Mentarit, do you think?'

'I don't see that it can do any harm,' Emerson replied. 'Certainly not to us, and if Mentarit is already under suspicion a casual inquiry cannot worsen her situation. See here, Peabody, you didn't leave any other noxious substances lying around, did you? We don't want another of the girls to be taken ill.'

'Speak for yourself, Emerson. If I knew for certain this young woman was not one of the few damsels loyal to Nefret, I would pour every noxious substance I possessed into her and feel not a single qualm. As for Amenit, you can spare her your concern. Her pulse was strong and steady, and her alimentary distress was subsiding. Naturally I cleared away the incriminating evidence while we were waiting for the litter, but I had better supervise the supervisor, to make certain she doesn't pry into my belongings.'

I found Reggie in my room, looking curiously at the bowls and jars set out on the chest I used as a toilet table. 'What was it she took, Mrs Amelia? I had no idea you sweet innocent ladies used such dangerous substances.'

'Any substance is dangerous if taken in excessive quantities or in the wrong way, Reggie.'

Reggie picked up one of the bowls and sniffed it – a futile

exercise, for I had carefully rinsed it out. 'She will be all right, won't she? I never saw such a face in my life!'

'It was only a rash; it will fade. You seem less concerned with her health than with her appearance, Reggie. I hope your promises to her were sincere. I would not like to think you a vile deceiver of women, like so many of your sex.'

Reggie put the bowl down and gazed earnestly at me. 'Few men would scruple to take advantage of a woman to win freedom for himself and his friends, or think it wrong to do so. As for me – I love, I worship, I adore that dear girl. Never will I leave her!'

'We had better continue this discussion elsewhere,' I said, with a significant nod at the handmaiden.

'Oh.' Reggie looked startled. 'Do you think she – '

'I think we should leave the girl to get on with her work.'

We retired to the sitting room, finding it unoccupied except by three of the rekkit who were setting up the tables for the evening meal. 'Where is the professor?' Reggie asked.

'I imagine he has gone to inquire of the guards whether there has been any sign of Ramses. I am a little curious myself, so if you will excuse me – '

'I will go with you.' Reggie shook his head. 'I hope the professor is not planning some rash attack on the guards. He is the bravest of men, but if you will permit me to say so – '

'No, I will not,' I replied shortly. 'Professor Emerson is not only the bravest of men, he is one of the most intelligent. No doubt your weaker wits are unable to follow the shrewd reasoning that guides his every action. I will brook no criticism of my husband, Mr Forthright – especially from you.'

To my surprise Reggie responded to my sally with a smile and a soft clap of his hands. 'Bravo, Mrs Amelia! It does my heart good to see such wifely devotion. Your poor opinion of my courage is understandable, after my failure to join you and Ramses and the professor in freeing Prince Tarek; but allow me to say a word in my own defence.'

'That is only fair,' I allowed.

'You have a gentle, womanly heart, Mrs Amelia; it is natural you should sympathise with Tarek, who wormed his way into your confidence when you were at Napata. No doubt he has assured you of his support and friendship. I take a more logical view of the case. I don't give a tinker's – er – curse which of these two savages rules this godforsaken spot, and I wouldn't trust either of them if he swore by every god in their endless pantheon. I beg you, ma'am, not to risk your life for Tarek. Think of yourself, your husband, your little son.'

'I am thinking of them,' I said, wondering how any man could be so obtuse. 'Come, if you are coming; stay if you prefer.'

He followed me, of course. 'Poor little boy,' he exclaimed. 'How frightened he must be, lost in that horrible place. But don't give up hope, Mrs Amelia. We will find him yet.'

'How do you propose to accomplish that?' I asked curiously. 'Amenit knows every foot of those passages.'

'But Amenit is not here, and the guards are.'

'It is unfortunate that she should be taken ill,' Reggie agreed. 'But you say she will recover, and when she returns we will carry out the plan she and I had discussed.'

'Which is?'

'I will explain later,' Reggie said. 'When the professor has joined us. We are almost there. . . Good heavens! What are they doing?'

He might well ask. Emerson and the two soldiers squatted close together, their backs to us, their attention focused on something on the floor in front of them. An odd rattling sound was heard, and then Emerson's voice exclaiming in Meroitic, 'Seven! It is mine!'

One of the guards made a profane reference to Bes, the god of jocular pursuits. 'Emerson!' I said severely. 'Are you corrupting these innocent savages by teaching them how to gamble?'

Emerson glanced at me over his shoulder. 'I didn't have to teach them, Peabody. I simply introduced them to a new game. I have already won two strings of beads and a knife.' Gathering up his winnings and the dice, he rose lithely to his feet. 'Farewell, my brothers; I go now.'

'At least leave us the magic cubes,' grumbled one of the guards – the one whose scabbard was empty.

Emerson grinned and slapped him on the back with a remark I did not understand. Both the men laughed, so I concluded it was as well I did not.

'Improving your colloquial command of the language, I presume,' I said, as Emerson escorted me out of the chamber.

'Among other things,' said Emerson, pocketing the dice.

'What of the boy?' Reggie asked. 'It is too bad of you, Professor, to prolong your wife's anxiety.'

'She knows I would have informed her at once if there had been any news, you blithering idiot,' said Emerson. 'Ramses has not manifested himself by sight or sound. It has only been a few hours, Peabody.'

'I know. Reggie has a plan,' I added.

'I can hardly wait to hear it,' said Emerson in the same tone.

Hear it we did, in the cool of the evening, as twilight spread her violet veils across the garden and the languorous lily fragrance died upon the air. A tawny form lay stretched upon the tiles when we entered; seeing us, it spat and growled and leapt like a streak of softest gold upon the wall and over.

'Ramses's cat,' I said. 'Is it angry with us because we have lost him, do you think?'

'Don't be fanciful, Peabody,' said Emerson in the gruff voice he uses when he is trying to hide a softer emotion.

'Do you want to hear my plan or not?' Reggie demanded.

'May as well,' said Emerson. 'Have a seat, Peabody.'

Seated upon a carved bench with the scent of the lotuses perfuming the air and the sleepy chirp of birds as background, we listened to Reggie. His plan had some merit – or would have done, had we not known a few things he did not.

As soon as Amenit had arranged for camels, supplies, and guides, we would, that same night, drug or distract the guards and descend into the subterranean maze in search of Ramses. Reggie was convinced the lad would come out of hiding when he heard me and his father assure him it was safe to do so. When we had found him we would all proceed by secret ways Amenit knew to the tunnel leading to the outside world and the waiting caravan.

'Not bad,' said Emerson judicially, after Reggie had finished. 'I see a few potential stumbling blocks, however. Suppose we fail to find the boy? Mrs Emerson and I would never leave here without him.'

'I tell you, Amenit knows every inch of the way. She will find him, even if he is unconscious or – or – '

'I suppose if he were – 'or' – we would have no reason to remain,' mused Emerson, stamping heavily on my foot to prevent me from expressing my indignation. 'But it sounds a formidable undertaking, Forthright. There must be miles of those passages. How can we search them all in a single night? Less, in fact, for unless we are far away from here by daybreak, we have no hope of avoiding recapture. We will certainly be pursued – '

'Why should we be?'

'Oh, good Gad,' Emerson muttered. 'What have I done to be afflicted with idiots? Because, Mr Forthright, the age-old laws of the Holy Mountain forbid people from leaving. You told us that yourself.'

'We have already been condemned to death,' Reggie said angrily. 'We could be no worse off.'

'You are missing the point, Reggie,' I said. 'Which is, that we cannot expect to complete the search and get well away in a single night. If we are lucky we will find Ramses right away, but luck, my young friend, is not a commodity on which successful plotters count.'

Reggie considered this, his expression both sulky and bewildered. Finally his face cleared. 'I see. Yes, I understand. Then we must find the lad first – is that what you are saying?'

I nodded. Reggie nodded. Emerson snorted. 'Fair enough,' Reggie went on. 'It is a pity Amenit is ill; we could have begun searching tonight. I will have to consult with her.'

'Naturally,' said Emerson. 'Now I believe we are being called to dinner; I suggest you refrain from continuing this discussion in front of the others.'

The prohibition was sensible, but it put a damper on conversation. Reggie brooded over his food and spoke hardly a word. Having finished, he jumped up and left the room with a mumbled apology.

'Alone at last,' said Emerson whimsically.

'Except for . . .' I indicated the veiled form of the handmaiden, and the servants.

'They don't annoy me as much as Forthright. He is trying my nerves outrageously, Peabody. I wish he would go away.'

He got his wish, and in a way I daresay not even he had expected. Reggie returned only too soon, and we passed the next hour or so in dismal silence. Reggie paced the floor, Emerson smoked furiously, the servants stood around trying not to look directly at us, and I . . . I tried to think, to plan, but my thoughts kept returning to Ramses. Reggie might be correct in assuming that he had remained close to the stairs and would respond to my call, but it seemed equally likely to me that he had gone off on some harebrained search for another exit. He might be hopelessly lost; he might have blundered into the hands of the priests; he might have tumbled into a pit or been bitten by a bat or eaten by a lion or . . . The possibilities were endless, and all were horrid.

The ominous sound of approaching men broke into my dark imaginings. 'Not again!' exclaimed Emerson, putting his pipe aside. 'This is too much. I shall complain to the management.'

But this time we were not wanted. The soldiers had come for Reggie. He accepted his destiny with calm fortitude, remarking only, 'I hope this means that they have found the lad and will bring him back to you, ma'am. Pray for me.'

'Oh, she will,' said Emerson. 'Come along, Peabody, let us see him to the door.'

The guards made no objection to our following them. 'Go back,' Reggie called. 'Don't risk yourselves, you cannot prevent them from taking me.'

'Touching concern,' remarked Emerson, strolling along with his hands in his pockets.

I knew his real intent and I was as curious as he to see how far we could go before we were stopped. We had actually passed through the great doors and stepped onto the terrace before the officer summoned up courage enough to order us to halt. Even then he did not touch Emerson or point his weapon, only held it in front of him like a barrier.

Night had fallen. The air had cleared, and a million sparks of diamond light brightened the dark canopy of the sky. Emerson turned aside and went to the edge of the terrace. 'Look there, Peabody,' he said, pointing. 'Something is going on in the village.'

Indeed, the area was alive with moving lights – not reflections of the pure brilliance of the stars, but ruddier, smokier, and more ominous. 'Torches,' Emerson said. 'They are searching the place.'

'For Ramses?'

'Tarek, rather. They must be getting desperate. He wouldn't go to ground there.'

'I hope they won't burn the huts,' I said uneasily. 'Or hurt anyone. Do you think your performance today could have prompted this?'

'I would certainly like to think my performance, and other actions of ours, have stirred up trouble for Nastasen. Look at that poor devil of a guard trying to wave his spear and make magical protective gestures at the same time. He'll trip over the cursed thing if he isn't careful. We may as well go in.'

With a last glance at Reggie and his escort, who were descending the staircase, we returned to our quarters. 'Now he's out of the way, we can go about our business,' said Emerson briskly. 'Have you any trinkets you can spare, Peabody? I think it's time for my luck to turn.'

We had to search Ramses's little bag to find something enticing, for I had of course abandoned most of my luggage and I was loath to give up any of my accoutrements. I was astonished at some of the odd things Ramses had clung to, even in the face of death in the desert. A few marbles, a broken bit of chalk, a mummified mouse (his greatest achievement in his study of that art), the stubs of two pencils, a moustache (bright red in colour), a set of false teeth (very large and very yellow), and several pieces of India rubber were among them; I forget the rest. Several items I had expected to find were missing, including Ramses's battered notebook and the spool of thread he had lent me. I could only speculate on what other bizarre objects he had taken with him, but I found their absence reassuring, particularly that of the notebook. Ramses never went anywhere without it. If he had had time enough and wits enough to collect such impedimenta before he was forced to take flight, his situation might not be as desperate as I had feared.

Taking the false teeth, the moustache (which proved, he later informed me, a great hit), the marbles, and the pencil stubs, Emerson went whistling off, leaving me to my task of winnowing information from Amenit's replacement.

I decided a long, soothing bath would be just the thing. Women are more inclined to wax confidential during the ritual of the toilette, and I felt I deserved some pampering after the varied excitements of the day. The effect was certainly soothing, the women carried out their duties punctiliously; but it brought home to me more clearly than words how our position had changed. Formerly the women had chatted freely, trying their phrases of broken English and giggling over my attempts at their language. Now, though my command of Meroitic was much more fluent, they responded with 'yes' and 'no' or not at all. It was obviously impossible to attain confidentiality when they were all together; so after my bath I dismissed the rest and requested the assistance of the handmaiden in preparing for bed.

She might as well have been dumb as a post. I could not persuade her to unveil; my fascinating little bottles and jars of lotion interested her not at all. She did tell me her name was Maleneqen, and after insistent questioning about Mentarit she unbent so far as to ask why I wanted to know. I explained that Mentarit had been kind and amiable – that her nursing had saved my life. 'We English are grateful to those who help us,' I went on. 'We return kindness with kindness, not good with evil deeds.'

There was no visible or audible response to this sententious speech, and very little to my further efforts. When a cheery whistle heralded the approach of Emerson I was glad to dismiss the girl and seek my couch.

Emerson was not long in joining me, but he had quite an argument with Maleneqen before she consented to leave us alone. (She did not consent, in fact; she left the room under Emerson's arm, kicking and squealing. But she did not come back.)

'Cursed female,' growled Emerson, climbing into bed. 'They get progressively more inconvenient. Were you able to learn anything about Mentarit?'

'You first, Emerson.'

'Of course, my dear.' He drew me close and kissed me gently. 'I regret I have nothing to report. I persuaded my fellow gamesters to let me open the trapdoor by telling them the simple truth – that I hoped to find some sign that Ramses had come back. There was nothing, Peabody. I managed to leave a note for him, though.'

'I fear it is too late, Emerson. I fear he has gone – into the darkness, lost forever. . .'

'Now, now, my love. Ramses has got himself out of worse spots than this – and so have we. We'll have a look for him ourselves, tomorrow night.'

'Oh, Emerson, is it possible? Have you won the confidence of the guards to that extent?'

'To the extent, at least, of persuading them to join me in a friendly cup of beer. I took a jar along this evening. It was harmless, but tomorrow's jar will not be – if you still have your supply of laudanum. Now then, did you discover anything of interest from that surly young woman?'

'Her name is Maleneqen, and I had the devil of a time getting that much out of her. She must be one of Nastasen's allies, Emerson, I gave her every opportunity to confide in me. All she would say about Mentarit is that she has gone.'

'Gone? where?'

'I don't know. That was the word she used, and she refused to elaborate. And then – this, I believe, you will find interesting – she said . . . good heavens!'

That was not what Maleneqen had said and Emerson knew it, for he had felt the same phenomenon that had prompted my exclamation – movement, sly and slinking, across the foot of the bed. Emerson tried to free himself of the bedclothes and only succeeded in entangling both of us. The thing, whatever it was, turned and glided towards the head of the bed. It made absolutely no sound. Only the pull of the linen fabric and the sense of something moving betokened its slow, inexorable approach. With a sudden bound it was upon me, muffling my breath, filling my mouth and nose with . . .

Fur. Purring hoarsely, the creature fitted itself into the narrow space between us in the fluidly pervasive manner cats have in such situations.

The soft sound that emerged from Emerson might have been a chuckle, but I am inclined to believe it was a short burst of stifled profanity. I myself was strangely moved; once I had got my breath back, I whispered, 'I would not want you to think me superstitious, Emerson, but I cannot help feeling there is some strange, occult significance in this visitation. After fleeing from us before, the cat now exhibits an uncharacteristic affection, almost as if it were a manifestation, in some sense I dare not contemplate, of – of – '

'Cursed if I don't think you are right, Peabody,' Emerson breathed. 'Didn't you tell me the cat wears a collar?'

That brilliantly incisive question dispelled the clouds of superstition. As one man, so to speak, we fell upon the cat, but with the circumspection Bastet had taught us to exhibit towards felines. While I stroked the cat and complimented it, Emerson managed to undo the collar, and almost at once let out a muffled cry.

'Are you missing any hairpins, Peabody?'

'That is an impossible question to answer, Emerson. One is always missing hairpins. Have you found one?'

'I just pricked my finger on it. It has been used to fasten a bit of paper to the collar. Here, hold on' – to the cat, he meant; it had indicated its intentions of leaving – 'I had better put the collar back on.'

The cat submitted with relative grace; after it had slid away I sucked my scratched finger and asked, 'Is it a message? Who is it from? What does it say?'

'It is paper, not the local imitation,' Emerson replied. 'That is in itself suggestive, but further than that I cannot say without reading it. Dare we light a lamp?'

'We must take the chance,' I whispered. 'Suspense weighs heavily upon me. Wait, I will get a match.'

Emerson did not wait, he followed me while I located my belt, the tin box, the matches within, and one of the small pottery lamps. In the wavering light, heads together, we read the words on the paper.

'Tutus sum, liber sum, et dies ultionis meae est propinqua. Nolite timere pro filio vestro fortimissimo et astutissimo. Cum summa peritia et audacia ille viam suam ad me invenit. Conviemus in templo in die adventus dei. Usque ad illud tempus manete; facite nihil.'

'Thank heaven,' whispered Emerson. 'Our son is safe. The handwriting is his. He must have written this at Tarek's dictation.'

'Certain of the expressions strongly suggest that Ramses not only wrote it but composed it,' I replied. '"Astutissimo," indeed. I suppose he used Latin to prevent the message from being understood if it were intercepted.'

(For the benefit of those few among my Readers whose command of the language of the Caesars is weak, I append a translation; 'I am safe, I am free, and the day of my vengeance is near. Fear not for your very brave, very clever son. With consummate skill and daring he found his way to me. We will meet in the temple on the day of the coming forth of the god. Till then, wait; do nothing.')

Emerson blew out the lamp. 'Back to bed, Peabody. We have much to discuss.'

351

'I have an uneasy feeling that we are being watched, Emerson.'
'That is almost a certainty, my dear. I am glad we took the risk, though; I can sleep more soundly knowing that Ramses is with our friend. It will be hard to wait, though. We must find out when the ceremony is to take place.'
'That is what I was about to tell you, Emerson, when the cat arrived. The ceremony is in two days' time – the day after tomorrow.'

The message opened endless avenues of speculation. How had Ramses managed to find his way to Tarek? Where were they now? What precisely were the prince's plans? He sounded very confident that matters would work out to his advantage, but we agreed we would feel easier if we knew what he intended. Emerson expressed some indignation over Tarek's (or Ramses's?) order to refrain from action. 'There is a decided suggestion of criticism there, Peabody, don't you think? As if we had done too much already. And how does he expect us to sit twiddling our thumbs for two cursed days? It is not humanly possible. What if his plans go awry?'
They were legitimate questions, but unfortunately I could no more think of sensible answers than could Emerson.

The following day stands out in my mind as unquestionably the most unpleasant of the entire adventure. Dying of thirst is not an activity in which I would care to engage again; anticipating the violent death of Emerson was extremely painful; the anguish of believing that Ramses had vanished forever into the rocky bowels of the cliffs tried my nerves severely. But on the whole, activity of any kind is preferable to waiting, especially when one has some reason to believe that waiting may end in a sticky death.
We made what preparations we could. I made certain my little revolver was loaded and my knife readily accessible, and

prepared myself for the physical exertion that might be necessary by exercising my limbs vigorously. This procedure had an unexpected advantage, for as soon as I began jumping, skipping, and swinging my arms, the attendants incontinently fled. I suppose they mistook my actions for magical gestures.

Finding ourselves alone, Emerson and I made the best possible use of our time. Indeed, our enjoyment of one another's company was the only thing that made that long day endurable. The cat did not come back, though I stood by the garden wall for some time calling it. There was no word from Reggie or from Amenit. No one came to threaten or reassure us.

Fortunately we were not called upon to endure another such day. It was mid-morning when they came for us, and as the curtain was thrust aside Emerson heaved a mighty sigh of relief. 'As I hoped and expected. High noon is the time.'

We were forced to sit around for an hour or more, since we flatly refused to go through any ceremonies of purification or put on the handsome robes that had been supplied. 'If we go down, we will go down fighting, and attired like an English lady and gentleman,' I decreed.

Emerson looked me over from head to foot, his lips twitching. 'A proper English lady would faint dead away seeing you attired like that, Peabody.'

Alas, he was correct. I had done the best I could to press and brush our travel-stained garments, but I could not mend the rents or sew on missing buttons. I had searched in vain for the grubby spool of thread Ramses had lent me. It required no great stretch of the imagination to understand why he had taken it with him, but it was deuced inconvenient. Emerson's shirt was beyond repair; he was wearing one of the locally produced substitutes and I must admit it was unexpectedly becoming to him, especially since it had been made for a much slighter individual.

'I hate to think what a proper English lady would do on seeing you, Emerson,' I riposted with a smile. 'Are you sure you don't want to borrow my knife?'

'No, thank you, my dear.' Absently Emerson flexed his arms. One of the attendants, who had timidly advanced towards him waving a pleated kilt like a parlormaid shaking a rug, jumped back with a squeak.

'Your costume requires something, though,' I said, frowning. 'Why don't you put on that beaded collar? And some of the bracelets.'

'I will be cursed – ' Emerson began loudly.

'Some of the beautiful *heavy* gold bracelets,' I said.

'Oh,' said Emerson. 'Excellent idea, Peabody.'

Once this had been done – and the effect, let me add, was very fine – we were ready. However, our escort was not. I don't know how they knew the time, having no clocks or watches, but apparently we were early. A debate ensued; it ended with the decision that it would be better to be too early than too late.

'Have we everything, Peabody?' Emerson asked, knocking out his pipe and putting it carefully in his trouser pocket.

'I think so. Notebooks' – I felt the front of my blouse – 'my belt and accoutrements, my weapons, your pipe and tobacco . . . I am ready.'

As the guards closed around us I cast one final look at the room where we had spent so many painful and yet fascinating hours. Whatever ensued, it seemed unlikely that we would return. We had decided that Tarek probably intended to wage an attack upon his brother's forces during the ceremony. We would of course support our friend to the uttermost; but if he went down and his cause with him, we would make a break for it. The details of that action were necessarily vague, for they depended on too many unknown factors, the most important of which was whether Ramses and Nefret would be present. If we could scoop them up and take them along, we would try to get over or through the cliffs, steal camels and supplies, and ride hell-for-leather (if the Reader will excuse the vulgarity) for the Nile. Otherwise we would have to hide in the tunnels until we found both children, for as Emerson had said, we would as soon have abandoned Ramses as the golden-haired maiden whose courage and beauty had won both our hearts.

The weather was certainly propitious. The sun beamed down from a cloudless sky; not a breath of wind or haze of sand broke the still, clear air. As we marched along, hand in hand, closely surrounded by a heavy guard, Emerson began to whistle and my spirits soared. We were about to go into action, and when the Emersons act in concert, few can stand against them. Something was bound to turn up.

I do not know whether I have made the plan of the Great Temple clear to the Reader, who may not be as familiar as we were with the design of such structures. It was in essence very like its ancient Egyptian models. The progression was from light to darkness, from openness to mystery. Passing through the great entrance pylons, the visitor entered an open court with surrounding colonnades. Through deepening shadows the worshipper proceeded from hall to chamber to passageway until he reached the holy of holies, the sanctuary in which dwelt the god himself. This was the simple, basic plan; over the years, in Egypt as here, additional halls and pylons and chambers had been added wherever space allowed. Like the temple of Abu Simbel, this one was for the most part carved out of the cliffs themselves, and because the area of the city itself was so limited, the rock-cut chambers had greatly increased in number and in function.

I suspected that there were chambers even more secret and sacred beyond the ones we had seen, for the ultimate mysteries of the god could not be observed by common worshippers, only by priests and priestesses assigned to his service. Since this was a public ceremony, I expected it would take place in the outer courtyard, and so it proved. The hypostyle hall was filled with people. They were packed like sardines into the colonnades on either side and spilled out into the open space in the centre. Files of armed guards kept a passage free; down this we marched towards the pillared colonnade opposite the gateway. This area was reserved for the elite and their attendants – priests of the highest rank, with shaven heads and pure white robes; nobles of both sexes, glittering with gold and jewels; musicians holding harps and pipes and drums; and our unworthy selves. We took the seats indicated to us and surveyed the scene with, I hardly need say, considerable interest.

'I wonder if I might smoke,' said Emerson.

'It would be rude, my dear. After all, this is a religious edifice – of a sort.'

'Hmph,' said Emerson. Like mine, his eyes were fixed upon the object that dominated the space before the arcade – a massive block of stone whose carvings were almost obliterated by time and by the ugly stains that formed grotesque patterns on its top and down its sides. It seemed to me that a dark cloud hung over it, as if the bright sunlight shuddered away from its surface. Human sacrifice had not been practised in ancient Egypt; the blood that stained the altars had been that of poor terrified cattle or geese. But here . . . Well, no doubt we would soon find out.

Turning to more seemly sights, my eyes moved across the gaily dressed group of nobles. There were children among them – girls with gold rings woven into their dark hair, little boys whose single braids shone lustrous as a raven's wing in the sunlight. One looked so much like Ramses that my heart skipped a beat. Then he turned to stare at me and the resemblance was gone.

It had been foolish of me to think he might be here. Tarek would not allow so young a lad to risk himself in battle. I wondered where Tarek's men were assembling. Nastasen's soldiers were everywhere, surrounding the spectators and mingling with them; the flash of spear points dazzled the eyes. He too must expect an attack in force. It appeared to me that the odds were with him, not only in numbers but in the strength of his position. It would be hard to break through that narrow opening, well guarded as it was.

The pick of Nastasen's men, tall, muscular fellows in the prime of life, surrounded the throne-chair and the strange little kiosk behind it. It was made of woven reeds, picked out with gold and heavily curtained. In shape it resembled those I had seen in Egyptian reliefs, with a sloping roof and cornice. I poked Emerson, who was morosely scanning the ranks of the spectators. 'Is she there, do you think?'

'Who? Where? Oh, there. Hmmm. It is quite possible. At this moment I am more interested in where Ramses might be.'

I explained my reasoning on that subject. 'No doubt,' Emerson said irritably. 'I wish they would get on with it, though. We will probably have to sit through most of the cursed ceremony; if Tarek is any sort of strategist, he will wait until the climax, when the attention of the audience is distracted.'

A surge of the crowd and a rising murmur of interest indicated that something was happening. Situated as we were, we could not see the entrance, so it was not until the new arrival was face-to-face with us that we recognised Reggie. Even then I had to take a second look. He was dressed like a nobleman, even to the wig of coarse dark hair that covered his fiery locks.

The Reader may have noted that in our plans for escape we had not considered Reggie. This was not as callous as it might seem. However the day went for Tarek, Reggie had a greater chance of survival than the rest of us. If Amenit could not save him, it was unlikely that we could do better. Should we succeed in getting away, we could and would mount another expedition; but the welfare of the children, Ramses and Nefret, had to take precedence.

Happily unaware of this somewhat cold-blooded assessment, Reggie greeted us with a brave smile. 'So here we are, at the end. At least we will die together.'

'I have no intention of dying,' said Emerson with a snap of his teeth. 'You look ridiculous, Forthright. Why did you let them stuff you into those clothes?'

'What does it matter?' Reggie sighed. 'The only thing that concerns me is the fate of that poor little boy. Even if he still lives, how can he survive without his parents?'

'I prefer not to discuss the subject,' said Emerson. 'Ah – I believe the performance is about to begin.'

Nastasen emerged from the entrance to the inner court. He was dressed like a simple priest, except for his long black hair. Following came a small group of high officials, including the two high priests, more guards – and another individual whose appearance made me wonder whether the events of two days past had been only a horrible nightmare. He looked exactly like the Hand of the Heneshem whom Emerson had dispatched – the same squat, heavily muscled body, the same coarse face, the same shining spear and scanty loincloth.

'Curse it!' said Emerson, sitting upright. 'I thought I had killed the b-----d.'

'Language, Emerson, please. It is not – cannot be – the same man.'

'Must be his brother, then,' muttered Emerson. And indeed, the hideous leer the new Hand bent upon my husband suggested an anticipatory pleasure stronger than simple pride in one's professional skill.

Welcomed with music and dancing, the rattle of sistra and the cries of the worshippers, the god came forth.

Emerson leaned forwards, his eyes shining. 'Good Gad, Peabody, look at that. It is the bark of the god – the ship shown in the ancient reliefs. Have ever scholars had such an opportunity as we?'

Readers who are interested in the meaning of ships in ancient Egyptian religious ceremonies should refer to Emerson's article in the *Journal of Egyptian Archaeology*. Here I will say no more than that the object in question was a model of the sacred barks upon which the god sailed to visit various shrines. At the curved prow and stern were carved heads of the god – Amon-Re, wearing the horned crown and the disk. Long poles carried the insignia sacred to Amon, and in the centre of the ship was a shrine or tabernacle of light wood hung all around with curtains. Model though it was, it required twenty-five or thirty bearers to carry it.

Normally hidden from the eyes of the vulgar, the god was on full display now; the curtains had been pulled back. It was a most curious statue, unlike any I had ever seen, and it must have been of immemorial antiquity. Approximately four feet in height, it was carved of painted, gilded wood. The arms were crossed upon the breast, the hands held the twin sceptres. A garment of fine linen covered the naked limbs; a collar six inches wide adorned the broad breast.

Emerson's fingers twitched. He was aching to take notes. To see such a ceremony, often described but never depicted in detail, was like travelling back in time. Almost I forgot the dread purpose of this ceremony and its hideous culmination.

Bowed under the weight of the gilded structure, the carriers proceeded slowly down the aisle towards the temple gates. Roughly the guards pushed back the spectators, who seethed like a nest of ants. They cried out in appeal and adoration; they held children high in their arms, thrusting them forwards over the heads of those in the front rank so their tiny hands might touch the sacred vehicle; they struggled and pushed for favourable positions. For the first time I realised fully the power of superstition, and knew that the religion I had studied with scholarly detachment had been, and was, a living, breathing force. These people believed. They would accept the decision of the god and defend his chosen one.

Partway down the aisle the carriers stopped, and a man stepped out of the ranks of the spectators, the guards parting to let him through. I could not hear what he said, for the cries of the crowd drowned him out, but I assumed it was an appeal or a question – and that the guards, and the bearers, had been well-bribed not only to let him address the god but to ensure the correct answer. I rose to my feet and stood on tiptoe, trying to see how the god would reply; unfortunately 'his' back was to me and the people in front were milling about. All I saw was the recoil of the questioner, who staggered back with his hands to his head. A gasp of wonder rose from the crowd. After a moment the ship moved on.

The same thing happened twice more. I saw even less on these occasions. Then the ship reached the gate, turned, and started

Elizabeth Peters

on its return trip. It came more quickly now and did not stop. The crowd noise died into a breathless silence, and the melodious basso of the high priest boomed out. 'O Aminreh, king of the gods – the pharaoh awaits you. Give him your blessing, O Aminreh, that the land may live and flourish with His Majesty.' Nastasen stepped forwards, smirking. Where was Tarek? This was the moment, when every eye was bent upon the bark and the god, when even breath had stopped in anticipation. I could not take my eyes off the grotesque wooden statue. The painted face stared straight ahead. The hollow eye sockets . . . They were hollow, not painted or filled with crystal. But they were not empty. Something glimmered within them. I noted that the arms of the god were not carved in one piece with the rest of the body, but were separate pieces of wood – and at that moment, when the ship had almost reached the spot where Nastasen stood awaiting it, the god's arm moved. The heavy wooden flail came down on the shoulder of the nearest bearer. He let out a cry and stumbled, losing his grip on the pole and falling forwards against the man ahead of him. The whole structure swayed to a stop as the other bearers struggled to retain their footing and their grip. The god's arm lifted – not the same arm, the other, the one that held the crook. It came gently to rest upon the head of a man who had suddenly appeared beside the shrine, emerging from the ranks of the spectators. The white robes were those of a minor priest. The face was Tarek's.

Into the stunned silence a voice rose like a brazen trumpet's blast. 'The god has spoken! Behold your king, people of the Holy Mountain!

360

'Sleep,
Servant of God'

I recognised the voice – so Murtek was Tarek's man after all!
His timing had been perfect. As the spectators stood frozen
with astonishment, Tarek ripped the formal curled wig from
his head and flung off his robes. On his brow shone the twin
uraeus serpents, the symbols of kingship; on his breast lay the
sacred insignia – scarab and cobra and nekhbet-vulture. Pulling
his sword from its scabbard he raised it high, shouting, 'I am
the king! Bow down before the chosen of Aminreh, he who
brings ma'at to the land, defender of the people!'

Throughout the courtyard other men were stripping off their
disguises, drawing their weapons, taking red feathers from
hidden folds in their garments and thrusting them into their
headbands.

'Bravo!' exclaimed Emerson. 'What a strategist! I couldn't
have done better myself!'

It was a masterstroke, and for a moment I thought Tarek
would bring it off, winning his crown without violence and
civil war. But the red feathers were outnumbered by the leather
helmets of Nastasen's guardsmen, and the High Priest of
Aminreh was not the man to let power slip through his fingers.

'Treason!' he bellowed. 'Blasphemy! This criminal has no
name. He is not the chosen of Aminreh but a traitor condemned
to die. Seize him!'

Pandemonium broke out. Nastasen's men sought to carry out the command of the high priest and the rebels sprang to defend their leader. Neither bow and arrow nor the long-shafted spears could be used in such close quarters; it was hand-to-hand fighting with sword and knife. Emerson was stamping with excitement. 'Curse it, Peabody, let go my arm! I need a sword! I need a feather!'

I had to scream to be heard over the battle cries and the clash of weapons. 'Emerson – look!'

Above the heads of the struggling men the bark of the god swayed like a real boat in a stormy sea. One by one the bearers lost their footing and went down under the press of bodies. The ship dipped at the prow and fell with a crash. The brittle, ancient wood snapped into a hundred pieces. The shrine collapsed like a matchstick toy. The statue cracked and broke apart, disgorging, like a butterfly from its chrysalis, a small body that rolled helplessly under the very feet of the combatants. With a mighty roar Emerson plunged into the maelstrom and emerged with Ramses clutched in his arms.

I drew my pistol and fired point-blank at the soldier who was about to bring his blade down on Emerson's head. Emerson leapt to my side and dropped Ramses unceremoniously at my feet. 'Good Gad, Peabody, watch where you're shooting! That cursed bullet came so close it parted my hair.'

'Better than having it parted by a sword,' I replied. Another of the leather helmets was bearing down upon us. I aimed at his arm but I must have missed, for he kept on coming, and I decided I could not, under those circumstances, afford to be discriminating. The second shot dropped him, practically on top of Ramses. Emerson snatched up his fallen sword just in time to parry a vicious cut from another attacker. Others were rushing towards us but several of our guards now displayed the red feather, and they leapt to our defence. I felt I could spare a moment to address my son.

The interior of the statue must not have been cleaned in years. Cobwebs festooned Ramses's hair (what there was of it) and his kilt was filthy. I saw the distinct print of someone's sandal on his stomach, which probably helped to explain his silence. I shook him. 'Are you injured, Ramses?'

'Whoop,' said Ramses, trying to catch his breath.

Pistol at the ready, I turned to see if Emerson was in need of my assistance, and found he was managing nicely. He must have been taking fencing lessons on the sly, for his skill had improved considerably since that never-to-be-forgotten day when he had fought the Master Criminal for my humble self.* In fact, I felt sure he could have put an end to his opponent quite handily if he had not been trying to incapacitate rather than kill the man.

One of our defenders fell, splashing my boots with his blood. Another bullet from my trusty little pistol put his killer hors de combat. Hastily I reloaded. The battle was waxing hot. I saw Tarek, his diadem bristling with red feathers, trying to fight his way towards his brother, who had taken refuge behind the throne. A fierce struggle seethed before it, where Nastasen's loyal guardsmen battled to hold off an attacking force of rebels. Even Pesaker had drawn his sword and entered the fray.

But in all that shrieking, clashing, groaning battle, there was one focus of quiet: the curtained kiosk at the back of the colonnade. Before it stood the Hand, leaning on his great spear. No one came near him; it was as if he and the structure he guarded were enclosed by an invisible, impenetrable wall.

The carnage was frightful. Twisted bodies and puddles of spilled blood covered the floor. Who was winning? I could not tell. Many of the valiant on both sides had fallen. It was a tragic, a terrible waste. Sick at heart, I yearned to succour the wounded and comfort the widow and orphan.

I do not know whether it was the same noble aim that inspired Tarek, or the fear that he might be losing. I prefer to believe it was the former. Beating down the last of his immediate attackers, he raised his voice over the sounds of combat. 'Too many brave men have died for you, my brother, while you hide behind the throne you wrongly claimed. Come forth and fight me man-to-man for the prize. Or are you afraid?'

*Lion in the Valley

Silence fell, broken only by the moans of the wounded and the panting breaths of the fighters as they lowered their swords and awaited Nastasen's response. On the faces of many I saw the lust of battle replaced by a deadly sickness and horror. This had truly been a fratricidal struggle, friend against friend, brother against brother.

Emerson's blade was crimson to the hilt. I could not truly regret his actions, for the men he had killed had been intent on slaughtering us, but I could and did regret the sad necessity. Not all the blood that stained his garments was that of his opponents. A glancing blow had laid his cheek open to the bone; he would have a nasty scar unless I could stitch it up soon. Of the other wounds that had marked him, the worst seemed to be one on his forearm. It was bleeding heavily. I returned my pistol to the holster and took out the square of linen I used as a handkerchief.

'I seem to have ruined another shirt,' remarked Emerson, as I reached for him. 'Not my fault this time, Peabody.'

'I cannot complain, my dear, when your rents and your wounds were incurred in our defence. Let me tie up your arm.'

'Don't fuss, Peabody. This is not over yet. I want to see what . . . Ah, here comes Nastasen. He could hardly refuse the challenge, but he looks like a man on the way to visit his dentist, doesn't he?'

The spectators had fallen back, leaving an aisle between Tarek and his brother. Tarek was bleeding from a dozen wounds, but his bearing was kingly and a grim smile touched his lips. The contrast between the two – one marked by the scars of honourable battle, the other in his pristine and delicate robes – brought a murmur from the watchers, and not all came from Tarek's followers. It may have been the realisation that he was losing the loyalty of his men that fired Nastasen's courage; it may have been his brother's visible contempt, or the hope that Tarek was worn and weak from loss of blood. Nastasen unfastened his jewelled girdle and threw it and his robe aside. 'I have no weapon,' he said. 'Kill me, defenceless and unarmed, if you will – brother.'

Tarek gestured to one of his men. 'Give him your sword.'

Nastasen took it, with an ironic bow towards the giver. He made a few passes, as if testing the balance and weight; then, without warning, he rushed at Tarek. Tarek had no time to parry; only an agile leap to the side saved him.

The spectators closed in, jostling one another for a better look, like men watching some sporting event. It was a disgusting display of the savagery that lies palpitating in the male breast, and it also prevented me from watching the duel. Ramses climbed onto a chair and stood on tiptoe, trying to see over the heads of the audience. I caught his arm. 'Get down from there this instant, and stay close by me. If I lose you again I will punish you severely. Emerson, will you . . . Oh, curse it! Where has your father gone?'

'There,' said Ramses, pointing.

Emerson had rushed to join the audience. His head kept bobbing up and down and he was shouting advice which I fear was lost on Tarek. Words like 'feint' and 'lunge' could have meant little to him.

The business went on a great deal longer than I had expected, and I began to grow anxious. The clang of meeting blades and the shouts and groans of the watchers were the only clues I had as to what was going on. I did not doubt Tarek's superior skill and courage but his brother was fresh and unwounded. If Tarek fell, what would happen to us? I hope I will not be considered self-serving if I admit that I began to consider possible courses of action.

Glancing around, I realised that Ramses and I were alone. The guards had gone to watch the fight, and Reggie . . . When had he left us? Had he joined the strife? He was nowhere to be seen. The mysterious kiosk now appeared to be unoccupied; at any rate, the Hand no longer stood before it.

A great shout went up from the spectators. A mighty blow, perhaps a mortal blow, had been struck – but by whom? Cursing my lack of inches, I scrambled up onto the chair. With that advantage I could see the head of one combatant. Only one was still on his feet. My heart plummeted, for the face was that of Nastasen. And then – ah, then! I saw the gush of blood from his open mouth, saw him stiffen and fall; I saw Tarek rise to his full height after the mighty lunge that had dispatched his enemy. For a moment he stood victorious, streaming with blood, the valiant feathers of his headdress slashed and broken. Then his eyes closed and he fell fainting into the press of arms and bodies.

I jumped off the chair and ran towards him, dragging Ramses by the arm. Other mothers may condemn me; the sight I expected to see was certainly not suitable for the eyes of a young lad. But those mothers have never had to deal with a young lad like Ramses. I was afraid to let him out of my sight for an instant.

With his enthusiastic cooperation and the aid of my trusty parasol I forced a path through the crowd and beat his admirers off the fallen form of our princely friend. As I had hoped, he was not dead; a nip of brandy from the flask at my belt soon brought him around, and the first sight his opening eyes beheld was Ramses, who was bending over him breathing anxiously into his face. 'Ah, my young friend,' he said with a faint smile. 'We have won, and you are a hero. I shall raise a monument to you in the court of the temple – '

'Save your strength,' I said firmly, giving him another sip of brandy. 'If you will have your men carry you to your home, I will come and tend your wounds.'

'Later, Lady – though I thank you. There is much to do before I can rest.' He lifted himself up and stood erect. 'But where is the Father of Curses? I would thank him too, for his words of wisdom and deeds of daring won many to my standard.'

I am ashamed to confess that I quite lost my head once I realised Emerson had vanished. I ran to and fro calling him, turning over fallen bodies, staring into ghastly faces. Litter bearers had already begun carrying the wounded from the court; I barred their path, demanding to see for myself it was not Emerson they carried.

'How could he have disappeared?' I cried, wringing my hands. 'He was here a moment ago, unwounded – not severely wounded – at least I thought he was not . . . Oh, heavens, what has happened to him?'

Tarek put a bloody but gentle hand on my shoulder. 'Fear not, Lady. We will find him, and if he has been harmed I will kill his abductors with my royal hand.'

'A fine help that will be,' I exclaimed. 'Now do stop shouting, everyone, and be calm. He can't have vanished into thin air. Someone must have seen something! Who could have taken him? For I will never believe he left of his own accord without telling me.'

'Not all my brother's allies were slain,' Tarek said slowly. 'They will revenge themselves on me if they can; they have good reason to hate the Father of Curses.'

'They may have taken Reggie too,' I exclaimed. 'Not that I give a curse about him. . . Murtek! Where have you been hiding?'

The venerable priest came towards us, stepping fastidiously over fallen bodies and holding his skirts high to avoid the pools of blood that stained the floor. 'Behind the throne,' he said, unabashed. 'I do not fight with swords. Now my prince wins, and I come to praise him. Hail to thee, Mighty Horus, ruler of the – '

'Never mind that. You were in a point of vantage, you must have seen something. What has happened to the Father of Curses?'

Murtek's eyes shifted. He licked his lips. 'I did not – '

'Your face betrays you,' I cried, brandishing my parasol. 'What did you see?'

'Speak,' Tarek ordered sternly. 'You are my friend and my loyal supporter, but if you know aught of the Father of Curses and keep silent, I will not protect you from the Lady Who Rages Like a Lioness When Her Cub Is Threatened.'

Murtek swallowed. 'I saw . . . I saw the guards of the Heneshem carry a litter into the temple. The form upon the litter was covered, even to its face, like a corpse being carried to the embalmers. The Hand . . . the Hand went beside it.'

It was the strange title Emerson and I had failed to understand. Why comprehension should have come to me then, with the sudden illumination of a lightning bolt, I do not know, but I expect my mental powers were strengthened by intense anxiety. Over the passage of many centuries the words had become slurred and run together, but they were – they could be nothing other than – the ancient title of the High Priestesses of Amon who ruled in Thebes under the pharaohs of the late dynasties. Had not the great Cushite conqueror Piankhi forced the high priestess of his time to adopt his daughter in order to strengthen his claim to the throne of Egypt?

'Hemet netcher Amon,' I repeated, giving the words their modem, stylised pronunciation. 'How could I have been so blind? It was also a title of the queen – her designation as royal heiress, as I have always believed. . . Not only her divine dignity but her extreme corpulence would necessitate the appointment of surrogates to perform her mundane functions – the Hand to execute criminals, the Voice to express her commands, the – er – the Concubine, that scantily garbed female who made such explicit gestures to the god's statue. . . She is the true power behind the throne here, the ultimate authority – the queen, the Candace – '

'No, Lady,' said Tarek. 'No. You do not understand.'

'I understand that she has taken my husband, and that is all that matters. Lead me to her at once, Tarek.'

'You cannot. . . You must not go there, Lady. If the Heneshem has taken him – '

'Must not, to me?' I thundered. 'How dare you, Tarek? Take me there at once.'

Tarek's broad shoulders sagged. 'I cannot refuse you, Lady. But remember when you see . . . what you will see . . . that I tried to spare you.'

Naturally this ambiguous warning only fired my determination to proceed, though it did arouse certain unpleasant images in my mind. What could I see that would be worse than the slaughter I had beheld that day? The lifeless corpse of my spouse – but if they meant to kill him they could have done so, a stab in the back like the cowards they were, while all were intent upon the titanic struggle of the brothers. A scene of slow, painful torture – but if that was their intent, the more need for haste. The God's Wife clinging to Emerson like a gigantic vampire bat, draining the blood from his living veins . . . I told myself not to be silly. It was not my husband's blood that dreadful woman wanted.

I am sure I hardly need say that even as these thoughts passed through my mind I was hastening towards the inner precincts, urging Tarek along with my parasol. Ramses trotted beside me; bringing up the rear was old Murtek, his apprehension overcome by the insatiable curiosity that was his strongest characteristic.

As we penetrated deeper and deeper into the bowels of the mountain, through corridors dimly lit by smoking lamps, I could hear rustles of furtive motion; and I thought this must be how a cat would feel if he could creep into the tunnels of mice and moles. They would flee before him as the inhabitants of this sunless maze hid from us – uncertain of their fate, and fearing the worst.

As we walked side by side, Tarek spoke in an urgent whisper. 'You must be far distant from this place, Lady, before tomorrow's sun greets the day. The caravan gathers; it will guide you to the oasis and set you safely on your way. I will not ask for a vow of secrecy from you, for I know your word is stronger than another man's oath; I only ask that you keep our secret until I have had time to prepare my people for the inevitable time when the wolves of the outside world fall upon us. You may take what you will – gold, treasure – '

'I don't want your gold, Tarek, I only want my husband – and the girl for whose sake you have endured so much.'

'Yes, Lady, that was why I brought you here, and although her leaving will extinguish a light that brightens my life, the white does not mate with the – '

'Tarek, don't talk nonsense. You are babbling like a nervous actor. What is wrong with you?'

Tarek stopped. The air of the tunnels was chill and clammy, but his face glistened with perspiration. 'Lady, I beg you. Do not go on. I will – I will go, and bring the Father of Curses back to you.'

My reply was curt and pungent. Tarek looked despairingly from me to Murtek.

'The gods decree this,' said the old hypocrite. 'How can you stop the wind from blowing, or a woman from having her way?'

'Especially this woman,' I said, taking a firmer grip on my parasol. 'Hurry, Tarek.'

Tarek made no further protest. At first his pace was so quick, Ramses had to run to keep up. Gradually it slowed; and as we entered an antechamber, richly furnished with embroidered hangings and cushions, he came to a stop. Lamps burned in alcoves, but there was no one present. Silently Tarek gestured towards the curtains at the far end of the room. Shifting my parasol to my left hand, I drew my pistol and plunged through them.

In this secret and secluded chamber had been gathered the richest treasures of the kingdom. Every surface of every article of furniture was covered with beaten gold and set with gems and enamel. Embroidered hangings hid the stone walls. The vessels on the tables were all of solid gold and heaped with food of every variety. Animal skins covered the floor. In a curtained alcove stood a low couch. Emerson lay there, his eyes closed, his face ruddily lit by a lamp that burned in a niche above. And over him bent the veiled form of a woman.

I had beheld such a scene before, through the eyes of imagination, but this was a grotesque parody of the original. My husband's ruggedly masculine features bore no resemblance to those of the golden-haired hero of the classic novel, and the shape that hovered over him would have made four of the immortal She. It was as squat and square as a huge toad.

As I stood gaping, Emerson opened his eyes. The most extraordinary grimace of horror and surprise passed over his face, and he promptly fainted again.

My parasol fell from my nerveless hand. Soft as it was, the sound of its fall alerted the creature to my presence. Moving with the ponderous deliberation of a giant slug, she straightened and started to turn.

I heard the rustle of draperies behind me and knew Tarek had entered the room, but I could not take my eyes off the sight before them. I had been wrong; this monstrous thing could not be the queen It must be something indescribably horrible to have caused the bravest of men to lose his senses. The living image of one of the beast-gods of ancient Egypt? The wizened, mummified countenance of a woman thousands of years old?

What I saw was infinitely worse, and in that moment of revelation I understood Emerson's shock and Tarek's warning. The face was only that of a very fat woman, her features dwarfed by ballooning cheeks. But it was *white* – the pallid dead-white of a stiffening corpse. The hair that streamed over her shoulders almost to the floor was silvery gold; the eyes squinting at me through folds of flesh were the soft blue of cornflowers in an English meadow.

Remote as the sky whose colour they had borrowed, they contemplated me with inhuman detachment. So might a normal woman have viewed a fly that had dared to light on her hand. Through the fog of horror that clouded my mind I seemed to hear Emerson's voice repeating the words he had spoken only a few months earlier, on a rainy evening in England. 'An exquisite creature, looking no more than eighteen; great misty blue eyes, hair like a fall of spun gold, skin white as ivory . . .'

'Mrs Forth,' I gasped. 'Is it – can it be – you?'

The vast white expanse of her brow rippled. 'I know that name,' she said in strongly accented Meroitic. 'It is the name of one I hate. Go away, woman, and do not speak that name again.'

The truth, the pitiful, painful truth, was clear to me now. She *had* died after the birth of her child, in all but body. From such cases come the old legends of demonic possession, when a man or woman unable to endure the pain of existence retreats from reality into a new identity. She was not Mrs Willoughby Forth. She was the God's Wife of Amon. She had forgotten her daughter, her husband, the world from which she had come.

Could I restore her? I could but try. And of course it was unthinkable that I should not make the attempt.

I addressed her in the strongest terms. I assured her that I felt only the tenderest compassion for her (despite her unlicensed attraction to a married man). Moved as I was by intense emotion, I believe I have never risen to greater oratorical heights. Emerson's eyes remained tightly closed, but I knew he had regained consciousness. He had wisely decided to refrain from joining in the conversation.

Her face remained unmoved until I made what, in the light of later developments, I must confess to be an error in judgment. 'We will take you away with us, Mrs Forth. A home awaits you, where you will be tenderly cherished – your husband's father lives only to clasp you again in his arms – '

She let out a shriek. 'Away? From my temple, my servants? You speak when I have told you to be silent. You remain when I have told you to leave me. I would have been merciful, but you try my patience, woman! Kill them! Kill the blasphemers!'

From the shadows at the far end of the room came the Hand, his spear poised and ready, his face set in a hideous smile. Emerson rolled off the couch and bounced to his feet.

'Get out of the line of fire, my dear,' I called, leveling my pistol.

'Oh, good Gad, Peabody – no – don't – '

He made certain I would not by dashing impetuously at the Hand. Light streaked along the blade of the spear as it plunged towards Emerson's breast. With catlike grace he ducked aside and caught hold of the haft of the weapon, just above the blade. Clutching the other end of the haft, the Hand strove to pull it from Emerson's grasp. Back and forth they swayed, matched in strength, the wooden shaft between them like a rope stretched taut by a titanic tug of war.

I pushed Ramses into Tarek's arms. 'Hold on to him,' I ordered, and began to circle around, trying for a clear shot.

Murtek had retreated behind the curtains but no farther; his eyeballs rolled as he watched in fascinated horror. The God's

Wife (for so, alas, I must call her) shook so violently, her draperies flapped up and down; she was screaming curses and orders. She reached out a mammoth arm as I edged past her, but her movements were so slow I easily evaded her.

Emerson appeared to be winning the tug-of-war. Fighting every inch of the way, his face twisted with effort and disbelief, the Hand was being pulled slowly towards his mighty opponent. What Emerson meant to do with him when he had got him within arm's reach I did not know, but evidently the Hand feared the worst; suddenly he let go of the spear and reached for the long knife at his belt. Emerson staggered back, recovered, and drove the butt end of the spear into the midsection of his opponent with such force that the Hand flew backwards like a stone shot from a catapult. He hit the wall with a crash and fell to the floor.

'Oh, well struck, Papa,' called Ramses.

'Is he dead?' Tarek asked hopefully.

'I trust not.' Emerson was breathing in great gasps, and the napkin I had tied around his arm was drenched with blood. 'This is becoming tiresome. Peabody, my dear, do me the favour of holstering your pistol before you embrace me.'

I had intended to throw my arms around him, not only because it is a favourite habit of mine, but because he was swaying on his feet. Something held me motionless, however, and that something was the face of the unfortunate woman who called herself the God's Wife of Amon. No longer was it pale as snow. Dark blood suffused it. No longer was she screaming in outrage. A dreadful bubbling, gabbling gurgle issued from her gaping mouth.

She toppled, like a great boulder pushed from the top of a cliff, slowly at first, then with gathering momentum, striking the floor with a hideous, sodden thud.

The magnitude of that fall had about it an air of heroic tragedy that held us all frozen for several seconds. Then Emerson whispered, 'Oh, good Gad. Is she . . . is she . . .'

I went through the motions, kneeling by the body and trying to find a pulse, but I had seen death take her even as she stood.

Amid the bloated, purple congestion of her face her blue eyes stared emptily into mine. In medical terms her demise could be attributed to the effect of frustrated fury – for since she had assumed her exalted station her will, I suppose, had never been thwarted – upon a body worn out by excessive eating and lack of healthful exercise; but I was inclined to give credit to Another, more Beneficent Source. 'She is gone,' I said solemnly. 'A merciful end, Emerson – all things considered.'

'As always, the Lady speaks well,' said Tarek. 'It is the only possible end to her troubles and ours, for you would have tried to take her away and she would have fought to stay. Now Nefret need never know the truth.'

I drew a fold of her robe across that terrible face. 'You lied to Nefret, Tarek, as you lied to us?'

'It was not a lie, Lady. She went to the god of her own will, denying her former self. Nefret was only an infant. Why should I tell her her mother had turned away from her, after trying twice to kill her?'

'I have heard of such things,' I said sadly. 'There is a sickness that afflicts women sometimes after the birth of a child.'

Murtek squatted beside the great still bulk and began intoning prayers.

'Come away, Lady,' Tarek said. 'You can do no more for her.'

'You have done quite enough already,' said Emerson. I looked sharply at him, suspecting sarcasm, but his face was grave and sympathetic. It was also ghastly pale. The sooner he received my medical attention the better, and yet I lingered, unwilling to leave the unhappy woman without some final word of farewell. But what word? The noble phrases of the Christian burial service seemed somehow inappropriate.

As he so often does, Emerson came to my rescue. Softly and sonorously he intoned, 'Sleep, Servant of God, in the protection of God.'

So speak the angelic judges of the Moslem faith to the new-born souls of true believers who have passed the test and are destined to breath the sweet air of Paradise.

'Very nice, my dear,' I said. 'Whatever their origin, the words are beautiful and comforting.'

'And general enough to cover all the contingencies, Peabody.'

'You don't deceive me, Emerson,' I said, taking his arm – and quickly releasing it, as he yelped with pain. 'Your cynicism is only a mask.'

'Hmph,' said Emerson.

Tarek led us to a handsome suite of rooms which must have been the living quarters of one of the high-ranking priests.

'Rest and restore your strength, my friends. Whatever you wish shall be given unto you; you have only to ask. Forgive me if I leave you now; there is much to do. After night has fallen I will return, to lead you to the caravan and bid you farewell.'

He hastened out before I could ask even one of the many questions that were bursting for utterance. 'Don't bother him now, Peabody,' said Emerson, sinking gratefully onto a soft couch. 'A successful usurper has his hands full.'

'He is not a usurper, but the rightful king, my dear.'

'Pretender, usurper, rightful heir – the key word is "successful," Peabody. Is there anything to drink? My throat is dry as a bone.'

Reminded thus of my own duties, I hastened to relieve my suffering spouse. Servants, who treated us with the awe accorded royalty, supplied my requests for water and food, wine and bandages. Not until Emerson's wounds had been tended, and I had seen the colour return to his cheeks, did I allow him to talk. There was no dearth of conversation, however, since Ramses had a good deal to say.

I permitted this – nay, I encouraged it – since I was somewhat curious as to how he had managed to get from the tunnel to the interior of the statue. I did not even complain when he talked with his mouth full. As he ate voraciously of the roasted meats and fresh fruit with which we had been supplied, he explained it was his first meal for almost twenty-four hours. 'Approximately half of the carriers of the god were supporters of Tarek's. They smuggled me into the temple before daylight. As you may have observed, Mama and Papa, I am not unlike the people of this place in physical appearance; in the darkness of the sanctuary I was able to pass for the individual who had been selected (by Nastasen and the high priest) to manipulate the statue. He was – er – removed by Tarek's men. I was assured he would come to no harm.'

He paused to swallow a mouthful of grapes that would have choked a normal boy, and his father said interestedly, 'But how did you get in touch with Tarek?'

'Thanks to your warning, Papa, I was able to hide a number of useful articles in the tunnel before I had to retreat there myself. I had, of course, observed how Amenit opened the trapdoor – '

'Of course,' I muttered.

'Adults underestimate children,' said Ramses, looking smug. 'She was careful to prevent *you* from seeing what she did, Mama, but she did not care if I saw. Also, Tarek had told me, during the dinner party when I had the honour of sitting with him, that there was a means of escape through the tunnel should we need to employ it. Additional messages, giving further details, came to me tied to the collar of the cat.'

'Of course,' I cried in deep chagrin. 'Ramses, why did you not share this information with your parents?'

'Now, Peabody, don't scold the lad,' said Emerson cheerfully. 'I am sure he had excellent reasons for doing as he did. I want to hear how you found your way through that maze of tunnels, my boy.'

On the occasion of our visit to the false High Priestess, and again when Mentarit took us to Nefret, Ramses had marked the path by means of the chalk he carried in his pocket or pocket pouch. He was therefore able to retrace his steps to the room where Nefret had met us. Not only had he taken my matches and candle, he had squirrelled away a lamp and an extra pot of oil, several small jars of water, and a packet of food. He was thus equipped for a fairly prolonged stay, should this be necessary, once he reached the room aforementioned. The message he had sent Tarek, via the cat, informed the former that that was where he could be found should it be necessary for him to retreat into the tunnels. He had beguiled the time of waiting by exploring other passages, using trails of thread to avoid losing his way.

'I discovered a number of interesting tombs,' he explained. 'And of course I took copious notes.'

'Were you there, all alone, until last night?' I asked, forgetting my annoyance with him in maternal pride. I would never have told him so, for he was vain enough already, but I felt certain few lads of his age could have behaved as courageously.

'Not alone,' said Ramses. 'Not all the time.'

'Tarek visited you there?'

Ramses nodded. 'Tarek and . . . and . . .' His prominent Adam's apple bobbed up and down.

'And who? Mentarit?'

Again Ramses nodded and swallowed. His face had the same vacant look I have sometimes observed on the features of Evelyn's infants. 'And. . . SHE . . .'

The capital letters are not an affectation of mine, dear Reader. Only thus can I begin to convey the intensity with which Ramses pronounced the pronoun.

'Oh, dear,' I said.

'Nefret?' Emerson asked interestedly. 'What a brave little girl she is, to take such a risk.'

'SHE,' Ramses began. 'SHE . . .'

I was tempted to kick him, as I have seen exasperated owners of motor cars kick the engine when it won't start. Fortunately Emerson changed the subject.

'Well, my boy, I am proud of you, and I know your mama is too. That you should have pursued your archaeological research under those conditions is really splendid. Where are your notebooks?'

'Tarek has them,' said Ramses, who was glib enough on every subject but one. 'I hope he will remember to return them before we go.'

'We can trust Tarek to do whatever is necessary,' I declared. 'He is willing to trust us in an equally important matter, and I think we must give him our word that we will never speak or write of what we found here.'

Ruefully, Emerson nodded in agreement. 'Tarek is right. Treasure hunters and adventurers, not to mention the soldiers of the European powers, would descend on this place and wreak havoc. We must and will keep silent. But curse it, Peabody, what a lost opportunity for research! It would make us the most famous archaeologists of all time!'

'We are already that, Emerson. And even if we were not, we could not build our reputations on the destruction of an innocent people.'

'Very true, my dear. And,' Emerson added, brightening, 'we have seen enough and taken enough notes to throw a very useful light on ancient Meroitic culture. So we are agreed, eh? Let's drink to that.'

So we did – Ramses in water, despite his objections – and it will now be clear to the Reader why the map that accompanies this text and the description of our route, have been deliberately designed to mislead. The day will come, no doubt, when new inventions will allow the exploration of the western desert, and the hidden valley will be opened to the outside world; but never will this come about through the breaking of his or her word by an Emerson.

Though I urged my valiant spouse to snatch a few hours of needed sleep, he insisted he did not need it. 'We must be ready to leave as soon as Tarek comes for us. We aren't in the clear yet, Peabody and Tarek knows it – that's why he is waiting until night to get us away. Not only will Nastasen's disappointed allies be burning for revenge, but there is probably a party, composed of people like Murtek, who would love to keep us here, picking our brains and using our prestige to enhance their authority.'

'You are right, Papa,' said Ramses. 'I heard Murtek arguing with Tarek – most deferentially, of course – on that very topic. Not even Murtek knows that – SHE – is going with us. The priests believe – HER – to be the incarnation of Isis, and would not willingly give – HER – up.'

I had a feeling that Ramses's capitals were going to get on my nerves, but this was not the time to raise the issue. 'Poor child,' I said, 'she has had a terrible time and I am afraid she will find it difficult to adjust to a new life. We must do all we can to help her. Ramses, you must never ever mention that her mother – '

'Please, Mama,' said Ramses in tones of freezing dignity. 'I am deeply hurt that such a thought should enter your mind. The happiness of – of' – he choked, but managed to get the words out – 'of Miss Nefret is as vital to me as my own. I would – I would – er – do anything to ensure it.'

'I beg your pardon, Ramses. I believe you.' It would have been impossible not to; his eyes had the fearful shine of a religious fanatic's. Deliberately I went on, 'But it won't be necessary for you to do anything more. She has a loving home awaiting her, and a great fortune as well. When I think of the joy of her dear old grandfather – '

'Hmph,' said Emerson, clearing his throat. 'Ramses, my boy, why don't you go and have a nice wash?'

'It seems a waste of time,' objected Ramses. 'I will be dirty again almost immediately. The desert journey – '

'At least you can start out clean,' I said. You don't want – HER – curse it, I mean Nefret – to see you so grubby and dishevelled, do you?'

Ramses had opened his mouth to protest. He closed it again, looked thoughtful, and left.

'Oh, dear,' I said, sighing. 'Emerson, I am afraid we are in for it. Did you see how Ramses – '

'I saw Ramses go, which was what I intended. I don't want him to hear this.'

'What, for heaven's sake? You alarm me, Emerson.'

'There is no cause for alarm, Peabody – not for us, at any rate. It is that poor child, for whom I feel the same loving concern that Ramses, to his infinite credit, has displayed.'

'Not quite the same sort of concern,' I murmured.

'I beg your pardon, Peabody?'

'Never mind. Go on, my dear.'

'I don't think you quite grasp all the implications, Peabody. Remember Willoughby Forth's innocent raptures about his pure young bride, and a certain phrase in his letter to his father. Consider again what you said to that poor woman just before she flew into a rage. Recall the date of Nefret's birth – Forth's rejection of his former life – the infanticidal madness of his wife – the reputation of that old rip his father . . .'

'Oh, no, Emerson,' I gasped. 'Surely not!'

'We may never know for certain,' Emerson said, 'and I, for one, would prefer not to know. But I will not hand that shining child over to her old villain of a . . . whatever he may be. He is no fit guardian for an innocent young girl. If what we suspect is true he might even be cad enough to tell her; and I would never sleep soundly again if I had been a party to such a dreadful thing. It would shatter the child. She has had anguish enough. What she needs . . . But I needn't tell you, Peabody, you know.'

I had to clear my throat before I could speak. 'No, Emerson, I don't believe I do. That is – what do you think it is she needs?'

'Why, a normal, ordinary, loving home, of course. The tender care of a mother, the protection of a strong yet gentle father, playmates of her own age and intellectual capacity . . . Ah, but I can safely leave all that to you, my dear. I have every confidence in your ability to make the proper arrangements.'

He did not seem to expect a reply, which was just as well. I do not believe I was capable of articulation.

When Tarek came for us, we were ready and waiting. The servants had brought a fresh shirt for Emerson, and robes, like those of the Beduin, for us all. There was nothing more we could do to prepare, but I must say that Ramses was as clean as I have ever seen him.

Tarek was dressed like a soldier, with sword and dagger, bow and quiver. His only insignia of rank was a narrow fillet of gold, with the twin uraeus serpents on his brow. He sank wearily into a chair. 'The moon has not yet risen. There is a little time before you must go; let us talk together, for my heart tells me we shall not meet again.'

'Bah,' said Emerson. 'Don't be such a pessimist. We will honour our promise to keep the Holy Mountain a secret, but life is long and full of surprises.'

Tarek smiled. 'The Father of Curses speaks wisely.' He placed an affectionate hand on the shaven pate of Ramses, who had sat down on the floor beside his chair. 'The stonecutters have already started to work on the great pylon which will honour you and your noble parents, my young friend.'

'Thank you,' said Ramses. 'What about my notebooks?'

'Ramses!' I exclaimed. 'Is that any way to talk to His Majesty?'

'The servants have brought them,' said Tarek, laughing. 'And also the things you left in your rooms.' He reached into the pouch at his belt and took out a book, which he handed me. 'I return this in person, Lady, since it was I who stole it from you.'

I glanced at the title, smiled, and handed it back. 'It is yours, Tarek. I can easily get another copy. Mr Haggard's books are very popular in England.'

Tarek's face lit up; for the first time he looked as young as he really was. 'It is mine to keep? A great gift, a noble gift. It will be one of the treasures of my house.'

'Oh, good Gad,' growled Emerson. 'Amelia, if you have finished corrupting the literary tastes of a royal house, I would like to ask a few sensible questions.'

'Ask,' said Tarek, tucking the copy of *King Solomon's Mines* carefully into his pouch.

'We know now why you were so anxious to bring us here, and some of the tricks you used,' Emerson began. 'But why the devil did you go through such intricate manoeuvres instead of simply telling us the truth from the start?'

Tarek's face hardened. 'Would you have believed me?'

'Certainly!' Emerson caught my eye and had the grace to blush. 'Well – perhaps not immediately. But you could have convinced us, given time – '

'Time was what I did not have,' said Tarek gravely. 'Nor did I have the knowledge of you and the lady I have now. By the time I had travelled to Cairo and then to England, I had learned how those of your colour treat those of mine.'

I would have denied it, but I could not. Shame, for my nation and my race, brought the colour flaming to my cheeks. Emerson bit his lip. 'You are right,' he said. 'What can I say?'

'You need say nothing. There is no hatred in your heart or that of the lady – but there are few like you.'

Tarek went on to explain that by the time he reached England he was sadly embittered by the contempt with which he had been treated – he, who was a prince in his own land. Nevertheless he persisted, overcoming the obstacles he met with rare courage and intelligence, until he found himself unable to deliver Forth's letter. The servants drove him from the door, and the police threatened him with arrest if he returned to that aristocratic neighbourhood.

'I did not know what to do,' Tarek said simply. 'I crept back by night and left the packet on the doorstep, but for all I knew it might have been ignored or thrown away. I had seen the young one with the fiery hair come and go from the house; I learned he was the son of Forth's brother, but I was afraid to speak to him there, for the soldiers in blue [the police] had threatened me with their dungeon. I followed him instead, to your house, though I did not know it was yours until I asked a man passing by. Forth had told me of you, and I thought, That is why the young one has come here. The old one showed him the message and he seeks the help of Emerson. So I waited, hiding in the darkness, and saw the old one come, and knew I had been right.'

'All the more reason for you to approach us directly,' said Emerson. 'You would not have been driven from our door.'

'I know that now,' said Tarek. 'I did not know it then. And you have not heard the rest.' He hesitated for a moment, as if searching for the right words. 'I had not come alone to England. Two came with me. One you know – Akinidad, who was with you for a time in Nubia, and who carried my orders back to my

scouts at the oasis. The other . . . The other was my brother
Tabirka, the son of my father by his favourite concubine. He
was closest to my heart of all my brothers.

'He was at my side that night. When the carriage of the old
one left, I tried to stop it, but the coachman struck at me with
his whip and would have run me down. For many hours we
stood by the gate, my brother and I, discussing what to do.
There was no one about; the rain had stopped and the lights in
your house burned late. "Go to them," my brother urged. "The
men of Egypt say that Emerson is great and good, not like the
other Inglizi. He was the friend of our father Forth. He will
listen. We do not know what lies the others may have told him."'

'At last he won me over. The lights still burned in your house.
But when we approached the gate, there was a sharp cracking
sound. My brother cried out and clapped his hand to his arm. It
was only a small hurt, but as we ran away – for I had no weapon
and I knew the sound of the bullets that can strike from afar –
there were more shots, and my brother would have fallen had I
not caught him up and carried him away. I laid him upon the
ground while I went to get the cart and horse we had hired.
When I came back he was . . . I heard your voices, calling, but I
could not leave him like a dead animal, without the rites of burial.
I took him away; and later I stole a spade from a farmhouse and
buried him deep in the woods, near a great standing stone. When
you return . . .'

'Yes, of course,' I said gently. 'I know the place. No wonder
you did not trust us! You must have thought we fired those
shots.'

'I saw no one else. Later, after I had followed you to Egypt I
spoke with many men, learning of your plans, and learning as
well that men had naught but praise for the Father of Curses
and his Lady. I sent Akinidad ahead, to bring another of my
men from the scouts, directing them to meet me at Gebel Barkal.
There, at last, we spoke face-to-face, the three of you and I, and
I learned to love and honour you.' He covered his eyes with his
hand, briefly, then rose. 'But come; the hour is upon us. My

heart is sore to lose you, and parting prolonged is made more painful.'

'Nefret,' I began.

'She will meet us there. Hasten.'

Accompanied by several soldiers, we hurried along through endless winding corridors until we reached a door, barred and blocked and heavily guarded. As we approached, the men grounded their spears, dropped to their knees and bent forwards till their foreheads touched the ground. From one averted face came a muffled voice that said, 'We are your men, Father of Curses. We will follow you through life unto death.'

'I say, Peabody,' Emerson exclaimed in high delight. 'It's Harsetef and his chaps; they came through alive after all. Splendid, splendid!'

The men got to their feet and I said, 'Yes, Emerson, I too am delighted, but I hope they don't mean that literally. It would be frightfully inconvenient to have them following us through London and down to Kent, especially dressed like that.'

'Do you really think so? I was rather looking forward to introducing them to Gargery. He enjoys this sort of thing so much. And Peabody – only imagine the look on Lady Carrington's face the next time she calls to complain about Ramses and is greeted by this lot, in full uniform. . .'

'No, Emerson.'

'No?' Emerson sighed. 'I suppose you are right. Hear then, my brave men, the last command of the Father of Curses. Serve King Tarek faithfully as you would serve me. The eye of the Father of Curses will be upon you and the blessing of the – '

'Emerson, do cut it short!' I begged, for Tarek was fairly dancing with impatience. Emerson gave me a reproachful look but obeyed, giving Harsetef his pipe as a memento. 'I am out of tobacco anyhow,' he explained, as the young soldier regarded the sacred relic with awe.

We followed Tarek along the winding ways. The tunnel was only wide enough for two people to walk abreast; a few men could have defended it against a multitude. Finally we emerged into a courtyard open to the sky and walled with towering cliffs. It must have been a ravine or cleft which had been widened over the centuries until it was now large enough to serve as a corral. Cubicles cut out of the rock wall served as stables and storerooms. In the pale moonlight I saw that a dozen camels were waiting. Several of the men had already mounted; others, clad in the loose robes used for desert travel, gathered around at Tarek's low-pitched call. He uttered a few curt instructions, and they scattered to finish the final loading

Tarek turned to us. 'Now is the moment my heart dreads,' he began.

I poked him, not ungently, with my parasol, for I knew that if he and Emerson got to exchanging compliments, we would be there all night. 'Our hearts are heavy too, my friend, so let us get it over with. You must go back to your duties.'

'True.' Tarek smiled wryly. 'There are pockets of rebellion still to be overcome, and my uncle Pesaker is yet untaken. I will also have to deal with Murtek and the other priests when they discover I have violated the oldest law of the Holy Mountain. Farewell, my friends, my saviours – '

'Where are the others?' I interrupted.

'They come.' Tarek gestured, and I saw a pair of white-clad forms emerge from the tunnel. 'Again and yet again, farewell.'

He embraced me and Ramses, and would have done the same to Emerson had not the latter avoided it by grasping Tarek's hand and wringing it vigorously. 'Good-bye, Tarek, and good luck. You are a good chap. Come and see us if you are ever in England.'

Tarek nodded and turned away. He was incapable of speaking, I believe, for an even more painful farewell was yet before him. But as he started towards the veiled figures a reverberating boom echoed from beyond the cliffs and a tongue of flame shot skyward. Tarek let out a ripe Meroitic curse. 'It is as I feared. I am needed. Hasten, my friends; one day we may meet again.' He ran for the tunnel entrance even as he spoke, followed by his guards.

The two women glided towards us. Emerson caught me around the waist and attempted to lift me onto one of the kneeling camels. 'Just a moment,' I cried, resisting. 'What about Reggie?'

'Oh, come, Peabody, surely you can't entertain any further doubts about that young villain. He is – '

'Here!' With a diabolical laugh one of the veiled figures flung back its swaddling. Leaping upon Ramses, Reggie seized him and pressed a pistol to his head. 'So, Professor,' he went on, 'you were not as gullible as your trusting little wife. I always was a favourite with the ladies.'

Cut to the quick, I exclaimed indignantly, 'I have known for a long time that you were not what you pretended, and if I had entertained any doubts, they would have been removed by Tarek's story of his brother's murder. You tried to kill them both to prevent them from reaching us. You did not leave our house that night with your grandfather, you had come before him, in your own carriage. Did you know Tarek was there, or were you skulking about in the hope of murdering us?'

'I wouldn't do anything so stupid,' said Reggie contemptuously. 'You underestimate my intelligence, Mrs Amelia – you always have done. Of course I knew Tarek was there. My grandfather had shown me that confounded message from Uncle Willie. I tried to convince him it was a fraud, but he wouldn't listen to me. Then one of the obliging constables in Berkeley Square warned me about the "nigger," as he politely termed him, who persisted in hanging about the house. I spotted Tarek without difficulty; there aren't many men of his height and colour to be found in that neighbourhood, and as soon as I saw him I realised it must have been he who brought the message from Africa. The constable assured me he would be arrested if he tried to speak with Grandfather, so that was all right, but when the old man took it into his head to consult with you, I knew I was in trouble. I could keep Tarek from Grandfather, but I couldn't prevent him from approaching you. The message itself might not convince you of its truth, but the testimony of the messenger certainly would, for you were among the few people in the world capable of weighing that testimony correctly. I had no choice, therefore, but to dispose of the messenger. He had been trailing me all over London and I was careful not to lose him when I drove to your house. I lay in wait for him after I left you; unfortunately you came rushing out before I could finish him off, and I had to make myself scarce.'

The moonlight shivered along the folds of his sleeve as he tightened his grip on the pistol. There was no response from Ramses; indeed, the poor lad could not have moved, for Reggie had him by the throat; but Emerson growled and tensed as if to spring. I caught his arm.

'You counted on inheriting your grandfather's fortune,' I said. 'You could not endure the idea that there was another heir living. When you failed to silence Tarek, you must have feared he would find us in Egypt or in Nubia and persuade us to change our minds – which of course we would have done had we known the truth. You couldn't take that chance, for you were well aware that when the Emersons set out to do something, they do it. So you followed us to Nubia. Your transparent attempts to turn us against Tarek failed, so you and your Egyptian servant tried again to kill him when you found him with Ramses that night. To your dismay – and, I expect, to Tarek's surprise – the broken arrow convinced us of the truth of Mr Forth's story. Realising that we were now determined to pursue the quest, you announced your intention of doing the same – but your real motive was to lure us into the desert where, following the false map you had left with me in lieu of the accurate copy you stole from Emerson, we would perish miserably of thirst. The messenger you sent back –'

'Was well-coached in his role,' said Reggie. 'Unfortunately shortly after he left us, we were captured by one of Tarek's patrols. They had been warned to watch out for me.'

'How did you fall into Nastasen's hands?' I asked.

'Good Gad, Peabody, this is no time for long-winded explanations,' Emerson burst out.

'Oh, I am in no hurry,' Reggie replied. 'I must wait until my dear little cousin joins us so that I can make a clean sweep.'

Another explosion echoed from beyond the cliffs, and Reggie's teeth gleamed in a smile of evil satisfaction. 'A few sticks of dynamite provide a useful distraction, don't they? Tarek was the only one who might have recognised them for what they were and luckily I and my luggage were safely in his brother's custody by the time he returned. I hope one of the charges blows him to Kingdom Come! I can't count on that, however, so I must make sure of Nefret before I leave. Even with you out of the way, Tarek might find a means of getting her back to England, and I can't risk that, not after all the trouble I've been to.'

'So you did know about Nefret,' I said.

'From the first. Amenit told me.' The second woman lifted her veil and I saw the dark, handsome face of the First Hand-maiden. The rash had faded, but the expression with which she regarded me showed it had not faded from her memory.

'Nastasen simply kidnapped me from his brother's men while Tarek was gadding about with you,' Reggie went on. 'He thought I could be of use to him – and I knew he could be of use to me, once I understood the situation. Our goals were the same. He wanted Tarek dead and little coz in his harem; that suited me very well, for without Tarek she didn't stand a chance of getting away. I assumed you had gone astray in the desert. Confound it, I had taken every means possible to ensure you would – the false map, poison in the camel's medicine, and my trusty (and well-paid) servant Daoud to persuade your men to desert you. Imagine my chagrin when you turned up after all. Then, of course, I had to think of another plan. Damn it, where is that stupid girl?'

He turned his head to glare at the tunnel entrance.

I could hear Emerson growling like the beast of prey he would become if anyone harmed his son. His body quivered like a taut bowstring, but he dared not attack while the pistol pressed against Ramses's head. The camel drivers stood staring in bewilderment; they had not understood a word, and even if they had, they would have been as helpless to act as we.

As Reggie turned, there was a sudden movement from the rider of the camel nearest him. Some object I could not clearly discern hooked around the arm that held the pistol and jerked it sharply up and away. The sound of the shot reverberated from wall to rocky wall like a Gatling gun; before the echoes died, Emerson had borne Reggie to the ground. Amenit drew a dagger from her swathings. As she struck at Emerson's back I brought my parasol down on her head. She dropped the dagger, and I caught her in a wrestling hold and held her until the drivers, now belatedly aware of the danger, could come to my assistance. I then managed to pry Emerson's fingers from Reggie's throat. The young villain was unconscious and his tongue was protruding.

'What shall we do with them?' I asked breathlessly.

'Tie them up with their own swaddling and leave them for Tarek,' Emerson replied. 'He'll think of something ingenious, I expect.'

'Better he than you, my dear,' I said.

'Yes; thank you for stopping me, Peabody. At least I think I thank you. . . Now where the devil is that girl? We'll have to go looking for her if she doesn't turn up soon.'

'I am here,' said a sweet, familiar voice. The rider whose quick gesture had saved the day threw back the hood of her robe and the starlight glimmered in the twisted braids of her hair. 'It was Ramses's idea that I disguise myself thus, and steal away unobserved,' Nefret went on, glancing down at Ramses, who had attached himself to the front leg of her camel and was staring at her with a particularly sickening expression. 'Had it not been for his wise advice, I might never have got away. But hurry! We dare not linger, dawn will come sooner than we like.'

'Quite right, my dear,' said Emerson, prying Ramses off her camel's leg and tossing him into a saddle. He was as limp as a stuffed doll. 'Ready, Peabody? Good. It is a pleasure to have you with us, young lady. What did you use to hook that bas – er – that rascal's arm so neatly?'

From the folds of her robe Nefret took a strange object. I had to look twice to recognise it – the crooked sceptre of the pharaohs of ancient Egypt, and of the god Osiris in his capacity of king of the dead. 'I brought all the artifacts I could gather up,' she said coolly. 'I thought you might be interested in studying them.'

Bereft of speech, Emerson beamed at her in silent admiration. That made two of them. I gave my camel a sharp blow. With a grumble and a lurch it moved forwards. The others fell in behind me. The great rocks that hid the entrance rolled aside, and the caravan turned into the winding path that traversed the outer ring of the cliffs. Fantastic rock formations lined the way, but overhead the stars shone bright, and a keen night breeze caressed my cheeks. Free! We were free! Ahead lay the desert with all its perils, and civilization – with even greater perils. The strange foreboding that had seized me had nothing to do with perils of either kind. There was one consolation, though. Nefret was the only individual I had ever met who could strike Ramses dumb. One could only hope that state of things would endure.